FLYING TIME

FLYING TIME

A NOVEL

Suzanne North

BRINDLE
& GLASS

Brindle & Glass Publishing Ltd.
brindleandglass.com

LIBRARY AND ARCHIVES CANADA CATALOGUING IN PUBLICATION
North, Suzanne, 1945–, author
Flying time / Suzanne North.

Issued in print and electronic formats.
ISBN 978-1-927366-23-3

I. Title.

PS8577.O68F49 2014   C813'.54   C2013-906013-8

Editor: Lynne Van Luven
Proofreader: Heather Sangster, Strong Finish
Design: Pete Kohut
Cover images: Paper cranes: Pete Kohut
Background texture: Billy Alexander, stock.xchng
Author photo: D.J. Buckle

Brindle & Glass is pleased to acknowledge the financial support for its publishing program from the Government of Canada through the Canada Book Fund, Canada Council for the Arts, and the Province of British Columbia through the British Columbia Arts Council and the Book Publishing Tax Credit.

MIX
Paper from
responsible sources
FSC
www.fsc.org   FSC® C016245

The interior pages of this book have been printed on 30% post-consumer recycled paper, processed chlorine free, and printed with vegetable-based inks.

This book is a work of fiction. Names, characters, places, and incidents are either products of the author's imagination or are used fictitiously. Any resemblance to actual events or locales or persons, living or dead, is entirely coincidental.

1 2 3 4 5 18 17 16 15 14

PRINTED IN CANADA

To my sisters, Gwen North and Ruth Caldwell.

Assignment #1
FILL FIVE PAGES

I'M WAITING FOR MEGGIE TO finish putting on her makeup. Our memoir writing class starts at two, and it's already one forty-five. Nothing much happens around here before two because we all take a nap after lunch. Around half past one we get helped up for the second time in the day, have a pee and a wash, and struggle into our public selves, or what's left of them. Meggie always repaints. She never leaves her room in anything but full makeup and I do mean full—foundation, eyeshadow, mascara, blusher. You name it and Meggie's been slapping it on since the day she left the convent school—and that's a good seventy years, even if you spot her a few. She's here because she had a stroke. She's doing pretty well, but the left corner of her mouth still droops a little so she paints it back where it belongs with her trusty tube of Scarlet Passion. Her hands shake too, so it's largely a matter of chance where everything ends up. But, what the hell, Meggie thinks it's important, and I'm beginning to agree. She calls her full makeup job "showing the flag."

Today we are off to review the difference between memoir and autobiography. As far as I can figure, from what our instructor said last time, your memory doesn't have to be so hot to write memoirs. According to Janice, it's how you remember your life that counts, not the dates and facts and figures that measure it out. This is an encouraging point to make if you're teaching a class where half your students couldn't tell you what they ate for dinner last night without prompting from the audience. But even if we can't remember yesterday worth a damn, most of us can tell you what the weather was like on our sixteenth birthday, or at least what we think the weather was like. That, in a nutshell, is the difference between memoir and autobiography. Write a memoir and it rains or shines as you recall. Write an autobiography and you're in the public library looking up old weather reports.

Which reminds me: last class Janice read us part of an essay on how to write. It was by some American mystery author who says you should never start a story with the weather. What a crock. In Calgary we never start anything without the weather. Even Meggie and I talk about the weather, and we haven't been outside since the Labour Day blizzard. Meggie says it was only a brush of wet snow, but it looked like a blizzard to me. And, in my memoirs, I get to call the meteorological shots. Not that these are my actual memoirs. They're just part of the assignment Janice set for us this week. We are to write the first thing that comes into our heads and keep on writing until we've filled at least five pages of our notebooks. We're not to worry about grammar or spelling because this is only an exercise to get us started. It's supposed to limber up our writing muscles, warm us up so we're ready to tackle the real thing. Janice says filling five pages should give us the same great feeling that a physical workout gives our flesh and blood muscles. I guess Janice never spent a morning in physio.

Meggie is done dabbing, so we're ready to roll. Literally. Meggie pushes my wheelchair, and I call directions because she refuses to hide her eye makeup behind glasses. I won't say she's blind as a bat without them, but she could give Mr. Magoo a run for his money. My eyes are fine since I had my cataracts done, so the no-glasses business is okay with me as long as she turns when I tell her and we don't run into walls. Our arrangement suits Meggie too because my chair makes a good substitute for her walker, which she hates using, and I mean hates as in loathes and detests. I don't really understand why she feels like this because from where I'm sitting, a walker looks like a pretty good deal. The prospect of getting out of this chair and being mobile again is what gets me through physio mornings. I've promised myself that I'll be galloping around here on a walker of my own by Halloween and back home before Christmas.

So off we go. Meggie says we look like something you'd see in a bad stretch at the Stampede parade—an old clown pushing a bag of rags in a wheelie bin.

Time to navigate.

Assignment #2
WHAT WAS THE MOST IMPORTANT
DAY OF YOUR LIFE?

THAT'S OUR ASSIGNMENT FOR THIS week. I suspect your children may never speak to you again if you don't make it the day they were born or the day you met their father. Meggie says don't show them what you've written. Eventually, when you're off warbling in the feathered choir, you won't be around to speak to anyway, so why worry? After a few swigs of gin and tonic, I found myself agreeing with her. Give the pair of us a second gin and we'd have been raring to publish in the *Herald* and be damned, but it was time for dinner—that's five o'clock here at Gimpville—so we tottered off to our macaroni and cheese. Well, some of us wheeled off, if you're going to be a stickler for accuracy.

By the way, this assignment is only another exercise, not our real memoirs. I'm beginning to wonder when we'll get to those. Someone should tell Janice that around here it doesn't do to dawdle. I don't think she understands that if we don't get down to business soon, some of us may reach The End before our memoirs do. All in all though, I have to admit I only signed up for the class so I'd have something to occupy my mind until I go home. Hang around this place long enough and you realize that "dying of boredom" is not just an expression.

I can see I'm going to have to watch myself. That boredom business sounded pretty negative, didn't it? I vowed when I had to come to Foothills Sunset that I wouldn't be a whiner. I fell off a chair and broke a few bits and pieces. Nothing will change that. But if you give in and start to dwell on all the things that get you down, you'll only make yourself miserable and go gaga quicker. At least that's what Meggie claims. She's been here longer than me and says that she's seen it happen more than once. According to her, it's whine today and wither away tomorrow. So get well, go home, get on with my life. That's the plan. In the meantime, I've decided to go all Norman Vincent Peale and think positively.

All right. Time to get organized and buckle down to this Most Important Day stuff.

For me, there's no thinking required. The most important day of my life was the day I went to work for Mr. Miyashita. Period. It certainly wasn't something I'd planned on doing. Strange how a decision made on impulse, a morning's whim really, can have such a profound effect on the rest of your life. I'm such a dithery old thing now that my spur-of-the-moment choice to take the job seems nothing short of miraculous. But on that winter morning all those years ago, it was simply a case of boredom meets opportunity. And what an opportunity! My time with Mr. Miyashita opened a new world to me, a world I could not have imagined before I met him. Thanks to him, I got an education, one that instilled in me an intellectual curiosity that I like to think has not diminished over the years. He also sent me on the greatest adventure of my life, a trip to Hong Kong on the Pan American flying boat in the fall of 1941. That journey changed my life, although if I'm to be honest, I'd have to admit not all the changes were happy ones. Still, it was an adventure on a grand scale, and I got to live it. How many people can say that?

Compared with my days at Miyashita Industries, I suppose the rest of my life has been pretty ordinary. Not that it's been an unhappy life. Far from it. On the whole, I'd say I've had more than my share of happiness—or at least as much as anyone with a brain and a conscience can reasonably expect. But no one who has been around as long as I have can escape at least a small helping of the misery that the world has on constant offer, especially those of us who lived through the war. Believe me, in the months following my trip to Hong Kong, sometimes my helping didn't feel all that small. The morning I stood and watched a train take the Miyashitas away to the New Denver camp was the morning I learned what it means to be sick at heart.

There I go, rambling all over the place again. One thing I know with absolute certainty is that the ability to concentrate definitely diminishes with age. At least it has in my case. I can see that from now on I'm going to have to do my best to collect my thoughts and begin at the beginning if I want the rest of this assignment to make any sense.

I turned nineteen in February of 1939. I still lived at home with my parents and my brother, Charlie, who was two years younger than me. I'd been working as a typist at the Greer & Western Coal Company for a little over five months. Greer & Western is long gone, but back then it was a thriving concern and our department was kept very busy. Still, typing is typing, and my days had become so routine that those five months felt more like five years. Every morning Mum packed me a paper bag lunch, and every morning I'd catch the streetcar from east Calgary to Greer & Western's downtown office. There, every morning on the dot of eight-thirty, I'd sit down at a desk in a room with three other girls, lift the cover off my Underwood, and go to work. I'd type until lunch, then after lunch I'd type some more. At five-thirty I'd cover my machine and catch the streetcar home. Same thing day in day out, except on Saturdays, when the office closed at noon. It was about as exciting as our days here at Foothills Sunset. But you have to keep in mind that this was at the end of the Great Depression, when you were lucky to have a job at all, as my dad was so fond of telling me. Especially if you were a woman. He always added that.

Most of my time at Greer & Western is now a blur of indistinguishable days, except for the Thursday I got the job with Mr. Miyashita. I'll say this for Janice, until I began to work on her assignment, I had no idea that even its smallest details had stayed with me all these years. Startling to be caught unaware by your own memory, ambushed by colours and smells and sounds rushing in all of a tumble, from God knows where. Made me feel a bit shaky at first to discover that whole day still rattling around in my old brain.

When I said goodbye to Mum that morning, the mercury in the thermometer outside our kitchen window huddled near the forty below mark. With every drop of moisture frozen from it, the air was so dry that little snaps of static electricity sparked off everything I touched. I even got a shock from Mum when she kissed me goodbye. It was only two blocks from our house to the streetcar stop, but it always felt farther when I was wearing my winter gear. That morning, I'd piled on an extra sweater, my heavy overcoat, two pairs of mittens, wool stockings, and felt-lined boots. A wool toque pulled down over my ears and a big scarf pulled up over my nose completed the ensemble. God, what a lot of effort it took to go out in the cold back then. If you ask me, down-filled wind-proofs, all warm air and no substance, are one of the wonders of the modern world, and Thinsulate is a preview of heaven. I only had to wait for the streetcar a minute or two, but by the time it trundled up to our stop my fingers ached and my toes had begun to numb. A gust of air stirred up by the slowing car made my eyes water. Tears trickled down my cheeks and froze the instant they hit the scarf.

The ride from our house to downtown took fifteen minutes. That morning, frost on the overhead wires made the trolleys a little temperamental, but we still pulled up to my stop by The Hudson's Bay at eight-twenty, right on time. Greer & Western Coal occupied the top two floors of a brick building on 9th Avenue across the street from the Palliser Hotel, so ten minutes left ample time to walk there and get settled at my desk.

Despite the bitter cold, it was a relief when the driver opened the doors and I stepped out into fresh air, away from the fug of cigarette smoke, old sweat, and wet wool that hung in the crowded cars on bitter days. Sometimes, depending on where you sat, you got whiffs of the coal fire in the driver's little heater, and in the evening, the reek of fish and chips in their greasy wrappings, riding home for someone's supper. Those fifteen minutes between home and downtown with all the windows shut could leave you feeling pretty queasy, especially if some man at the back in the smoking compartment lit a cigar. Matter of fact, just sitting here thinking about it is enough to make my stomach churn. Or maybe what's really upsetting me is having to admit that I remember a morning all those years ago more vividly than any morning last week. That is one of the classic signs of old age, and it's supposed to happen to other people, not to me.

I see me at my desk in a room with high ceilings and three tall sash windows. I hear the clatter of typewriters punctuated by the bangs and hisses of reluctant pipes as steam blasts through them on its way to the radiators. Again the smells. This time it's clouds of Evening in Paris wafting off to battle the powerful forces of Raleigh's Medicated

Ointment and Life Buoy soap. The lower panes of the windows glitter with frost ferns while the upper glass remains clear and the morning sun shafts through, turning dust motes to floating specks of light and warming my shoulders as I type a letter to the transportation manager of the Portland Distributing Company on the subject of the proposed delivery date for a shipment of Drumheller bituminous.

The four of us had been at work for an hour. I had just put a new sheet of carbon paper between Greer & Western's best linen bond and the cheap stuff we used for copies when the big boss, Mr. Calthorpe himself, appeared at the typing room door. Everyone stopped working and looked up as he creaked across the oiled hardwood to the front of the room, followed by Miss Bayliss, the Simona Legree of the typing pool.

"Girls! Your attention!" Miss Bayliss ordered in her clipped and chilly tones. Since this was the first time Greer & Western's president had ever set foot in the typing room, we knew it must be something important.

"Good morning, girls," Mr. Calthorpe began. His smile was genial if a trifle strained. "I've come to ask a favour of you. A friend of Greer & Western's is in difficulty, and I'm hoping one of you young ladies will be able to help us help him." He paused for effect, letting us prepare for the enormity of what he was about to say.

"As you may already know, Mr. Hero Miyashita is the head of the Canadian branch of Miyashita Industries. His private secretary was taken ill a few weeks ago and has had to return home to Japan. Until the company can arrange for a new man to be sent from their headquarters in Hiroshima, Mr. Miyashita is in need of some crackerjack secretarial help. That's why I'm here today. I have come to ask one of you charming and talented young ladies to volunteer to work for Miyashita Industries. Of course, it would be a temporary arrangement, a few months' secondment to tide Mr. Miyashita over until his new permanent secretary arrives."

"Secondment" made it all sound very grand, but even without the lofty language and the sweet talk, we knew the request must be important to Mr. Calthorpe as this was the only time he had ever spoken to us directly. Usually, it was Miss Bayliss who hired us and fired us and issued all the orders in-between. That morning she stood a deferential step behind Mr. Calthorpe, doing her best to gaze up at him with rapt attention. This demanded some intricate contortions on her part because she was a good three inches taller than our roly-poly, red-faced little boss. That morning he looked even more flushed than usual.

"I would like the four of you to decide among yourselves which of you will volunteer to work for Mr. Miyashita as his temporary secretary." He paused again, this time to mop his brow with a large white handkerchief. He folded it carefully and put it back in the pocket of his suit jacket. I suppose, if any of us had stopped to think, we wouldn't have been surprised at his taking such a personal and sweaty interest in Mr. Miyashita's business welfare. I'd typed enough contracts to know that to a small company like Greer & Western, Miyashita Industries would be a hugely important customer. Not that I'd ever typed any contracts or even any correspondence with them, but maybe Mr. Calthorpe had hopes for the future.

"I'm sure that bright young ladies like yourselves will already know Mr. Miyashita by reputation. He's a respected member of Calgary's business community and a valued citizen of our city. Just ask any of the local charities he supports so generously and they'll tell you the same." Another pause, another mop.

Mr. Calthorpe continued in this vein for a while, emphasizing that not only was Mr. Miyashita generous, he was a gentleman too. I think this was a roundabout way of telling us that even though Mr. Miyashita was a foreigner, and a Japanese foreigner to boot, he was so wealthy and his company so huge and important that local businessmen had to treat him with outward respect, no matter what their inner reservations.

"Here at Greer & Western, we're very proud of our staff. We have a reputation for hiring the best, and I'm certain that's why Mr. Miyashita spoke to me first about finding a replacement. I must emphasize that it is only a temporary position, but don't let that worry you. The girl who volunteers for this assignment will have a job waiting for her back here at Greer & Western. You have my word on that." He gave us his best avuncular smile, unaware of the storm clouds gathering over his head in the shape of Miss Bayliss. "Right now, I'd like the four of you to go to the lunchroom and decide over a pot of tea which one of you will be that volunteer. Take your time and think carefully. There's no need to rush your decision."

This was radically democratic of Mr. Calthorpe. Miss Bayliss looked ready to spit in his eye. She even straightened her knees and glared down at his glistening bald spot, but unlike her, Mr. Calthorpe didn't have eyes in the back of his head so he took no notice.

"Let my secretary know when you've decided who will get the job. I'd like that girl to be at my office this afternoon at one o'clock sharp in order to meet Mr. Miyashita." He pocketed the handkerchief for the last time. "I'll say no more for now except that I have confidence in every one of you. No matter which of you young ladies takes on this job, I know she will make all of us here at Greer & Western proud. Young ladies of your character would never let their company down."

I don't think Mr. Calthorpe knew much about young ladies.

The four of us trooped off dutifully to the junior staff lunchroom— Verna Ainsworth, Heather MacGregor, Irene Jackson, and me. See what I mean about every last detail? I don't suppose I've thought about any of them for sixty years, but here they are, names and all, still young and pretty and happy. An old kitchen table with a white enamelled top and wobbly legs stood in the centre of the room. We sat around it on mismatched wooden chairs held together by bits of stove wire and God knows how many layers of paint. Those chairs weren't furniture so much as organized kindling.

Before we put the kettle on and brewed our pot of Lipton's, we shut the door to the lunchroom so Miss Bayliss couldn't eavesdrop. It's a good thing we did because if she'd heard, she'd have sacked us on the spot. Our conversation was brief, but it was a real humdinger.

"I'm not working for a Chink, and that's final." This from Irene.

"He's not a Chink, he's a Jap." Heather's contribution.

"You girls shouldn't use slang. It makes you sound cheap." Verna's.

"I'll work for him." Mine.

And that, to the best of my recollection, is how I got the job. No one else wanted it.

You wouldn't dare use those words today; even "girls" can land you in hot water. It's "young women" now. But that was the way the world worked back in 1939. No one then would have blinked an eye, let alone raised an eyebrow. Even Miss Bayliss wouldn't have cared about the sentiments, only the slangy language. Using slang was considered vulgar, downright fast if it was racy enough, in the same league as smoking a cigarette on the street. It would never have crossed the minds of the young women in that lunchroom that the words themselves were anything worse than unladylike. That is if they'd thought about it. As I recall, thought seldom raised much of a ripple in our typing pool.

Still, before I get too snooty about that conversation, I don't remember me rearing up on my hind legs to voice an objection. All I can say for myself is that I was young, naive to the point of simpleminded, and had never been farther away from home than a one-time camping trip to Revelstoke with our church young people's group. I was not what you'd call a woman of the world, even by Calgary standards. But I was smart enough and adventurous enough and bored enough to jump at a change. Chink, Jap—it didn't matter to me. He could have been a Martian, for all I cared. And believe me, in the Calgary of 1939, a wealthy Japanese businessman was only marginally less exotic than a Martian.

Our conversation lasted under a minute. We had everything settled before the tea in our cups was cool enough to drink. Even so, we didn't jump up and rush back to work, not when we were lounging around the lunch room in the middle of the morning with the president's permission. That tea was a luxury. We stretched it out until, after half an hour, Miss Bayliss couldn't stand it any longer and barged in without so much as a perfunctory knock on the door.

"And which of you do I have to replace with no notice?" she said in a voice that could have etched glass. "I assume that after all this time you've come to a decision." Miss Bayliss was a great one for assuming.

Dumb-cluck me was about to stick up her hand when the quicker-witted Irene chimed in. "Not yet, Miss Bayliss, but we're almost ready to take a vote."

"Then do it quickly. And, by the way, I assume there will be no complaints from the rest of you about having to take up the slack while I'm short a typist."

According to office legend, Miss Bayliss had started at Greer & Western as a lowly typist herself, but now that she was ruler of the room, her fingers never touched a key, not even to fill in when one of us was sick. However, she did proofread all our work. It made her day when one of her girls had to stay late and redo a letter or, better still, a nice, long contract full of numbers. Miss Bayliss was the original kiss-up, kick-down kid.

"And don't take forever. There's a morning's work still waiting that I assume you plan on finishing." Miss Bayliss turned abruptly on the heel of her black oxford and huffed out on a note of aggrieved resignation. She left the door open a crack. Irene got up and closed it.

We made that tea last until after eleven. I was a little hurt that none of the others wanted to talk about my new job, but it was no longer of interest to anyone but me. The matter was settled and that was that, so we moved on to a topic of conversation in which our interest never flagged. We talked about men. Irene and Verna were both engaged, and pretty little Heather had boyfriends galore. I had a steady boyfriend myself. We weren't officially engaged, but Norman had us both on a strict savings plan that he hoped would allow us to set enough aside to be able to make an announcement within the year.

As I remember, our conversations never varied much. Invariably, Verna's favourite topic was her hope chest. She'd spent the years of her long engagement embroidering so many sheets and towels and tablecloths with her future initials that she could have opened a small hotel. She even crocheted dishcloths on her lunch break. Of course her Robert (whom Irene referred to as Boring Bob when Verna wasn't around) was a perfect gentleman. Probably watching Verna crochet those dishcloths was more effective than cold showers. But Irene's Pete was a bit of a beast, if she did say so herself—and she did at every opportunity. Nothing Irene liked better than to recount her latest adventures with what she called Pete's Roman hands and Russian fingers. He plied her with chocolate and the occasional minute bottle of Evening in Paris to no avail. According to Irene, she always called a halt before "things" went too far. She did admit that once or twice "things" almost got out of hand. She said Pete got so excited you'd think he had a broom handle up his trousers. I laughed along with the rest, but I honestly didn't understand what Irene was talking about. Amazing when you think that I was almost nineteen years old. Told you I was naive bordering on simple, didn't I?

I wasn't so simple that I was about to rush home and ask my parents about Pete's broom handle. Even I knew better than that. I asked my brother instead. That evening, I went to Charlie's room, where he was busy with his homework. After much hemming and hawing, I finally managed to put the question. When Charlie finished laughing, he explained the male erection to me in detailed and clinical terms. Imagine having to ask your little brother about the facts of life. I asked him if he'd ever had a broom handle himself, but he told me to buzz off and let him finish his history essay. I'm not certain where Charlie obtained all this scientific information of his. I'd love to have asked him someday, but Charlie and I never got a someday.

When we'd squeezed the last drop of tea from the old Brown Betty, the four of us strolled back to the typing room. The others went in to work while I knocked on the door of Miss Bayliss's tiny office across the hall. Everyone called her cubby-hole an office, but all it needed was a sink and a mop and it could have been the janitor's closet. Still, that hadn't stopped her from having her name and title stencilled in gold letters on the door. Miss T.E. Bayliss, Head, Typing Dept., did not ask me to sit.

"So it's you, Miss Jeynes," she said, looking up from her proofreading. "I can't say as I'm surprised. Well, I hope you won't live to regret going to work for an Oriental." She looked at me as if she expected a reply. I kept quiet mainly because I didn't know what to say. "I'll inform Mrs. Tanner that you're the one who has decided to leave Greer & Western. And now I assume you will want to get back to your machine and finish your morning's work." I took this as a dismissal and turned to leave, but she called me back.

"Mrs. Tanner also requested me to inform you that she will have a final pay envelope ready for you when you go to Mr. Calthorpe's office this afternoon." Miss Bayliss was bitterly jealous of Mrs. Tanner, who held the coveted post of private secretary to the president. "If it were up to me, I'd dock you for today. You haven't put in anything like an honest day's work and, in my view, that means you don't deserve an honest day's wage. I assume you'll be able to live with your conscience."

Really. That's what she said to me. Word for word. In retrospect, I can see that old Bayliss had a screw or two loose, but I still can't work up much sympathy for her.

I managed to live with my conscience quite comfortably while I bashed out the last of my morning's letters. It was almost a quarter to one by the time I finished and the others were out at lunch. I ate my sandwich at my desk, a practice Miss Bayliss frowned on, washed my hands and face, combed my hair, and went upstairs to Mr. Calthorpe's office. Until that afternoon, I'd never been in the executive offices. I was impressed and more than a little intimidated by their size. You could have put the entire typing room into the outer office where Mrs. Tanner worked. A pretty patterned rug covered the hardwood, and a couple of comfortable-looking armchairs sat in front of a big window that had proper drapes, not just pull-down blinds like we had in the typing room.

Mrs. Tanner sat at a large desk beside the door to Mr. Calthorpe's inner office. A widow of about the same age as my mother, she was my ideal of the well-dressed woman. Still is, for that matter. Tall and slim with a figure made for clothes, she livened her tailored office outfits with a succession of silk scarves that she tied with a panache I envy to this day. She smiled up at me across an acre of mahogany and greeted me by name, which was a bit of a startler for someone accustomed to Miss Bayliss's style of employee relations. She handed me a long white envelope with my name written on it in a graceful copperplate and told me that Mr. Calthorpe had asked the accounting department to put in something extra along with my pay as a bonus for helping out when it was needed. I thanked her and put the envelope in my purse, but oh, how I wanted to rip in and start counting. Mrs. Tanner motioned me to an armchair and proceeded to do her best to put me at ease. Had I been outside over the lunch hour and was it still so very cold? I managed to stammer a few words back, but I was so nervous I probably didn't make any sense.

At exactly one, Mr. Calthorpe opened his office door. By that time, he knew my name. He asked me to step into his office, which was even grander than Mrs. Tanner's. His carpet was a real British India, his armchairs were upholstered in leather, and you could have waltzed on his desk with room for a comfortable twirl. A dozen liquor bottles and a soda siphon sat on the marble top of a handsome mahogany sideboard. Sometimes, at Christmas, Dad managed to buy a bottle of whisky that he doled out to our holiday visitors in little tots, with a few fumes held back for Mum to flame the pudding. Until I clapped eyes on Mr. Calthorpe's sideboard, I'd never seen so much liquor in one place. The sheer lavishness must have mesmerized me because I don't recall noticing Mr. Miyashita until he got up from a chair by Mr. Calthorpe's desk and walked over to shake my hand. I'm sure Mr. Calthorpe introduced me to him, but it didn't register then, and I certainly don't remember it now. The most important introduction of my life is a complete blank.

I did have the presence of mind to shake his hand. To be honest, Mr. Miyashita looked so distinguished that I damn near curtsied. I don't know what I had expected—Mr. Moto maybe—but Mr. Miyashita was a complete surprise. I'd never seen anyone like him before. He was even more amazing than the liquor bottles. He was perfect, right from his neatly parted silver hair to his double-Windsored silk tie and bespoke navy blue suit. I had no idea that something as ordinary as a business suit could be that beautiful, but then I'd never seen Savile Row tailoring before. Beside it, Mr. Calthorpe's clothes looked saggy and old. For that matter, so did Mr. Calthorpe, although he must have been a good fifteen years younger than Mr. Miyashita.

"Thank you for volunteering to work for me, Miss Jeynes. I hope you will enjoy your time at my office, and that you will find your work both interesting and agreeable." Maybe I'd been expecting him to sound like Mr. Moto too, and in truth, Mr. Miyashita did have an accent—an English one. Nothing like my Northumbrian parents' broad Geordie talk, though. Mr. Miyashita spoke perfect BBC.

He bowed politely as he released my hand. I think that respectful little bow, not much more than a slight nod of the head, won my heart. No adult had ever treated me as if my work or my feelings about it mattered. The urge to curtsy struck again, but fortunately Mr. Calthorpe piped up and broke the spell.

"What time would you like this little gal of ours to start work tomorrow?"

"Please, would you be at my office tomorrow morning at ten, Miss Jeynes," Mr. Miyashita said. "I will outline your duties then."

"Thanks, Kay," Mr. Calthorpe chimed in by way of dismissal. "You're a swell kid. I know you're going to do Greer & Western proud." He grasped my hand in his sausagey fingers, gave it a damp squeeze, and I was out the door. Why is it that these big, life-altering occasions seem to last about ten seconds?

"Everything set?" Mrs. Tanner asked.

"I think so," I said, still a little awestruck by my new boss.

"Have you anything planned for this afternoon?"

"Go back and type, I guess."

"That won't be necessary, Kay. I mentioned earlier to Mr. Calthorpe that you'll have things to do to get ready for tomorrow, and he agreed you should take the rest of the afternoon off."

"Thank you, Mrs. Tanner." The day was getting better and better. "There are some things I'd like to do."

"And by the way, if anyone should ask why you're leaving early, tell them to talk to me." I was pretty certain I knew the anyone she had in mind. Then she stood and walked from behind her desk to shake my hand. "Congratulations on your new job, Kay. And good luck."

I liked Mrs. Tanner. She was what my mum used to call a real lady, and she was a smart one too. Nowadays, she'd be running the company. During the war, she took a job in Ottawa working for some bigwig on a very important, hush-hush project. As a matter of fact, it was Mrs. Tanner who got me my job in Ottawa in 1942.

The first thing I did on my impromptu afternoon off was whip downstairs to the ladies' washroom, close myself in a cubicle, and open my pay envelope. A regular week's salary was all there, including Friday's pay—along with twenty dollars extra. I could hardly believe my eyes. Twenty dollars all at one time! Now, before you laugh, you have to realize that twenty dollars was a fortune to me back then, almost two weeks' pay. I'd had my eye on a dress I'd seen in The Hudson's Bay that looked just like the one Ginger Rogers wore in *Shall We Dance*. I wanted it desperately, but the eight-dollar price tag put it way out of my range. Even a meal at Eaton's cafeteria was something I could only afford on special occasions. There, a meat and two veg lunch, including soup, a bun, coffee, and a piece of pie, cost twenty-five cents. I know because a few days before Christmas, the Greer & Western girls had splurged on the turkey dinner special. At a fancy place like the Palliser, you could eat that same meal for a couple of dollars. Not that I had ever poked my nose in the door of their dining room. But that afternoon, with my twenty dollars in hand, I could have booked a suite at the Palliser and swilled champagne. I was rich. Instead, I stuffed my money back into my purse and left for home.

On my way to catch the streetcar I stopped at Harry's News and Tobacco, where I lavished a little of my new fortune on a bag of liquorice allsorts for Mum, a small tin of pipe tobacco for Dad, and a *Popular Photography* for Charlie. After all, I had something to celebrate, didn't I? To be honest, I wasn't altogether certain what kind of reception my big news was going to get at home, and I wanted to make it clear that I regarded getting the job with Mr. Miyashita as a significant step up. Not that a few ounces of candy and a bit of tobacco would convince my family of anything. Still, it never hurts to smooth the way a little, does it?

I got home a little after two. At first Mum thought I'd felt sick at work and left early. When I told her the real reason, she hit the roof.

"How could you, Kay? How could you up and leave a good steady company like Greer & Western to take a chance on some foreign lot nobody's ever heard of?"

"But, Mum, everyone's heard of Miyashita Industries. It's one of the biggest companies in the world."

"And how can you be so sure your old job will be waiting when things fall through with this Mr. Nanki Poo or whatever his name is?" She continued as if I hadn't spoken. "Do you ever stop to look before you leap? Oh, Kay, what a girl you are! Rush in where angels fear—that's you." She shook her head. "I'll bet it never entered your head to ask Norman what he thought."

Mum scored a bull's eye with that one. It hadn't occurred to me to ask Norman's opinion, and right then, I realized I wasn't going to tell him about my twenty dollars either. After her first flash of anger, Mum simmered down to mutters and mumbles for the rest of the afternoon. She did eat the liquorice though.

I told Charlie my news when he got home from school. He was all for it, which made me feel good, but at the same time, I knew his opinion didn't count for much compared with Mum and Dad's. I kept quiet about the twenty dollars until after dinner when we were alone upstairs. I gave Charlie five for his enlarger fund, which bought his silence but didn't stop him from teasing me.

"Elder sister is very generous." He made a stab at a Mr. Moto voice. "Five dollars for her brother's enlarger fund is most welcome."

"Give up, Charlie. That's the worst Mr. Moto imitation anyone's ever heard." My brother ignored me. Instead, he bowed just like Peter Lorre did in the movies. "And how much does her honourable boss pay his new typewriting girl?"

I had to admit that, stupid as it sounded, I'd forgotten to ask.

"Such negligence not only sounds stupid. It is stupid. Until the answer to this important question is revealed, your loyal brother cannot begin to dream of a larger enlarger."

Charlie bowed his Mr. Moto bow again, then left to do his homework. I heard him laughing to himself as he sat at the little table that served as his desk. A short time later he reappeared in my room, this time to tell me a story about Mr. Motoshita, the famous detective, and his new, incredibly dumb girl sidekick, Kayo. Then, every twenty minutes or so until bedtime, he'd pop back in with yet another thrilling adventure featuring Calgary's newest team of crime fighters. As the evening went on, his improvisations got ever more wild and elaborate until they were almost one-man skits. And very annoying they were, which is exactly why Charlie did them. Still, I have to admit, he was pretty funny. That annoyed me even more.

Dad was neutral. He agreed with Mum that what I'd done was rash, but then you can't put an old head on young shoulders, can you? He told her she didn't have to worry about Miyashita Industries, that it was one of the biggest companies in Japan. He also said that Greer & Western had treated me fairly so far and he couldn't see any reason why Mr. Calthorpe would lie. If Mr. Calthorpe said there would be a job for me back at Greer & Western, then there would be a job waiting. But maybe things wouldn't come to that. He'd heard good things of Mr. Miyashita too. Why just last week, Dad read in the *Albertan* that Mr. Miyashita had donated the money to buy some new X-ray equipment for the Holy Cross Hospital. So who was to say he mightn't be a decent fellow in his own way, even though he was an Oriental and a Jap at that? Besides, it was only a temporary arrangement, wasn't it? And what's done is done, so let's make the best of it and wait and see. He did agree with Mum that I should have consulted Norman.

Of course Mum and Dad asked about my new salary. They weren't impressed when I told them that in the excitement of getting the job I'd forgotten to ask. Still, all things considered, breaking the news hadn't gone so badly. The day ended one for, one against, and one neutral. That was one neutral better than I'd expected.

Assignment #3
WHAT WAS THE BEST OR WORST JOB YOU EVER HAD?

THIS WEEK'S ASSIGNMENT IS MADE to order for me to carry on telling about Mr. Miyashita although I've never really thought of my time with him as merely a job, best or worst. The three years I spent in his office changed my life. There's so much to tell about that time, I wasn't sure where to start. Janice's advice? Keep it simple, begin at the beginning, and tell how I got the job. I tried to explain that I'd already done that in our Most Important Day exercise, but she didn't understand what I was getting at. The poor child wasn't all there this morning. Decidedly vague. Fit right in with the rest of us. She's booked for a root canal this afternoon, and the guilty tooth must have been giving her hell. Or maybe our readings numbed her wits.

At the start of the session she asked if any of us would like to read part of what we'd written to the class. Strictly volunteer. I didn't. During the readings, everyone listened politely, but you could see they all found their own Most Important Day riveting and other people's a big yawn. Me too, except for Meggie's. Her Most Important Day was the day she left her first husband and ran off with a Swiss mountain-climbing guide from Lake Louise. She even considered marrying him but discovered in the nick of time, so to speak, that his hobby was collecting cuckoo clocks. He had more than thirty of them. Noons and midnights were such hell that she had to dump the poor fellow. I don't quite believe that this really was Meggie's most important day, but at least it was entertaining, especially compared with The Day Our Emily Was Born or The Day I Met the Lovely Girl Who Became My Wife.

After we'd heard from the last volunteer, Janice told us we should try to loosen up and write like we're talking to our best friend, not our high school English teacher. She said that if we imagine our best friend is right there beside us listening to what we're saying, it might help make our writing more natural, more like a conversation. That's when Dave, the most literal-minded old fart in Calgary, stuck up his hand and informed us that Janice's suggestion was impossible for him because his best friend had died last year. Passed on, as he put it. Janice said that maybe Dave was interpreting her suggestion too narrowly. Why couldn't he simply imagine his best friend was alive and talk to him anyway? Poor Janice—big mistake. Dave took this as his cue to rattle on about how, as far as he knew, the only man ever to rise from the dead was Jesus Christ, who by the way and thank you for asking even if you didn't, just happens to be his own Personal Saviour. I could see he was revving up for a big bout of witnessing when Meggie rode to the rescue and batted her new false eyelashes at him. An end of the left one had come unglued so it really did flap up a breeze. She said she could think of any number of defunct friends she'd love to chat with, but if Dave's imagination wasn't up to that, then he should try chatting to himself. Why didn't Dave pretend he was his own best friend and start talking?

"That's ridiculous," Dave said. "I can't sit around talking to myself."

"Why not?" said Meggie. "Around here, who'd notice?"

Janice just nodded and popped a couple more aspirin. I wonder how much they pay the kid to teach our class. Not enough, I'd guess.

There I go, rambling again, putting off the moment when I actually have to buckle down to this week's assignment. Time to stop the nonsense and get to work. So here's my stab at The Best Job I Ever Had.

I woke early on the morning of my first day at Miyashita Industries, and the world was a different place. Yesterday I had been bored; today I wasn't. I felt a happy rush of anticipation at the thought of going to work. Even the weather was a joy. Either that or my memory has slapped on some first-rate meteorology in honour of the occasion. A chinook had blown over the mountains during the night. By the time I left for work, the thermometer outside our kitchen window read forty degrees above, more than seventy degrees warmer than the morning before. It's a phenomenon that still astounds me.

I decided to skip the streetcar and walk to work. Or maybe that should be float. For me, a warm wind in February blows with it an exhilaration that verges on the euphoric. It's difficult to understand if you've never felt the full force of a big Alberta chinook blasting down from the Rockies. To those of us who live half the year in the prairie's desiccating cold, the wind brings a relief from winter that is a joy in itself. At times, it almost seems as if this imitation spring carries with it an imitation spring fever. By half past nine, I was striding down 9th Avenue with scarf and toque stuffed in my pockets and my unfastened coat billowing in the wind. Clouds arched over the Rockies in the classic chinook formation. Sunlight dazzled off shrinking snowbanks and runnels of meltwater gurgled down storm drains. By noon we'd see the mercury in the sixties, bare patches of brown grass, and the gutters running streams. The world had already begun to smell of mud and sublimating snow.

I arrived for work fifteen minutes early. The Miyashita Industries office was in the Grain Exchange Building, a handsome place with wide, arched windows on the ground floor and an elaborately carved sandstone entrance that I'd passed every morning as I walked from the streetcar to Greer & Western. I muscled open one of the heavy oak and bevelled-glass doors and made my way to the elevator. Back then, elevators were not automatic; actual people ran them, usually women. The Grain Exchange elevator girl didn't wear a uniform like the girls in Eaton's, but she did have the same thick white cotton gloves. With those gloves on and her hair collected in big clumps of ringlets over each ear, I remember thinking she looked like Minnie Mouse. She was cheerful and chatty and let me off at the fourth floor. The Miyashita Industries door stood shut, its frosted-glass window dark. I knocked.

"He's not in yet," the elevator girl called to me. "He never gets here before ten."

"Where's everyone else?" I asked.

"There is no one else since Mr. Tanaka got sick and went home to Japan."

"You mean no one works here but Mr. Miyashita?"

"Nope. Just him. You want to wait or you want to go back down? He'll be here in ten minutes."

We rode to the main floor in silence. I was a little taken aback. I had expected there would be other employees, an assistant or two or even an office boy. But I was it. I waited in the lobby for a few minutes, then stepped back outside into the wind to watch for him. I couldn't believe Mr. Miyashita never got to work before ten. That really was foreign. In Calgary, people prided themselves on getting a good early start to the day. It was considered virtuous in itself not only to be an early riser but to arrive at least ten minutes beforehand for every appointment. In my parents' eyes, if you were five minutes early you were five minutes late. And starting work at ten? Not unless you'd been gravely ill.

At two minutes to ten, I saw my new boss striding up from the 1st Avenue underpass, coattails flapping in the wind, one gloved hand carrying a briefcase and the other clamped firmly on his grey homburg. He waved to me, and a gust swept the hat into the air. The hand shot up and caught it with the careless grace of long practice.

"Good morning, Miss Jeynes." He opened the door for me and leaned against it to keep it from blowing shut. As I walked past him into the lobby, I noticed that he was wearing spats. Believe me, even in 1939, there weren't many men in Calgary who wore spats. Later I learned that Sterling's Shoes kept them on special order for him, and that his wife would not allow him out of the house from mid-October to mid-April without them. On bitterly cold days, particularly when there was lots of snow, Mr. Miyashita wore big, felt-lined boots like everyone else, and very odd they looked poking out from under his Savile Row trousers. No odder than the spats though.

"Is this not a splendid chinook we have blowing, Miss Jeynes?"

As we waited for the elevator, I owned as how I thought the weather was pretty wonderful compared with yesterday, sir.

"You know there are those who find these *foehn* winds intolerable," he said in his beautiful English voice. I hadn't a clue what *foehn* meant. "They can make people feel very testy and out of sorts. Some get headaches too."

"My mother doesn't like chinooks much," I said. "Especially if they last for any length of time. They don't give her headaches, at least not the physical kind. It's her tulips. They start to grow and then they get frozen when the cold comes back. Either that or the dog next door comes over and nibbles off the little green shoots." I managed to stop my nervous babbling.

Mr. Miyashita smiled. It made him look much younger. Hard to believe that he was thirty years younger than I am now. He seemed so old to me back then.

"That is an aspect of chinooks I had not considered, but then I am not a keen gardener. That is Mrs. Miyashita's bailiwick. Are you a gardener, Miss Jeynes?" Before I could answer, the elevator arrived and whisked us up to the fourth floor.

Mr. Miyashita paused at the door to the office, set his briefcase down, and took a key from his pocket. "This key is yours, Miss Jeynes." He held it in both hands as he presented it to me, almost making a little ceremony of the occasion. "Your first duty every morning will be to open the office door at ten. Would you care to begin?"

"Thank you, sir." I accepted the key with equal gravity and unlocked the door.

I had never seen anything like the reception office at Miyashita Industries. I suppose I should stop saying that right now or this exercise is going to be full of never seen anything likes. But I hadn't. The office was an art gallery, a fifteen- by twenty-five-foot space filled with paintings and large photographs, all of the Rocky Mountains. I had been expecting something like Greer & Western. As a nod to decoration, the reception office there featured a big map of Alberta with a couple of gold stick-on stars that marked the location of the company's mines.

I stood staring at the paintings, probably with my mouth hanging open. I think I spent the better part of that day with my mouth open.

"Perhaps you are familiar with some of these mountains," Mr. Miyashita said.

"I know Mount Rundle," I said, pointing to a small watercolour of the famous ridge. "And there are the Three Sisters. This one is of Mount Stephen, but I only know that because I read the little brass plate underneath. I think it's near Field. May I ask who painted them, sir?"

"An Englishman named Marmaduke Matthews," he replied. "Mr. Van Horne issued passes on the CPR to a number of artists so they could travel and paint landscapes along the route. Matthews did that one of Rundle in 1894. I first saw his work when I travelled across Canada on the CPR myself, on my way to study in England. Decidedly old-school European in style and perhaps a little too romantic for some tastes, but very skilled all the same, I think. Van Horne was an amateur painter himself, you know, and a very good one. Are you interested in painting, Miss Jeynes?"

"I don't know much about it, but I really like these watercolours." I pointed to a half-dozen smaller paintings, their colours more separate and distinct than those in Matthews's work.

"They are by another Englishman," he said, "a young fellow named Walter Phillips. However, they are not watercolours. They are coloured woodcuts, and you can see the influence of the *ukiyo-e* masters in Phillips's technique. Perhaps that is why I am so fond of them."

Again, I didn't know what he was talking about. I added *ukiyo-e* to my don't-have-a-clue list, right under *foehn* winds. I'd look them up in the Britannica when I went to the library on Saturday. If I could figure out how to spell them.

"I do hope you are fond of the mountains, Miss Jeynes. As you can see, you will be working in the midst of them. This is your desk. After you get settled in, we will discuss what will be expected of you in your new position here." He disappeared into his own office.

My corner of the outer room was very ordinary, and I remember feeling a bit disappointed. I don't know quite what I'd expected but certainly something a touch more exotic and Japanese than the plain oak desk and the same model Underwood that I'd typed on at Greer & Western. I hung my coat on the wooden rack beside the door, ran a comb through my wind-snarled hair, and went to have another look at the art on display. I liked the photographs best, perhaps because I knew a bit about photography, thanks to Charlie, but more probably because I was familiar with their subjects. Most of them had been taken in the mountains between Canmore and Golden. Many were of places around Banff where I'd gone hiking and fishing with Charlie and our friends, but in the photos they seemed different, not exactly sinister but certainly forbidding. Maybe scale had something to do with it. These were not postcard-pretty alpine scenes. The enlargements were big, some up to four feet wide, and nothing in the stark, black-and-white images acknowledged a human scale. Here the Rockies were cold, dangerous, and incredibly beautiful. In one, a jagged line of spruce trees cast black shadows across the layers of a limestone cliff. I found myself forgetting to make sense of its subject and looking instead at shapes and patterns. The next enlargement was a study in curves and contrasts with wind-sculpted snow curled over itself against a backdrop of black shale. But the one that really caught my eye, a composite of twenty small studies of strange-looking fossils, was more scientific illustration than art. I later learned that Mr. Miyashita had taken them at the Burgess Shale, where he had spent a summer with Walcott.

Before I could move on to the next photo, Mr. Miyashita emerged from his office, looking every bit as well tailored as he had the day before, this time in a dark grey suit and polished black oxfords. The suit was another work of art, and the shoes weren't far behind. Later, after I started to keep the books and paid a few of Kilgour, French and Stanbury's bills, I discovered just how much it cost to look like a million bucks in bespoke suits from Cary Grant's favourite tailor and handmade shoes from New & Lingwood. A single pair of those shoes cost more than all the shoes I'd worn in my life. I made myself stop staring at his feet.

"Are you a photographer, Miss Jeynes?" he asked.

"I like looking at pictures, but my brother is the family photographer. He's a real shutterbug. He even develops his own prints. Right now he can only do contact prints, but he's saving up to buy the parts to build himself an enlarger." I felt myself in the grip of another bout of nervous blathering. "I wish Charlie could see these. I've never seen photographs like them. They're wonderful. And so big. Who took them?"

"I did," he said. "And thank you for your enthusiasm." He smiled and looked young again. "Now, if you are ready, perhaps you would care to see the rest of the office before we begin our morning's business."

Miyashita Industries occupied four rooms—the reception office, a photographic darkroom, a storage room, and Mr. Miyashita's private office. We started with the darkroom. It crossed my mind to wonder why a business office would need a darkroom, but the art gallery in the reception area had prepared me for subsequent oddities. I guessed this must be where Mr. Miyashita printed his mountain photos. The black interior was immaculate, with all the equipment neatly stowed. And such equipment. Even my untrained eye could see that it was the Aladdin's cave of darkrooms. I couldn't help thinking of Charlie's darkroom, otherwise known as our cellar. That's where he printed his contact sheets, developing them in a set of chipped trays, hand-me-downs from a professional photographer who went to our church. He warmed the developer on an old hotplate and washed the prints in our kitchen sink. I suspected Charlie's enlarger fund was in for a long haul before it caught up with even the smaller of Mr. Miyashita's Elwoods.

"I do not expect you will need to do much in this room, Miss Jeynes," Mr. Miyashita said. "But you must remember that when the red light over its door is on, the darkroom is in use. The door must not be opened then."

"I'll be very careful, sir." I'd had Charlie yell at me enough times when I'd forgotten he was printing and turned on the cellar light to know the gravity of this photographic sin.

The storage room held its own surprise, although this one had at least something do with business. A glass-domed stock ticker sat on a stand in the middle of the floor, chattering to itself as it spewed tape into a wicker basket at its base. I'd seen one before when my bookkeeping class went on a field trip to James Richardson & Sons, the stockbrokers.

"Do you know how to read ticker tape, Miss Jeynes?"

"Sorry, sir."

"The closing results for the stock exchange that are printed in the newspaper, perhaps?"

"Yes, I do know how to read those." At last, something I actually knew. "I learned in bookkeeping class."

"Then you will learn how to read this in no time." He reached down and scooped up a tangle of tape. "It is very simple." He stretched out a length for me to inspect, revealing a meaningless string of letters and numbers. "The tape provides the same information as the newspaper figures but in a different form. You will soon acquire the knack."

Cabinets full of drawers crowded one another on every wall of the room. The place was packed with drawers—big drawers in a map cabinet, medium drawers in four filing cabinets, and little drawers in a cabinet that looked a lot like the ones library card catalogues used to occupy before computers took over.

"These files will be your responsibility," Mr. Miyashita said. He opened a drawer and pulled out a big white envelope. In it was a contact sheet of a dozen photographic images plus a smaller envelope that held their negatives stored between glassine sheets. The filing cabinets were crammed with them. Some of the envelopes held only one eight-by-ten print or maybe a couple of four-by-fives along with their large negatives. Most were labelled in English, but a few were in Japanese only. Almost all the images stored in them were of the mountains.

"Frankly, Miss Jeynes, the photographs in these files are in considerable disarray. At the time I printed them, I would simply mark their envelopes with locations and dates and then stuff them in a file drawer. My hope is that you will bring order to this chaos."

I wondered why Mr. Miyashita's previous secretary had allowed the files to get into such a state. I knew that unless the next incumbent took at least a year to travel from Japan, I hadn't a hope of sorting the mess in those cabinets before I went back to typing at Greer & Western. Mr. Miyashita opened a drawer in the map cabinet. It was full of enlargements like the ones on the wall in the outer office.

"You will find this cabinet and its counterpart in your office are both in a bit of a state as well, but I'm sure you'll have the lot of them sorted out in no time. The cabinet with the small drawers is for negatives only, but we will get to those later. And that is the office. Do you have any questions?"

I had so many I hardly knew where to start. "Office supplies, sir? Pencils, paper, typewriter ribbons?"

"My goodness, how remiss of me." Mr. Miyashita shook his head. "That is all kept here in the bottom drawer of this cabinet behind the door. Anything you need that you do not find in the drawer you may purchase at Osborne's. Now, if you will be so kind as to find yourself a pad of writing paper, we will go to my office and discuss your duties. Mrs. Tanner tells me you are very skilled in the Gregg system of short-hand writing."

"Yes, sir." I wasn't sure if I was agreeing to go to his office or acknowledging my expertise at shorthand, but before I found a note pad, someone knocked at the door.

"Ah, that will be the Carlton fellow," Mr. Miyashita said. "He brings coffee every morning."

Indeed it was the man from the Carlton Café, a coffee shop around the corner on 9th Avenue, carrying a picnic basket that held a thermos and two thick crockery mugs that he put on my desk.

"I took the liberty of ordering a cup for you, Miss Jeynes," he said as the deliveryman pocketed his tip and left. "I hope that is satisfactory."

"Thank you, sir. It's very satisfactory."

"Then enjoy your coffee and please join me when you've finished." He poured his own cup and retreated to his office.

And wasn't that the cat's pyjamas, stripes and all? Mid-morning coffee sent in to the office—the lap of luxury in those days. The girls at Greer & Western simply wouldn't believe me when I told them. It didn't matter that the coffee wasn't very good. Who cared when there I was, me, former typist Kay Jeynes, now private secretary, albeit temporarily, to the head of Miyashita Industries Canada, sitting at my desk, sipping coffee amid the splendour of the Rocky Mountains and feeling very sophisticated. I tell you, right then I impressed myself no end. Nevertheless, all triumphal moments pass. I put my empty cup back in the Carlton's basket, collected a pencil and writing pad from the supply drawer, and went to work.

Mr. Miyashita's office was as surprising as the other rooms if only because it was so plain. I'd been expecting something at least as impressive as Mr. Calthorpe's office, but Mr. Miyashita's was much smaller and the furniture, while comfortable, was as unremarkable as mine. Only two things struck me as at all out of the ordinary. The first was a tiny jack pine in a shallow pot on the desk. I took it for a seedling, a very sickly one. Its thready roots clung to a chunk of rock, and its gnarled and twisted trunk made the poor wee thing look as if it had started life high on a windy ridge in the Rockies. Even then, when I was a good deal more sentimental than I am now, I don't think I had feelings for plants, but that jack pine was so stunted and scraggly that I felt quite sorry for it.

The second thing I found unusual was another picture, this one a stylized portrait of a Japanese man dressed in a dark purple robe with a white X inside a white circle on the left shoulder. His right hand was clenched in a fist and his left clutched the scarlet scabbard of a sword. The man looked angry or maybe anxious, I couldn't decide which. I mistook his tonsure for a funny-looking light blue hat. At first I thought it might be another water colour, a very simple one, but the luminous, almost shiny, grey background made me wonder. I found myself fascinated by the face, especially the eyebrows. Who'd have thought that two black rectangles could say so much? It fascinates me to this day, the face of my old friend Tokuji. I brought him to Foothills Sunset with me and a great comfort he is. He's watching as I work on this assignment.

How did we come to this, you and I, my dear Tokuji? Yes, you're right, the answer is obvious. We are here because one of us found it irksome to fetch the stepladder to change a ceiling light bulb in the kitchen. But that wasn't my question, as well you know. Oh for God's sake, Kay, stop this drivel. Talking to a picture. And you think poor old Dave is missing a few bats from his belfry. Get a grip, woman.

Outlining my secretarial responsibilities did not take long. Answer the phone, open the mail, pass on all Japanese correspondence to Mr. Miyashita, read and sort the other letters, type Mr. Miyashita's dictated replies, and manage some simple bookkeeping and bill paying—an accounting firm did the complicated stuff. Starting the next week, he would teach me how to read ticker tape. Still, all these tasks seemed incidental compared with the photographs. For him, the images stored in the files were far and away the most important things in the office. He wanted me to set to work immediately organizing his jumble of prints and negatives, but I knew I'd be out of my depth. I'd have to ask someone, probably a librarian, how best to tackle the chaotic contents of those cabinets, or I'd simply create a new and different mess.

"I'm going to have to get some advice on setting up a proper filing system for your photos because I don't know how to do it. I'm sorry, sir."

"Miss Jeynes, you need never apologize for not knowing something, only for not learning it. You must consult whomever you need to set up our system. And if there is anything else here that you are not certain about or do not understand, I would like you to ask. I will do my best to help you find answers to your questions."

"What's a *foehn* wind, sir?"

"A *foehn* wind?"

"Remember, you said earlier that some people find *foehn* winds intolerable."

"So I did," he said.

"Well, I don't know what that word means. I don't even know how to spell it."

"*Foehn*," he said. "F-o-e-h-n." And then he explained in clear and simple terms the physics of a chinook. That was the first of many explanations I got from Mr. Miyashita. He was a born teacher, and I was his first and only pupil.

THAT EVENING AS we sat down to dinner around our kitchen table, everyone wanted to know about my first day at work.

"Come on then. What are the other girls like?" Mum asked as she dished out the steak and kidney.

"There aren't any other girls. There's just me."

"You're the only girl in the whole office?" Her serving spoon stopped halfway to a plate. "That's unusual, isn't it?" In my parents' lexicon, unusual was synonymous with suspect.

"Now, Judith, like as not they do things a different way in Japan," said Dad. "Maybe they don't hold with hiring women to work in their offices. Kay did tell us that his last secretary was a man. Isn't that so, Kay?"

"Then what about the men?" Mum asked. A blob of gravy fell from the spoon onto the tablecloth, but she didn't notice.

"There aren't any men, except for Mr. Miyashita," I said.

"You mean to tell me there's just the two of you?"

"Just us," I said, casual as all get out. I turned my attention to spooning some mashed turnips onto my place. "Turnips look good, Mum."

"Same as always." She wasn't about to let me change the subject. "If this Mya-whata-me-not Industries is such a big noise, then why are there only the two of you in that office?"

"I don't know," I mumbled, keeping my eyes on my plate.

"Your mother's right to worry, Kay. Big company like that. And your Mr. Miyashita, a son of the founder and all—at least that's what it said in the *Albertan*. Him running a piddly two-person office makes you wonder."

I don't think my parents were worried about my working alone with Mr. Miyashita because they feared for my maidenly virtue, although come to think of it, on one of her more dramatic days, my mother might have entertained visions of him popping me into a laundry hamper bound for white slavery. No. What did disturb them was the fact that the Canadian headquarters of the mighty Miyashita Industries empire was such an insignificant place. I could tell they were worried that something about Mr. Miyashita wasn't quite on the up and up.

Later that evening I heard them talking in the kitchen. Norman was dropping by to take me to a movie, and I had come downstairs to wait for him. They changed the subject as soon as they saw me, but I did catch the words "remittance man" before I came into the room. I learned early that there were certain things about my new job and my new boss I'd be wise to keep under my hat.

While I didn't exactly lie to my parents—at least not very often— I didn't exactly tell the truth about my new job either. Most of the things I kept secret were things that made me feel uncomfortable myself. The ten o'clock start, for one. That always worried me. I knew Mum and Dad would be shocked if they found out, so I made sure they didn't. I became the shining example of the good early start. I got up an hour earlier than I had in my Greer & Western days and was at my desk by seven-thirty every morning. Occasionally Mum would mutter something about foreign slave drivers, and Dad would nod and say that I did seem to be putting in very long hours. Then they'd agree that it never hurt anyone to get a good early start. After all, I did get my Saturday mornings off now. Despite the slave-driving talk, I know they were both secretly relieved, even pleased, that Mr. Miyashita demanded such industry of his employee. At least it showed he was a hard-working fellow himself who expected value for money from his staff. Now that wasn't unusual at all, was it?

Not only did Mum and Dad keep their worries about my Japanese boss to themselves, they also defended their chick from anyone out-side our nest who ventured a criticism of my new job. I remember one sunny Saturday morning in early May, as I lay in bed with my window open to the spring air, I heard Mum chatting over the fence with Mrs. Sanders, our next-door neighbour. Mrs. Sanders's engaged daughter Alice was a salesclerk at Woolworth's.

"Kay having a sleep-in this morning, is she?" Mrs. Sanders said. "My, but she takes herself off to work early these days. That office of hers must be a very busy place."

"You've got that right," Mum agreed. "Her new boss demands an awful lot. But, to be fair, I have to say the man does pay an honest day's wage. Very honest." I could almost see the knowing nod that went with this last.

"I guess he has to, him being a Jap and all, or no one would work for him, would they?" Mrs. Sanders said.

"Or maybe he knows you get what you pay for," Mum countered very sharpish. "And our Kay is worth every penny she's paid."

Mrs. Sanders remained unconvinced. "I can tell you Alice's Jim wouldn't let her work for a Jap and that's a fact, not even for a hundred dollars a month."

Claiming her kettle must be on the boil by now, Mum bid a curt good morning to Mrs. Sanders and marched back to the house. I noticed that she had not corrected our neighbour's estimate of my new salary, but let me assure you, although I was earning substantially more than I had at Greer & Western, it wasn't anything like a hundred a month. I didn't learn exactly how much more until I'd been working for Mr. Miyashita for more than a week. He never mentioned money, and I was such a ninny I was too shy to ask. I finally found the courage the day Mum told me not to bother coming home from work until I knew my own wage. That afternoon I managed to put a tentative question to Mr. Miyashita about whether our office paid by the month or the week. He looked a little puzzled.

"My salary, sir. Do I get paid once a month or do I get paid once a week?"

"Oh yes, your salary," he said as if this were the first time he'd considered the subject, which it probably was. "What is your preference, Miss Jeynes?" he asked.

We settled on once a month. Then I screwed up my nerve another notch and asked how much I would be earning.

"How much did you earn at Greer & Western?" he asked. I think he may have felt uncomfortable too, but it wasn't until much later that I discovered I was the only secretary whose salary he ever had to pay for himself. His previous secretaries' wages had come directly from head office in Hiroshima.

I told him what I had earned typing.

"At this office your duties certainly encompass more than simple typewriting," he said. "Fifty dollars a month may be fair remuneration for that, but here I think you must receive a somewhat higher wage, one commensurate with your many new responsibilities. Would you consider seventy-five dollars each month to be acceptable?"

I think I managed to gasp out a "More than acceptable, thank you, sir." Acceptable? Acceptable? Seventy-five dollars a month? Acceptable, my eye—I was Rockefeller! I could hardly wait to tell Charlie. Mr. Motoshita and Kayo—ha! The only fly in the ointment was the question of how to break the news to Mum and Dad. To them, paying a nineteen-year-old girl seventy-five dollars a month would not just seem unusual, it would rank as insane.

"Then we are agreed that you will write a cheque to yourself for seventy-five dollars on the last day of every month and bring it to me for my signature."

"We're agreed, sir."

"Good. Now perhaps you would be so kind as to make us a cup of tea. And not the green leaves, please," he added. "This afternoon we will have real Canadian tea with sugar."

That night I told my parents and Charlie the good news. Both Mum and Charlie look pleased, but Dad was shocked.

"Sixty-five dollars a month? Why there's grown men with families make less than that and consider themselves lucky." He shook his head in dismay. "Sixty-five dollars for a girl not a year out of school. Makes a man wonder what the world's coming to."

Dad found my sixty-five dollars such a shock that I almost stopped feeling guilty that I'd kept quiet about the extra ten. I had decided to put that part of my new salary toward my university education and had opened a savings account at the Bank of Nova Scotia. However, I knew it would be easier to keep the family peace if I kept my ten-dollar-a-month secret because education was not a neutral topic at our house. Believe you me, the subject of Kay's Education had caused some right old dust-ups.

"I'll tell you what the world's coming to," Mum snapped back at him. "Kay got herself some education, that's what. She's a silver-medal secretary, not the downstairs skivvy."

For a sinking moment I thought Mum and Dad were going to put on the gloves and take the old fight another round. But that evening, since both Charlie and I were in the room, they put it away for later. Instead, Charlie turned on the radio, and we all listened to Lux Radio Theatre.

YESTERDAY MORNING AFTER physio I actually managed to work on this assignment. And didn't that make it a red-letter day if ever there was? The fact that I had enough oomph to do anything after physio amazed me. Usually, I collapse and sleep until lunch. But Darren, my physiotherapist, told me that I'm making real progress. For the first time, I believe him. Meggie says she can see I'm getting stronger too. Then again, I tell her that the droopy side of her face is looking much perkier these days, so maybe we're just encouraging each other with cheerful lies. Still, better a cheery lie than gloom and doom—isn't that so, Mr. Peale?

So, after (!) physio, I settled in to glance over what I'd written for this Best Job Ever exercise. I have to admit it gave me a bit of a shock. Until you actually read your own writing, you don't realize what a hash you're making of it. I saw that I was all over the place, telling what happened in February and then skipping ahead to May and jumping back to February again. My mind seems to dart helter skelter, chasing after every memory that pops into it. One memory leads to another, and that one leads to the next, and so it goes, scurrying on and on and on. It's a miracle I didn't find myself dashing around in 1963, wondering who I was and how I got there.

Perhaps that's why Janice has set us these exercises, so that when we do get to writing our real memoirs we'll at least have half a clue about where to start and what to put in. So I'm going to forget about order right now. I'll fling in whatever pops to mind and sort the whole mess later. That way I'll have everything written down on my steno pads, ready to be included in *Kathleen (Kay) Jeynes Hastings— Her Memoirs*. And my my, don't that sound grand? You know, I'm coming to the conclusion that maybe I haven't led a memoir sort of life. All in all, I think I might be more a reminiscence kind of girl. I'm sure reminiscences can be much messier than memoirs. Meggie and I discussed this over yesterday's gin and tonic. She says not to worry, that memoirs are simply reminiscences with the messy bits left out. Meggie thinks a messy bit is anything that doesn't make you look good.

As usual, she does have a point, especially her definition of messy bits. I know there are some pages in these exercises of mine that I would sooner set on fire than allow to see the light of memoir's day. I'd certainly like to forget that I lied to my parents about Mr. Miyashita. Not because I'm ashamed of the lying—show me a kid who hasn't lied to her parents. No, the messy bit is the fact that I felt the need to lie about him. I am ashamed of that.

But I digress, she said, which is the polite word for rambling. No time for that this morning because our class meets at one o'clock sharp today. We may even miss our naps. Gasp!

Meanwhile, back at the Best Job Ever . . .

It did take some time for Mr. Miyashita and me to settle into a routine at our office and begin to feel comfortable together. I guess that isn't too surprising when you consider that I was a wide-eyed Calgary kid of nineteen and he was a distinguished Japanese gentleman of sixty-one. But even as we got to know each other, there remained a formality to our relations that now, in the present age of first-name familiarity and easy bonhomie, would be considered quaintly old-fashioned. For many weeks, our conversation rarely ventured even to the fringes of the personal.

On a typical day, I'd arrive at work to find the *Albertan*, Calgary's morning paper, lying in front of the office door. I'd read the stock market page and make a note of yesterday's closing volume and prices for the companies Mr. Miyashita was following most closely. After I'd checked to make certain the stock ticker had plenty of tape, I'd settle in with my latest library book or work on the photo files until the mailman came and I'd sort the post. I loved working on those files. I must confess that I spent as much time looking at the photographs as I did cataloguing them.

Mr. Miyashita arrived every morning on the dot of ten; the Carlton coffee appeared shortly after. I think it was the coffee that first helped us to feel more at ease with each other. One morning toward the end of March he emerged from his office carrying his mug.

"I must say, this coffee leaves much to be desired, does it not, Miss Jeynes?" he asked.

Now here was a dilemma. The Carlton's coffee was pretty bad, but it might seem impolite to be too critical, seeing as he had been providing me with a cup of it every morning for the past six weeks. Then again, maybe it would be more polite to agree with him. I dithered.

"Come, Miss Jeynes. Do not dither. I would like you to give me an honest opinion."

So I did. "It's not very good, sir."

"Do you know how to make coffee?"

"I do," I said. "Although we don't have it very often at home. My parents are English and they like tea better."

"The English and the Japanese—both great ones for their tea," he agreed. "But early in the day, I much prefer coffee myself. Since you know how, perhaps you would make a pot for us of a morning. Would that be possible?"

"Absolutely, sir. But we'll need to get a pot and something to heat it on."

"Excellent. You may purchase any supplies you need at The Hudson's Bay. We have an account there. And perhaps you would include a packet of digestive biscuits as well. I confess that I developed quite a taste for digestives when I lived in England."

So I cancelled the Carlton basket and from then on made our coffee with water from the taps above the darkroom sink heated on a hot plate in the storage room. We drank it from bright yellow bone china cups that Mr. Miyahita bought at Birks one morning on his way to work. Sometimes, instead of drinking his coffee alone, Mr. Miyashita would invite me to join him in his office. Often this happened on mornings when I had asked him a question. I had taken him at his word, and when I didn't understand something at the office, I asked about it. Those cups of coffee marked the beginning of my real education.

It was pretty haphazard at first. For instance, my introduction to the art of bonsai came the morning I suggested to my horrified boss that with a new pot and regular watering, we could have that poor little jack pine of his growing properly in no time. I discovered origami on the Japanese holiday of Girls' Day. I was pretty long in the tooth for Girls' Day, but that didn't stop Mrs. Miyashita from folding a white paper crane, a symbol of good fortune, as a gift for me in honour of the occasion and sending it along with her husband to the office. Eventually, when I got to know her, she taught me some simple folds. I can still turn out a pretty snazzy little presentation box.

My questions about the portrait next to Mr. Miyashita's desk started us on the subject of *ukiyo-e*, Japanese woodblock prints, illustrations of the so-called floating world, the ephemeral world of famous actors and geishas, of courtesans and the heroes of legend. One morning as we drank our coffee, I asked the identity of the man in the picture.

"It is a portrait of Otani Tokuji. He was a famous kabuki actor in the late eighteenth century when Sharaku did this portrait of him. He is dressed in costume for one of his roles. I have had Tokuji with me for thirty years now," Mr. Miyashita answered. "The print was a gift to me from my uncle. He is a collector of *ukiyo-e* and knows how much I admire his Sharakus. I believe he has managed to acquire almost fifty of them now, mostly the actor portraits."

"Fifty portraits? Where does he find room to hang them all?"

Mr. Miyashita laughed. "He does not, Miss Jeynes. Putting pictures under glass and surrounding them with wood in order to suspend them on a wall is a Western custom. In Japan, *ukiyo-e* prints were sometimes bound into albums or, more often than not, simply left loose and wrapped together in a sort of parcel. When this portrait was made, *ukiyo-e* was popular art—inexpensive, ephemeral, tailored to the market—and publishers turned out prints by the thousands. Most were treated in an offhand way, rather like we might treat the pictures printed on calendars today. Even now there are still some connoisseurs of Japanese art who consider *ukiyo-e* prints like this portrait to be pretty shoddy stuff. But I daresay that would not surprise poor Sharaku. He wasn't much of a success in his own day either."

"Well, I'm glad your uncle isn't that kind of connoisseur or we wouldn't have Tokuji here at the office," I said. "How could anyone think his portrait is shoddy?"

"I agree wholeheartedly, and I shall pass your remarks on to my uncle Nori next time I write."

"Do you see him when you go home for visits?" It was my first gaffe.

"I am at home, Miss Jeynes," he said, all aloof and cold in an instant. I swear the temperature in the room dropped ten degrees as he spoke. "My home is here in Calgary. I am Canadian." He had never used that tone of voice with me before, and it hurt.

Nor was what he said true. Mr. Miyashita was not a Canadian citizen. He was a foreign national, a citizen of Japan. People of Japanese descent were not allowed to become full voting citizens of Canada until 1949, and that included people whose families had lived here for generations. Canada had always placed severe restrictions on immigration from Asia. Perhaps because he was Japanese and had grown up in a society with similarly xenophobic attitudes, Mr. Miyashita did not find our racist exclusionary laws shocking or even particularly remarkable. Even if he had, that would still not have stopped him from loving Canada because he was a Canuckophile, or whatever it is you call the Canadian equivalent of a Francophile or an Anglophile. Maybe there's never been a Canuckophile except for him, and that's why there isn't a real word for it.

No matter what the word, Mr. Miyashita was one and had been since 1898, the year he turned twenty and travelled from Japan to Britain to study at Oxford. He sailed across the Pacific to Vancouver, where he embarked on the next leg of the journey, a train trip to Halifax in a private car laid on by the CPR as a favour to his family. Three years later he retraced the same route on his way back to Japan. That time the trip took him six months, four of which he spent in the Rockies between Banff and Golden. He fell in love with a landscape and never recovered. His years in Calgary were simply the continuation of a love affair with Canada that lasted all his life. I know Mr. Miyashita truly believed that in every way that mattered, he was a Canadian. I learned later that he had never been back to Japan in the thirty years he'd run the Calgary office, not even when his mother died. I can see now why my question about home had stung.

The next day, perhaps by way of making amends, he gave me a book from his own library, a brand-new copy of Henderson and Ledoux's *The Surviving Works of Sharaku*, a catalogue of the prints of that most elusive of *ukiyo-e* artists. It's still in my bookcase at home with its attached silk ribbon marking Tokuji's place. He is number ten, and there are two pages devoted to him. Like everything else I read back then, I soaked up that book like a sponge And don't I wish I could do that now.

NOT ALL THE subjects we discussed were Japanese. In our office classroom, there were no boundaries, no limits on questions asked. Curiosity started me on a journey, and Mr. Miyashita was my guide. I had been interested in rocks and fossils for as long as I could remember, but I credit him with introducing me to geology as a serious study. I was middle-aged before I finally earned a master's degree in palaeontology. But my questions to him about his photographs of the Burgess Shale fossils, the ones that had caught my eye on my first day at his office, started me on the path. He had taken them in the summer of 1910 while he and his wife were on holiday in the mountains. One evening, as they sat down to dinner at Mount Stephen House, the CPR's hotel near Field, a fellow student from his Oxford days appeared in the dining room quite by chance. Mr. Miyashita's acquaintance, now a palaeontologist with the British Geological Survey, had travelled to Field to visit Charles Walcott and was dining with him at the hotel that evening. At that time, Walcott was secretary of the Smithsonian Institution in Washington. He and his family spent their summers camping near the site of the Burgess Shale, where Walcott did his fieldwork. Over the years, Walcott amassed for the Smithsonian a collection of some of the oddest fossils ever studied, creatures dating from the Cambrian, the period of the first great proliferation of life on earth. And what glorious names those strange critters have—*Hallucigenia*, *Perspicaris, Anomalocaris, Wiwaxia, Amiskwia* . . .

Photography was also an interest of Walcott's, and he and his family took a liking to the quiet Japanese fellow with the cameras, and to his shy wife. That's how the Miyashitas came to spend the remainder of the summer taking pictures at Walcott's quarry. Every morning, Mr. Miyashita would haul his heavy photographic equipment from the campsite up a rough trail to the fossil beds. Most days, Mrs. Miyashita hiked up with him and helped carry the gear. They'd spend the day photographing the fossils in situ, then dismantle the camera, including the several auxiliary bellows Mr. Miyashita had rigged to extend the lens, and pack the whole kit back down the mountain. Some days he remained at the campsite with Mrs. Walcott, photographing the specimens after she had prepped and catalogued them for transport. The Burgess fossils proved particularly difficult to capture on film, being tiny and not much more than thin smears on the rock. He tried everything from dipping the rock in water to spreading a film of oil over its surface, but to his perfectionist's eye, nothing seemed to work. I couldn't see it myself. The photos looked good to me, and the ones I found in the files of Walcott at work were fascinating. There was also a lovely one of a young Mrs. Miyashita standing with Walcott's wife. They are smiling and holding up enamelled tin mugs to the camera in salute. Mr. Miyashita returned to Field in subsequent summers to help with the collecting. He took more pictures of Walcott and his family, but he never again attempted to photograph the fossils.

My questions about the Burgess Shale led to his passing along to me a copy of Geike's *Text-Book of Geology*, the text he had used forty years before at Oxford. I got the impression that he had wanted to continue his geological studies, but that natural science was not part of the plan for a scion of the practical-minded Miyashita family. Still, he did manage to pass on his love of the subject to his student. Over the next couple of years, we spent many mornings, very happy ones for me, discussing the history of the earth before what Mr. Miyashita sometimes referred to as that noxious ape, *Homo sapiens*, infested it.

I began to read newspapers too, and not just the funnies. Mr. Miyashita subscribed to the *Wall Street Journal*, the *New York Times*, the *Financial Post*, the *Manchester Guardian*, the *Times*, and both Calgary dailies. The American papers took a week to arrive, and the English ones often travelled for a month or more. In those days, although many people had radios, we still considered newspapers the best and most trustworthy source of news.

With such a glut of them arriving, it didn't take long for back issues to accumulate in the storage room, where they sat, all neatly stacked, waiting for me to dispose of them. I salvaged the English papers every week and took them home. Dad sat down with the *Manchester Guardian* the minute it came through the door, and as for Mum, I know she thought there was something pretty posh about spending an hour or two with the *Times* after Sunday lunch, even if it was six weeks out of date. Mr. Miyashita subscribed to several Japanese newspapers as well, but with them, if it hadn't been for the photos, I'd never have known which way was up.

Back in 1939, as the world crept closer and closer to the brink, newspapers were not happy reading, not that newspapers ever are. I had only been at Miyashita Industries a few weeks when the *Calgary*

Herald reported that Germany had annexed what remained of Czechoslovakia in direct contravention of the Munich Agreement.

"And there, Mr. Chamberlain, is your peace in our time." Mr. Miyashita threw the paper down on his desk in disgust. "Surely he must resign, a man so foolish as to believe Herr Hitler would follow the rules on his little piece of paper. The fellow is doolally." Coming from Mr. Miyashita, this was strong stuff. With him, restraint was practically an art form.

"But, sir, how could Mr. Chamberlain have known this would happen?" I said. "He took a risk when he gave them the Sudetenland, but it could have worked, couldn't it?"

"No, Miss Jeynes, it could not. All of Czechoslovakia would not satisfy Herr Hitler any more than all of China will satisfy my former countrymen. It is thanks to this benighted policy of appeasement that the nation of Masaryk and Capek no longer exists. These are dark times. God is not in His heaven, and all is far from right with the world."

"But surely . . ."

For the first time since we had begun our coffee tutorials, he held up a hand to stem the discussion. Then he smiled. "Now tell me how you are getting on with that old geology book of mine?"

Often our coffee-break discussions lasted until well after twelve, when Mr. Miyashita would look at his watch and remind me to eat the sandwich and apple Mum packed for me every morning. He rarely ate lunch himself. After lunch he would occasionally ask me to accompany him to Richardson & Sons. Ostensibly, I went with him to take shorthand notes of the meeting with his stockbroker, but I think the real reason was so I would learn more about the workings of the market. After a while, we added the stock market to our topics under discussion and that paved the way for lessons in the principles of investment. The first and most important of these was an admonition.

"Remember always, Miss Jeynes, that you are making an investment, not having a flutter. There is a difference."

I have never been able to decide whether that statement is true or not. Besides, Mr. Miyashita himself once indulged in a spectacular

flutter early in his investing career when he put money into a long-odds Turner Valley oil venture. He was lucky and the gamble paid off handsomely, but by the time I went to work at Miyashita Industries, my boss's high-risk days were long past. Nevertheless, under his conservative tutelage, I did manage to amass quite a profitable, if imaginary, portfolio of my own. Although I've never been as clever at it as Mr. Miyashita, over the years I've made some pretty decent profits in the market, thanks to the lessons I learned in his office. Of course I would go and marry a man who believed it was impossible for a woman to have a head for finance. Ken thought the most complex financial decision women were capable of was whether or not to clip the coupons on their Canada Savings Bonds. I had to wait until I inherited some cash of my own before I got into the market and made some real money. Ken maintained that my success was sheer luck, and he kept waiting for me to lose the lot. But luck had nothing to do with it. The fundamentals of investment I learned from Mr. Miyashita hadn't changed.

I certainly didn't tell my parents anything about my accidental education. They would never have understood those coffee breaks. Besides, I did do real office work as well, work that would have met with their approval. With help from a librarian at the Calgary Public Library, I managed to start a proper filing system for the photos. By way of thanks, Mr. Miyashita sent a donation to the library's book purchasing fund along with a personal note to the librarian. I also helped him look after his charitable donations. Aside from the Red Cross, all of them were local. I once remarked on this.

"I believe in being generous with causes close to home," he said. "It is especially important for someone not born in Canada to lend support to other Canadians. It is a way of saying thank you, a tangible way for a newcomer to pledge his commitment to his chosen place."

Mr. Miyashita was a generous man, but I think his donations were also a way of getting people to accept him in spite of their prejudices against Orientals in general and, at that time, their fear of the Japanese in particular. After all, only a fool would be overtly nasty to a rich man who might give money to his cause. To some extent, this tactic

worked with the business and professional communities, at least on the surface, but it bought Mr. Miyashita little or no acceptance socially. I did notice an oddity about the donations too. Like the cheques for my salary, the ones I made out to charities were always drawn on his personal account, never on the Miyashita Industries account.

And that was another thing that puzzled me: how very little actual work we did for Miyashita Industries. We rarely got mail from them, maybe three or four letters a year that Mr. Miyashita opened for himself and read in his office. After a letter from Japan arrived, he was always irritable and out of sorts for the rest of the day.

Now that I think back on it, in all the time I worked at Miyashita Industries, I probably typed fewer than a dozen letters to do with their business. I do remember that we arranged for a couple of shipments of malting barley and, on one occasion, pork. I guess beer and trotters weren't on the strategic materials list. Eventually, everything but grain and pulping timber required elaborate export permits, and by early 1941, virtually all Canadian trade with Japan had come to a halt. After that, Miyashita Industries Canada did no business whatsoever. This didn't concern my boss in the slightest. If anything, he did his best to forget about the company. The only evidence we had ever done any business in their name was the bank account we used to facilitate our occasional exports. Mr. Miyashita's quarterly remittance allowance was deposited into this account as well. The money went from headquarters in Japan straight to the bank in Canada, bypassing our office completely. Mr. Miyashita hadn't drawn on those funds for years, so the account had a substantial balance. I know because I was the one who kept track of it. I'd dutifully type out a statement at the end of every month and leave it in an envelope on his desk. He never bothered to read it. I'd find the unopened envelope in his wastepaper basket when I put it out for the janitor.

Our workday began to develop a rhythm. Mr. Miyashita would arrive at ten. We'd have our coffee, then he'd work on his investments, read the papers, and often spend part of the afternoon in the darkroom. From time to time, he dictated a letter or two. For my part, I soon needed my extra couple of hours in the morning to do my reading for

coffee break. I'd get to work at seven-thirty, read until Mr. Miyashita arrived, and then make the coffee. After lunch I'd take care of whatever secretarial work needed to be done, then go back to work on the photo files. Mr. Miyashita did care about those. Occasionally, we'd have a cup of tea in the afternoon. Put like that, it doesn't sound like much, does it? But, believe me, it was the best job I ever had.

Assignment #4
HAS RELIGION PLAYED A ROLE IN YOUR LIFE?

WHAT HATH OUR JANICE WROUGHT this week? I don't think the kid realizes that Foothills Sunset is a hotbed of religion. Seething with belief, we are. This isn't too surprising when you consider that What Comes After is of some immediate, not to say pressing, interest to people around here. It makes us easy prey, and not a day goes by that you don't see some priest or minister or rabbi prowling the corridors. Sometimes they hunt in packs. Ecumenism in action. Well, at least Dave is going to have a field day at our next read-aloud session.

For Meggie and me, this is a tough assignment. These days, we're both confirmed old atheists, although Meggie objects to the term. She prefers heathen. However, no matter what you call it, we weren't always non-believers. I'm an Anglican who lapsed. Meggie was brought up Presbyterian, but that didn't stop her parents from shipping her off to a convent school when she was fifteen. Meggie says that John Knox followed by three years with the nuns were enough to push anyone over the religious brink. Personally, I don't remember anything so dramatic. I think my religious beliefs simply drifted away without my noticing until one day they were gone.

That supposes I had beliefs to drift. Surely I must have had some as a child—most children do—but, for the life of me, I can't recollect what they were. I know I went to Sunday school and later to church at St. Chad's Anglican in east Calgary. I have memories of flannel boards and pennies for the missionaries, of confirmation classes and sipping communion wine from the same chalice as everyone else, a practice I always thought was highly unsanitary and still do. And that's about it. Except for the towering prose of the old *Book of Common Prayer*: Cranmer's words will be with me forever. Then again, so will the words to "Jesus Wants Me for a Sunbeam."

As for my family, Mum attended the eleven o'clock service every Sunday and was a staunch believer. Dad didn't believe in much of anything. His time in France during the First World War put an end to any religious faith he may have had, but he wasn't militant about it. He certainly didn't object to Mum taking Charlie and me to church with her; sometimes he even came along. I know he liked and respected our minister, Canon Giles. I couldn't tell you what Charlie believed. It mustn't have been a topic that interested either of us much because I have no memory of ever talking with him about religion. We were too busy in this world to worry about the next. And that's about it for me and what Janice so annoyingly persists in referring to as my spirituality.

I should add, though, that I liked Canon Giles too. I think everyone did. Years later, when he was long retired and I was married with children of my own, I would sometimes run into him at the Central library. If I had come without the children, we'd have cup of coffee together, and although the Canon was not one for wallowing in nostalgia, our talk would occasionally go back to the old days at St. Chad's. He had been a friend of Mr. and Mrs. Miyashita, and sometimes we talked about them too. He first met the Miyashitas when I introduced him to them at one of the St. Chad's talent nights. Charlie and I had invited our boss and his wife to come watch us perform our version of a Fred Astaire and Ginger Rogers dance routine.

By the time of that November talent night, I'd been working for Mr. Miyashita more than nine months. Charlie had begun to work for him as well, printing contact sheets from the negatives stored in the file drawers. Earlier that autumn, I'd asked Mr. Miyashita if my brother could please come after school one day to see the mountain photos in our office gallery and maybe have a look at the darkroom too. Mr. Miyashita gave his permission, and Charlie knocked on the door shortly after four on a Thursday afternoon in late September.

"Hello, Charles." Mr. Miyashita shook my brother's hand. "How kind of you to take the time to come have a look at these photographs of mine."

"May I ask what kind of camera you used to take that one of the pine trees, sir?" Charlie asked.

And they were off, lost in their discussion of the finer points of lenses and f-stops and exposure times and other arcane technical details so dear to photographers' hearts and so mind-numbing to the rest of us.

After work, Charlie and I walked home from downtown, following our long shadows in the slanting light of late afternoon. I asked him what he thought of the darkroom and of the photographs on the office wall.

"The darkroom is the best you can buy." He stated this as if it were an obvious fact, which I suppose it was to him. "And Mr. Miyashita's photographs are the best I've ever seen outside a book. They'd publish them in *Popular Photography* in a minute."

"Do you really think so?"

"I know so," he said. "I've read every book on photography in the public library, and I keep up on all the photo magazines they get. I've never seen anything better than Mr. Miyashita's pictures. And they're not just good shots, the prints are amazing too. I think he's as good as Ansel Adams." For my brother, to mention another photographer in the same breath as Ansel Adams was his ultimate accolade.

The next week, Charlie chucked his *Herald* route and from then on spent Tuesdays and Thursdays after school, and the occasional Saturday morning, working in Mr. Miyashita's darkroom. Our parents never commented on this move of his, which I thought rather unfair, considering the reception I'd got for doing the same thing. By then, I don't think small beer like Charlie's paper route concerned them much. They were too preoccupied with the war, which had begun in earnest when Germany invaded Poland on the first of September. Two days later, Britain declared war. Canada waited a week, then did the same. No wonder Mum and Dad were worried. They had family and friends back in England, "at home," as Mum always called it. Until the day she died, when my mother said "at home" you knew she wasn't talking about Calgary. Her parents still lived in Morpeth. So did her auntie Phyl and her uncle Jimmy, her school friends Nora and Peggy, her cousin Dave and his dog, Flash, the wee whippet bitch, and all of the others who to me were no more than names on an envelope or faces in a snapshot. But they were my mother's childhood, and in 1939 she feared for them.

"I thought we'd done for the bloody Germans last time round." Dad sat in the living room reading the *Calgary Herald* the day after Canada declared war. "'War to End All Wars,' that's what they told us. Didn't reckon with yon Adolf, did they?"

"Thank God our Charlie's too young to be caught in this one," said Mum.

"Charlie's seventeen."

"And it'll all be over and done before he comes eighteen. You mark my words."

Dad didn't have the heart to contradict her. He said no more and went back to his paper.

Mr. Miyashita was as upset as my parents. It rained the day after Britain declared war on Germany. That morning, he arrived at the office dripping wet.

"And so it begins, Miss Jeynes." Without another word, he picked up the *Albertan* from my desk and walked into his office. Later, when I took him his coffee, I found him still in his raincoat and hat, sitting at his desk, staring out the window. He didn't notice when I put down the cup. For the next few weeks, he became obsessed with the news and waited impatiently for his international papers to arrive. During that period I think he even began to find our coffee tutorials irksome, especially on mornings when the mailman brought a British paper and our discussion interfered with his reading. After Charlie started to work at the office, Mr. Miyashita seemed to come round a little. Perhaps talking about photography distracted him. I know he enjoyed studying the newly printed contact sheets. The pair of them spent many happy afternoons planning how the photos' deficiencies could be addressed on future trips to the mountains.

One afternoon in early November Charlie arrived at work with a brown paper parcel under his arm. He put it on my desk.

"Mr. Leaman finished the shoes," he said. "I ran over to Sunnyside at lunchtime and picked them up." He untied the string and pulled back the paper to reveal what may have been the oldest pair of gentlemen's patent leather dancing shoes in the world. "Look how Dad's taps are attached. They're perfect." He took off his school boots and put on the shoes. Then he began to dance his way across the office's hardwood floor.

"Charlie, no! Mr. Miyashita's in there reading his papers."

But I was too late. Mr. Miyashita was now standing in his doorway watching.

"What are you wearing on your feet, Charles?" he asked, genuinely curious.

"Tap-dancing shoes, sir. I'm sorry I disturbed you. I didn't realize they'd sound so loud in here."

"Tap-dancing shoes. You mean like the ones Fred Astaire wears?"

I must confess I was a little surprised at Mr. Miyashita's casual mention of Fred Astaire.

"Well, not quite like Astaire's," Charlie admitted. "An old gentleman at our church gave me the shoes. They're pretty ancient. He told me he brought them with him when he moved here from England just after the Boer War. My dad made the taps. Here, have a look." Charlie pulled off a shoe and handed it to Mr. Miyashita. A toe poked out of his sock, and I thought how that would embarrass Mum if she knew.

"Your father made these metal pieces?"

"Our dad's a blacksmith. He can make just about anything from a piece of iron," Charlie said.

"It produces a quite remarkable sound, does it not?" Mr. Miyashita rapped the shoe's toe on my desk. "How did your father know to shape the metal this particular way?"

"We went to Ingraham's one Saturday afternoon and they showed us a pair of real tap shoes they had for sale," Charlie answered. "They were girls' shoes, but that didn't matter because all we needed was a pattern. After Dad saw those taps, he knew what to do. He made these ones on his dinner break at work."

"And how neatly they attach to the soles. Amazing."

"A shoemaker on 10th Street did that."

"It is excellent work." Mr. Miyashita handed the shoe back to Charlie. "I did not know you were a dancer, Charles."

"I'm not really. I've never taken lessons or anything. I just like to fool around. Kay and I promised we'd do a dance at the next talent night at

St. Chad's, so that's why Mr. Ledger gave me the shoes and Dad made the taps."

"And you dance too, Miss Jeynes? This afternoon is full of surprises."

"I'm not nearly as good as Charlie," I said. "But it's loads of fun. Charlie's made up a whole dance to 'Pick Yourself Up.' We're supposed to be Fred Astaire and Ginger Rogers."

"I didn't make the whole thing up. I tried to copy the dance Penny and Lucky do in *Swing Time*," Charlie said in a burst of honesty. "I only made up the parts I didn't remember." He did not add that most of the parts of Fred and Ginger's dance that he didn't remember happened to be the ones that were far too difficult for us. For that matter, we probably didn't get the easy steps right either since neither of us knew the first thing about real tap dancing. Nevertheless, we rated full marks for enthusiasm and that went a long way in making up for our technical deficiencies.

"No, no, Charles. Do not put the shoes away," Mr. Miyashita said. "You and your sister must show me this dance of yours. Is there enough room here?"

So Charlie sang the tune and we danced around the little gallery while Mr. Miyashita stood by my desk and clapped his hands in time to the music. Then the phone rang. What was all the hammering about? demanded the secretary from the lawyer's office below us. Did we realize we were making such a racket they couldn't hear themselves think down there?

"Sorry. We were hanging some pictures," I answered a little breathlessly. "But we're finished now."

I hung up and the three of us burst out laughing like naughty children who'd been caught in the act. Our boss laughed loudest of all.

"Is this not exactly like *Top Hat* when Jerry dances in the hotel room directly above Dale's?" And wasn't that a jaw dropper? "Rest assured," Mr. Miyashita continued, fully aware that he had caught us both with his detailed knowledge of Charlie's favourite movie. "I will most certainly tell Mrs. Miyashita about my afternoon with Fred Astaire and Ginger Rogers. She is very fond of their films. I have taken her to all of them. Sometimes she likes to watch them three or four times."

"Why don't you both come to talent night and see us dance?" Charlie asked. He sat on the floor changing from the tap shoes back to his boots. "We'll have our costumes then and real music too. Our friend Terps Plaxton is going to play the piano for us, and she's really good." I thought Charlie's invitation was pretty forward.

"Thank you, Charles. How kind of you. Mrs. Miyashita and I would be delighted to attend."

Talent night was on a Saturday in mid-November. The religion may not have stuck, but I do remember the social occasions at St. Chad's. They were a real source of enjoyment for our whole family. In those Depression days, when nobody we knew had much money, our social life revolved around the church—the other families we met there, the picnics, the socials, the Christmas concerts, the young people's group, the talent nights. In the days before television, it's where we got together and made our own entertainment.

Aside from the Christmas concert, talent nights were everybody's favourite. Talent night demanded a lot of preparation, at least it did if you were new to the game, like Charlie and me. Mum helped us with our costumes. Charlie planned to wear full evening dress, or at least our home-invented version—white tie and tails à la St. Chad's basement. Along with the dancing shoes, Mr. Ledger had given him a tailcoat, white vest, and trousers. Mr. Ledger was pushing eighty, and judging by their faint greenish tinge, it's likely that his evening clothes had last mustered for active duty to celebrate Queen Victoria's Diamond Jubilee. When Charlie brought the suit home, it reeked of mothballs and was miles too big around the middle. However, by the time Mum had taken it in, sponged it up, and pressed the seams, the old thing didn't look half bad in a dim light, although the mothballs lingered on. Mum was clever at making something out of not much. Her redemptive needle had transformed the sturdier bits of an old white shirt of Dad's that was bound for the ragbag into a convincing starched dickey and a bow tie. She even rigged some studs out of little pearly buttons that she'd salvaged from her button box.

I wore a dress like the one I'd been looking at so longingly in The Hudson's Bay, with a cowl neck and a skirt full enough for dancing.

Mum helped me sew it from material we'd found on sale at The Beehive. It didn't have the same big sunflowers as Ginger's dress and the skirt wasn't as long, but when Mum finally managed to get the drape of the collar set, we both thought my blue circles and triangles looked every bit as smart. As a surprise, Mum made me a new petticoat to wear under it. She sewed extra lace and frills on the bottom so they'd flounce and look pretty when I twirled. And did I feel wonderful in that dress. With my hair curled, a dab of cologne behind each ear, and a pair of real silk stockings inside my high-heeled shoes, I was Ginger Rogers.

Charlie and I must have practised that dance for a month. Like Mrs. Miyashita, Charlie was an avid Fred Astaire fan. He'd seen every Astaire movie at least five times, often more. Those were the days when you could go to the movies before noon on a Saturday and sit through the show from news reels and cartoons through the feature as many times as you liked until the theatre closed. Charlie only left Astaire movies because he knew Mum would be very annoyed if he didn't make it home in time for supper. Poor Mum. After one of his Astaire marathons, Charlie would nearly drive her mad for the next few weeks tap, tap, tapping around the house, trying to teach himself the steps he'd seen in the movie. It was all noise to her, but I could sometimes tell what song he was humming to himself from the rhythm of the taps. "I'm puttin' on my top hat" was unmistakable. By the time Charlie volunteered us for talent night, he was a pretty good tapper. After Dad and Mr. Leaman had finished with those shoes, he was a pretty loud one too. I wasn't a bad dancer myself in those days, and I did my best to keep up with him, but really, in my tapless pumps, I was just along for the ride.

Canon Giles let us do our rehearsing in the church basement. There was an old Heintzman upright there, kept in tiptop condition by Mr. Satterthwaite, a piano turner who belonged to our congregation. Our friend Terps—Terpsichore Plaxton, to give it both barrels— played for us. And wasn't that a name to saddle the poor kid with? Terps's mother was nuts. Mrs. Plaxton had artistic aspirations and three daughters, whom she named Clio, Thalia, and Terpsichore. I kid you not. Mr. Plaxton was a successful builder, which meant his wife could afford to spend money on lessons for her daughters. So plump and clumsy Clio suffered the indignities of ballet classes—her Clio was a student of The Dahhhnce, as Mrs. Plaxton always said—while the adenoidal Tally laboured under the curse of elocution lessons—the art of Melpomene, my dear. Terps was the only one with any real talent, and by some miraculous accident, Mrs. Plaxton set her last-born muse to learning the piano. The Plaxton girls also had a little brother, who, thanks to his dad, was called Fred. Fred grew up to be a carpenter. Had she but known, Mrs. Plaxton would probably have named him Jesus.

In spite of her crazy mother, or maybe because of her, Terps was one of the most down-to-earth kids I've ever known. She was also the most talented and had played the piano at every talent night since she turned eleven, not just for her own solos but for everyone else too. Singers, dancers, fiddlers, choirs—it didn't matter, Terps accompanied them all. She was seventeen and already a fine musician. I've never seen anyone who could sight-read like her. That skill got her a Saturday job at Heintzman's. In those days, every good music shop had someone on staff who could sit down at the piano and play the score you were thinking of buying so you could hear exactly what you were getting. There wasn't a piece of pop music Terps couldn't sight-read, and she came to pretty respectable grips with a lot of classical stuff too. Later on, she earned a living in Calgary as a music teacher and accompanist. We remained good friends for more than sixty years until her death from cancer in 1998. I'll always remember how very accommodating she was about playing for those dance practices of ours. She even brought her dancing sister Clio along one Saturday afternoon to help us with the trickier steps. I'm sure Charlie thought Terps put all that time and effort into our dance because the pair of them were such good pals, but I knew the real reason. Terps was in love with him.

The big Saturday night finally arrived. Charlie and I got to the church early so we'd be in plenty of time to meet Mr. and Mrs. Miyashita. It had snowed that afternoon, and some of the men were busy cleaning the walks while others were in the basement pushing the Sunday school tables against the walls and setting up rows of chairs in the middle of the floor. When the audience began to arrive, Charlie and I went outside and stood on the church steps watching for the Miyashitas to walk up from the streetcar. Lights shone behind the curtained windows of the tidy little houses across from St. Chad's. People made their way in groups to the church, the happy chatter of their voices punctuated by the scrape of shovels and the barking of a small dog behind a fence somewhere down the street. The sounds were as clear and crisp as the winter air that carried them.

As Charlie and I waited, a long black sedan pulled up in front of the church. A silver archer, the Pierce-Arrow company's hood ornament, pointed the way with his drawn arrow. The rest of the chrome work—and there was plenty—gleamed in the moonlight. I could see the streetlamp reflected in the polished paint of the body panels. I swear that car actually glowed with the lustre of wealth and luxury. The only time cars like it ever stopped at St. Chad's was for funerals, but even McInnes & Holloway's poshest limousines were nowhere near as grand as that Pierce-Arrow. Mr. Miyashita climbed out from behind the wheel and went round to open the passenger door for his wife. Mrs. Miyashita linked her arm through his, and together they walked up the path to the church. I tell you, if Cleopatra herself had sailed up to the steps of St. Chad's in her barge, she wouldn't have caused anything like the stir raised by those two small Japanese people and their big car. The shovels halted in mid-scoop. People stood and stared. Even the dog stopped barking.

I don't know why, but it hadn't occurred to me that the Miyashitas would come by car. I knew Mr. Miyashita owned one. I remember him telling me that he had chosen a North American make because he thought a British one might be too conspicuous. Later Charlie told me I must be the only person in Calgary who hadn't noticed the Pierce-Arrow. Well, I certainly noticed it that night. I stood and stared with the rest until Charlie poked me in the ribs and we went to greet its passengers. Canon Giles had arrived by then too, so I introduced him to the Miyashitas. The kindness of his welcome set the tone for the evening. He led them down the steps to the basement and the best seats in the house.

The curious stares continued as the audience sat down around the Miyashitas. Everyone came to talent nights: old, young, and in-between. The crowd settled in with much scraping of chairs and shuffling of feet and calling of greetings to friends across the room. The Miyashitas sat in the midst of it all, completely unaware that they looked as exotic as hibiscus blossoms on a caragana hedge. Earlier in the week, Mr. Miyashita told me that Mrs. Miyashita had asked him to inquire what people generally wore to talent nights as neither of them had ever been to one. That's how I knew they had made an effort to dress in a way they thought would make them blend in with the crowd. They hadn't the foggiest notion of how odd they looked in their conservative but oh-so-costly Western clothes, sitting on the old wooden chairs, surrounded by the congregation of St. Chad's dressed in its cheap and cheerful Saturday night finery. That basement had never seen a suit like Mr. Miyashita's blue pinstripe, or silk like the stuff of his wife's dress with its delicate pattern of fans and flowers. The Canon sat and chatted with them as the room filled.

I saw Norman come in. He waved and went to sit with Mum and Dad. I don't remember what he did for rest of the evening, and that probably sums up how I felt about him. Poor Norman. I don't think I treated him very well.

Like everything that went on at the church, talent night always started with a prayer, and that night's blessing is one I do remember. After the usual polite Anglican thanks for this and that, the Canon put in a request for God to keep the men of our armed services safe from harm and bring the war to a speedy end. Then he returned to the evening at hand and asked God to be with the performers and their audience. He even put in a special word for Terps, pointing out to the Almighty that she had worked harder than anyone to bring us enjoyment that evening. Finally, the prayer became an oblique lecture on how he expected his flock to behave toward the Miyashitas. The Canon laid it on.

"We pray, Oh Lord, that soon all in this war-torn world will meet in the spirit of peace and friendship that blesses our gathering here tonight. That people of all nations, of all colours and creeds, might come together before Thee in the true harmony and brotherly love, in the tolerance and good will that is with us now in this room." Then he went back to the expected, ". . . pray that You will bless this evening and all who sail in her blah blah blah. Amen."

With the amen still ringing round the room, we opened our eyes and it was curtain time. Of course, all curtains at St. Chad's were strictly imaginary. No dressing rooms either. Not even a stage. The performers, including the ones in costumes, sat with the audience until the Canon, always the master of ceremonies, consulted his list, called them up to the front, and introduced their act. Not that most of the acts needed any introduction. There were usually enough new performers to add a bit of spice to the evening, but one of the great things about talent nights was their predictability. Many of the performers who trod the boards in St. Chad's basement were regulars. The whole audience knew exactly what to expect from them and enjoyed every minute of it.

That November talent night is so clear in my mind it's as if I'm looking at snapshots in an album. I don't know why I see it this way. Perhaps because I've thought so often lately of Charlie and Mr. Miyashita and their passion for photography, it seems natural. In reality, I suppose it's quite the opposite, very unnatural indeed. After all, photographs are supposed to trigger memories. Memories are not supposed to trigger photographs. Except mine do.

The first snapshot in my album is of Mr. Birch dressed in his Sunday suit, wearing a boater hat and carrying a bamboo cane. Mr. Birch always kicked off the show. He sang the same song every time, something about a man who "something something dum de dum, at Baden-Baden Spa." His English accent was so richly plummy that no one could understand a word he sang, but that didn't matter because his audience had never heard of either Baden-Baden or its spa and would have been equally mystified had they caught the lyrics.

"Needs his tonsils pruned, that one," Mum would remark later at home. "Sounds like he swallowed a hot potato," Dad would agree. Only once did Mr. Birch detour from the road to Baden-Baden. That time, thanks to a couple of nips of neat whisky provided by Mr. Moore in the furnace room before the program started, he favoured us with a song he'd learned as a lad on holiday in the islands of the Firth of Clyde, sung to the old tune "Cock o' the North." Fortunately, Mr. Birch's tortured vocables ensured its lyrics were similarly unintelligible to everyone except my dad, who had soldiered with a couple of fellows from Millport in the last war and knew "Auntie Mary Had a Canary Up the Leg of Her Drawers" when he heard it.

The photo of Mr. Moore is a touch blurry, just as Mr. Moore himself often was, when after too many visits to the furnace room, he'd walk a little unsteadily to the front and tell a funny story. It usually began with an Englishman, a Scotchman, and Yank sitting in a pub and ended when Mr. Moore got so muddled that he couldn't remember what came next. At that point the whole audience would applaud to make him feel better, which often gave him the pleasant illusion that he'd finished his story after all. Then he'd sit down, and everyone was happy.

Mrs. Appleton's photo is an eight-by-ten glossy as befits the star soprano in the church choir. Compared with Mr. Birch, Mrs. Appleton's repertoire was vast and so was she. She'd quiver her chins through "Who Is Sylvia" or "The Night Has a Thousand Eyes" or, on rare occasion when a coyly romantic mood struck, "The Lass With the Delicate Air." Charlie always called it "The Lass With the Delicate Rear," which, in Mrs. Appleton's case, was not kind.

Talent nights weren't all singing though. There's a very dramatic shot in my album of Mr. Jackson, who taught English at Central High School. He's wearing a crown. Miss Anderson, the Latin teacher at Western Canada, stands beside him, staring at her hands. They always acted scenes from Shakespeare together. Mum and Dad thought they were particularly splendid that night as Macbeth and his missus. In real life, everyone at church wondered why the pair of them didn't get married. It was some years before it dawned on me that Mr. Jackson was gay.

The Sillies have a group photo. Mr. Laidlaw is dressed to play Red Riding Hood in a cape the size of a small tent. At six-foot-something and a good two hundred and fifty pounds, he's the biggest man at St. Chad's, and his huge fists dwarf the dainty wicker basket he holds in front of his frilly apron. Mr. Timms and Mr. Burton both carry cardboard axes so they must be the handsome woodsmen. I can tell by the grey felt ears and fur mittens that Mr. Redfern is the wolf. He has a painted-on Hitler moustache too. And there's Mr. Collins in Grandmama's lacy nightcap and gown. The five of them put on a skit every talent night. They'd spoof popular movies or act out fairy tales to poke fun at current politics, but no matter what they did, at least two of The Sillies did it dressed in women's clothes. The Widow Twankey and her sisters were alive and well in St. Chad's basement. The Sillies were a huge audience favourite.

And there's Terps, smiling up at me in black and white although her mop of hair was the colour of flame and her eyes blue as the azure ribbon that held it back from her face. She's just finished her solo, the "Minute Waltz" by the look of all those watches whipped out to time her. Now she's playing for the singsong that always follows the last act. The audience calls out favourites to her—"Annie Laurie" and "Oh, My Darling Clementine," "K-K-K-Katy" and "Home on the Range."

Then the album becomes a jumble of photos that aren't sharp enough to warrant pasting on a page, of faces I can no longer match with names I can't remember. Even Charlie and I seem a little faded, although I know we were a great hit and won the prize for Best of the Evening. Everyone praised Mum and Dad for having such clever children. And weren't those costumes of theirs first-rate? Mr. Ledger visited his old suit and patted its shoulder with pride.

When the last song had been sung, and Terps stood up from her piano to a well-earned roar of applause and cheers, the Sunday school tables were hauled back into action to hold the tea. This was always a potluck affair coordinated by the Women's Auxiliary: those who could brought what they could. Enormous pots of tea and plates of cookies and cakes flowed from the church kitchen, and everyone sat around the tables eating and drinking and enjoying the performances all over again by talking about them.

To this day, I have no idea what the Miyashitas made of it all. They sat smiling politely and sipping their tea as they talked with my parents, who like the Canon, had met them for the first time that evening.

Conversation at our table was somewhat strained to begin with, but after a few false starts, everyone seemed to relax, at least a little. We all enjoyed hearing Mr. Miyashita's story of how he had been taken to see a performance at a famous London music hall when he was a student, especially when he concluded that, all in all, he found our St. Chad's talent night much more enjoyable. Mrs. Miyashita's English wasn't nearly as good as her husband's so she didn't say much, but she did seem pleased to be there with us in the stuffy basement. She drank a whole cup of milky, brown liquid and pronounced it most refreshing, although I'm sure it bore no resemblance to anything she would recognize as tea.

Somehow, everyone knew when it was time to go home. Mothers stuffed children into leggings and coats and searched for mittens. The rest of the ladies tidied up and washed the dishes while their husbands set the chairs and tables ready for Sunday school next morning. The Canon came with Charlie and me as we accompanied the Miyashitas to their car. We climbed up from the bustle of the basement into the calm of a perfect winter night. The new snow lay pristine under a sky full of stars, and the air was so still that a puff of smoke from the Canon's pipe drifted up and hung in a ring above his head like a pillowy halo.

"I'm so pleased that Charlie and Kay asked you to come to our talent night," he said to the Miyashitas as we made our way to the street. "It was good to have you with us and I hope that you—" The Canon stopped in mid-sentence.

"What's happened to the car?" Charlie said, although it was plain to all of us exactly what had happened. Someone had scratched the words JAP CRAP in large capital letters along the side of the Pierce-Arrow. The scratches were wide and so deep they went through the paint right down to the metal. The hood and fenders had not escaped and were etched with squiggles and curlicues, the nonsense marks used in cartoons to denote curses.

"Mr. Miyashita, I don't know what to say," the Canon began, his voice shaking with anger. "I am deeply ashamed that anyone in our congregation would . . ."

"Please, Canon Giles." Mr. Miyashita held up his hand to stem our minister's apology. "Even in a small city like Calgary, one takes a risk in leaving a motor car unattended in the street. No member of your congregation would do this, and I doubt that we will ever discover the identity of the passing thug who is responsible."

But we all knew, and so did Mr. Miyashita, that what he said was not true. This had not been done by any passing thug. Some very nice, respectable member of St. Chad's had slipped out of the church and vandalized the car while the rest of us sat inside laughing and applauding. The Canon insisted that the police be called. Mr. Miyashita wouldn't hear of it.

By this time, a crowd had gathered behind us. One look from the Canon and they knew to keep their mouths shut. None of us had ever seen him this angry before. It was frightening. I think that anger, more than anything, impressed his flock with the gravity of what had happened. Mr. Miyashita shook the Canon's hand and thanked him again for talent night, the tea, and his kindness. As he did, Charlie walked around the car, checking the tires. Then Mr. Miyashita helped his wife into the passenger seat and drove her home. The Canon, without so much as a glance at his silent parishioners, walked back into the church and closed the door behind him.

Mum and Dad were as appalled as Canon Giles by what had happened, but they said nothing as the four of us walked home. None of us did. It wasn't until we had entered the house through our unlocked door and started up the stairs to bed that Dad broke the silence.

"We've come to a pretty pass when a man can't leave his car on the streets of Calgary for an hour or two."

"It wouldn't have happened if Mr. Miyashita was a white man," Charlie said. No one contradicted him.

"Bloody cowards," Mum said. "I hope poor Mrs. Miyateesha is all right."

"Miyashita," I corrected, and the subject was closed for the night.

Monday morning, Canon Giles arrived at the Miyashita Industries office as I was making coffee. He had come to arrange for the repair of the car. Mr. Miyashita flatly refused his offer, stating again that since no one knew the vandal's identity, no one could be held responsible, least of all the parish of St. Chad's. I think the Canon realized it would be futile to pursue the argument.

"I drink a cup of coffee at this time of the morning," Mr. Miyashita said. "Would you care to join me, Canon Giles?"

"How kind of you to offer, Mr. Miyashita. I'd be delighted."

The Canon followed my boss into his office for what would be the first of many conversations over coffee or lunch or, on rare occasion, a glass of sherry. They were both well-educated, well-read men and enjoyed each other's company. In time, Mr. Miyashita began to rely on the Canon's advice regarding the allocation of his charitable donations. If anyone knew who needed money in Calgary and where it would be well spent, Canon Giles did. In turn, Mr. Miyashita helped his friend make some decent investments with the bit of money he had inherited from his father. Years later, the Canon told me he and Mrs. Giles retired far more comfortably than they had any right to expect, thanks to Mr. Miyashita's financial acumen.

The car was soon repaired and restored to its former glory, but the memory of the ugliness scored into its metal could not be painted over quite so easily. As a matter of fact, that's what I recall most clearly about the whole incident. I can still see those enraging squiggles and curlicues scratched into the fenders, the prim and proper stand-ins for curses. That's Anglican vandals for you, nasty as the rest and prigs to boot.

Assignment #5
TELL ABOUT YOUR EDUCATION
(TRY TO INCLUDE SOME DIALOGUE)

I GOT A JUMP ON this assignment. I've already told a bit about my education and used some dialogue to do it so I'm feeling chuffed. I must say though that Janice's kicker about dialogue did cause some rumbling in the ranks. How can we possibly remember conversations word for word, especially conversations we might have had seventy years ago? We'd end up inventing everything that was said and then we'd be writing fiction, made-up stuff, not our real memoirs. However, Janice claims that in memoirs, reconstruction of dialogue (that's her way of saying "inventing") is perfectly permissible as long as you remain true to the spirit of the original conversation. I took this to mean that you shouldn't put words in people's mouths that they'd never have said in a million years, let alone a mere seventy.

"Our Kay is such a bright lass that her mother and I told her to get on up to Edmonton and study history at the university," said Dad. "And while you're at it, Kay, dear," said Mum, "you should dump that dreary Norman and find yourself something a bit more exciting by way of a love life."

Remaining true to the spirit. That is the difficult part all right, and not only when it comes to conversations. I'm finding it a real temptation to blur what Meggie calls the messy bits with a touch or two of self-serving varnish—a dab here to make me look more honest, a dab there to make me seem braver, a big thick blob to cover the bits I'm ashamed of. Give me a day or two and I'd be convinced my glossy new version was true. Who knows, maybe I've been telling lies and don't realize it. Then again, there are things I think it's pointless to dredge up unless you are one of those who actually believes that confession cleanses the soul, a kind of spiritual Metamucil. Come on, Kay, time to get on with this education business.

To be perfectly honest (ha ha), it's no exaggeration to say that my real education started the day I went to work for Mr. Miyashita. However, I'd never have got the job without my year at Albertson's Secretarial College. I credit Albertson's with making me into a top-notch secretary. Well, all right. Maybe they only made me into a very good secretary, but I always thought of myself as top-notch. After all, I did graduate top of the class. By the time I got that silver medal (which, by the way, was so small it rated a mention in Ripley's and which, also by the way, I still have in a box at home), I was a whiz at shorthand and bookkeeping, and a dab hand at the typewriter too. My typing landed me the job at Greer & Western, and I've already told how that set me up with Mr. Miyashita. What I haven't said is that I never ever intended to become a secretary. It was another of those things that just happened. The more I work on these assignments of Janice's, the more I'm beginning to think that a good part of my entire life just happened. Don't misunderstand. I didn't end up in secretarial college because I lacked ambition—I had plenty of that. What I lacked was money. After I graduated from Western Canada High School, I wanted to go on to university and study history. That was in 1937, and my Great Depression timing couldn't have been worse. Something as grand as university was not in the picture, at least not for me. According to Mum and Dad, I was a very lucky girl to get to Albertson's. It took a lot of arguing, but they finally did agree on that.

Looking back after all these years, I think it's likely that my parents' own educations played a big part in their arguments. Mum had one, Dad didn't. Maybe the difference wasn't quite as black and white as that, but Mum had graduated from high school and been an assistant teacher whereas Dad left school at the age of eleven and apprenticed as a blacksmith. Probably it would be fairer to say that it all boiled down to money for them too. Mum's family had some, Dad's didn't.

I can see now that Mum's parents were part of the fight as well. Her father had made a good thing of a grocery business in Morpeth, the town in Northumberland where they lived, and he wasn't stingy with his only child. Both he and my grandmother had some progressive views on education for women, at least they were progressive for those days. Not that they were social reformers—Mum told me that Grandad had opposed giving women the vote—but they did want to do the best they could for their daughter. They made certain Mum finished high school, which was more than either of them had done. She took a job as an assistant teacher at an infant school in the village of Pegswood near the mine where my dad worked.

Dad had served his blacksmith's apprenticeship at that same mine. By the time Mum started teaching, he was a fully qualified member of his trade. Nowadays, mention blacksmiths and people only think of horses, but at the mines back then the job had a much broader scope. Certainly the blacksmiths kept the pit ponies shod, but they also made parts and fittings for all manner of machines, including the huge shaft elevators and their cages. If it was metal, the blacksmiths at the mine made it and maintained it. Men like Dad were really practical engineers. He could turn his hand to anything. In his time off from the CPR, he worked as a volunteer for the Calgary Zoo, where he built and mended the iron cages and fences. He even made Charlie and me toys when we were little. I ran miles whipping my iron hoop along the pavements in Inglewood. He made us skates too, and those taps on Charlie's dancing shoes were nothing short of ingenious.

Dad was twenty-two years old when the First World War broke out, and like millions of other young men, he joined up to fight for King and Country. As far as I know, he never fired a gun in battle, and the only armed German he saw was a pilot whose plane had been forced down behind British lines near the barn where he was shoeing horses. Corporal Jeynes served three years in France, smithing for the army and observing the carnage around him. After the war, Dad went back to his job at the mine. He never talked about his time in France except to tell about helping to pull the German pilot from the wreckage of his downed plane.

If it weren't for Mum's education, she and Dad would never have met. She still lived with her parents in Morpeth when she got her teaching job—unmarried daughters did not live on their own—so she commuted to Pegswood and back every day on the train. One wet morning Dad saw her on the platform at the Pegswood station struggling with a reluctant umbrella and too many books. He took charge of both and walked her to school through the rain. For him, that one walk is all it took. Looking back, I think it's pretty certain that my grandparents didn't approve of Dad, that they thought their only child was marrying beneath her. However, I suspect that even then Mum must have been a force to be reckoned with; she got her way and married him.

I have a picture of my parents on their wedding day, both looking as stiff and starched as their wedding clothes. It's the earliest photo I have of Dad. There are none from his childhood, not even one of those studio portrait things that Mum's family went in for on big occasions. Her lot loved photos—posing for them, taking them, pasting them in albums. Who knows, maybe it's hereditary and that's what started Charlie off on photography. After we moved to Canada, they used to send us little black-and-white pictures by the bushel.

We moved to Canada in 1924 when I was four years old and Charlie had just turned two. Dad didn't get on with his family—I never did know why—so there were no regrets there, but Mum's parents took it pretty hard, their daughter and their grandchildren moving thousands of miles away across the ocean to the wild west. Morpeth to Calgary was a long and costly trip, and they only managed it once, in the summer of 1929 when I was nine. Then the Depression hit and Grandad's business interests took a beating. After that came the war and no one travelled, at least no civilians. By the time the war ended, they were too old and too sick to make the trip, although they were both a good twenty years younger than I am now. I think people must have got old earlier in those days. At least that's what I'm telling myself. Maybe missing their daughter aged them as well because I know they never got over losing her to Canada. Mum never got over leaving England either.

Dad worked for the CPR as a blacksmith in the Ogden shops. We lived in east Calgary, not far from Colonel Walker's old place that's now the Inglewood Bird Sanctuary. Our house isn't there any more—torn down to make way for an infill sometime in the 1990s. The whole district has gone upscale, which I suppose is good for the neighbourhood but bad news for funny little places like ours. I was sorry to see it go, although in practical terms, it was no great loss, nothing to get the heritage society up in arms. It was small by today's standards—a kitchen and a living room downstairs, two bedrooms upstairs with a bathroom tucked in between them. When Charlie and I got too old to share a room, Dad put a wall down the centre of the biggest bedroom and made it into two small rooms. I got the side with the west window because it had the closet. For some reason I've forgotten, girls were thought to need a closet more than boys. Charlie kept his shirts and trousers on hangers on the wall of his room like decorations. His socks and underwear sat on shelves inside a curtained apple-crate that did double duty as a nightstand. He didn't have many clothes so this worked quite well.

I know it doesn't sound like much, but that little house did for the four of us, and what's more, it was all ours. We owned it. I know Mum's family helped with the buying because it was more house than a CPR blacksmith could afford to buy outright, especially during the worst of the Depression when the company laid off scores of men at Ogden and cut the remaining workers' hours to the bone. Many only worked ten hours a week, and they were lucky to get that. Truth be told, my grandparents probably did most of the buying. Early on, when we first came to Canada, they sent money for coal every winter too, so the house was warm even on the coldest January day. Later, they provided the money to have the furnace converted to natural gas, and after that, they paid the monthly gas bill. It galled Dad to take money from Mum's parents, but during the Depression, pride was a luxury not many could afford, not unless they wanted to see their children suffer for it. So my grandparents helped with the house and the heat, and eventually poked their financial fingers into our schooling as well. Thanks to them, Charlie's university education was safely tucked away in the Bank of Nova Scotia. Grandad's business may have declined after 1929, but he still managed to set enough money aside for Charlie to study medicine. I don't remember anyone ever asking Charlie what he wanted, but Grandad had his heart set on my-grandson-the-doctor. The old man's money didn't stretch to two educations, and there was no doubt as to who'd be getting his brass. So much for enlightened views on women and education. This time it was Mum's turn to resent her father's money.

It's plain to see now that by the time I left high school the stage had been well and truly set for the battle over what to do with Kay. I know Mum thought that if we really scrimped there might be enough for university for both Charlie and me. Living was cheap during the Depression, so if you had any money at all you could spread it pretty thin and still survive. Our mother could squeeze a dime so hard the King cried uncle, but Dad wouldn't have it. The pair of them argued, usually late at night after Charlie and I had gone to bed. I can hear them now, their Geordie voices at it hammer and tong. The angrier they got, the more Northumberland they got.

I've tried and tried, but I don't seem to be able to put their argument down on paper in a way that lets you hear those Geordie sounds. Or is that see the sounds? This dialogue business is a lot trickier than you might think, especially when you start messing with accents. Besides, I'm not altogether certain that my parents spoke real Geordie, although that's what they called it. Years ago, I think it might have been in the early 1960s, I was seated at a dinner party next to a linguistics professor from the University of Alberta. It was a long and tedious journey from the jellied consommé to the floating island. Somewhere around the overdone roast beef he informed me that my parents' accent was not Geordie at all but another dialect called Pitmatic that originated in the coal districts of Northumberland and Durham. On my next visit to the old house in Inglewood, I passed this nugget along to Mum.

"Man's a regular Henry Higgins, isn't he?" She sniffed. "And while he was at it, did Professor Poncey try to tell you 'Weel May the Keel Row' is a Scots song?" That ended that discussion.

GEORDIE, PITMATIC, WHAT'S to choose when even my best efforts at writing their voices make Mum and Dad come across like a couple of eee-by-gummers in a bad British sitcom. That's not what they were like, not at all. I've ripped those pages out of my exercise book and I'm going to start over. This time I'll tell you what they said in plain

Canadian. If you know what Geordies sound like you can add the accents for yourself. If you know Pitmatic, give yourself a medal.

"Our Kay's a clever one," said Mum. "She's got a good head on her shoulders and the get-up-and-go to use it. It's not right to let a brain like that go to waste." Maybe Mum wished she'd had a chance to make more of her own education. I know she had loved her teaching job.

"Don't be daft, woman. You don't have to tell me our Kay's smart as a whip. But even clever lasses get married and have children. What use will her university be to her then? Believe you me, she'd be better off learning to look after a house and a husband than having her head stuffed with stories about dead kings and their old wars."

"So you want to see your daughter charring for her living, do you? Because that's what she'll be good for without an education. And you tell me where she's going to meet this fine husband of hers while she's out scrubbing other women's floors. You tell me that, Albert Jeynes."

"Now you're spouting rubbish. What about yon Norman? He's a good steady lad and she met him all right. And no one's talking about Kay scrubbing floors, for all that it's honest work and nothing to be ashamed of."

"Scrubbing's honest work all right, honest enough if you can't get better. But Kay can do better by a long chalk. She'll go far if we give her the chance."

"All the way up a church aisle more like, and her grand university degree wrapped up in a bouquet she'll toss at the end of the day."

So it went, round and round and always the same. I don't remember when they came to their compromise, but finally it was settled—Charlie got university and I got a year's secretarial training. As it turned out, Charlie never did get to medical school. He joined up the day after he turned eighteen. And oh my, the fireworks that bombshell of Charlie's set off could have lit the sky for a week. The fuss over my education was a tempest in a teapot by comparison, and a tiny teapot at that.

I know I felt resentful and angry that my parents wouldn't send me to university, but mostly I think I felt very sorry for my poor wee thwarted self. I didn't begrudge Charlie his education, but I wanted my own. I can see now though that I didn't want it badly enough. If I had, I'd have found a way to get that history degree, a way that didn't depend on Grandad's money. I couldn't admit it to myself back then, but those dead kings and their old wars weren't worth quite enough to me. Many years later, I did get a degree, two in fact. I paid for part of my middle-aged studies with money I inherited from my parents, money that included the funds earmarked for Charlie's education.

ALL THINGS CONSIDERED, perhaps Albertson's Secretarial College was the best thing that could have happened to me then. That place was an education in a lot more than typing and shorthand, although those have come in handy over the years. I've been using the shorthand to write these assignments. I'd type them up too, but my left arm still isn't strong enough for that. Soon, I hope. Still, I think Miss Duffren would be very pleased with my recent efforts, pages of Gregg all neat and tidy and a credit to the school. Duffy was the shorthand teacher at Albertson's. Not that any of us students dared to call her Duffy to her face. That would have been considered far too familiar and, even worse, unladylike. The staff at Albertson's prided themselves on turning out refined young ladies. Sometimes the place felt like the poor kids' version of a Swiss finishing school. I know it's hard to believe, but we actually had to wear gloves and a proper little hat to class every day. My friend Susan got expelled for hiding a couple of Sweet Caps in the flowers of her best summer straw. They'd never have noticed except one split its paper and leaked tobacco down her ear. Sneaking a smoke in the washroom was never the same without Susan. She had the last laugh though. She was smart and pretty and landed a job with the Alberta Wheat Pool, where she eventually became executive secretary to the president. After that, Albertson's forgot they had expelled her. They even invited her back to give a talk to a graduating class.

Albertson's was a great preparation for Miss Bayliss too. There must have been half a dozen old bags exactly like her teaching there, the kind who resented us simply because we were young and pretty and had our lives ahead of us. Those old biddies didn't just give Susan the boot, they enjoyed it. Except Miss Duffren. She wasn't like that. Her heart was in the right place, and in her own peculiar way—believe me, Duffy was peculiar—she was a good teacher. At least she tried to encourage us. I think she was one of the army of spinsters whose sweethearts had been killed in the First World War. She was little and plump and dressed in flowing silky things, all vivid colours: scarlets and yellows and iridescent blues that shimmered under the overhead lights. I can still see her standing at the front of the class, wrapped in a drawer's worth of gossamer shawls, her hands fluttering as she chanted her mantra and we practised writing our symbols.

"Remember the three Cs, girls—concentrate, concentrate, concentrate. And soon the words will flow, flow, flow, in through your ears, out through your fingers, and on to your pad. You are the scribes, the recorders of history, the keepers of secrets. You are the secretaries. Now concentrate, concentrate, concentrate." How we ever managed to learn a thing with Duffy babbling in the background I do not know, but we did.

What a very strange place Albertson's seems when I think about it now. Victorian really. That makes sense though when you consider that the Calgary of the 1930s was a lot closer to the Victorian age, both in time and in spirit than to the present. Poor Miss Duffren would faint if she could see the girls today with their bare midriffs, rings in their navels and tattoos God knows where. Nothing was bare at Albertson's except the furnishings. But for all its airs and pretensions, it did turn out some first-rate secretaries, of whom, as I have previously and so modestly mentioned, I was one.

I didn't get to university until my own children were grown. I got a degree in geology and had my head stuffed so full of rocks that I went on to do a master's in palaeontology. Graduated with distinction too. But much as I enjoyed my dabbling in Devonian seas, I can't say that university changed me in any fundamental way. I could put Master of Science after my name, but I was still the same Kay, the Kay Jeynes who got her real education at Mr. Miyashita's office by way of Albertson's Secretarial College.

I'VE NEVER FORGOTTEN what I learned in those coffee-break tutorials with Mr. Miyashita, although I must admit that some of our discussions are clearer in my memory than others. A few, like the time we talked about Tokuji and his creator, are so vivid I can recall them almost word for word or at least well enough to practise a little of Janice's reconstruction of dialogue. Perhaps it's because Tokuji is still with me that I remember our Sharaku morning so clearly. I know that I had just finished reading the book about him that Mr. Miyashita had given me.

"How did Sharaku do so many prints in such a short time?" I put the coffee tray on Mr. Miyashita's desk and settled into my usual chair across from him. He had taken Tokuji's portrait off the wall and propped it up next to the bonsai pine where both of us could see it as we talked. For that morning, Tokuji became a third member of our group.

"Perhaps he didn't," Mr. Miyashita answered.

"But it says in the book that he only worked for ten months in 1794 and 1795, and that he produced over one hundred and forty prints." I was quite the little quoter of chapter and verse in those days—really rather a pain. "That's almost four a week."

"It is true that his prints were published during those ten months, but could it not be that Sharaku had worked on his designs for a much longer period? For all we know, he may have had a portfolio full of them by the time he found a publisher. Keep in mind, Miss Jeynes, that it is a long journey from the initial design to the final print." Mr. Miyashita put down his coffee cup and began to number the stages of that journey on his fingers.

"First, Sharaku would have to find a publisher, someone who thought he might make some money on the designs. Then the publisher would have to see to the carving of the individual woodblocks. That step was an art in itself. Every colour required a separate block. Next came the actual printing, and you can see in the portrait of Tokuji that it was no small undertaking. I should think working with powdered mica to produce that lovely sheen in the background must have been a very tricky business."

"So Sharaku did the designs, but other people did the rest?"

"That would be most likely. And it is the same today, is it not? The people who draw the funnies we read in the *Calgary Herald* do not do the printing."

Somehow, I couldn't quite picture Mr. Miyashita as an avid *Dagwood* reader; nevertheless, he made his point.

"Why did he quit?"

"We don't know that he did stop designing prints, only that no more were published. At least none that have been discovered. You see, we know even less about Sharaku's life than we do about Shakespeare's. We can tell from his prints that he was familiar with the world of the theatre. Some think he may have been an actor himself, although that is far from certain. And if he did stop designing—and that, too, is far from certain—perhaps it was because his prints did not sell very well. Ultimately, Sharaku's work had to make its way in an exceedingly tough and crowded market. There was no room for work that did not turn a profit. Sadly enough, one thing we do know for certain is that Sharaku's publisher dropped him. It is the last we ever hear of him. He simply disappears."

"Why do you think his prints didn't sell?"

"Who can say? Too true to life, would be my guess." Mr. Miyashita smiled at Tokuji. "Sharaku captured his subjects as he saw them, not as they wanted to see themselves. Remember, kabuki actors were the film stars of their time, and they did not care to be seen as weak or nasty or ugly or, I suppose, even as ordinary humans. Their public did not want to view them that way either. They wanted heroes. But Sharaku did not do portraits of heroes. His subjects are human beings with all their human flaws and failings. So his prints did not sell. Heroes are always in demand, Miss Jeynes—humans not so much."

Time ultimately proved Mr. Miyashita wrong on that point. Sharaku prints sell extremely well these days. I read last year that one of the actor portraits sold at an auction in Paris for more than half a million dollars. I'll bet my Tokuji would fetch at least as much. Not that I have any intention of selling him, nor of telling anyone how valuable he is. I know my children think that he's a reproduction of one of those funny old Japanese things Mum's so fond of, and as long as I don't tell them any different, we'll all be happy. If they knew he was the real deal, a mint Sharaku worth hundreds of thousands, I assure you Tokuji would not be hanging on my wall here at Foothills Sunset. He would be insured up to his expressive eyebrows or locked up in some airless vault. Probably both. Not that my children are grasping or mean-spirited. It's just that they have a rather literal way of valuing things. Probably inherit that from their father. And speaking of inheriting, I've left Tokuji to the Honolulu Academy of Arts in my will. They have a superb collection of *ukiyo-e*, so he will feel at home there among friends. Besides, many years ago, I fell in love in Honolulu. I feel I owe the place something in return.

I would like to write more about my coffee-break education for our class tomorrow, but this was a physio day and I really do feel a bit punk and shivery. I think I'll knock off and go to bed. I'll probably feel much better in the morning and be able to continue in a cheerier frame of mind. I haven't even started on the question Janice asked us—did our education prepare us for life or whatever it was. I can't remember exactly, and right now it's too much bother to look it up in my notes.

Listen to yourself, Kay. "Too much bother!" Now isn't that a prize bit of whining. You've really got to watch yourself around here, especially when you're feeling down, or the whines creep their way into everything you do. I swear that if I ever get around to writing my real memoirs and not just these notes, I'll chop every word that so much as hints of a snivel. Three cheers for retroactive self-improvement.

74

Assignment #6
IS THERE A PERSON — NOT A FAMILY MEMBER — WHO WAS PARTICULARLY IMPORTANT IN YOUR LIFE?

THANKS TO A BOUT OF bronchitis, I missed our last two classes and got behind in the assignments. What's really frustrating is that now I'm behind on my physio as well, so Christmas at home is looking less and less likely. Meggie gave me a talking to on how this is very negative thinking, and if I keep it up, I'm going to turn into one of those poor old zombies they prop up in front of the CBC News Network every after-noon, doomed to watch *Question Period* for the rest of my days.

On the positive side, this week's assignment gives me the perfect chance to carry on telling about Mr. Miyashita. I can't say I'm altogether sorry I missed last week's class. We were supposed to tell about what Janice called an experience that opened our hearts. Maybe the kid didn't take enough time to explain exactly what she meant by this because at today's read-aloud session poor literal Dave treated us to a detailed account of his triple bypass operation. We got the full story of the lead-ing up to and the coming back from, but mercifully skipped the surgery itself because, as Dave pointed out, he was unconscious for that. The rest of us were not similarly blessed during his reading.

After we'd all recovered from Dave's operation, several other people read their stories. One old girl (look who's talking) who rarely says much of anything read her account of the time a small hawk flew into her kitchen window and hurt its wing. As she and her husband nursed the bird back to health, it became quite tame and friendly and took to traipsing around after her while she did her housework. At one point, it even laid an egg in its hospital box but nothing came of it. Although she longed to keep the hawk with her, when its wing had healed, they let it go. It flew away, and she never saw it again. I don't know why I found this story so touching. Meggie says it's because we're all suckers for that first fine careless raptor, which may not be the worst pun in the world but is certainly a contender.

I should know because I'm an expert on bad puns, thanks to Mr. Miyashita. He loved every corny play on words the English language is capable of sustaining, no matter how tenuously. He took pride in being so fluent in English that he understood the interplay of multiple meanings needed to appreciate the jokes. He used to crack some awful groaners himself, and although most of them were older than time, he thought they were all his own invention. I remember the morning he told the elevator girl that her job must have its ups and downs. He was particularly pleased with that one, so pleased that he told it to me the minute he stepped into the office.

"Ups and downs! Not bad at all, I think, Miss Jeynes. I must remember to tell it to Charles this afternoon. Ups and downs." He chortled his way into his office. I was tactful enough not to tell him that Mabel probably heard it at least five times a day.

It took months for Mr. Miyashita and me to get to know each other well enough to venture something as intimate as sharing a joke. I think the breakthrough came the Monday after talent night when he arrived at work, and I tried to apologize for the damage to his car.

"You must not assume guilt for things that are beyond your control, Miss Jeynes," he said. "You are not responsible for the damage to my automobile, so there is no need for you to apologize."

"I'm sorry it happened."

"As am I. But that is no reason to look so glum. Cars can be repaired. When the fellows at Sunnyside Auto Body have finished with mine, it will be as good as new. So we will talk no more of this unfortunate business." He swept the air with the back of his hand as if brushing away the subject. "Instead, we should discuss your very enjoyable talent night. I must say, I did appreciate The Sillies' political satire. It was not only funny but cleverly pointed, especially the Bad Wolf with his Hitler moustache."

"Everyone likes The Sillies," I said.

"May I ask you why men playing the roles of women automatically become objects of laughter here in Canada? I find this puzzling, perhaps because I come from a country where men act all the characters in plays, including those of women, and it is not considered in the least funny."

I didn't have the foggiest notion how to explain the humour in drag acts. "I guess you either think it's funny or you don't. I can't explain it."

"Quite right too," he said. "Humour is nearly impossible to explain, and if you could manage an explanation, then the joke probably would not be funny any more. It would be like dissecting a butterfly to find out how the creature works. In the end, you would have body parts and perhaps an explanation, but the butterfly itself would be quite dead."

I don't know how dead butterflies worked their grim way into a chat about church basement humour, but sometimes conversations with Mr. Miyashita took a peculiar turn.

"I must say, your dance required no explanations at all," he continued. "You and Charles were the highlight of the evening for everyone. Mrs. Miyashita thoroughly enjoyed it and so did I." He paused for a moment and then grinned. "Miss Jeynes, that dance was a real lollapalooza."

"A lollapalooza?" I couldn't help it, I started to laugh. Mr. Miyashita laughed too.

"Lollapalooza," he repeated. "That is American slang for something extraordinary or excellent."

"I know the word, sir. It's just that I didn't expect to hear you use it."

"I must confess, I cannot resist English words with a great many Ls in them. It could be that I am a touch doolally about the letter L. You see, when I was a student at Oxford I got a terrible teasing because the English are convinced that no Japanese can pronounce an L properly. As a consequence, I made certain my Ls were the most perfect in all of England. Now I fear I am very vain about them. Lollapalooza is a lovely word, is it not?"

"Lovelier than Lilliputian or Lancelot?" I asked.

"By far. Lollapalooza is a word worthy of Queen Liliuokalani, the Honolulu lady who played lullabies on her ukulele."

"I give up, sir. You win. Hands down."

"But I have only just begun, Miss Jeynes. I know so many words brimming with Ls that we could continue well past lunch."

LOOKING BACK, I am amazed at Mr. Miyashita's sense of humour. Corny as his own jokes were, he had managed to develop a love of

English word play and a feel for what was funny in a totally different culture. I think our shared laughter over that silly word game cemented a bond between us. Still, there's no denying that my boss was not an easy man to get to know. As I've said, there were the obvious cultural and racial barriers between us, as well as our differences in class and wealth and age. But take those away and he was still an odd fish. I wrote in our Most Important Day exercise that back in the Calgary of 1939, Mr. Miyashita might as well have been a Martian and that's not as far-fetched as it sounds. There really was something not quite of this world about him. He was always odd man out in Canada, but I don't think he fit in any better back in Japan or, for that matter, in his own family.

Soon after I began to work for him, it became clear to me that he was on the outs with his powerful relatives. They were a formidable lot, the Miyashitas of Hiroshima, important enough to have considerable political clout and ambitious enough to use it. Mr. Miyashita was the second in a family of four brothers. The eldest, along with their father, who must have been getting on for ninety in 1939, led the family's business empire. And make no mistake, Miyashita Industries was an empire. Dad and his *Albertan* articles got that spot on. Over the years the company had spread its tentacles through heavy industry, shipbuilding, chemical plants, and all manner of manufacturing from airplanes to textiles.

Long before Mr. Miyashita came of age, he knew that he would have no part to play in ruling this empire. From the time he was old enough to form opinions, his religious and political views set him at odds with his family. Even as a boy, he had no use for the cult of militarism and the inevitable glorification of war it fostered. As an adult, he came to loathe the kind of men it bred too, men like his father and brothers, puffed up with their dreams of conquest and empire and Samurai honour. In return, they detested him and what they considered his dangerously radical political notions. In reality, these were quite tame by the standards of the day, even for Japan.

Grand philosophical differences aside, I suspect the final rift had a much more mundane cause. In the family's eyes, Mr. Miyashita had married beneath him and, by doing so, had betrayed them and stained their honour. He also married for love, which they probably considered bad form as well. Not that Mrs. Miyashita was the simple peasant girl of myth and legend who won the heart of the handsome prince. She came from a perfectly respectable, well-to-do, upper-middle-class family. Her father was a prominent engineer and the owner of a company that sometimes did work for Miyashita Industries. That was the problem. In the world of the mighty Miyashitas, you didn't go marrying the help. Shortly after Mr. Miyashita's unsuitable marriage, Papa, with the help of eldest brother and the blessings of the younger two—one an up-and-comer in the government and the other an officer in the Imperial Navy—banished him and his embarrassing wife from the family and from Japan. In their view, the second son was uncooperative, unpredictable, and untrustworthy. His continued presence was simply too disruptive to tolerate. There is an old and often-quoted Japanese proverb that says, "The nail that stands up must be pounded down." If there was ever a nail that got pounded, it was Mr. Miyashita. Having concluded that Vancouver, with its large population of ex-patriate Japanese was not isolated enough, his family packed him off across the Rockies to Calgary in 1909 to open the Canadian branch of Miyashita Industries.

Outwardly, this seemed an eminently respectable undertaking for a younger son, but at the same time, it kept him safely stashed where he couldn't upset any more family apple carts. My parents hadn't been so far off the mark after all. Mr. Miyashita was a remittance man—a black sheep exiled to a faraway place and paid to stay there. Paid exceedingly well, I should add. Miyashita Industries believed in keeping up appearances. They bought a mansion in Mount Royal, one befitting the Canadian representative of the company, and sent him a hefty allowance. This allowance was the source of the seed money for his first investments. Over the years, by dint of canny and occasionally inspired management, he parlayed his remittance payments into what would be a respectable fortune even in today's inflated dollars.

Luck had played a part too, at least at first. Picking the right oil company to back in a high-risk oil drilling venture provided the foundation for his subsequent investments, the ones where he made his real money. Following the success of the Dingman #1 well, literally hundreds of little companies staked claims in the foothills around Turner Valley. Most of these ventures came to nothing, but a few made wealthy men of lucky investors like Mr. Miyashita. After Royalite bought the company at the height of its success, he took his profits and never played such a high-risk game again. His newly conservative investment strategies served him well when he moved his oil money into the stock market. He more than weathered the crash of '29, and thanks to his prudence and a shrewd sense of timing, he continued to make money all through the Depression. When I went to work for him, Mr. Miyashita was a very rich remittance man indeed.

After I got to know Mrs. Miyashita, she told me that with the exception of his mother and his mother's brother—the uncle who had given him the Sharaku print—the family had not communicated with him for years, even on business matters. This was delegated to underlings, perhaps as a way of emphasizing his lowly status as an outcast. If the family silence was supposed to cause Mr. Miyashita any grief, it didn't. As far as he was concerned, the less he heard from headquarters, the better. It was enough that he had to endure the presence of the so-called secretary. From 1909 until I went to work for him, Miyashita Industries had sent out a succession of men from Japan to fill this position, but any secretarial duties they performed were incidental. In reality, the secretaries were Mr. Miyashita's minders, the family's eyes and ears in Canada, sent to make certain the wayward son toed the line. I know it sounds impossible, but they kept this up for nearly thirty years. Or maybe they just forgot about him and nobody bothered to change whatever arrangements had been put in place all those years ago. Who knows? I still find the whole business amazing. However, during the time the Miyashitas had lived in Canada, much had changed politically, and by 1939, it was almost certain that no new family spy would be sent to reclaim the job I had taken. Since the Japanese invasion of China in 1937, Miyashita Industries had concentrated all its might on that war and on preparations for the larger conflict they knew was coming.

The loss of their trivial Canadian trade meant nothing to them and the future of their black sheep brother even less. I'm certain they never knew he'd hired me and wouldn't have cared if they had. As a matter of fact, the idea that he could hire a secretary for himself did not occur to Mr. Miyashita until the day he sat next to my former boss at a Rotary lunch and mentioned that he had seen Mr. Tanaka off at the CPR station that morning. Mr. Calthorpe, in an effort to ingratiate himself with the Canadian head of Miyashita Industries, immediately volunteered the services of one of his Greer & Western typists. Ultimately, this sycophantic generosity didn't sell one lump of coal for Greer & Western. On the other hand, it did wonders for Mr. Miyashita's photo files and for me too.

I NEVER KNEW the whole story behind Mr. Miyashita's exile, and I certainly never learned any of it from him. Most of what I know I found out from Canon Giles during our public library encounters. I picked up some bits and pieces from my mother too. Mum and Mrs. Miyashita became good friends, which must have surprised them both. It certainly did me. Looking back, I can see that despite the barrier of language and the obvious divisions of race and class and money, the similarity of their circumstances made for a natural sympathy between them. Each had left a warm, close-knit family to follow a beloved husband, a man estranged from his own family, to a new life in a new country. They had both been ripped from deep roots and thrown down in Calgary to get on with life as best they could. At least Mum spoke English and had children to console her. Mrs. Miyashita had neither. To this day, I can't begin to imagine that kind of isolation, or how lonely she must have been for most of her life in Canada. Many years later, my mother and I would occasionally talk about the old east Calgary days and her Japanese friend. I know she didn't tell me everything. I'm certain that she took some of Mrs. Miyashita's most intimate confidences to the grave.

I didn't get to know Mrs. Miyashita until after talent night. Up to then, I had only spoken a few words to her on the phone and a few more on the rare afternoons when she dropped by the office in order to walk home with her husband after shopping at The Hudson's Bay. I know she was ashamed of her English with its heavy accent and haphazard syntax, and this made her hesitant to engage in even the most basic conversation. Nevertheless, Mrs. Miyashita's English was still better than my non-existent Japanese, so we made do.

On a grey mid-week morning the week after talent night, Mr. Miyashita called the office from home to say he had a cold and would not be coming to work. I hardly recognized his voice. He sounded truly ill. My boss was no hypochondriac, but he would often stay home with even a slight case of the sniffles because he did not want to upset his wife by going out in the cold air. Mrs. Miyashita fretted constantly about his health and not altogether without reason. Along with his colds, he had a tendency to develop bronchial infections and, on one exceedingly unpleasant occasion, pneumonia. Those were the days before antibiotics, so if you caught something as serious as pneumonia you either recovered on your own or you didn't. The new sulpha drugs had improved things considerably, but before penicillin, old ladies didn't bounce back from bronchitis in a week like I've just done. Back then, recovery could take a long time, longer than many old people had. All right, so maybe I didn't exactly bounce and maybe it's taking longer than a week, but I am back.

Earlier that morning, a messenger had delivered some papers from Richardson's that could not wait for Mr. Miyashita's signature. I mentioned them when he called.

"Would you be so kind as to bring them to my house this afternoon, Miss Jeynes," he croaked. "I will sign them, and you can drop them off at Richardson's on your way back to the office."

That afternoon, I missed the two o'clock streetcar to Mount Royal by seconds. I watched it trundle down the track without me and decided to walk rather than stand and wait for the next car. It was cold, not as cold as the morning I wrote about in our Most Important Day exercise, but still very bitter and windy with it. Altogether, it was little more than a fast-striding twenty minutes to the Miyashitas', but by the time I climbed the flight of stone steps to their front door, my toes and fingers had passed tingle and moved on to pain. Thanks to the wind, the fronts of my legs were rapidly going the same way in spite of my wool stockings. Mrs. Miyashita must have seen me coming because she opened the door before I lifted the knocker.

The head of Miyashita Industries Canada lived in a handsome house set well back from the street on a large, sloping lot surrounded by a fieldstone fence. An eccentric turn-of-the-century Alberta entrepreneur, who made it big in one of the province's booms and then went broke in the inevitable bust that followed, had built it when the boom was at its loudest. Despite some of the entrepreneur's wackier flourishes—a life-sized buffalo head carved in stone over the front door pops to mind—the house was beautifully proportioned with arched windows in groups of three on either side of a similarly arched entrance. Like many of Calgary's public buildings from the same period, it was constructed of Paskapoo sandstone, a warm brown-grey stone quarried near the city.

To someone accustomed to our little place in east Calgary, the Miyashitas' Mount Royal house seemed enormous, although compared with some of today's suburban mansions, its two floors and five bedrooms would probably look modest. The old place is long gone, demolished in the 1960s to make way for an apartment block. That really was Calgary's decade for architectural barbarism, wasn't it? Remember the Royal Doulton gargoyles on the old *Calgary Herald* building? Hacked off to make way for marble slabs and modernization. Fortunately, the Palliser Hotel was a little luckier. At least the mess the renovation hooligans made of its lobby was reversible. Not so the *Herald*'s gargoyles or the Miyashitas' house. They are gone forever. I sometimes wonder what happened to all that dressed sandstone and to the dear old buffalo that Mr. Miyashita had, of course, named Bill. Surely the wreckers wouldn't just have carted Bill off to some rubble dump and turned him into landfill. I like to think of him, forgotten and covered with moss, sitting at the bottom of some long-gone workman's garden, patiently waiting to be rediscovered and enjoyed all over again. No one will know how he got there or where he came from. He'll be the Mystery Buffalo, but I'll bet you any money they call him Bill.

Dear me, there she goes again, digressing all over the place and with a vengeance. Perhaps all the coughing and antibiotics have addled my old brain. At least that will be my excuse this time. Meanwhile, back in the warmth of the Miyashitas' front hall . . .

Mrs. Miyashita opened the door, and a dog started to bark from somewhere inside the house. It continued its racket as I followed her in and began shedding my winter paraphernalia. Although I towered over her, Mrs. Miyashita helped me off with my coat. I bent to undo the clips on my overshoes and noticed that she was wearing slippers so I took off my shoes as well. Later, she told my mother that this showed I had very good manners. I'm afraid that right then I felt anything but mannerly. As a matter of fact, next to Mrs. Miyashita, so dainty and neat in her silk kimono, I felt like an enormous dowdy lump. There I stood in my thick grey stockings, tweed skirt, and sensible wools, clutching the papers from Richardson's in a cold, red-knuckled fist. Mrs. Miyashita offered me a pair of her slippers, but besides being sizes too small, they were divided by a thong between the first and second toes. She was wearing a pair of white stockings that had the same divided toe.

I had never seen Mrs. Miyashita in Japanese clothes before. She always wore Western dress out in public and reserved her kimonos for home. That day she had on a sky-blue silk with a pattern of alternating mauve and rose dragonflies. To someone who had just come in from the white-on-grey world of a cloudy winter afternoon, that kimono was a sight to lift the spirits. All Mrs. Miyashita's kimonos looked gorgeous to me, but I did eventually learn to tell the difference between those for everyday wear and the fancier ones she wore for special occasions. Later, I was flattered to discover that she had worn one of the fancy kimonos for my call, that she regarded my bringing business papers to her house as an event worth formal acknowledgment.

"Miss Jeynes, you are very cold," she said. "After you speak to my husband, we will drink tea and you will be warm." It was more a promise than an invitation. "Please follow me."

I know I cannot write down what Mrs. Miyashita said in the exact way she said it so I'm not going to try. If I couldn't get my parents' familiar Northumbrian voices on paper, I don't have a hope of writing her Japanese voice. And even if I could get the voice, I'd still have to describe the simultaneous game of charades that accompanied most of our conversations. But with a combination of words and pantomime, we did manage to communicate. To be fair to Mrs. Miyashita, I should add that through time and practice with my mother, her English did improve. Unfortunately, the improved version isn't any easier to write down because Mrs. Miyashita's Japanese accent acquired distinctly Geordie overtones. Only the Evel Knievels of memoir writing would dare to attempt a reconstruction of that amazing mishmash. As for me, except for *hello*, *goodbye*, *please*, and *thank you*, my Japanese remained non-existent.

That afternoon, I followed Mrs. Miyashita up the stairs and tried not to goggle at my surroundings on the way, although they were worth a stare or two. I'd never been inside one of the big houses in Mount Royal before, but I don't think the Miyashitas' was in any way typical. For starters, the furnishings were an odd mix of traditional Japanese, late Victorian English, and very modern art deco. I know that sounds like a mess, but it wasn't. Each piece sat comfortably with its odd neighbours on big Persian rugs. A cheerful wood fire burned in the grate of a Rundlestone fireplace. More of Mr. Miyashita's photos and several large oil paintings of the mountains hung on the oak-panelled walls, along with a couple of Japanese scroll paintings. An unusual Gissing of a Turner Valley oil derrick occupied pride-of-place above the mantel. I've wondered since whether the well in that painting was the one he had invested in so successfully. Overall, the house seemed far more Western than Japanese, although I remember noticing how spacious and uncluttered the rooms looked for a time and place that loved fussy ornament and plenty of it. That restraint, I am certain, was Japanese.

Mr. Miyashita was in his study reading, propped up on a tubular chrome and black leather chaise longue that would still be considered modern today. He wore a silk dressing gown with a cravat at the neck. It made him look like a Japanese Noel Coward, although the sophistication came to an abrupt end at the loud tartan travel robe Mrs. Miyashita had tucked around his legs. In a small corner fireplace blue flames licked at the ceramic grid of a gas heater. From either end of the carved oak mantelpiece, two beavers locked eyes across a central Alberta rose, another of the entrepreneur's eccentric touches.

"Good afternoon, Miss Jeynes." Mr. Miyashita sounded even more hoarse than he had over the phone. He marked his place in *Great Expectations* and took off his reading glasses. "No, please, do not come in here. You must not risk catching this cold." A croup kettle steamed on a low table in front of a radiator, adding much-needed moisture to the parched winter air. The room was very warm.

I stood on the threshold while Mrs. Miyashita took the papers in for me. She spoke to her husband in Japanese as she brought him a fountain pen from a desk near the window.

"My wife tells me that you walked here."

"Yes, sir. I missed the streetcar and thought walking would be warmer than standing waiting for the next one."

"And now I expect you are thoroughly chilled. Why did you not take a taxi cab?" He sounded almost angry. I couldn't think what I had done to irritate him so I put it down to his feeling unwell and out of sorts. "You know we have an account with Polley's, do you not?"

The thought of taking a taxi had simply not occurred to me. "I'm fine, sir," I said. "I walk in the cold all the time."

"You will not do so today. On your way back you will telephone for a cab and you will instruct the driver to wait for you at Richardson's while you deliver these papers. Then you will ride directly to your house. Those are boss's orders, Miss Jeynes," he added when he saw me about to protest.

While Mr. Miyashita read and signed the papers, Mrs. Miyashita opened a small cardboard box labelled in Japanese and, with a tiny wooden spatula, scooped some white powder from it, which she sprinkled into the croup kettle. The smell of camphor wafted through the room. After she collected the papers, I wished Mr. Miyashita a speedy recovery and the two of us left him to his book.

The barking began again as soon as we reached the bottom of the stairs. By the time we made it to the living room it was so loud that I had to raise my voice to be heard.

"You have a dog?" Considering the racket, this was a pretty dumb question.

Mrs. Miyashita nodded. "Nikkou." She almost had to shout the name. "Her name is Nikkou. Do you like dogs?"

"Very much."

"You would like to meet Nikkou?"

"Yes please, I would."

Mrs. Miyashita opened the door to the kitchen and a golden blur with a curly tail streaked out and circled our legs. The blur slowed and focused into a small dog of no particular breed with floppy ears and short, woolly fur. Dizzy with delight, it flung itself down at my feet and rolled over on its back. Mrs. Miyashita knelt and scratched its belly.

"Nikkou enjoys company," she said, which seemed something of an understatement.

"I can see that." I added a few pats of my own to the fleecy fur. "How old is she?"

"I do not know for certain. We guess she is three years or maybe four. She was very small when she came crying to our door. She was lost and starved and dirty. Fleas too."

The belly under my hand was far from thin and the soft fur had the gloss of health. Nikkou had fallen on good times.

I sat in one of the easy chairs by the fire. Mrs. Miyashita left the dog to entertain me while she went to the kitchen to make tea. Some minutes later she reappeared pushing a very English mahogany tea wagon. It had the usual glass tray on which sat a teapot, two cups, and a plate of digestive biscuits. The digestives sparked Nikkou's attention. She flipped herself upright in order to focus on the biscuit plate with a gaze so intent that I half-expected her to raise a front paw and point like a bird-dog.

In keeping with the rest of the Miyashitas' house, our afternoon tea was a mix of Japan and Canada. The tea itself was from Japan, and Mrs. Miyashita brewed it in a Japanese teapot so small that in my family's opinion, it wouldn't have held enough water to dampen the leaves, let alone wet your whistle. Still, the soft yellow glaze painted with tiny flowers was very pretty. Mrs. Miyashita poured the pale green *gyokuro* into white cups made of such delicate porcelain that even when mine was full, I could see the shadows of my fingers through it. The cups had handles and saucers too, which was very Canadian, but there was no sugar or milk on the tea wagon, which was not. That was my first cup of green tea, and although it tasted odd, I thought it a very pleasant drink and still do. Until I accepted a digestive biscuit, that is. I don't recommend combining *gyokuro* and digestives unless you are interested in experiencing the clash of east and west first-hand. I noticed that Mrs. Miyashita did not eat the biscuit she took. She fed half to Nikkou and the other half remained in her saucer.

Our first real conversation got off to a slow start.

"This is lovely tea," I said.

"Thank you. My sister sends it to me from Japan."

"Is Nikkou a Japanese name?" I asked.

"Yes," said Mrs. Miyashita. "Nikkou means—"

And we were stuck. Mrs. Miyashita had forgotten the English word for sunlight. She pointed to the window. Unfortunately, it was a cloudy afternoon.

"So Nikkou means window," I said, thinking it a peculiar name for a dog.

Mrs. Miyashita shook her head. She pointed to the window again and then made a big circle with her arms.

"A round window?"

"Not window." This time she pointed both hands at the window and then moved her arms from left to right, fingers fluttering, as if she were playing an arpeggio on the piano.

"Rippling. Flowing. Streaming," I guessed. "Rain streaming down the window."

In desperation she pointed to the yellow teapot and went through the whole mime again. I may not have been the sharpest charades player in Calgary, but even I knew nobody would name a dog Tea-flowing-down-a-windowpane. She finished by pointing to the teapot's yellow, then to Nikkou's fur, and back to the window. I finally twigged.

"Nikkou means sunlight," I said. My God, I could be a dim bulb at times. Still can.

"Sunlight," a relieved Mrs. Miyashita repeated, only she pronounced it "sunright."

"Or sunshine," I added. "Sunshine means almost the same as sunlight."

"Sunshine is good," she said, obviously pleased to be relieved of the burden of the L.

"Nikkou is perfect for her," I said.

The little dog thumped her tail at the sound of her name, but her eyes remained riveted on the half digestive still in Mrs. Miyashita's saucer.

Conversations with Mrs. Miyashita might have been slow going, but they were always a pleasure. That afternoon we talked happily about dogs and kimonos and how much we enjoyed Fred Astaire's dancing until the chime of the back door bell interrupted us. Nikkou barked.

"You must excuse me, Miss Jeynes," Mrs. Miyashita said. "That is the boy from Phelps' with the groceries. Will you please hold Sunshine for me?"

I looped a finger through Nikkou's collar while Mrs. Miyashita went to answer the door. I should have held on with both hands. There were a good twenty pounds of fit dog under that fluff. She broke free and muscled her way through the kitchen door just before it closed behind Mrs. Miyashita. I followed and recaptured her as the grocery boy walked in the back door. It was Billy Trent, a classmate of Charlie's at Western Canada High School. He said a polite good afternoon to Mrs. Miyashita over Nikkou's din and put the grocery box on the kitchen counter next to the refrigerator.

"Hi, Kay," he said, obviously surprised to see me. He knelt down and held out his arms to Nikkou. I looked at Mrs. Miyashita, who gave me the nod and I released my hold on the collar. Nikkou stopped barking and ran to throw herself at Billy's feet.

"Nikkou likes Billy," Mrs. Miyashita said. I wondered if there were anyone Nikkou didn't like. "Nikkou does not like the postman," she added, as if she had read my mind. "Please wait," she said to Billy. "I will find money for you."

"What are you doing here?" he asked after Mrs. Miyashita had left the room.

"Delivering some papers to Mr. Miyashita," I replied, not that it was any of his business.

"Yeah, I heard you were working for the Jap."

"So are you," I said, pointing to the grocery box. "And that's a pretty sad-looking cabbage you've brought." The leaves were brown at the edges and the top was speckled with black mould.

"I don't pack the groceries, Kay. I just deliver them, so don't get mad at me."

"You like delivering garbage?"

"I like having a job. I can't help it if Mr. Phelps is down on Japs. He's the one who decides what to pack. Not me."

I looked in the box. The rest of the produce wasn't much better. The carrots were especially nasty, limp and speckled with the same black mould as the cabbage. Then I saw the bill tucked down the side of the box. It was even more disgusting. I didn't know much about shopping for food, but I did know cabbages didn't cost that much.

"How does Phelps get away with charging this kind of money? It's robbery."

"I don't know how much he charges them," Billy said. "I never collect when I deliver. It all gets put on their account."

"Then why are you waiting for money?"

"Because Mrs. Miyashita always gives me a tip." At least he had the grace to sound ashamed. "Kay, I'm sorry. I like her. She's a nice lady for a Jap. But what can I do? I need this job."

I FOLLOWED THE boss's instructions to the letter. After Mrs. Miyashita and I finished our tea, I telephoned Polley's and took a taxi to Richardson's and then on home. I tell you, a cab pulling up in front of our house caused more than a few curtains on the street to twitch, our own included. I explained to Mum why I had come home early and in such style.

"And what did that little ride cost?" Her first question.

"I'm not sure," I said. "Mr. Miyashita paid for it. I never thought to ask." That wasn't quite true. Actually it was a bare-faced lie. I knew to the penny how much that taxi ride cost, but I wasn't going to tell Mum when she so obviously regarded it as an extravagance and, even worse, as putting on airs. I could hear it all before she said it. And wasn't I Lady Muck herself, sitting in the back of Polley's cab? And me with two good legs. Think of all the things a girl with a bit of sense could have bought and done for the price of that one taxi ride. Right then, I couldn't face trying to justify the taxi or to explain that I'd signed for my ride on Mr. Miyashita's account. Besides, that would simply have earned me a lecture on paying as you go, cash on the barrel, and neither a borrower nor a lender be. I told her about my afternoon at the Miyashitas' instead. I started with the groceries.

"Everyone's heard of Phelps," Mum said when I had finished my story. "Fancies himself grocer to the upper crust—Calgary's answer to Fortnum & Mason. I'll bet Mr. La-di-dah doesn't try to pass off his mouldy cabbage on the rest of Mount Royal. The man's a chiseller and no mistake. Why does Mrs. M. bother with him?" Mum had given up trying to pronounce Miyashita.

"I don't know," I said. "Maybe because his store is close to their house?"

"How does he get away with it? Why doesn't she speak to him? Or take her business elsewhere?"

"You've heard Mrs. Miyashita talk. Her English isn't very good. I don't think she could speak to him." I had no answer to her last question.

"Poor wee soul. I've a mind to go down to that rubbish bin he calls a shop and give yon Phelps an earful myself."

Mr. Phelps's treatment of Mrs. Miyashita had really got Mum's dander up. Most likely this was because it upset her sense of justice and not because the man was a racist. As a matter of fact, I don't think my parents were any less racist than the average Calgarian of the time. For Mum and Dad, racism took the form of knowing in a general, unspecified way that white people were superior to all the rest, just as they knew that the English were the best of the whites. There wasn't a doubt in their minds that the Union Jack flew at the very top of the whole heap of humanity. But the Miyashitas were no longer part of some faceless generality. Meeting them at talent night had separated my boss and his wife from the heap and made them specific and individual. Now they were people my parents had spoken to and drunk tea with, people who had been good to Charlie and me. Mum and Dad knew the Miyashitas personally, and this shifted the racist equation. Why, Mr. M. spoke with an English accent, didn't he? Even if that accent was Oxford and a bit on the poncey side, he still sounded like a real Englishman.

"Before we do anything, I think I should talk to Mr. Miyashita first," I said. "Besides, maybe this isn't any of our business."

"Of course it's our business," Mum said. "You want to be like that spineless Billy Trent? Kay, you have to stand up for what's right in this world, and what that Phelps is doing isn't right. It's a swindle."

Secretly, I would have loved to see Mum go after Mr. Phelps. My mother on the warpath was a force of nature. Still, I tried to rein her in a little.

"At least let me talk to Mr. Miyashita first. I'll tell him as soon as he comes back to work. He probably doesn't know anything about what Phelps is doing."

"I wouldn't bet on it," Mum said. "After all, the man must eat that rubbish at his meals."

"I promise I'll talk to him as soon as he comes back to the office."

"Make sure you do. None of that shrinking violet business of yours like with your wages. You speak up. Japs or no, what that Phelps is doing is wrong."

"Mrs. Miyashita has a beautiful tea wagon," I said, thinking we could do with a change of subject. "And she made me green tea. She has a refrigerator too."

I DID TALK to Mr. Miyashita when he came back to work the next Monday. I waited until we were sitting in his office drinking our coffee.

"Sir, if a person knows something important but isn't sure that it's up to them to say anything about it, what should the person do? Say that person came to know something by accident and it's maybe not any of that person's business so if she stuck her nose in where it wasn't wanted other people might be offended and think she was interfering but if she didn't speak up then maybe . . ."

"Please, Miss Jeynes, please." Mr. Miyashita put a stop to my tortured ramblings. "Is something troubling you? You may speak freely. I am very difficult to offend."

Well, that last wasn't quite true, but it did make it easier for me to tell him about the groceries.

"And I'm sorry if I've stepped over the line, sir, but I thought I should make certain you knew," I said when I had finished. "I don't mean to be a busybody and interfere, but what Phelps is doing isn't right. That's why my mother said I had to tell you." Like any snivelling coward worth her piece of silver, I tried to shift some of the blame for my tale-telling onto Mum.

Mr. Miyashita said nothing. He sat back in his chair and gazed at Tokuji. Mr. Miyashita was a very private person, and at first I thought my speaking out on a problem involving his personal life had offended him so deeply that he was busy thinking of a polite way to fire me. At last he turned and looked at me.

"Your mother is right, Miss Jeynes," he said. "Thank you for telling me this." At least I still had a job. The silence continued for another minute or two. Finally, he seemed to come to a decision. He leaned forward in his chair.

"Miss Jeynes, do you know the origin of the word *secretary*?"

"It has something to do with *secret*," I said.

"Indeed it does. *Secretarius* is the Latin for 'one entrusted with secrets,' and, as you are my secretary, I have entrusted you with mine. That is why your mother was quite correct when she instructed you to tell me about Mr. Phelps and his shoddy practices. It is one of your duties as my confidential secretary to keep me informed of such things."

"Yes, I guess it is," I said, now wishing I hadn't given all the credit to Mum.

"I know there has been some difficulty with the groceries, but I did not know exactly what. It began shortly after my previous secretary returned to Japan. Tanaka's wife was a great help to Mrs. Miyashita, as were the wives of the secretaries before him. They all spoke some English, which was a condition of their husbands' employment, so they were able to help her with things like shopping for our food and keeping the household running smoothly. I know that without Mrs. Tanaka, shopping has become difficult for my wife, although she would never admit it."

It hadn't occurred to me that Mr. Miyashita's secretaries would have wives and families. To be honest, I hadn't thought much about my predecessors at all. However, I can see now that the loss of Mrs. Tanaka must have been a blow to Mrs. Miyashita and not just because she helped with the shopping. Although Mrs. Miyashita and the secretaries' wives may not have formed real friendships, language and loneliness would have drawn them together in that second-best facsimile, companionship.

Sometimes I wondered why the Miyashitas, particularly Mrs. Miyashita, did not make more of an effort to meet any of the few Japanese who lived in Calgary at the time. I once asked Mum about it.

"He doesn't want to, and she wouldn't know how, is my guess. You've got to realize that back home in Japan, Mrs. M. would be considered a very grand lady, being married to him and all. My guess is that after the first hello, none of the women here would know what to say to her and vice versa. Be like Mrs. Rockefeller popping round to our place for a cup of tea and a chin wag, wouldn't it?"

Privately, I thought—and still do—that Mum wouldn't have had the least difficulty in chatting with the millionaire's missus.

"But you're friends with Mrs. Miyashita," I pointed out. "The two of you don't seem to have any trouble finding things to talk about."

"That's different," Mum said. "I'm not a Jap."

So Mrs. Miyashita, the permanent exile, would watch the old secretary and his wife leave, and then a new secretary and a new wife would arrive from Japan, and the cycle would begin again. Except this time. As Mr. Tanaka was the last secretary, so Mrs. Tanaka was the last companion. I did not know this when Mr. Miyashita and I had our conversation.

"But, sir, couldn't you hire her some help," I suggested. "Maybe just somebody to go grocery shopping for her, until your new secretary and his wife get here?"

"I have broached the subject of help many times since the day we arrived in Canada, and every time my wife has refused to allow me to hire anyone. She would not hear of a cook or a housekeeper, so I stopped asking. She says she prefers to do these things herself, that

Canadians eat strange food, and that her English is not up to instructing a housekeeper. Personally, I believe she does not want strangers under foot all day long, and in this I have a great deal of sympathy. She does have a woman to clean the house two afternoons a week, and a man to shovel the walks in winter and do the heavy work in the garden in the summer—but that is all she will permit."

I could see Mrs. Miyashita's point. If she had a cook, a housekeeper, and a gardener, there wouldn't be anything for her to do. She'd be stuck sitting around all day long in her silk kimonos going berserk with boredom and loneliness while she issued misunderstood orders and ate badly cooked foreign food. No wonder she didn't want servants. Looking after Mr. Miyashita was her job.

"When Mrs. Tanaka left so suddenly to return to Japan, my wife was without an English-speaking associate for the first time in many years. I do not know why, but she has become hesitant to shop alone for our food. She now dictates her requirements to me. I write her list in English and drop it off at Phelps' Grocery Store on my way to the office. I opened an account there. Now you tell me they are cheating us."

"It's not just the money, sir. Some of those vegetables looked pretty grim."

"That is often the case with vegetables in Calgary during the winter," Mr. Miyashita remarked. He had a point. In 1940, the fresh vegetables available in grocery stores were limited to the basics—carrots, Brussels sprouts, parsnips, and the like—no raddichio or bok choy back then. And near the end of a long winter, even the most stalwart turnip could turn soft and spotty.

We lapsed into silence once more. This time I was the first to speak.

"Sir, I'd be glad to go shopping with Mrs. Miyashita on Saturday mornings," I offered. "I don't know all that much about buying food—my mum looks after that—but together we'd get better stuff than Phelps gives her and we'd get it at a fair price too."

"It is very kind of you to offer, Miss Jeynes, and I'm certain my wife would say the same. But I would not impose on you on your day off. That is out of the question."

"It's all right, sir. After all, it would only be until your new secretary arrives."

"No, no. You misunderstand me. I was about to suggest that you might do this on a weekday instead. If that is acceptable, I will speak to my wife this evening. I think she would like to go shopping with you. She most certainly enjoyed your visit to our house last week."

I WENT HOME in a bit of a panic that evening. I didn't know beans about shopping for food: it was something Mum did during the day while the rest of us were out. She did all of the cooking and most of the housework too, although I remember that when we were little Charlie and I both loved to help her bake. As we grew older, we were given a few household chores of our own, but there were never many, and the two of us split them evenly. We were expected to set the table and wash the dishes and keep our rooms clean. We shovelled the walks in winter and helped with the garden in the summer but that was about it. Unlike most of my girlfriends, I was never forced to do any more around the house than my brother simply because I was a girl. This was a radical attitude for the time, but when I think back on my parents' arguments about my education, maybe it's not all that surprising that my mother didn't push me into domesticity. Or perhaps she thought that looking after us and the house was her job and didn't expect her children to do her work for her any more than she expected us to nip over to Ogden after school and give Dad a hand with his smithing. She might have changed her tune if there'd been ten of us instead of two.

"How can you tell when fish is fresh?" I asked her that evening after Charlie and I had finished the dishes. Mum sat in her easy chair in the living room trying to read the newspaper. We had already discussed the basics of poultry selection and how to assess cabbage. "What should I look for?"

"If I were you, I'd just ask Mrs. M.," Mum said. "She'll have picked out a fish or two in her day. Probably knows her way around a cabbage too." She was losing patience with my questions.

"But I'm supposed to be helping her, not the other way round."

Mum laughed at this, which rather hurt my feelings. Nevertheless, she did tell me about buying fish.

"First thing, remember that Calgary is a long way from the sea so you only buy fish on a Friday."

"Why Friday?" I asked.

"Because of the Catholics," Mum said. "They aren't allowed to eat meat on Fridays, so they all have fish for their suppers instead. Fish is shipped to be at its best here on a Friday and you can thank the Pope for that." Now that I thought about it, when our family did eat fish in winter it was always on a Friday, but I hadn't realized there was a reason. "And you don't buy fish just anywhere. If you want the best, you go to the Billingsgate and you get there early."

"But how do you know if it's fresh?" I persisted. "Exactly what should I be looking for?"

"Oh for heaven's sake, Kay, you're after a bit of cod, not shopping for the Lord Mayor's banquet."

"Come on, Mum. I don't want to look too dumb. How do you know what fish to buy?"

"You meet me on Friday morning at the Billingsgate, that's how." She picked up her newspaper. "Be there at ten."

THAT FRIDAY, MRS. Miyashita met me at the office, and we walked the block to the fish market. It was a mild morning, not much below freezing, but Mrs. Miyashita was dressed for an Arctic expedition in a fur coat and matching fur hat. She wore her regular winter foot gear too—a pair of galoshes from Eaton's children's department stuffed with layers of woolly socks. They looked more than a touch peculiar with the fur coat; in the same eccentric league as her husband's spats.

We arrived at the Billingsgate at ten o'clock on the dot. I had debated whether I should tell Mrs. Miyashita that we were meeting my mother or let it seem like a coincidence. I was reluctant to admit that I'd never bought a fish in my life, and that Mum had come help me out. In the end I told her that my mother often shopped at the Billingsgate on a Friday morning, and we'd probably run into her there. She seemed pleased at the prospect.

In those days, the Billingsgate was right in the middle of downtown on 7th Avenue and Centre Street. There's still a Billingsgate Fish Market in Calgary and it still sells excellent fish, but it moved to new quarters years ago. What I remember most about the old place is white everywhere and all of it spotless—white-tiled walls, white-tiled floor, white-aproned clerks, white-enamelled trays of fish resting on ice in white coolers. And the smell. No one could forget that. The Billingsgate smelled of the ocean: fishy and clean and salt, all in the same breath. When you stepped through the door, you stepped from the prairie to the seaside.

Mum was in the store waiting for us. I can see her now as clearly as if it were last week. She is standing in a patch of sun near the big front window dressed in her green tweed overcoat and a winter hat she'd knit herself, a helmet affair with flaps that pulled down over her ears. She is holding her purse in one hand and a string shopping bag in the other. She beams a smile at me as I walk through the door. Mum was forty-one at the time, but how young she looks to me now.

"Hello, you two," she called, probably in order to avoid taking a run at Miyashita.

"Good morning, Mrs. Jeynes." Mrs. Miyashita removed a fur-lined leather glove and held out her hand. Mum took off her home-knit mitten and the two of them shook hands. It's my recollection that from then on they shook hands every time they met. At least they did when I was there to see.

"What looks fresh this morning, Mum?" I asked, trying to hustle the two of them to the counter.

My mother ignored me as she and Mrs. Miyashita continued to exchange pleasantries, first about the weather and then about what clever costumes Mum had sewn for Charlie and me on talent night, and how much Mr. and Mr. Miyashita had enjoyed our dance. Mum said how sorry she was about their car, and Mrs. Miyashita told her not to worry, it was all fixed and as good as new. And on they chatted. Mum's mangling of what she considered funny foreign words was a standing joke with Charlie and me, so I was surprised when she turned out to be much cleverer than I was at understanding Mrs. Miyashita's English and helping her find lost words. At last, when the two of them decided the proper time had come for business, we approached the counter.

"Good morning, Mr. Denzil." Mum greeted the clerk by name.

"Good morning to you, Mrs. Jeynes." Mr. Denzil, a dapper little man with a pencil moustache, wore a shirt and apron so white they'd have made new snow look dingy. "What may I get for you today?"

"I'm after a nice bit of sole," Mum said.

Mr. Denzil opened the glass-fronted cooler and propped up one of the enamel trays to display its glistening load. "Fresh off the train from Vancouver this morning. Took it off the ice myself. Filleted not half an hour ago."

"A pound and a bit will do nicely, thank you. And give us a peek before you wrap it, please."

Mr. Denzil placed two pieces of fish on a sheet of waxed paper, weighed them, and passed them over the top of the cooler to Mum. She held it for the three of us to inspect and then explained to Mrs. Miyashita that since I wasn't certain how to tell when fish was fresh, this would be as good a time as any for me to learn. Mrs. Miyashita agreed and proceeded to participate in my fishy education with genuine enthusiasm.

"Must be . . ." She made poking motions at the sole with her forefinger.

"Firm," Mum filled in.

"Yes. Firm is good."

"And it should spring back when you touch it too," Mum added, giving one of the fillets a poke for real. Mrs. Miyashita nodded her agreement. "And look for an even white. None of that blotchy stuff, thank you."

"Must smell good." Mrs. Miyashita augmented this remark with a couple of sniffs in the direction of the sole. "This is good."

"Smell is probably the most important thing of all. You want it nice and clean and fresh," Mum said. "Here, get a snootful of this." I leaned over and took a sniff. It smelled like fish to me.

Mum passed the sole back to Mr. Denzil and at Mrs. Miyashita's request ordered some for her. Mr. Denzil wrapped both orders in brown butcher paper and string, and marked the price on each with a grease pencil. While we waited, Mum and Mrs. Miyashita continued their seminar on how to choose the freshest and best. Inevitably, each had her own horror story of the time the fish was not fresh and the whole family came down with food poisoning. Not their own families, of course. Only the unfortunate relatives of those feckless women who had neglected to learn how to judge fish. I thought this was a bit rich on Mum's part, since until today, she'd never taken the trouble to impart this vital life lesson to her only daughter. Nevertheless, she and Mrs. Miyashita were enjoying themselves enormously.

"Would anyone like a cup of coffee?" I asked, more to put an end to the lecture than anything else. We went across the street to the Buffalo Café, where I bought Mum and Mrs. Miyashita a pot of tea and some coffee for myself. The Buffalo's coffee wasn't anywhere near as good as the coffee I brewed at the office.

Mum and Mrs. Miyashita hadn't stopped talking since they shook hands in the Billingsgate. I might as well not have been with them for all the attention they paid to me. However, I did learn all sorts of things about my boss's wife that morning and a few things I didn't know about my mother too.

"My gran taught me to cook fish," Mum said. "A hot pan and a bit of butter, then in, over, and out before it turns all dry and nasty."

"Our cook taught me fish," Mrs. Miyashita said. "She taught me all my cooking. Nara made the most beautiful sushi in Japan."

"You've got me there," Mum said. "I've never heard that one before."

"Sushi is special rice with mostly fish, sometimes vegetables, sometimes wrapped in seaweed too," Mrs. Miyashita explained. "It is all together in small pieces, and very pretty to see."

"How do you cook it?" Mum asked.

"Not cooked," Mrs. Miyashita said. "Sushi fish is . . ." Again, she searched for the English word. This time Mum was unable to help her find it. That anyone would eat uncooked fish was beyond her imagining.

"Raw?" I chimed in. "The fish is raw?"

"Yes," Mrs. Miyashita said. "That is the word."

"Raw fish?" Mum said with a wan smile. "That's a bit unusual, isn't it?"

Truth be told, I thought it was unusual myself and still do. I've eaten sushi in both Canada and Japan, and pretty as it is, I have to admit that I prefer my fish cooked.

"At home, everyone likes sushi," Mrs. Miyashita said. "It is my husband's favourite."

"Well, husbands all have their favourites, don't they?" I knew what Mum really wanted to say was that there's no accounting for taste. "Mine loves his bubble and squeak."

"Bubble and squeak?" Mrs. Miyashita looked puzzled. "This is a food?"

"It's an English dish," I said.

"About as English as food gets," Mum added. "If you don't count roast beef and Yorkshire pudding."

"I wonder if my husband ate this dish when he studied in England?"

"Like as not," Mum said. "At home, everyone enjoys a good bubble and squeak. Bit of cold beef, a few sprouts, and some spuds all mashed together and fried up in dripping, and you've got yourself a dandy dinner."

"And that is called bubble and squeak," Mrs. Miyashita said. This time the wan smile was hers. "How interesting." It didn't take me long to realize that Mrs. Miyashita's "interesting" meant the same thing as my mother's "unusual." Not that I didn't sympathize with her. If I never see a plate of bubble and squeak again, it will be too soon.

"May I get you some hot water for your tea, Mrs. Miyashita? Mum?" I thought it best to find us a new topic. They both refused my offer. "Mrs. Miyashita's sister sends her special tea. It's very good." I tried again, this time with more success.

"You have a sister," Mum said. "Where does she live?"

"Midori lives in Japan. In Hiroshima," Mrs. Miyashita replied. "That is the city where we were children."

"You must miss her," Mum said. "I know I miss my family."

And then they began to talk of their families, of the friends and places they had left behind to come to this city where neither snow drops nor cherry trees could survive and you never caught so much as a whiff of the sea except second-hand at the Billingsgate. At one point, I broke in to suggest that Mrs. Miyashita and I should probably get on with our shopping.

"Don't fret yourself, Kay. I'll see to all that," Mum promised with an airy wave of her hand. In the same breath she went on telling about her friend Nora, who saved copies of the *Morpeth Herald* and mailed them to her every few months, but who knew what was going to happen to the mail now, what with Hitler and all. Mrs. Miyashita's sister sent her copies of a Japanese fashion magazine they both enjoyed. Obviously, I'd been dismissed. I'm not sure either of them noticed when I put on my coat and left to walk back to work. Mum told me later that she and Mrs. Miyashita had indeed continued their shopping and found themselves some dandy vegetables in the Jenkins Groceteria on 8th Avenue.

The next Friday I went shopping again with Mrs. Miyashita. Again my mother met us in the Billingsgate. That morning, as the three of us sat in the Buffalo Café drinking our tea, Mum informed me that she and Mrs. Miyashita had decided they could manage quite nicely on their own from now on, thank you, dear, so I needn't bother taking any more Friday mornings off work. Then Mrs. Miyashita thanked me for all my help, which as far as I could see consisted solely of hooking her up with Mum. However, I knew when I wasn't wanted by the grown-ups and took my rejection with good grace.

I went back to the office and told Mr. Miyashita what had happened. I know he was pleased at the way things had worked out, and not just because his dinners improved.

Assignment #7
DID YOUR FAMILY CELEBRATE HOLIDAYS
AND OTHER SPECIAL OCCASIONS?

IT'S DECEMBER ALREADY, AND EVERYONE here is beginning to think of Christmas. Unlike me, Meggie has spent a Christmas at Foothills Sunset. She says it's a time when the joint could use a little cheering up, and she thinks this celebration exercise might be just the ticket. The way Meggie sees it, Christmas Present isn't up to much for most of the people here, and Christmas Yet to Come, if they do manage another, won't be any better, so having an excuse to visit a happier Christmas Past is a comparatively pleasant prospect.

This week, Meggie and I each had our own special occasions to celebrate. They will never be recognized on any official calendar but are of great significance to us. Sound a trumpet fanfare for Meggie, who scored an amazing financial triumph on eBay, and another for me, the old gimp who walked across the physio room by herself. By herself with a walker, that is. I got out of my wheelchair and made it from the centre of the room to the door—that must be fifteen feet if it's an inch. The physiotherapist applauded. I would have clapped too, but I couldn't let go of the walker. Darren says if I keep making this kind of progress, I'll be back in my own apartment by mid-February. I think I'll be there sooner.

Meggie was almost as pleased as me when she heard my news. Meggie is a brick. Even though she isn't making much progress in physio herself, she is always delighted to hear about mine. If I were her, I might be feeling a little discouraged or even resentful, but not Meggie. Human nature being what it is, I don't think there is a word that means the exact opposite of *schadenfreude*, but if there were, it would belong to her. She's already started planning my going-home party. I'm going to miss her when I leave Foothills Sunset, especially our drinks before dinner.

This evening, by way of celebration, instead of G&Ts we had

martinis—gin, vermouth, and olives, all paid for with Meggie's eBay money. Her youngest grandson sold her entire swizzle stick collection last week for eighty-two dollars. Can you believe it? Apparently Meggie had amassed a real slew of the things over the years and some were from very famous bars. Meggie split the take with Jerome, but that still left enough money to keep us in martinis for a good long while. Even though we can both afford to buy all the booze we care to drink, somehow the swizzle stick gin tastes better. Besides, Meggie says that her eBay sale has given her a whole new purpose in life. It is now her ambition to last longer than her bottle of Noilly Prat. I told her if she keeps on mixing martinis as dry as the ones we had tonight, she'll have to live to be a hundred and ten. Meggie replied that she refuses to bugger up her cocktails just to fix a win. Nothing she likes better than a long shot and a dry martini.

To tell the truth, neither of us is up to much drinking these days. Our G&Ts are long on the tonic and short on gin, and neither of us managed to finish our martini, although we did eat the olives, which thanks to the salt probably sent our blood pressure into the stratosphere. Ah me, the world is fraught. Still, Meggie says it's the gesture that counts, and that it's important for us to celebrate what we can, especially here at Foothills Sunset, where most of the residents have little reason to rejoice. So we celebrate because Kay walked fifteen feet and Meggie pulled off a coup on eBay. What does it matter as long as there's a friend to raise a thimble of gin?

Meggie's attitude reminds me of my mother's. Mum was a great celebrator too, and not just of the biggies like Christmas and birthdays. She never needed much of an excuse to whip up a cake, warm the big teapot, and call it an occasion. The first robin of spring or the last strawberry of summer would do, as long as there were friends to drink a cup with us. No gin in those days though. Who could afford it? And not much entertaining at meal times either. Where we lived, dinner parties, except perhaps the occasional potluck picnic, were unheard of. People in our neighbourhood considered themselves fortunate if they could feed their own families. But a cuppa and a little something sweet were a different story. Even in our poorest days, Mum and Dad always managed to conjure up a piece of cake and a pot of tea for our friends. If you could bank fun, we'd have been millionaires. I think the year I went to work for Mr. Miyashita was my family's best ever for parties, although my memory may have cast it in a particularly glowing light because of what came after.

The big teapot was in constant use all through 1939. As well as the usual celebrations, we had the added excitement of the Royal Visit in late May. King George VI and Queen Elizabeth came to Canada and, even better, stopped in Calgary for a few hours. This caused a great to-do. The whole city caught Royal fever. Some citizens succumbed to a virulent strain. Mrs. Jamieson, our neighbour across the street, produced a baby girl the day their Majesties arrived in Canada and named her Georgeanne Elizabeth. Good thing Ike and Mamie Eisenhower never came to town.

The papers were full of The Visit, as it became known. We knew every detail. Her Majesty's lady-in-waiting was Lady Nunburnholme; the ocean liner temporarily commissioned as the Royal Yacht for the Canadian trip was the *Empress of Australia*; its captain was Admiral Sir Dudley North. Please do not ask me why those names popped to mind. Do you ever get the feeling that everything you have ever seen, heard, read, or said is stored away somewhere in your brain? There it lies, like silt at the bottom of a pond, smooth and undisturbed. Then a pebble drops and churns it up and tiny particles float to the surface. But a particle like Sir Dudley North? Sometimes I worry me.

When the big day finally came, children got the day off school and many of their parents were given time from work so the whole family could come and wave as the King and Queen drove past in their open car. Mr. Miyashita gave me the afternoon, but he and Mrs. Miyashita didn't come to the parade. This was not surprising, as they never went anywhere large crowds gathered. I suspect that St. Chad's talent night audience was the biggest group they had ever been part of, and that venture had not ended well. However, my family and most of our neighbours were there along with the rest of Calgary, waiting behind the soldiers who stood lining the streets along the route. Some of the men in the crowd wore their service medals from the war to end all wars. Dad didn't. He said he'd lost his in the move to Canada, but I think he'd thrown them out. As the King and Queen went by, we all waved and cheered as loudly as we could, considering the lumps in our throats. Then we trooped home with our friends to toast their Majesties with tea and keep up our strength with a slice of sponge cake.

Next on our summer list was Mum's birthday, which she shared with Canada. As July 1 approached, she often got a little mopish for England and her family. That year, Dad's boss lent him his car for the day, and we planned to cheer her up with a birthday picnic at the Dominion Day Race Meet in Millarville. I ordered a cake from Picardy's. Charlie and I made sandwiches and a thermos of tea. Dad supplied bottles of ginger beer that we could put to cool in the little stream near the track. By ten o'clock, we'd packed the food and the plaid picnic blanket in the trunk of the boss's Pontiac and were on our way to Millarville and a perfect summer Saturday. Mum didn't have to do a thing except enjoy the drive out to the foothills and watch the races. She even had a bit of a flutter on a little grey horse named Okey Dokey, who won going away.

If I hadn't been a couple of years short of legal betting age, I'd have had a flutter myself on a sturdy bay named Shorty. That afternoon, Shorty provided me with an object lesson in the truth of Mr. Miyashita's caution regarding the difference between gambling and investment. Still, he was an appealing little horse and probably made up in endurance what he so sadly lacked in speed. I now find myself wondering just how much actual thoroughbred blood flowed in Shorty's veins, but back then, I don't suppose anyone at the Millarville track was overly worried about Jockey Club formalities. These days, their Canada Day Race Meet is all very by the book—registered thoroughbreds and racing colours and computerized parimutuels. They even have a proper starting gate. But in Shorty's day, a good many of the horses that stood behind the starter's tapes on July 1 were back herding cattle on July 2.

We drove home after the last race sunburned and happy from our afternoon in the weathered wooden bleachers. On the way, Mum treated us to ice cream cones out of her Okey Dokey winnings. She said this birthday was her best ever in Canada, although I think she was still a little shocked by the extravagance of the Picardy cake. I assured her I had some extra cash on hand since Mr. Miyashita had given me a bonus to celebrate Dominion Day.

It was no surprise that my Canuckophile boss celebrated Dominion Day. It was far and away his favourite holiday. Not only was July 1 his chosen country's birthday, it also marked the beginning of the month's holiday that he and Mrs. Miyashita spent every year in Banff. Mr. Miyashita took his cameras, Mrs. Miyashita brought along her fly-fishing rod, and the pair of them spent their days rambling the mountain trails, sometimes on foot, sometimes on horseback. Every night they'd go back to their suite in the Banff Springs Hotel. Mr. Miyashita would have been happy in a leaky tent with a tin of beans for his supper as long as he could spend time in his beloved Rockies, but Mrs. Miyashita was not keen on rough-ing it. She enjoyed their days on the trails; at night she wanted to dress for dinner and sleep in a real bed. Besides, in the best Japanese tradition, she and her husband both enjoyed a soak in the hotel's hot springs after a hard day's hiking, although I know they considered the Canadian custom of wearing bathing suits in the pool very odd. Back at the office, I had plenty to keep me busy, but July was a lonely month without Mr. Miyashita, especially at coffee break.

After Dominion Day, it was time for the Stampede. For my family that meant an evening or two on Scotchman's Hill watching the chuckwagon races with all the other non-paying fans. Norman usually came along, and the two of us would stay on after the races ostensibly to watch the fireworks that ended the Stampede day but really to hold hands, talk about our future, and exchange some not very fevered kisses.

Six weeks later, on August 24, we celebrated Charlie's seventeenth birthday with a fish fry over an open fire in the backyard. Under the watchful eyes of every cat in the neighbourhood, we cooked the trout he had caught that morning in the Elbow River. Terps and her sisters came and so did some of Charlie's other friends from school. Norman was there too, I think. It was our last party for some time. After Canada declared war on Germany that September, none of us felt like celebrating anything. In practical terms, nothing in our lives really changed right then, but there was a difference in the air after the declaration and we could sense it. Maybe it was apprehension, a feeling that we were living through the lull before the storm, bracing ourselves for something big, but none of us knew what. Still, by the time talent night rolled around in November, we seemed to have got used to the idea, if not the reality, of being at war, and we were ready for a bit of fun. After talent night, we began looking forward to Christmas. Thanks to my fatter paycheque, I was able to add an extra ten dollars a month to the twenty-five I already paid Mum for my room and board. Consequently, all our celebrations had become a touch more splashy. Christmas was my family's favourite holiday and that year's, while far from extravagant, was our most lavish ever.

Although Canada was at war, food rationing was still in the future. Mum had already squirrelled away some baking. She always baked her fruitcakes on a Saturday afternoon in November, which allowed them plenty of time to ripen before Christmas. I'm sure she made them on a Saturday so we'd all have a chance to be at home for a stir and a wish. Charlie and I helped with the baking just as we had when we were little. Not that either of us was allowed to do much more than we did back then. Mum managed all the complicated stuff. She decided how much of what to put into the big Medalta mixing bowl and in what order. Charlie and I were assigned to the basics. We picked over the currants and cut the glacé cherries in half. There was more fruit for the cakes than I ever remembered seeing before.

"That'll do, Charles." Mum rapped the back of Charlie's hand with her wooden spoon. "Keep that up and there'll be more cherries in you than in the cakes."

"That's not fair," Charlie protested as he licked batter off his knuckles. "Kay ate three."

"I never did," I said.

"And how old are you two?" Mum raised an eyebrow. We all laughed and went back to work. Neither Charlie nor I ate any more of the cherries.

During the final stage of preparation, when all the mounds of fruit and almonds had been mixed into the batter, Mum called Dad to the kitchen and we each had a stir and made a wish. We all watched as she spooned the mixture into three square pans of graduated sizes and popped them into the oven. That year, the cakes got their own small bottle of brandy. When they were baked and cooled, Mum sprinkled a generous dollop on each, wrapped them in cheesecloth, and put them away in a big biscuit tin in the cellar. Then, every Saturday until Christmas, she would unwrap them, douse them with more brandy, and wrap them up again to continue mellowing.

One Saturday in December, the day after her third or fourth shopping trip with Mrs. Miyashita, I helped Mum with the unwrapping. Charlie was sitting in the kitchen with us, drinking a glass of milk and reading *Popular Photography*. Since he had begun working for Mr. Miyashita, he could afford to buy himself a copy every month.

"I wish your dad liked marzipan," Mum said. "A nice layer of marzipan always makes a fruitcake look finished." She gave the smallest cake its tot of brandy.

"They look pretty good to me as is," I said.

"I wonder if Mr. and Mrs. M. like Christmas cake?" Mum said. "If I'd thought of it in time, I could have baked them one."

"I don't think fruitcake is very Japanese," I said. "But Mr. Miyashita probably ate it when he was a student in England. That's when he got to like digestive biscuits."

"Seems a shame, those two all alone at Christmas, and so far away from home, doesn't it?" Mum said.

"Mum, they don't celebrate Christmas in Japan," Charlie said. "Christmas is a Christian holiday. It's probably just like any other day for the Miyashitas."

"Besides," I chimed in, "Mr. Miyashita says that Canada is home, not Japan."

"Well it may be for him but it's not home for her, and I can tell you that for a fact."

"Mrs. Miyashita said that?" I asked

"Not out loud, she didn't," Mum admitted. "But it doesn't take Sherlock Holmes to see the woman misses her family. And even if you weren't born a Christian, in Canada Christmas is still a time for family and friends."

"I don't think Mr. Miyashita misses his family at all," I said.

"That's nothing to wonder at, is it?" Mum said, but she didn't elaborate.

THAT YEAR, CANON Giles helped Mr. Miyashita prepare for Christmas or perhaps that should be Mr. Miyashita helped the Canon. As they did every year, Canon Giles and the St. Chad's Women's Auxiliary planned to distribute hampers to the needy. This year the hampers were considerably more lavish than usual because Mr. Miyashita had volunteered to pay for them.

The hampers were not just for Anglicans. It didn't matter who you were or what you believed. If you needed a little help, you automatically qualified for one of the St. Chad boxes along with a "top of the season to you, missus" and no questions asked. I remember Canon Giles dropping into the office one morning to discuss the Women's Auxiliary's wish list with its underwriter. I brought them some coffee, and Mr. Miyashita asked me to pour myself a cup and join them so I could take notes.

The Canon read us the list, including the estimate of the cost per hamper. It was not cheap. The ladies of St. Chad's had really gone to town on Mr. Miyashita's nickel. Besides generous quantities of the usual food staples, they suggested there should be some Christmas treats too—candies for the children, tobacco for the men, bars of fancy soap for the ladies. Each hamper would also have a voucher from the Fairplay Meatateria for a turkey, and another from the Piggly Wiggly store for a box of that Canadian Christmas staple, mandarin oranges. In those days, everyone called them Jap oranges except for some diehard English holdouts like my mother who continued to refer to them as satsumas because that's what they knew them as back home. Come to think of it, ethnic and religious slurs were rife in the popular names of many of the foods that appeared around Christmas right from Jap oranges to the Pope's nose. Ask your grandmother what they called Brazil nuts when she was a girl. Anyway, the mandarins appeared on the St. Chad's list as Jap oranges.

"Well, Miss Jeynes?" Mr. Miyashita asked when the Canon had finished reading. "Will this do?"

"It's a very good hamper for a family, sir," I said. "But what about people who are alone at Christmas, especially old people? It wouldn't be so suitable for them, would it?"

"You know, you're right, Kay," the Canon agreed. "I can't see many of the old fellows on our list cooking themselves a turkey dinner."

"But I'll bet they'd like a tin of ham or a fruitcake," I said, thinking of our old friend Mr. Ledger.

"Then we must pack some hampers especially for the old, mustn't we?" Mr. Miyashita said. "And perhaps some for those who live alone too. I'm certain your Women's Auxiliary will know how many of each sort are needed. Would they be so kind as to prepare them as well?"

"I'll do my best to have their suggestions to you day after tomorrow," the Canon said.

"No, no. That will not be necessary," Mr. Miyashita said. "I can tell from the list you have shown me today that the ladies of St. Chad's know far better than I what is needed. I see no reason for me to stick my oar in."

"But surely you would like to know that your money will be well spent," the Canon said.

I think Canon Giles was accustomed to dealing with far more exacting donors than my boss, ones who probably wouldn't approve of fripperies like perfumed soap and cigarettes for the poor. Many years later, he confessed to me that he had instructed the Women's Auxiliary to lard the list a bit so that Mr. Miyashita would have something to cut. That way the frivolities could be tossed overboard, leaving the necessities a better chance of staying in the boxes. He said he felt ashamed of this when he realized that Mr. Miyashita gave gifts with no strings. Personally, I think the Canon may have been a touch naive in his assessment. Mr. Miyashita did not attach any strings to this particular gift because he had complete faith in Canon Giles. As a matter of fact, it wasn't long after Christmas that Mr. Miyashita enlisted the Canon's help in disbursing all his donations. That's when they became a team, their own little philanthropic foundation.

"I have no doubt the money will be put to very good use. No doubt at all," Mr. Miyashita said. "Please thank the Women's Auxiliary for their good work and tell them it is my pleasure to help them with their hampers."

The idea of the Christmas hamper seemed to have caught Mr. Miyashita's fancy.

"The giving of hampers to the needy—is this a common Christmas practice in Canada?" he asked me that afternoon as I brought him the latest stock prices from the ticker tape.

"Yes, sir, it is," I said. "Lots of churches do it." Despite having lived in Canada for thirty years there were still gaps in his knowledge of local customs.

"But I thought this was a Boxing Day tradition. Was the day not named for the custom of boxing up the remains of the Christmas feast and distributing them among the poor?"

"It was, but now Boxing Day is only a name. If people didn't get their hampers before Christmas, then they'd have nothing to celebrate with on the day, would they? Give them a turkey before Christmas, and they can cook it for themselves instead of waiting for rich people's leftovers."

"That is true," he said. "A hamper before Christmas could be considered a gift. By Boxing Day, it could only be regarded as charity."

Mr. Miyashita made a good point. People who didn't have much but their pride could be very touchy on the subject of charity. My family and most of our neighbours were poor, but we certainly didn't consider ourselves needy. After all, we were healthy, we had food in our mouths and a roof over our heads. In those days, that was more than enough to be grateful for—still is, for that matter. We all knew people who had been hit far worse by the Depression. They were the needy ones, not us.

"Besides, sir, hampers aren't just for the needy," I said. "You can give hampers as Christmas presents to your friends too. My mother makes up boxes of Christmas baking every year to give to people we know who live alone or can't bake for themselves. People like Mr. Ledger. She's given him a batch of mince tarts and some ginger snaps ever since I can remember."

Now that I think back on it, I don't know how Mum did it. No matter how tight the money, she always managed to bake a little extra for sharing. This year, with the Jeynes' exchequer in modest surplus, I knew her Christmas boxes would be generous ones.

A COUPLE OF Saturdays before Christmas, Mum didn't bother to re-wrap the smallest fruitcake after its brandy sprinkle. Instead, she added a layer of marzipan and decorated the finished product with piped icing and bits of green and red glacé fruit that she'd cut and arranged to look like a flower. She had just put the final piece in place when Norman and I came in from skating. She made a cup of tea to warm us up and gave us each a piece of the shortbread she'd baked that afternoon.

"That cake looks really good, Mum," I said. "But why did you put marzipan on it when Dad doesn't eat it?"

"This one isn't for us," she said. "It's for Mr. and Mrs. M. And that's a cherry blossom." She pointed to the decoration. "People in Japan are very fond of cherry blossoms. I read that at the library."

"I didn't know Orientals liked fruitcake," Norman said.

"Everyone likes fruitcake," Mum stated with a confidence I didn't share. "And the icing will be nicely set for you to take with you to work Monday morning, Kay."

Mr. Miyashita was delighted with the cake.

"A hamper, Miss Jeynes. A Christmas hamper from your mother." He leaned back in his chair and sat admiring the cake in its open box in the middle of his desk. "And so beautifully decorated. Your mother is an artist."

"The flower is supposed to be a cherry blossom," I said.

"That is obvious," Mr. Miyashita said. "And a cleverly done blossom it is. My wife will be very pleased."

"Mum says it's ready to eat now, but it will be even better if you leave it until Christmas."

"Then we will not touch so much as a crumb until the twenty-fifth." He replaced the lid on the cake's box and retied the string. "It will be a great treat for us both. You know, I do not think Mrs. Miyashita has ever tasted fruitcake. I have not eaten it myself for forty years. This one will recall many memories for me."

The next day at the office he presented me with an envelope made of heavy white paper inlaid with flower petals.

"For your mother, Miss Jeynes," he said. "From Mrs. Miyashita and me."

Mum couldn't get over the paper. "Have you ever seen the like? There are flower petals in it." She sniffed the envelope in case some of the flowers' perfume lingered on. "No smell though. I wonder what kind of flowers they are?"

"Come on, Mum. Stop sniffing and open it," Charlie said.

"Keep your shirt on. It's not like other envelopes. There's no glue. It's all folded together." She tugged one flap loose from its fold and the whole envelope fell open. Four scraps of paper fell to the floor. Charlie scrambled to pick them up.

"Look at these." He held up four origami cranes folded out of coloured paper. "Four little birds."

Much later, I learned that Mrs. Miyashita usually folded only white paper. At the time, I didn't realize that for her those brightly-patterned cranes were a real concession to Christmas.

"There's nothing else in it," Mum said. "The letter's written on the inside of the envelope." She read the note out loud to us.

Dear Mrs. Jeynes,

My wife and I thank you for your gift of a Christmas hamper. We are looking forward to eating a slice of your beautifully decorated cake on Christmas day although I know we will have great difficulty bringing ourselves to cut through the cherry blossom on its top.

Mrs. Miyashita has asked me to enclose four origami cranes that she has folded for you and your family. She hopes they may be suitable to hang on your Christmas tree. In Japan, the crane is a symbol of good fortune and these bring with them our wish of good fortune for you and your family.

Yours truly,

Hero Miyashita

"Isn't that a lovely letter," Mum said. "From the sound of it, you'd almost think no one had ever given him a Christmas present before."

"I don't think they have," I said. "I'll bet yours was the first."

"Come on, Kay. The man's lived here for thirty years."

"Maybe so. But I bet he's never had a present from anyone in Calgary until you sent that cake. Maybe he's had business gifts, but they're not the same."

"Give us a gander at those cranes, Charlie," Mum said. "Will you look at that. There's even a thread to hang them by."

A FEW DAYS before Christmas, Mr. Miyashita popped out of his office and stood by my desk. I looked up from the stack of photographs I was cataloguing.

"I was not familiar with the custom of the Christmas hamper, but I do know about the custom of the Christmas bonus," he said. "I believe many Canadian companies give their employees a bonus at this time of the year, do they not?"

"Yes, sir. Some do, but not all." At Greer & Western, they made do with letting us go home at two o'clock on Christmas Eve.

"My company is one of those that do. Please accept this with my thanks for your excellent work." He took a white business envelope from the inner pocket of his suit and presented it to me. "A very happy Christmas to you, Miss Jeynes."

"Thank you, sir," I said. "May I open it before Christmas?"

"It is now your envelope so you may open it whenever you wish." He smiled at me. "You may even open it before you make us both a cup of good, strong Canadian tea."

I did open the envelope before I made the tea and found five crisp five-dollar bills, considerably more than a week's salary, all in one lovely lump.

THE SATURDAY MORNING before Christmas, Charlie and I were just out the door on our way to a carol practice at the church, when a Polley's taxi pulled up to our house. We met the driver coming up our walk carrying a wicker basket, its top covered with a white cloth.

Charlie took it from him, and we turned back to the house.

"Whatever this is, it weighs a ton." He set it down on the kitchen table. "Look, there's a card with it. It's for you, Mum." Another flower petal envelope with Mum's name written on it poked out from under the cloth. The three of us stood around the table eyeing the basket. Charlie and I didn't even try to suppress our excitement. I could see Mum was as excited as we were, but she at least pretended to act like an adult.

"You two are going to be late for your practice if you hang around here any longer," she said. The St. Chad's young people's group went caroling every Christmas Eve, visiting the houses of those parishioners who were too old or too infirm to attend the midnight service.

"Mum, nobody needs to practise Christmas carols," Charlie said. "We already know them. And besides, half the people we sing for are deaf."

"That's no way to talk," Mum said. "We'll all be old someday."

"Maybe you could wait and open it when we get home from practice," I suggested, knowing full well that the hamper had pushed Mum far beyond that kind of patience.

"Well, I suppose ten minutes late won't hurt just this once," she conceded. "Come on, fetch us the scissors, Charlie, and we'll get this string off."

"Aren't you going to read the card first?" he asked, getting a little of his own back on Mum, who was a strict enforcer of the read before you rip law when it applied to her children.

"Don't be so cheeky, Charles Jeynes, or I'll pin your ears back for you. Now where are those scissors?"

While Charlie looked for the scissors, Mum opened the note.

"It's from Mrs. M.," she said. "I didn't know she could write English."

"She can't," I said. "She dictates to Mr. Miyashita. See, that's the same handwriting as the note about the cake."

"So it is." Mum read the message to herself, very slowly, drawing it out just to drive us crazy.

"Ah come on, Mum. What does it say?" Charlie handed her the scissors.

She passed him the note and began snipping the strings that held the brown paper over the basket.

"Dear Mrs. Jeynes," Charlie read. "Thank you for helping me do my shopping these past weeks. It is a happy thing for me. I hope you and your family will be happy together at your Christmas celebrations. Yours truly, Tose Miyashita." He made *Tose* rhyme with *nose*.

"It's pronounced Toh-see," Mum corrected him, but I wouldn't have put big money on her version being any more accurate than Charlie's.

Mum cut the last string and pulled the cloth off the basket, revealing a large, round parcel wrapped in brown paper. It sat in the middle of a bed of excelsior, surrounded by several much smaller packages. Charlie hauled the big one out and set it down with a thud that made the table jump.

"A basketball stuffed with lead would be my guess," he said.

Mum ripped open the paper. The three of us stood dumbstruck. She was the first to speak.

"It's a ham," she said, never a woman to shy from the obvious. "And what a ham. I've not seen one to beat it in all my life. Pig must have been a giant."

"It's even bigger than the ones they cook in Eaton's restaurant," I said.

"You could feed the whole neighbourhood with it, and there'd still be leftovers," Charlie said.

Mum looked at him and began to smile. "You know, that's a grand idea." As she spoke, Dad came in the back door.

"Ah no. Don't tell me your mother's been having ideas again." He pulled off his overshoes and wandered over to give Mum a peck on the cheek. Then he noticed the ham.

"Good Lord, who's that?"

"That's Mum's ham," Charlie said. "Mrs. Miyashita sent it to thank Mum for helping her shop."

"Thing's so big it should have a name," Dad laughed. "Well, I guess we know what's for lunch. And tea and supper and breakfast. Enough gammon on that bone for the neighbourhood."

"That's exactly what Charlie said. And I think that's just what we should do—feed the neighbourhood," Mum said. "We'll have a party, a real New Year's Eve party with a ham supper after midnight and everything."

And so the plan was hatched. We stood around the table discussing how many people we could squeeze into the house and what we'd serve with the ham. As we talked, Mum opened the smaller parcels, the ham's satellites—a bottle of Johnnie Walker's finest, a packet of green tea, and two porcelain cups and saucers just like the one I'd drunk from at the Miyashitas' house.

Dad put a hand on the whisky bottle and sighed. "It'll never stretch through a New Year's Eve unless we measure it out with an eye dropper."

"You know, I think it's best we don't serve any strong drink at the party," Mum said. Dad looked relieved.

"Does this party mean we can't have any ham before the New Year?" Charlie asked. "Not even a little for Christmas breakfast?"

"Pet, if you want, you can eat ham on Christmas morning till you burst. Even you won't make a dint." Mum gave the ham a little pat. "Now the pair of you had better get to that practice or it'll be over before you've sung a note."

CHRISTMAS EVE WAS just like the carol said, silent and calm and bright. Back then, when Calgary was small and streetlamps were scarcer and dimmer, the stars shone much brighter over the city than they do now. That night after supper, Charlie and I walked to the church under the Milky Way's broad river of light and counted constellations in the winter sky. We found the easy ones first—Orion and Cassiopeia, Andromeda and the Ursas, Major and Minor. We were about to start looking for Pegasus when Terps and her sisters caught up with us. Terps had brought along her flute—she played flute and clarinet as well as the piano—to accompany our singing. She stuffed it under her coat to keep it warm between houses, although that year, for the first time, we didn't have to walk everywhere we went. The Canon drove his car as did a couple of the wealthier dads, so we all piled in and were chauffeured from place to place. Very fancy.

At the Canon's suggestion, we started the evening in Mount Royal, singing for the Miyashitas by way of thanks for footing the bill for the St. Chad's hampers. I was surprised to see Buffalo Bill wearing a tinsel Christmas garland. It looped around his horns and cascaded down his great stone neck. But my surprise was nothing compared with Mr. Miyashita's when he opened the door to find a dozen St. Chad's Anglican Young People standing on his front steps singing "Good King Wenceslas." Mrs. Miyashita, dressed in her blue kimono, was right behind him, the barking Nikkou at her side. Nikkou at full blast was more than a match for carolling Anglicans. At least she was until the last verse when Terps launched into a very fancy flute descant that actually shut her up if only for a few seconds. She cocked her head and listened, eyes fixed on the flute. Then she pursed her little black lips, raised her muzzle to the sky, and let rip with a series of blood-curdling yodels. The flute spluttered to a stop as Terps burst out laughing. The rest of us followed suit and left the Good Page treading forever in his master's footsteps because we couldn't stop laughing long enough to finish the verse. Even Nikkou fell silent in mid-howl. I swear she looked a little embarrassed. The Miyashitas laughed with us.

After everyone had regained their composure, including the dog, Mr. Miyashita invited us in for a cup of tea. I know the others were curious to see inside the grand house, but the Canon declined on our behalf, explaining that the old people on our list tended to go to bed early. We had to get back to east Calgary to sing at their houses while they were still up. Then we launched into "Hark! The Herald Angels Sing," and as we sang, Mrs. Miyashita transferred the much-subdued Nikkou's leash to Canon Giles's keeping and disappeared into the house. She returned a minute later with Mr. Miyashita's overcoat and scarf, and only when he had put them on and fastened all the buttons did she reclaim her dog. When we finished, Mr. Miyashita applauded and Mrs. Miyashita smiled and nodded her approval. Nikkou made do with a single, restrained woof.

"I do not wish to keep you from your rounds, but I must ask if you are familiar with a carol about King David's city?" Mr. Miyashita asked. "I heard it sung one Christmas Eve in Oxford in the chapel at my college. I thought it very beautiful indeed."

So before we left, we sang "Once in Royal David's City," and again the flute wove over and under our voices as Terps blew its mellow notes into the cold December air on misty puffs of breath. This time Nikkou's yodels were infrequent and decidedly more mellifluous. At the end of the carol, Terps ruffled the little dog's ears and complimented her on her musical contributions to the evening, and we all laughed some more. Then Mr. Miyashita shook our hands and thanked each one of us for coming to sing at his house.

IN MY FAMILY we opened our presents before breakfast on Christmas morning, although this time we were torn between them and the ham, particularly Charlie. Ultimately, the parcels won. They deserved the victory because it was a truly boffo year in the worldly goods department. Mum had made us all new outfits—a pullover sweater and a shirt each for Dad and Charlie, a blue tweed skirt with a matching cardigan for me—and very smart they were. Charlie's presents were pretty generous too. Now that he could use Mr. Miyashita's darkroom, he really didn't need his own enlarger, so he dipped into the fund to buy me a radio that I'd been eyeing in the Eaton's catalogue, one small enough to fit on the shelf next to my bed. I had that little bakelite radio for years. Probably still would if I could get the tubes for it. He gave Mum and Dad a portable gramophone and some records to go with it. I noticed that the records were mostly dance tunes that Charlie himself favoured, but to give him credit, he did throw in some Fritz Kreisler especially for Dad. As for me, with my new salary and my Christmas bonus, I had a telephone put into the house and pledged to pay the monthly bill. There was much teasing about how I'd really got the phone so Norman and I could monopolize the line with long, lovey-dovey conversations. I laughed too, but truth be told, I didn't see much of a future for us, on or off the telephone.

Dad produced the best present of all. For most of December, he'd spent every Saturday morning working at the zoo. There was always some emergency that required his immediate attention—repairs to the tigers' cage, or a rusty bar that was a danger to the monkeys. After several weeks of this, Mum got a little restive, and I heard her mutter that if a man would only use his eyes, he'd find more than enough chores to keep him busy around his own house. But all was forgiven on Christmas morning when Dad opened the front curtains and pointed to the Model T parked at our curb.

"Thought it was time we had our own transport in this family. Not for everyday mind. Only for special occasions and fishing trips and the like."

"You mean it's ours?" Charlie asked, not really believing. "We own a car?"

"Tires and all. Even threw in a steering wheel."

"Where did we get the money?" Mum's first question.

"Didn't take money. I built a trailer for young Davey Evans. That's where I've been these last Saturdays. Davey wants to make some extra cash hauling coal with that truck of his, so he traded me the car for my work. All that car cost was my time. Davey and his brother towed it over last night after you lot got home from the midnight service and the coast was clear. Doubt those lads saw their beds before two."

"They towed it?" I said. "Why didn't they drive?"

"Well, the old girl's a bit long in the tooth and her motor isn't running in top form," Dad said. "Mind, it's nothing to worry about. Hasn't been driven for a year or two, that's all. Nothing that can't be put to rights. Charlie and I will have her running like new before you can say Jack Robinson. Mark my words—this year we'll be driving to the Millarville Races in our own car."

Starting with Mum, we all gave Dad a hug and told him he was brilliant. He did not disagree. Brilliant yes, but overly optimistic about the car. The poor thing was older than me, and as we later discovered, generations of mice had called its tattered interior home. However, Dad and Charlie did have it running by spring, if not like new then at least respectably enough to be called reliable. Mum and I were in on the repairs too. I stripped the inside down to the metal and helped her reupholster the whole thing from the seats to the padding on the doors. Despite all the refurbishments, a faint pong of mouse lingered for the entire time we owned the car. Many years later I cleaned out an old garden shed that stunk of mice. First whiff and there I was, back sitting in our old Model T.

AS HE DID every year, Mr. Ledger came home from church with us for Christmas dinner, which we ate around one-thirty. We stopped on the way into the house to give him a special tour of the new car.

"Well, dash my buttons!" Mr. Ledger is the only person I ever heard actually use that expression. "Your own motor." He walked around the car examining it from every angle. "And a fine one it is too."

"The poor thing's a bit of a shambles inside, I'm afraid." Mum indulged in a rare understatement.

"If I know you, Judith, you'll have it cleaned up and looking better than new in no time. Look what you managed with that old suit of mine. It was a shambles all right, and more than a bit."

Mr. Ledger brought presents. He gave us the same things every year—a little box of Olivier's chocolates for Mum, a jar of Gentleman's Relish for Dad (which he quite fancied himself), and a candy cane each for Charlie and me. In Mr. Ledger's eyes Charlie and I remained eight years old forever. Christmas dinner was turkey and all that went with it, including the crackers and silly hats. That year the pudding burned so bright and long on the last of the little bottle of brandy that the holly sprig stuck in its top shrivelled around the edges. At the meal's end, Mr. Ledger, who'd got a little tipsy before dinner on his two tots of Johnnie Walker, rose from his chair and made a very fine speech, thanking the cook and the provider of the feast and ending with a sentimental flourish about good food and good friends. While Charlie and I did the dishes, Mum and Dad went for a walk, and Mr. Ledger put his feet up and snoozed in Mum's easy chair. After Mum and Dad got home, Charlie and I went skating with Norman and Terps and her sisters until the light began to fade and the bare poplars behind the rink cast long blue shadows on the ice. We went home to turkey sandwiches and tea and slices of Christmas cake. When even my bottomless pit of a brother could not eat another bite, the pair of us walked Mr. Ledger, along with his box of Mum's baking, home to his tiny house near the church.

THIS EVENING, OVER our martinis, Meggie asked me what I'd written for our celebration assignment. I told her about Charlie's fish fry, and how funny the neighbourhood cats looked dotted around the yard, about the Christmas hamper and our new-to-us old car. Meggie said that either I was looking back through the thickest pair of rose-coloured glasses in history or our family had led an unbelievably idyllic life. I tried to explain that we'd had our tensions and even our fights like the ones about my education and Mum's parents and their financial meddling. She just laughed.

"Sweetie, those weren't fights. Those were domestic disagreements. Fights are when your parents scream at each other and don't give a damn who hears them at it. And if they're not screaming, they're not speaking. Mine used to have some of their best brawls at Christmas. I can't remember a single one that my mother didn't spend crying in her room and my dad didn't get drunk. Being shipped off to boarding school was a relief. The nuns were crazy, but at least it was it was quiet at the convent. You know, I don't think I was ever really happy until I married Hersh. For me, growing up was the pits. You were a lucky girl, Kay."

We sat and sipped our martinis in silence for a few minutes.

"All of them?" I asked.

"All of who?"

"The nuns. Every last nun in the place was crazy?"

"Well, maybe not quite all. Some of them were just nice repressed lesbians. And believe me, they were a big improvement on the religious ones. Sister Anne was really a good egg."

I've been sitting here back in my own room, trying to finish this assignment for tomorrow, but instead, I keep thinking about what Meggie said. About the rose-coloured glasses. I hope she's wrong. I admit I may be casting a bit of a rosy glow over the past but, all in all, I honestly think we were a happy family. Not an impossibly idyllic one by any means, but happy in a very ordinary way. As a matter of fact, I'd say my experience was the reverse of Meggie's. I don't think I knew what it meant to be truly unhappy until I grew up. Then again, I've always been a late bloomer.

I WAS TOO weary to keep writing last night so I didn't manage to finish "Holidays and Celebrations" in time for class today. Nevertheless, before I move on to something new, I would like to add that we did have our New Year's party and it was quite the shindig. Judging by the mounds of overcoats upstairs on the beds, we squeezed so many people into our house, the little place bulged at the seams. Norman and his parents were there and so were Terps and her sisters. Mr. Ledger came, and so did any of our neighbours who felt like popping in and that seemed to be most of them. Canon Giles and his wife dropped round for a few minutes, but they couldn't stay long because they'd promised their children they'd be home in time to welcome the New Year. Mr. and Mrs. Miyashita were there too.

Mum had invited them on the spur of the moment one Friday morning when she and Mrs. Miyashita were out shopping. The invitation was accepted. However, Mum hadn't consulted Dad beforehand, and he was taken aback when he heard the news. It became the subject of one of their more lively domestic disagreements. Their voices carried up the stairs as I lay in bed that night.

"Now, Judith, I don't know that it's our place to be asking Kay's boss to parties," Dad said.

"And why not?"

"Well, us inviting someone so grand and all to our little house." Even as he spoke, Dad must have known Mum would never swallow a line that flimsy, especially coming from him.

"It wasn't 'us' that did the inviting. It was me. And it's not His Nibs I invited. I asked Mrs. M. He'll be coming with her."

"You never stopped for a minute to think about the rest of the people who'll be here, did you?" Dad struggled to keep his voice even.

"What about them?" Mum snapped back. That's when Dad really flew off the handle.

"What are they going to think when they find themselves spending their Hogmanay with a couple of Japs? That's what!"

"So you'll eat the woman's ham all right, but you won't invite her in for a slice."

"Don't put words in my mouth. You know damn well that's not what I said."

"Then tell me what you did say because that's what I heard."

"For God's sake, woman, why can't you ever stop and use your head for two minutes? Like as not we'll be fighting the Japs someday. Look at what the buggers are up to in China!"

"And what's China got to do with Mrs. M.? You think she's going to come goose-stepping up 9th Avenue toting her rifle?"

"You know damn well that's not the point!"

"Then what is the point?" A coldness I'd never heard before had crept into Mum's voice. It frightened me. I think it must have shaken Dad a little too.

"Judith, I know you've grown fond of the woman, and there's no denying that he's a good boss to Kay and Charlie." Dad did his best to rein in his temper and be reasonable. "And if it were only us it would be fine. But you know as well as I do that some people are going to feel uncomfortable with the pair of them here."

"Then those people don't have to come, do they?"

"Those people are our friends," Dad said, but he knew that he was beaten.

"Mrs. M. is my friend too. She can't help it if she's a Jap, so the least we can do is ask her in and give her a bite of her ham. They're coming to the party and that's that."

And come the Miyashitas did. They arrived at half past nine in a Polley's taxi. Their entrance caused a stir. The Miyashitas were not east Calgary and that's putting it mildly. It wasn't simply that they were Japanese, although that was the biggest reason. They were rich and well educated and Mr. Miyashita talked posh too. What's more, they didn't dress like the rest of us. I knew that they had both done their best, just as they had on talent night, to wear Western clothes appropriate to the occasion, but this time they were even less successful, especially Mrs. Miyashita. Her royal purple dress put every other stitch of clothing in the room to shame, including her husband's perfect suit. As she walked into the room, its voluminous sleeves floated out behind her and the pattern in the watered silk rippled in the lamplight.

As Dad had predicted, the Miyashitas' presence did add a tension to the evening. Not that there were any rude remarks about Japs—at least none that I heard—but then no one invited to my parents' house would have dared to insult another guest. However, a few of our neighbours did leave, talking vaguely of something or other they had to do at home as they collected their coats and said their tepid thank yous. Mrs. Sanders from next door was the first to go. I noticed that her husband didn't leave with her. As Mum remarked to me later, if the Emperor of Japan and all his army had appeared at our party, they couldn't have routed Porky Sanders before he'd sunk his gnashers into a slice of that ham.

Terps and her sisters brought a stack of dance records to play on the new gramophone, so we pushed back the chairs and rolled up the rug. There wasn't enough room in our house to really let rip, but Charlie and Terps managed a pretty snazzy Lindy hop and that got everybody going. The surprise of the evening though was Mrs. Miyashita. Charlie asked her to dance and, instead of refusing as I thought she would, she followed him to the middle of the living room and the pair of them proceeded to give the rest of us a lesson in the art of the waltz. She looked amazing with her silk sleeves billowing and her face flushed with pleasure. An enchanted Mr. Ledger watched from his chair near the gramophone. When the record ended he walked over and, with a formal bow, claimed Mrs. Miyashita's next dance for himself. Forgetting age and aches, he whirled her around the living room. As people watched, some of the tension seemed to drain from the room. It was as if by dancing with their old friend, Mrs. Miyashita somehow became a little more like one of them.

"Get a load of Mr. Ledger," Charlie said to me. Mr. Ledger looked twenty years younger and his smile could have lit the streetlamps all the way to St. Chad's. He also looked taller, but that may have been because his partner was so tiny.

"What about Mrs. Miyashita? Where did she learn to dance like that?"

"In Japan," Charlie said. "A long time ago. Way back when she was a girl."

"How do you know?"

"Mum told me. She said Mrs. Miyashita's father made both his daughters take special lessons in Western-style dancing. Looks like she really took to it."

"Why would her dad make them do that?"

"Apparently he was nuts about all sorts of Western things. He was one of the first people in Hiroshima to drive a car. Smoked Cuban cigars too. Even took up fly-fishing. Say, maybe that's why Mrs. M. likes to go fishing on her holidays."

"But waltzing?"

"Who knows? Now watch this," he said as Mrs. Miyashita followed Mr. Ledger through a particularly fancy bit of footwork. "Can't do steps like that unless you know what you're doing."

"No wonder she loves Fred Astaire movies so much."

"Amazing when you think of how old the two of them are," he said. "You know, Mrs. Miyashita is even older than Mum."

I felt a little jealous that Mum had confided in Charlie but never mentioned a word about Mrs. Miyashita's dancing to me. "Why did Mum tell you all this?"

"Because she wanted me to ask Mrs. M. to waltz tonight. Mr. Miyashita doesn't dance at all, and waltzing's her favourite."

When the music stopped and neither Mr. Ledger's arthritic hip nor his asthma could be denied any longer, he escorted his partner back to her husband. With a small bow, he reluctantly relinquished her hand and wheezed his way over to Charlie and me.

"Passed along those shoes of mine too soon, Charles. There's a dance or two left in these old legs yet." He mopped his red face with a handkerchief. "What a charming woman," he rhapsodized. "Light as a feather in your arms. Like dancing with down."

"Let me get you something to drink, Mr. Ledger," I offered.

"Thank you, Kay. I wouldn't say no to a drop of punch." He sank onto one of the chairs near the door.

It got so hot in the house with the dancing and the crush of people and the ham baking in the oven that we had to open the doors to get some fresh air blowing through. Fortunately, it was a pleasant night, only a degree or two below freezing, so our improvised air conditioning worked well and the dancing continued until almost midnight. Mrs. Miyashita danced more waltzes, some of them with Charlie, and another with Mr. Ledger after he got his wind back. She even danced with Norman's father, a milkman who delivered in Mount Royal. Apparently, in the summer when Mrs. Miyashita was out in her garden and saw the Model Dairies wagon coming, she'd pop out with a carrot or a handful of dandelion greens for his horse, Gladys. In Mr. Johnson's books, anyone who was good to Gladdie had to be a bit of all right. I don't think Norman's mother agreed.

Before you knew it, it was nearly midnight and time to get things organized for First Footing. If the first person to cross the threshold in the New Year is a black-haired man, then you'll have good luck the rest of the year. It's traditional for him to bring a gift, often coal or a piece of wood for the fire. First Footing is an old custom in Scotland where Hogmanay is a far bigger celebration than Christmas. People like my parents who grew up near the border observe it too.

"Two minutes to midnight," Charlie announced. He switched on the radio so we could hear the countdown.

"Then we'd better get a wiggle on." Mum fetched the lump of coal that she kept in the box with the Christmas decorations. Our furnace had long since been converted to gas, but she'd saved a small piece of coal that we used every year. She held it up for everyone to see. "Who's going to be our black-haired man for 1940?"

"How about Mr. Miyashita?" Dad said. I think it was his way of apologizing to Mum for what he'd said about her new friend.

"But, Mr. Jeynes, I have not been a black-haired man for a good few years." Mr. Miyashita laughed and held up a lock of his silver hair for inspection.

"But your hair was black at one time," said Dad.

"Very black indeed," Mr. Miyashita agreed.

"Then you'll fill the bill."

"But what must I do?"

"Charlie'll keep you company and tell you all about it. Come on. Time to get yourself outside. Don't forget the coal." Dad bundled my smiling, if bewildered, boss out onto the front steps just as the radio announced one minute to midnight. Charlie followed, and Dad shut the door behind them.

"Where goes my husband?" an anxious Mrs. Miyashita asked me. "And why does he hold . . ." The word for coal eluded her. I tried to explain First Footing, the dark-haired man and his gift, but she was so worried I don't think she understood a word. "His overcoat," she fretted. "He is without his overcoat." As the radio announcer counted down the last ten seconds, I could see Mrs. Miyashita mentally stoking her croup kettle and spooning out the camphor powder.

At the stroke of midnight, the shouts of "Happy New Year" nearly drowned out the sound of Mr. Miyashita's knocks. Mum opened the front door, and she and Dad welcomed in their First Footer. We all sang "Auld Lang Syne." Then the hand shaking and kissing and back slapping began in earnest. Mr. Miyashita stood smiling and self-assured, shaking any hands that were offered to him, and a surprising number were. Mrs. Miyashita pressed close to her husband's side, looking for all the world as if she'd like to hide under his jacket. She seemed so bewildered and uncomfortable that I felt I should do something. Mr. Ledger beat me to it. The picture of old world gallantry, he bowed to Mrs. Miyashita, wished her all the best for the New Year, and kissed her hand. Then Mum whisked her astonished friend off to the kitchen, where some of the women were busy setting out food on the table.

"If you wouldn't mind slicing that bread for me, Tose, it'd be a big help," Mum said. Wrapped in one of Mum's aprons, her big sleeves pinned back by a couple of clothes pegs, Mrs. Miyashita stood cutting perfect, even slices from the big loaf and listening to the chatter of the other women. "Kay, go find your dad. Tell him it's time to carve the ham."

Our 1940 started with a meal the like of which people in our neighbourhood hadn't seen in years. The whole of the kitchen table was covered with food. Mum put out a spread of salad and pickles and bread, but everyone who came had brought food, Christmas baking, or some other specialty of theirs. I remember Mrs. Jamieson arrived with a big jar of her famous beetroot pickles, and Mrs. Jones had baked a mound of Welsh cakes. Norman's dad brought bricks of ice cream from work and stashed them in a snowbank in the backyard until they were needed. That ice cream went down very well with a spoon or two of Mrs. Costa's canned Saskatoon berries on top. But the true ruler of the table was Mrs. Miyashita's magnificent ham. Studded with cloves, its fat scored in perfect diamonds and glistening with red current glaze, that ham reigned as undisputed king of the feast.

The Miyashitas left soon after they'd had a taste of it and a little salad. I'm not certain they actually liked glazed ham. I have a feeling that Mrs. Miyashita regarded it as funny foreign food, perhaps not as ghastly as bubble and squeak but in the same league. The party carried on until half past two. In those days, the last to leave pitched in and helped with the dishes and the cleaning up before they went home. When the rug was back in its proper place, when the last plate was dried, and we had closed the door on the last guest, Dad uncorked the bottle of whisky and poured a tot for Mum and one for himself. He opened bottles of ginger beer for Charlie and me. Then the four of us stood and drank our own toast to the New Year.

"And may this war be over by summer," Mum added.

"I'll drink to that, old girl. I'll drink to that." Dad raised his glass, but he didn't look convinced.

Assignment #8
DISCUSS A SINGLE YEAR IN YOUR LIFE THAT
YOU CONSIDER PARTICULARLY SIGNIFICANT

MEMOIR CLASS WAS CANCELLED CHRISTMAS week. Then Meggie and I missed the next one because Jerome and his girlfriend took us on a jaunt to Banff. I like Jerome—he never makes you feel like you're his good deed for the day—and being in the mountains again, even for a few hours, was lovely. Meggie says these days she enjoys any outing that isn't a funeral. We stood the kids to a slap-up lunch at the Banff Springs Hotel and were back with our weary old bods tucked up in our rooms by half past four. That was far too late for class, but conscientious Janice had left us a note outlining our new assignment, "Nature and You: Is Nature Important to You?" Neither of us got very far with it. Not that Banff was our only excuse. I have to admit that it took me a lot longer than a week to finish working on "Holidays and Celebrations." Add to that an extra physio session, plus a visit to the orthopaedic surgeon for yet another check-up, and I was left with half a day for the Natural World. As for Meggie, she was delighted to give the whole thing a miss. She has a real downer on Ma Nature these days because of what happened last Thursday when she got up in the middle of the night to have a pee. And what did she spy with her myopic old eyes but two thumping great centipedes having a fight on the edge of the sink, or maybe it was sex. Whatever it was, Meggie did not approve of large insects making either love or war in her bathroom at three in the morning, so she whipped off a slipper and beat the crap out of her false eyelashes.

While she was explaining our new assignment, Janice gave us a little pep talk on writing. We're supposed to cut way back on the modifiers. Janice says that adjectives are to prose what candies are to diabetics. If that's true, then it's a wonder the entire class wasn't in a coma by the end of our "Nature and You" readings. Meggie disagreed with the comparison. She thinks it may be more apt to think of adjectives as the olives in a martini. The right number adds a perfect touch of salt—too many and there's no room left for the gin.

Speaking of martinis, we're still working our way through the swizzle stick gin. Meggie says her swizzle stick sale should be a lesson to us that we're never to throw anything away before we get Jerome to check it out on eBay. I'm going to phone my granddaughter and ask her to go to the condo and bring me my old snow-boot box next time she visits so I can sort through the odds and ends I've tossed in it over the years. I know there are old theatre programs and menus and tourist brochures, all from before the war. Apparently things like that are fetching a price these days. According to Jerome, the return half of my Clipper ticket, the part from Hong Kong back to San Francisco that I didn't use, would be worth at least a hundred dollars, maybe more. There are also some photos of the mountains that Charlie took on one of our trips to Banff. I know they'd have triggered a few memories for "Nature and You."

In a way I'm sorry that I didn't have time to work on that assignment. As a palaeontologist, I spent a good chunk of my adult life studying nature. I even wrote two books on the subject. Nothing so grand as scientific monographs—just popular stuff describing the fossils you can see in highway cuts on day drives from Calgary and another on the fossils in the city's building stones. They sold rather well too, on a modest, local level.

My formal studies did not begin until my lessons with Mr. Miyashita, but rocks had fascinated me since childhood. I was six years old when I saw my first fossils in an outcrop near Banff. As a CPR man, Dad had a pass for the train, so he and Mum occasionally took Charlie and me on day trips to the mountains. I remember that at first I thought the perfect little brachiopods embedded in that outcrop were actually alive. When Dad explained what fossils were and how they came to be in the rock, I thought them mysterious and beautiful beyond words. I still do. As a matter of fact, I think those fossils were the first of the ties that have bound me to the mountains for life. I once lived away from Calgary for a few years, and every time I looked at a sunset and did not see peaks along the horizon I'd miss them the way you miss beloved friends.

Here at Foothills Sunset, the big window in my room has a clear view to the Rockies and the horizon never disappoints. Even on cloudy days, I know the mountains are there. They do not return my regard, and that is another of their charms.

I think my interest in history also led me to palaeontology. After all, geology is history on a gigantic scale, or I suppose if you're going to be pedantic and define history as the study of mankind, then it's pre-history. Whatever you choose to call it, it's measured in billions of years, not the paltry thousands of *Homo sapiens'* existence. Mr. Miyashita once explained it to me this way: Consider the whole of the day that has just passed. Now blink. That blink at the end of the twenty-fourth hour is the span of human history compared with the age of the earth itself. Your own three score and ten don't even register. I know the received wisdom on this observation is that it drives home the humbling realization of how insignificant we are. But for me, the vast scale of geological time has always been a comfort. For my graduate degree, I studied one tiny tributary of the great river of life. The more I learned about my Devonian brachiopods, the more I came to realize that the world is a place of infinite wonders, not the least of which is that an inconsequential agglomeration of atoms like me is conscious of it.

I shall depart for the nonce on that highfalutin note as I've just noticed it's four-thirty—time I walked down the hall to Meggie's room if we're going to manage a drink before our five o'clock dinner.

Note that: Walk! Still with a walker but on my own two pins. And the pain is far less than it was even a week ago. If I keep this up, Darren says it's home by Valentine's for sure.

AFTER DINNER, MEGGIE and I spent some time discussing this "Year in Your Life" assignment. Meggie has decided to write about a year with Hersh, starting on the morning of their first wedding anniversary when she woke up and suddenly realized that for the first time in her life she was truly happy and had been happy for that whole year. Apparently, it was a revelation to be able to put a name to this lovely, if unfamiliar, state. "I'm happy!" She said the words out loud, then started to laugh. Hersh sat bolt upright in bed. He told her it was very startling to be woken from a deep sleep by a gal laughing her head off in your ear. Then they stopped talking and made it an even happier morning to remember.

I don't recall anything as dramatic as Meggie's anniversary epiphany. I certainly never woke up one morning and discovered I was happy. For me, happiness was the normal state; at least it was during my childhood. Call it the innocence of the overprotected, but that, plus a little luck and a lot of naiveté, got me to the age of twenty before I began to realize my world might not always be the safe and gentle place Mum and Dad had made for me.

Perhaps the first glimmer of my new understanding came the week after our New Year's party when Norman joined the army. He came over to the house that evening to tell us the big news. I remember his announcement took me by surprise, although I can't think why. By 1940, many of the young men I knew were talking about doing the same thing even if they hadn't actually signed up. But Norman had never so much as whispered a word of his plans to me. Still, I remember that Charlie and I made a big fuss over him. Joining the army seemed such an adult thing to do. We were both impressed with his new importance, Charlie especially. Mum and Dad were more reserved.

"Good luck to you, lad." Dad shook Norman's hand. "Keep your feet dry and come home safe and sound."

Mum gave him a hug. "We're going to miss you, and that's for sure."

Norman protested that he wasn't going anywhere for a while. He didn't even know when they'd call him up for basic training.

"By the way, do they ask you to prove how old you are at the recruiting office?" Charlie inquired, casual as all get out.

"Don't you go getting ideas, Charles Jeynes." Mum's hackles were up before you could blink.

Norman began his basic training near Calgary that spring, and I only saw him when he had leave. In late June he began specialized training on tanks. Just before this, he took me out dancing at Bowness, the Calgary Transit park on the Bow River at the end of the streetcar line. I haven't been there for years so I can't tell you what it's like now, but in those days there was something for everyone at Bowness Park—canoes, picnic tables, a swimming area, the dance pavilion, a merry-go-round for the children—all to be had for the price of a streetcar ticket. The Bowness merry-go-round that Charlie and I used to ride when we were little is now at Heritage Park. These days, its galloping mustangs travel at a much more sedate pace than they did back in my childhood when they were young and wild.

After a picnic supper, catered by Norman's mother, we went canoeing on the lagoon. You never actually went anywhere when you canoed at Bowness—it was pure as opposed to applied paddling, something to occupy the time between supper and the start of the dance. On warm summer evenings, the lagoon was filled with canoes circling the central fountain to the tinny strains of recorded music. Like the other girls out in the boats, I didn't do any of the paddling. That was part of the etiquette: the lady languished in the bow, propped up on a little backrest, trailing her fingers in the water as she gazed back to the stern where her gentleman sat doing the actual work. We thought it was romantic as all get out.

The June evenings of my youth were always long and lovely. The sun still hadn't set when the fountain's coloured lights were switched on so you could barely see their pallid glimmer on the spray. But, as twilight gathered, the lights began to shine brighter and brighter until by dark, plumes of colour cascaded onto the black surface of the lagoon. Norman took us so close to the fountain that we floated through a blue mist that changed to green and then to gold before we emerged on the other side.

It was well after nine by the time we paddled back to the landing and strolled to the pavilion. The dance had already begun. A couple of the men were in uniform, looking very proud of themselves. Norman wore civvies. Much later in the evening, on one of the band's breaks, we walked partway round the lagoon and sat on a bench to watch the fountain. After the jostling bodies and noise, it was cool and peaceful by the water. The splash of the fountain muffled the sound of voices that drifted from the pavilion.

"Good band tonight," I said.

Norman nodded, but he seemed a million miles away.

"Kay, there's something I have to say to you." He looked so earnest that for one heart-sinking moment I thought he was going to ask me to marry him right away. Such egos, the young. "I'm going to be sent overseas."

"But you're not finished your training."

"I didn't mean right away. It won't happen for a while yet, but this war isn't going to end anytime soon and someday I'll be sent to fight in it. You can bet real money on that. And when they do send me, I might not come home for a long time." Norman did not add the "if ever," but it hung in the air. "That's a fact, and right now we've got to face facts whether we want to or not. We don't have any choice." He sat staring out across the water. Then he squared his shoulders, took a deep breath, and turned to look at me.

"Kay, I think we should call off our engagement. I know we've never made an official announcement or anything formal like that, but it doesn't matter because we both know we're as good as engaged. At least that's how it feels to me. But with things as they stand right now, I think we have to call it off." I'm almost certain Norman had planned what he wanted to say very carefully, but he was still finding the going heavy weather. "It's not fair for me to ask you to wait. Maybe somewhere down the road, everything will work out, but we can't count on it. At least not now."

I didn't know what to say, but that didn't matter because Norman hadn't finished.

"I don't want you to think I'm saying this because I don't love you. You know I do. And maybe I shouldn't have sprung it on you out of the blue, but I didn't know how else to tell you. I sure hope I haven't got you all upset."

"I'm not upset," I said.

"Well, you look pretty upset. You aren't mad at me, are you? You know I love you."

"Yes, I know." It seemed so ungenerous not to tell him I loved him back, but the words wouldn't come. They would not have been true, and at the time, I suppose that mattered to me. "I'm not mad at you.

It's just that the thought of you being sent overseas makes it real. The war, I mean."

"It is real. They made that pretty clear to us at training camp. This war is real, and it's going to get a lot more real before it's done."

"Are you afraid of going? Of fighting?" I asked him. "I would be."

"Of course I am. You'd have to be a fool not to be afraid."

Norman was sent overseas in June of 1941, a fully fledged private in the Calgary Tanks, and I did not see him again for a very long time. His regiment took part in the Dieppe Raid, the disastrous attack on the French coast launched by the Allies on August 19, 1942. Norman's tank got hopelessly bellied in the shingle and did not make it off the beach. Nor did most of the other tanks. The ones that did were stopped by the seawall and by concrete barriers placed by the Germans to block the way inland. Still, the immobilized tanks kept firing their guns right to the end, providing cover that enabled what was left of the infantry to retreat to the ships. Most of the tank crews either died in battle or became prisoners of war. Norman was one of the lucky ones. He lived. His left arm was severed below the elbow, but he lived. Nine hundred and seven of the Canadians who went into the battle at Dieppe died. The whole gruesome fiasco lasted only a matter of hours. At its end, 3,379 Canadians were listed as dead, wounded, or taken prisoner. Only 2,210 returned to England, many of them badly wounded. I know the numbers because I got Jerome to look up the Dieppe Raid on the Internet for me. It's enough to make you wish there were a hell so the architects of that catastrophe could rot in it for all eternity. With the gift of hindsight, the raid's planners justified their deadly incompetence by claiming they learned vital lessons at Dieppe, lessons that helped make the invasion of Normandy a success. When you get right down to it, hell is probably better than they deserve.

Norman spent the remainder of the war in a prison camp. When the camp was liberated, he was sent to a hospital in Essex, where he fell in love with an English girl, one of the nurses on his ward. They were married in England in 1945. I met Molly soon after she came to join him in Canada, and I liked her very much. I know Norman had a happy life with her, far happier than he would ever have had with me.

I CAN'T HONESTLY say that Norman's absence changed my life much. I sometimes felt guilty because I only really noticed that he'd been away when he came home on one of his infrequent leaves. My social life certainly didn't suffer. There always seemed to be a fellow around to take me dancing or out to a movie when I felt like going.

I was very busy at work that winter. The photograph files were taking shape. It gave me great pleasure to see the drawers of the cabinets filling with neatly labelled folders, each one's contents carefully recorded, described, and cross-referenced on four-by-six cards. My coffee-break tutorials continued too, although Mr. Miyashita and I seemed to be spending less and less time discussing the news. He still obsessed over his papers, but I think he found their contents so depressing that he did not care to spend time talking about them, at least not with me. As the war went on, it became increasingly difficult for him to get his foreign publications. The American newspapers still arrived in a reasonably timely fashion, but before long, the British papers got pretty erratic. I know Dad really missed the *Manchester Guardian*. For a short period, I brought the *New York Times* home for him instead, but that didn't work out. He was not interested in the opinions of a bunch of weaselly Yanks who were only too willing to sit on the sidelines and watch Britain fight Hitler. While he did not express them in such vivid terms as my father, I suspect Mr. Miyashita shared some of Dad's opinions.

That February the first squadron of the Royal Canadian Air Force arrived in England. Mr. Miyashita sat reading about it in the *Albertan* one morning when I brought him his coffee.

"It is not enough, you know," he said, shaking his head as he folded the paper. "And it never will be enough until America joins us in this fight."

"Some Americans are joining the Canadian Army," I said. "There are two fellows from Montana training with Norman."

"It is not simply their men we need, Miss Jeynes. We need American industry even more." He paused for a moment as he thought how best to explain this point to me. "You and I both spend considerable time studying the New York stock market, do we not?"

"Yes, sir." I was flattered that he included me as a fellow student of the market.

"Now imagine what would happen if all those American companies listed on the New York exchange were put to work producing goods for our armed forces—ships, airplanes, oil, munitions, tanks, all the matériel of war that is in such desperately short supply at the moment. Until we have that industrial power on our side, until America joins us, we can have no hope of victory."

"Do you think the Americans will come into the war?" I asked.

"Someday," he said. "It is inevitable. I do not know what it will take to precipitate their entry, but something will goad them to action."

Perhaps because of this conversation, I remember being a particularly diligent student of the stock market that winter. I followed my imaginary investment portfolio as if the family fortune depended on it, and the market was often a subject of discussion during our coffee-break tutorials. However, our major subject was geology. As the war slowly but inexorably gained momentum, I think Mr. Miyashita took comfort in the fact that mere human beings have no influence on geological events. Certain of the more cataclysmic, like earthquakes and volcanic eruptions, may be the cause of much human misery, but as he pointed out to me, unlike war, that is simply a by-product of the event and not its purpose. I learned from Mr. Miyashita that nature does not intend us harm, that nature has no intentions either good or bad. Nature simply is. I think that for him, our coffee tutorials on my latest reading in his geology books were a refuge from the realities of the news. For me, they opened whole new dimensions of a subject that has absorbed me all my life.

The tenor of our days at the office changed with Charlie coming to work in the darkroom after school on Tuesdays and Thursdays. Those winter afternoons in 1940 were the happiest I spent at Miyashita Industries. I'd sit at my desk working on the photo files while Charlie developed prints in the darkroom and Mr. Miyashita read his papers or worked on his investments in his office. I know it can't have snowed every Tuesday and Thursday that winter, but in my memory there are always fat flakes drifting past my window in the fading light of late afternoon. It is always quiet too, with the hush peculiar to snowy afternoons cocooning us from the noise of the traffic on 1st Street. The only break in the stillness is the clatter of Charlie's boots on the hardwood as he strides along the corridor from the elevator to the office.

Mr. Miyashita often asked me to put the kettle on when Charlie arrived. Then the three of us would sit in his office drinking tea and chatting while he encouraged my brother to eat far too many digestive biscuits. No matter how many digestives Charlie packed away, they never seemed to spoil his appetite for dinner, a phenomenon I did not witness again until my own sons were teenagers.

At half past five we'd call it a day and head for home. On the coldest days, mostly to humour Mrs. Miyashita I suspect, Mr. Miyashita took a taxi and would drop Charlie and me off at our house even though it took him well out of his way.

I LEARNED TO drive that spring. Early in April, Mr. Miyashita asked me to use his car to take my mother and Mrs. Miyashita on one of their shopping expeditions. Apparently the pair of them had decided to go farther afield than the Billingsgate and Jenkins. He was a little taken aback when I told him I didn't know how to drive.

"Until this Christmas we didn't have a car," I offered by way of explanation. "So I never had a chance to learn."

"Perhaps your mother drives?"

And perhaps you're desperate because you don't want to get stuck driving them yourself, I thought.

"I'm afraid not," I said.

"And neither does my wife," he said, very down in the mouth.

"Charlie told me that Mrs. Miyashita's father was the first person in Hiroshima to drive his own car. I'm surprised he didn't teach her to drive as well."

"Thanks to her father, my wife is a woman of many accomplishments, some of them most unusual for a Japanese lady of her age and station."

"Like dancing and fly-fishing?"

"Exactly. But waltzing is one thing, Miss Jeynes. A man's automobile is another." He smiled and leaned back in his chair. "My wife's father was a remarkable fellow. He was a great believer in practical experience. I think that is partly what made him such an exceptional engineer. As a consequence, my wife and her sister were not merely taught pastimes like fly-fishing and dancing. They were also schooled in the everyday tasks of life. For instance, he insisted they both learn to cook so that they would have practical knowledge when it came time for them to supervise households of their own. Believe me, I thank him for those cooking lessons every time I sit down to my dinner. They were taught to garden as well, so if their circumstances changed, they would know how to grow their own food. Unfortunately, this emphasis on the practical stopped at his motorcar. He loved that machine the way other men love precious works of art. I think seeing a novice behind its wheel, especially one of his daughters, would have been too great a strain for him."

"I bet Charlie would drive Mrs. Miyashita and Mum if they don't mind waiting until Saturday morning to go shopping," I suggested. I knew Charlie would jump at the chance to drive the Pierce-Arrow.

"So Charles drives?"

"He's a really good driver," I said. "Canon Giles taught him so he could chauffeur some of the old people to church on Sundays."

I did not add that Charlie was soon an infinitely better driver than his teacher. As a matter of fact, Canon Giles, whose mind tended to wander in every direction but the road in front of him, was a well-known menace on the streets of Calgary. Charlie claimed that as soon as they caught sight of the Canon's old Nash, others drivers pulled over to the side of the road, and pedestrians crossing the street ran for the sidewalks. I never knew whether to believe him or not.

"A Saturday or two with Charles might work as a stopgap," Mr. Miyashita conceded. "At least until you learn to drive and obtain a licence. Of course, that is something we must see to immediately. I will ask Charles to begin your instruction this afternoon."

My first lesson with Charlie in Mr. Miyashita's car began on a quiet country road near the Glenmore Dam. Charlie was a good teacher, and we both enjoyed our outings in the big car. Come to think of it, I'm probably safe in claiming that I am the only person living in Calgary today who learned to drive on a Pierce-Arrow. I loved driving, and was soon as good a driver as my brother. I had my licence by May. Dad was a little dismayed when he realized that meant he would have to give me a crack at the Model T. It had taken him hours of work to get our Christmas car humming along, and he'd developed quite an affection for the "old girl," as he always called it. I'm sure the thought of seeing me behind her wheel gave rise to the same apprehensions that Mrs. Miyashita's father had felt. However, Dad could hardly let Charlie drive the old girl and then refuse me, not unless he wanted an earful from Mum.

LATE THAT MAY, Mrs. Miyashita discovered root cellars. Mum had heard about a market garden near Midnapore. It was far too early for any vegetables, but she and Mrs. Miyashita decided they should scout the place out for later in the season. So off the three of us went, with me at the wheel of the Pierce-Arrow. Today Midnapore is part of Calgary, all suburbs and shopping malls, but back then it was out in the country. Lines of poplar trees flanked both sides of the road from town. They ran for miles, all apple-green and fresh in the spring air, a sight that would no doubt have pleased Pat Burns, who had them planted back when the Macleod Trail was only a narrow, two-lane road along the border of his Bow Valley Ranch. The Burns poplars were chopped down years ago when the highway was widened, but they were lovely while they lasted. So were the meadowlarks, and I swear that morning there was one on every other fence post belting out its song. There's nothing like a meadowlark on a fine May morning to convince you that all's right with the world.

The market garden turned out to be a small grain farm where as a sideline the farmer's wife cultivated an enormous vegetable plot and sold the produce from it, along with honey from her own beehives and fresh eggs laid by the flock of industrious red hens we saw pecking for bugs in the yard. The hens scattered with much indignant flapping and clucking as we walked past the barn and on to a big root cellar dug into the side of a hill. That root cellar was the high point of Mrs. Miyashita's morning. She was so taken with it that the farmer's wife let her go inside and look around. She was enchanted by the big barrels full of sand and sawdust where the vegetables were stored over winter, and by the wooden shelves with their rows of glass jars filled with honey and preserves.

"So beautiful," Mrs. Miyashita said, pointing to a rosy jar of crab apple jelly. "You have the summer in your cellar." The woman seemed a little nonplussed by this observation, although I think she understood that Mrs. Miyashita was paying her a compliment.

Mum and Mrs. Miyashita each bought a dozen eggs and a jar of honey, then we headed for home. The pair of them chatted happily in the backseat. They always sat in the back when I drove. It made me feel like a chauffeur, which, come to think of it, is exactly what I was.

"You could build a root cellar in your own garden, Tose," I heard Mum suggest. We didn't have a root cellar ourselves. Dad had built a cold room in a corner of the cellar that worked almost as well. "That yard of yours is so big you'd never notice it was there."

"But there is not a steep hill in our garden," Mrs. Miyashita said. "Only a little . . ."

"Slope," Mum filled in for her. "And it would do very nicely. Besides you don't need a hill to have a root cellar. The Jamiesons across the way from us have one that's dug straight down. It has a trap door and a ladder. I've seen bigger ones too, with little staircases in them and even electric lights."

Mrs. Miyashita agreed that a light and a staircase, perhaps one with a proper handrail, had definite appeal. By the time we reached Mount Royal, the pair of them had decided not if, but where and how big the root cellar would be. All that remained was to find someone to build it. This proved more difficult than they had anticipated. The odd-job man who kept the Miyashitas' walks shovelled in the winter and managed the heavy work in their garden claimed he had no time that spring for extra tasks. Perhaps if Mrs. Miyashita was willing to wait until August, he could find time to dig then. But he didn't pretend to be any kind of a carpenter and she'd have to get someone else to build her shelves and bins. So the project was put on hold until later in the summer. Nevertheless, that year Mrs. Miyashita planted her garden with a view to winter storage in her new root cellar.

ON DOMINION DAY, Charlie drove us to the Millarville Races, this time in our own car. We packed Mum another birthday picnic, and Terps came with us, which made the day even more fun. Mum renewed her profitable acquaintance with Okey Dokey, although his odds weren't nearly as good as they'd been the year before because too many other people had remembered the little grey's spectacular win. I looked for my pal Shorty, but he wasn't entered in any of the races—probably couldn't get the day off work. I drove us home. Dad survived the trip. Just.

When we got home from Millarville, it was time for Charlie and me to finish packing for a month in Banff. The Miyashitas had invited us to accompany them on their summer holiday. Mr. Miyashita said this was to be a working trip for the two of us. Charlie would be busy with his duties as assistant photographer, and I would be responsible for keeping a detailed record of every photo taken. According to the boss, we were simply moving the office to Banff for the month. Neither of us fell for this line. I knew it wouldn't take me more than a few minutes a day to log the photos, and as for Charlie, there was nothing he'd sooner do than help his mentor take pictures in the mountains. Still, I think Mr. Miyashita honestly did believe it was a business trip, and so did Mum and Dad. I'm sure he discussed his plans with them before issuing the invitation because our parents would never have given us permission to spend a month idling around Banff on something as frivolous as a holiday. But work was a different matter.

Not only did Mum and Dad give us permission, they even volunteered to look after Nikkou. This delighted Mrs. Miyashita. She was always unhappy about leaving her little dog behind at a kennel. I knew the regulations regarding dogs in National Parks were very strict, but I still wondered why she didn't take Nikkou with her. I asked Mum and she explained that Mrs. Miyashita was convinced Nikkou would slip her leash and be lost in the forest where grizzly bears, assisted by wolves and cougars, would devour her in an instant.

Charlie and I were thrilled at the prospect of a whole month in the mountains. I have to admit that I found the prospect of a month at the Banff Springs Hotel pretty thrilling as well. We were each to have a room of our own, a room with a bath. For a couple of kids from east Calgary who had never stayed in a hotel before, we sure did start at the top.

Late in May, Mr. Miyashita called us both into his office.

"Do you own a dinner jacket, Charles?" he asked. I'm sure he already knew the answer, but he was a very diplomatic gentleman so he asked the question anyway.

"No, sir, I don't." Charlie probably wouldn't have known what a dinner jacket was if it hadn't been for all those Fred Astaire movies.

"I suppose a young fellow of . . . what age are you now Charles? Seventeen? Eighteen?"

"Seventeen, sir. Eighteen in August."

"I suppose that a fellow of seventeen really does not have much call for a dinner jacket, does he?"

"None at all," Charlie said. In our neighbourhood, people considered themselves fortunate to have dinner, never mind special clothes to eat it in.

"Then we must find you one before we leave for Banff. You will need it at the Banff Springs. Better meet me at Kilpatrick's Tog Shop tomorrow after school."

"I'm sorry, but I can't afford Kilpatrick's, sir. Maybe we could meet at Woolworth's."

"There is no question of your buying yourself a dinner jacket, Charles. Since you must stay in Banff in order to do your work, it is my obligation as your employer to provide you with any equipment or clothing out of the ordinary that you may need on the job. A dinner jacket and suitable trousers are required for the hotel dining room, but it would not be fair for you to be out of pocket for them. Not fair at all. Remember, this is a business trip and, as such, it includes all business expenses."

Faced with such a tour de force of sophistry, who could refuse? Mr. Miyashita applied the same reasoning to my wardrobe and enlisted Mrs. Miyashita to take me to her dressmaker, a middle-aged, no-nonsense Scot named Janet Peebles, and have her run up a few of what he called suitable evening frocks. I thought Mum might be hurt by this because she always sewed my clothes, but it didn't faze her in the least. Maybe the fact that my fancy new dresses were work clothes (ha ha) made a difference. She even came with Mrs. Miyashita and me to Miss Peebles's shop to choose patterns and fabrics and great fun it was for all of us.

I did get Mum to help me make some casual clothes for the trip. She whipped up a blouse and a wrap-around sports skirt from material I'd bought on sale. As a surprise, she also made me a pair of hiking breeches, nipped in tight at the knee but very roomy, not to say voluminous, in the bum. Charlie and Dad thought they were hilarious. They called them Kay's fart catchers. Mum laughed too, until she remembered to give them an earful about their vulgar language.

The Miyashitas picked us up on the morning of July 2. The arrival of the Pierce-Arrow caused a sensation on our street. Our neighbours didn't bother to peek from behind the curtains—they marched right out and stood on their front steps to get a better look. All the children were on holiday from school, and some of those steps were pretty crowded. Dad had already left for work so only Mum was at home to see us off. Mr. Miyashita took Nikkou's travelling gear out of the trunk—a case of Dr. Ballard's, a hairbrush, and a blanket—and carried it up the walk. The little dog danced after him on her leash, pulling Mrs. Miyashita behind her. Mrs. Miyashita and Mum shook hands.

"I am grateful that you will mind Nikkou," she said. "You are kind, Judith."

"But, Tose, I told you, she won't be any trouble at all." Mum took the leash. "She'll get Albert and me out for a nice walk of an evening. Now off you go and enjoy your trip. And see these two behave themselves." She gave Charlie and me each a kiss, and as the car pulled out from the curb, she waved us on our way with a big smile and a call of "happy journeys." So did the neighbours.

It wasn't until I had children of my own that I realized Mum's jaunty goodbye must have been a wrench for her. This was the first time her chicks had ventured from the nest for more than a day or two, and here they were, flying off on their own for a whole month. I don't think she worried that any real harm would come to us, or at least no more than any other protective parent with an imagination for disaster. And for a woman who had taken me to task for getting above myself on the strength of one ride home in a Polley's taxi, she didn't seem at all concerned that we might have our heads turned by fancy new clothes and a month in a posh hotel. Still, a whole month was a long time, and she would be lonely for us. She'd also worry about us feeling out of place and being homesick and missing her and Dad. Not that she wouldn't be pleased if we did miss them a little. It didn't occur to me that I might be homesick, probably because I'd never had occasion to discover what homesickness felt like. In any case, I would certainly have considered myself far too mature and sophisticated for anything so childish.

We checked into the Banff Springs shortly before lunch. For all my trips to Banff, that was the first time I'd set foot in the CPR's Castle in the Rockies. I was prepared for something grand, but this was grand on a scale beyond my imagination. I found it daunting at first. I've read that Van Horne wanted his hotel to impress its guests with a building equal to the magnificence of its surroundings. He certainly succeeded in impressing me. However, the hotel in 1940 was nothing like the original that first opened under his supervision in 1888. Over the years, the Banff Springs has been burned down, rebuilt, added to, and renovated, until it has evolved into the gargantuan mishmash of styles that stands today. The hotel is a blend of Scottish castle and Loire chateau mixed with timbered Tudor, Norman gothic, Spanish Renaissance, and anything else that happened to catch the CPR's outsized fancy. In the spirit of Van Horne himself, all of it is larger than life. Turn a corner and there's another massive stone staircase or a towering vaulted ceiling or an elaborately carved fireplace big enough to roast a moose. It should be ludicrous, but somehow this outlandish hodgepodge of parts merges into one great and glorious architectural extravaganza. For me, the Banff Springs will always be the grandest hotel in Canada. Only the Chateau Frontenac, on its bluff overlooking the St. Lawrence, can compete. And did I mention that those staircases are made of Tyndall stone, an Ordovician limestone teeming with fossils?

The Miyashitas had their usual suite overlooking the golf course and the Bow Valley. My single room was right next to theirs. Charlie's was a few doors down. We all had the million-dollar view, not that it mattered much because we spent so little time in our rooms. Except the private bath mattered. At least it mattered to me. If anything could have turned my head that was it—my very own white-tiled bathroom with its enormous claw-footed tub and all the thick white towels I cared to use. What's more, I could wallow in the bath as long as I liked without someone pounding on the door. I took a bath every morning, then another lavender-scented one before dinner. Finally, I'd end my ablutionary day with a bubble bath last thing at night.

It took me a while to adjust to the fact that people do things for you at a hotel, that doing things for you is their job. I never did manage to get to the point where I could leave my unmade bed for the chambermaid without suffering pangs of conscience. On the other hand, Charlie was an instant study. He was overjoyed when he found that the chambermaid would not only make the bed, but fold his pyjamas, hang up his clothes, and tidy the room as well. He didn't make his bed for a month.

We'd been in Banff a few days before I asked Mrs. Miyashita where I should wash my clothes. She explained that if I put my laundry in the special bag, it would come back clean and pressed the next day. Amazing. But the best thing of all, next to my bathroom, was the room-service breakfast. At home, we never got food on a tray unless we were sick in bed. Then it was invalid food like dry toast and ginger tea, or maybe a little cream of wheat or a boiled egg when we were on the mend. But at the Banff Springs, a phone call brought a morning tray of whatever you fancied—grapefruit, toast, porridge, bacon, ham, kippers, eggs, even a steak—all served elegantly on CPR china with coffee in a big silver pot. Everything from the cutlery to the heavy linen napkins had the old CPR logo on it, and lovely stuff it was.

We spent most of our days out in the mountains. Often, Mr. Miyashita and Charlie would strike off with the cameras while Mrs. Miyashita and I rambled the streams stopping at likely fishing holes. Wearing the tiniest pair of hip waders I've ever seen, she'd stride into the freezing water, rod in hand, and begin flicking faux insects over the surface. Mrs. Miyashita could dance a fly across water so convincingly that rainbow trout elbowed each other out of the way to bite. She tied her own flies too, and had great success with several of her own invention. She never took more fish than she could use, and many of those eager trout were tossed back to bite again another day. She taught me how to fly-fish that summer, but I've never achieved anything like her level of skill.

We drove to places like Johnson's Canyon or Lake Minnewanka or Lake Louise and rambled the trails there. Once, we got up very early and drove to Field, where we climbed the long, steep trail up to the Burgess Shale. Mr. Miyashita took a photo of me standing on the site of Walcott's quarry. That's when I knew for certain that someday I would be a palaeontologist.

On the morning we had planned to go hiking near Castle Mountain, we woke to pouring rain. It was cold too, the kind of dank chill-your-bones cold that the mountains can manage even in July. Not that you could see any mountains with the clouds socked in to a few hundred feet. We hung around the hotel for most of the morning, reading and watching the rain pelt down. By lunch, Charlie and I were so bored we couldn't sit still any longer. It was either go outside or go nuts, so we made up our minds to hike around the deserted golf course. Our boss decided to join us, saying that his legs could use a good stretch. It was obvious that Mrs. Miyashita, ever mindful of his health, did not approve of him walking in the rain. She herself opted to stay in her sitting room, reading in front of the fire.

We got back to the hotel shortly after three, drenched but happy and more than ready for a long wallow in the hotel's hot pool. However, that afternoon we deserted the Banff Springs for the public pool at the Upper Hot Springs. Canon Giles and his wife had driven to Banff with their children for a picnic and a swim, and we had made arrangements to meet them in the pool at half past four.

"A most invigorating tramp despite the rain," Mr. Miyashita informed his wife. "And we still have plenty of time for tea before we leave to meet the Giles family. A pity it rained on their picnic, but the weather will not matter once we are all warm in the pool."

He called room service and ordered sandwiches, cake, and coffee while Mrs. Miyashita filled her little electric kettle at the bathroom sink. Whenever she travelled, Mrs. Miyashita brought along her kettle, a supply of green tea, and a proper Japanese pot to brew it in. By that summer, she was using her tea sparingly, as it had become almost impossible to get. I remember suggesting that she might be able to find some in one of the Chinese grocery shops at the bottom of the Centre Street Bridge before I realized the utter foolishness of my words. In the Calgary of 1940, no Japanese would have dared set foot in a Chinese shop, especially not after Nanking.

Mrs. Miyashita waited for the coffee and food to arrive before she poured boiling water over her precious leaves. While the tea steeped, she nibbled a corner of a dainty fish paste sandwich. The rest of us, including Mr. Miyashita, attacked those bits of bread and bloater like they were our last meal. Not surprisingly, Mr. Miyashita and I ran out of steam before Charlie.

"Please do finish the sandwiches before we go to the pool, Charles," Mr. Miyashita insisted. "It is a long time until dinner." Obviously, our boss had never heard of the no-swimming-for-an-hour-after-eating rule that my parents enforced so rigorously.

"And the cake too," Mrs. Miyashita urged.

Charlie obliged.

YOU CAN SMELL the pool at the Upper Hot Springs before you can see it. The stench of rotting eggs pervades the whole place, but the reek of sulphur dioxide has never discouraged avid bathers like the Miyashitas. That afternoon, when I emerged from the locker room into the rain and cold, it didn't bother me either. The water might smell like it was pumped straight from hell, but at least it retained the heat of its source. I could hardly wait to get in and get warm. There weren't many other people in the pool—two or three soakers clinging to the edge plus a group of four young fellows about Charlie's age horsing around in the deep end. As I walked down the steps into the water, the boys took time from turning somersaults to aim a few loud wolf-whistles in my direction. Of course, I stuck my nose in the air and pretended that they were simply too juvenile for a sophisticated older woman like me to notice. They found this hugely funny, and added a few big laughs to the whistles. Then I saw Billy Trent's head bob up in the middle of the pack. I caught his eye, but he turned and floated off in the opposite direction, pretending he hadn't seen me or heard his pals laughing. This annoyed me so much that I waved and called, "Hello there, Billy," in a little flirty-girl voice. That succeeded in making him the object of the group's laughter.

By the time the Miyashitas got into the pool and submerged themselves beside me in the shallow end, Billy's friends had tired of ragging him about his bathing-beauty girlfriend and returned to perfecting their underwater handstands.

"Where's Charlie?" I asked.

"Still in the locker room," Mr. Miyashita answered. "Canon Giles came in as we were changing. Charles is helping him get the twins into their bathing costumes. My, but they are a pair of live wires."

"Live wires" was the euphemism used to describe children like the Canon's demonic five-year-olds before the term *hyperactive* was invented. The Giles twins were ahead of their time.

"Gee! This place stinks worse than usual today," the largest of the somersaulters called to his friends. He had paddled halfway across the pool and stood up to his chest in the water, staring at us. He was a tall, good-looking blond, a little older than the rest.

"I bet you any money that Bill did it," another of them joked as he swam up beside his friend. "Told you not to eat beans for lunch, Trent."

"No, I don't think it's Bill this time," the tall one said in a loud voice. "This stink is yellow, and it's coming from the shallow end."

"Yeah, you know I think you're right about that, Ed," the other one said. "The shallow end does have kind of a yellow stink, doesn't it?"

The others had swum up to join them, except for Billy, who remained treading water in the background. They continued their remarks about the stink and whether or not the yellow would leave a stain on the nice white pool. Each new wisecrack was followed by loud guffaws. The whole scene only lasted a matter of seconds, and it took me a few of them to realize what I was hearing. When I did, I stood up and began to wade toward them. I was so angry I didn't know what I was going to do, but it would be something that pack of idiots wouldn't forget. I was angry at the lifeguard too, for sitting in his high chair sheltered by an umbrella, looking the other way. I had gone about two steps when Mr. Miyashita spoke to me.

"Please, do come back, Miss Jeynes." He sat with his back against the side of the pool, as relaxed as if the commotion in front of him were not happening. Mrs. Miyashita huddled beside him, submerged to her chin. Her eyes were shut tight.

"But, sir, I can't let them . . ."

"You will catch cold if you continue to stand out of the water like that. Come back and sit down with us and keep warm." It was an order, not a suggestion.

As I waded back, I saw Billy hoist himself out of the pool and slink toward the locker room. He almost ran into Canon Giles and Charlie and the twins as he disappeared through the door. The Canon left his children with Charlie and strolled to the side of the pool. Oblivious to his presence, Billy's friends continued their bullying banter.

"That stink is so yellow, I bet you could set a match to it," the big blond said. "No wonder fire crackers come from China. All they do is . . ."

"Good afternoon, Edward," the Canon called. Even though he stood in the chill air in nothing but his bathing trunks, he still managed to project an aura of clerical authority.

"Canon Giles," the blond stammered. "Good afternoon, sir." I watched him deflate. "I didn't know you were here." Long pause. "Sir." His three companions shrivelled beside him.

"Perhaps before you leave the pool you would like to introduce me to your friends."

The blond mumbled their names. Canon Giles repeated each one in his best pulpit-to-back-pew voice.

"Thank you, Edward. I'll do my best to keep those names in mind, so when I see your father at our next Rotary lunch, I'll be able to let him know what an amusing time you and your friends were having in Banff. Now don't let me keep you. I know you were just about to leave. Do give my regards to your parents."

The boys splashed out of the pool, stumbling over themselves to follow Billy into the locker room. By this time, Mrs. Giles and their three little girls had joined the Canon. She gave him a questioning look, but he simply shook his head and helped them into the pool. Charlie brought the twins, and we made quite a party in the shallow end. Mrs. Miyashita was still shaken. She remained submerged and silent until Mrs. Giles put her in charge of her two-year-old daughter while she taught the older one how to float. Children always cheered Mrs. Miyashita. Even the antics of the terrible twins made her smile. I could see she felt a little steadier by the time we were ready to return to the hotel and dress for dinner.

Mr. Miyashita and I never spoke about that afternoon at the Upper Hot Springs. It was as if it had never happened.

EATING IN THE hotel's dining room was a big treat for Charlie and me. Our family never ate in restaurants, so to us, dinner at the Banff Springs every night was living the high life. I know Mrs. Miyashita enjoyed it too. She was not an adventurous eater, and the hotel kitchen would do their best to cook whatever she wanted, including the fish she caught with her fly rod. The Banff Springs dining room might not rise to sushi, but at least she was safe from the likes of bubble and squeak. I think she also enjoyed the opportunity to wear her evening dresses.

Most nights after we had eaten, Mr. Miyashita liked to attend the Toronto Trio's hour of classical music in Mount Stephen Hall. The group's leader, Murray Adaskin, went on to become one of Canada's leading classical composers. I met him in the early 1970s in Saskatoon, where he was a member of the music faculty at the University of

Saskatchewan. He was tickled when I told him I had heard him play at the Banff Springs all those years ago.

Finally, Charlie and I would round off the evening with some dancing in the ballroom. The hotel always hired top-notch bands for the summer, as good as any we'd ever heard, even on the radio. We both felt a little shy, so for the first night or two we danced mainly with each other. Charlie looked handsome in his new dinner jacket, and when the girls saw how well he danced, he had his choice of partners. If I do say so myself, I didn't do too badly in that department either.

We got to be friends with a brother and sister from Philadelphia who loved dancing as much as we did. Tom Wilson had just graduated from Harvard and his sister, Margaret, was a student at Radcliffe. They were in Banff, "on vacation" as they called it, with their parents. We also met the senior Wilsons, both of whom made it clear they did not approve of the Jeynes kids. They were pretty snooty to us, which I know embarrassed Tom and Margaret. Mrs. Wilson had it in for me particularly. I'm certain the old bat thought I had gold-digging designs on her son. I have to admit it was obvious that Charlie and I didn't come from the Wilson's financial class, that we weren't the sort who regularly summered at the hotel. The new evening frocks I had thought so splendid paled beside the designer gowns that crowded the dance floor. Peebles de Calgary couldn't compete with Chanel de Paris, so it's just as well it never occurred to me to try to pass myself off as anything but exactly what I was. However, Ma Wilson wasn't to know that. I'm sure she spent the entire three weeks of her stay in an agony of apprehension.

The Wilson parents didn't approve of the Miyashitas either, or of our relationship with them. They were not the only ones. Many of the other guests treated the Miyashitas coolly or simply pretended they didn't exist. In a way, it was the high-hat version of the boys at the swimming pool. This was unusual for the Banff Springs, which was a very cosmopolitan place and attracted its wealthy guests from all over the world. However, that July, the Miyashitas were the only Japanese in the hotel. During their previous stays, there had been plenty of guests from Japan and staff too. As a matter of fact, for years most of the Banff Springs' bellboys were Japanese. But that changed at the start of the Sino-Japanese War. By 1940, the Japanese bellboys were long gone. I know Mrs. Miyashita missed them.

Some evenings the Miyashitas accompanied us to the ballroom. Mrs. Miyashita would dance the occasional waltz with Charlie but mostly they seemed happy to sit and watch us. They always left for bed before ten. Charlie and I seldom danced past midnight ourselves because we had to be up, breakfasted, and out on the trails by seven or earlier, depending on what Mr. Miyashita planned to photograph that day.

We didn't spend all our time with the Miyashitas. Although they never came right out and said it, they needed time to themselves to catch a breath away from the overwhelming energy of youth. I now understand that need all too well. But back then, Charlie and I were of an age that regards resting as a waste of time, especially holiday time. We were always up to something. I learned to golf on that trip. As a treat, Mr. Miyashita arranged for us to have some lessons with the hotel's course professional, and also stood us to as many rounds as we could find the time to play. I was a natural. I couldn't hit the ball as far as Charlie, but I could hit it straight, and ultimately that was what counted. Charlie spent so much time in the woods searching for lost balls that I regularly beat him by at least five strokes, sometimes more. Tom and Margaret often played with us.

Despite this constant busyness, I did find time to be homesick, mostly when I wanted to tell my parents about something I'd seen or done. There were other times too, when I simply missed having them around. Although I was sorry when our month came to an end, I was happy to be going home to Mum and Dad. I would not have admitted this for anything.

THE MIYASHITAS DROPPED us off at our house late on a Friday afternoon, along with two trout caught by Mrs. Miyashita and me that morning and kept fresh in a waxed cardboard box full of ice provided by the hotel. We'd wrapped the box in a ground sheet so it wouldn't leak all over the trunk.

Mum lifted the lid. "That's a fine-looking pair of fish, and both of them Rainbows too."

"Kay caught the big one," Mrs. Miyashita said.

"Mrs. Miyashita is teaching me how use a fly rod."

"Well that one's a real credit to your teacher. Must be getting on for three pounds."

"Three pounds, four and a half ounces." The hotel kitchen had weighed it for me.

Charlie lifted the box out of the car. Water from the melted ice trickled out its corners and onto his trousers.

Mum invited the Miyashitas to stay for a cup of tea, but Mrs. Miyashita wanted to get home and unpack. She and Mum made a date to get together the next afternoon instead. After all, the pair of them hadn't had a proper visit for more than a month.

"I think yon Nikky's caught a whiff of those trout." Mum laughed. Nikkou had begun to bark from behind our screen door the minute the car pulled up to the curb. Her yapping rose to a frenzy when Charlie started up the walk with the fish. "You'll be wanting to take her home with you, so I'll run in and get her things," Mum said. "I can tell you, we're going to miss her. She's been good as gold."

The second Mum opened the door Nikkou bounced out. After a brief pause to assess her chances with Charlie and the fish, she tore down the walk, threw herself at Mrs. Miyashita's feet, and pawed the air.

"Nikkou is beautiful. Her fur shines. She was happy with you, Judith. Thank you."

Hysteria aside, Nikkou did look very fit and sleek, but she still wasn't what you'd call slim.

"Nikky's no whippet and that's the truth," Mum remarked to me as the Miyashitas drove off. "Got a bonny coat on her though."

Twenty minutes later the phone rang. Mum answered. I heard her say, "Hello, Tose," and that was it. For the next five minutes, a flood of Mrs. Miyashita's Japanese-Geordie English poured from the receiver. I'd never heard her say so much so fast so loudly. I wasn't standing all that close to Mum, but I caught every word. Even so, I can't say I understood many of them. I did manage to make out "root cellar" repeated at least ten times, although her excitement made the Ls a bit hit or miss. As usual, Mum seemed to follow her friend better than I did, and every so often she'd try to get a word in.

"I'm glad you . . . Albert and I thought . . . No trouble at . . ." Finally Mum gave up and stood in silence until the torrent ran dry.

"Tose, the cellar was a little way for Albert and me to say thanks for being so kind to our children. It was a pleasure for us to build, and I'm happy you're pleased with it."

This brought another rush of words from Mrs. Miyashita, during which Dad arrived home from work. More minutes passed before Mum finally managed to hang up the phone and say a proper hello to him.

"That was Tose," she said to him. "She thinks her new root cellar is a beautiful place."

"Nothing but a hole in the ground with a few sticks of wood in it," Dad said, but I could see that he was pleased.

"If that root cellar's nothing but a hole in the ground, then the *Queen Mary*'s nothing but a leaky old tub," Mum said, which pleased him even more. "You did a grand job on it, Albert, a grand job."

The next afternoon I drove Mum to the Miyashitas' for tea. I'd no sooner stuck a foot out the car door before Mrs. Miyashita whisked me off to inspect the root cellar. In her rush, she even forgot to shake Mum's hand. I have to say that as root cellars go, it was spectacular. It measured a good eight feet long by five feet wide and at least seven or eight feet deep. A trap door set at an angle opened to a staircase so steep and narrow it was not much more than a glorified ladder. Still, it did have the requisite handrail. Three bins waiting to be filled with the fall crop of root vegetables occupied the length of one wall. A set of wooden shelves ran along the wall opposite them. The top shelf was no higher than my chin, and I wondered if Dad had run a little short of wood. Then I realized he had built them to Mrs. Miyashita's diminutive scale. The smell of fresh-sawn spruce and damp clay filled the dark interior. The only thing missing was a proper light—I'd done my inspection by flashlight—but the next week, Mr. Miyashita hired an electrician to install the wiring. My boss was nearly as delighted with that root cellar as his wife. I wouldn't have been surprised if he'd asked the electrician to hang a crystal chandelier. I know that he entertained the idea of getting his uncle to send him some special paper lanterns, but Canada's ever-deteriorating relations with Japan made that a non-starter. Eventually, he settled for the usual overhead bulb although he insisted on augmenting it with a strand of Christmas lights strung along the top shelf. Once he saw them, even my practical dad had to admit those coloured lights would add a festive element to fetching a spud for supper on a winter afternoon.

That evening Mum and I went for a stroll by the river. She was so proud of the root cellar she couldn't stop talking about it.

"Digging the hole was a bit of a job for your dad, especially when we hit clay, but after that it was plain sailing." A fine bit of understatement from someone who hadn't had to go at the clay with a pickaxe. Dad was a strong man and blacksmiths tend to be a pretty fit lot, but digging that cellar must still have been one hell of a job.

"We used the wood from Naylor's place. Remember the big stack of boards Dad lugged home the day he helped George tear down that old shed of his? Well, I sanded them up good as new. All that root cellar cost is a bag of nails and a little time and sweat. Besides, it kept your dad and me busy of an evening so we didn't miss you lot too much. It's good to have you home though, pet."

She put her arm around me, and we walked home through the summer twilight listening to the sounds of our street—the slap of skipping ropes on pavement, Porky Sanders's booming laugh, Mrs. Jamieson calling her children home to bed.

"Mum, why do you think the Miyashitas never had any children of their own? They seem to like kids."

"They did have a child," Mum said. "A little girl. She died in the flu epidemic."

"How old was she?"

"Just gone seven. Her name was Midori."

"And they never wanted another?"

"Tose had a bad time when Midori was born. She couldn't have another."

AFTER WE CAME home from Banff, Charlie and Mr. Miyashita continued to take photographs on day trips to the foothills. I think Mr. Miyashita was relieved to get away from the office and escape his newspapers with their dismal reports of the war—the Battle of Britain was underway and things were not looking good for the Allies. I often went with him and Charlie on these excursions and took along the fly rod Mrs. Miyashita had loaned me. One August morning just before dawn, we drove to a spot west of Bragg Creek to photograph a tall pine tree that had been blasted by lightning into a shape Mr. Miyashita found particularly interesting. I couldn't see the damaged tree's fascination myself, but it was near some excellent fishing so I was happy to tag along. As we drove, the sky turned from black to grey and the stars began to fade from view.

Mr. Miyashita led us by flashlight through the woods to a large clearing. His tree stood isolated near the centre, its silhouette now visible against the eastern sky. To the west, vestiges of night still cloaked the mountains. It was too dark for the trout to be up and biting, or for me to make my way down the steep bank of the stream that flowed along the south side of the clearing. Instead, I stood and watched while Charlie set up the view camera on its tripod. Mr. Miyashita fiddled with some last adjustments. Then we sat on a fallen log and waited for the perfect light. Even in summer, early mornings are cold in the foothills so we warmed ourselves with hot coffee from a thermos flask. We waited while the soft grey shadows gradually retreated and colour crept back to the world. I don't know how long we sat before Mr. Miyashita deemed the sun's rays to be at the perfect angle. Finally, after one last tweak to the focus, he tripped the shutter. At Charlie's urging—"Better bracket it, sir, just to be on the safe side"—he took a couple more shots, but I could tell he knew the first one was enough.

Before he packed the camera away, Charlie disappeared into the bushes to relieve himself of some of his three cups of coffee. He returned carrying an enormous moth on his open hand. It was so big it covered his palm.

"Have you ever seen anything like it?" He held his hand out to us. "Hard to believe it's real."

The wings were a pale, almost luminous green, and each had a tiny dark circle like an open eye at its centre. The back wings tapered to long swallow tails that trailed down Charlie's fingers. He gently lifted the moth from his own hand and placed it on the back of mine, where it sat motionless, like some exotic piece of jewellery. I felt the strange prickle of insect feet on my skin, but they did not move.

"Is it alive?" I asked.

"I think so," Charlie said. "I found it on the trunk of a poplar tree."

"If it's alive then why didn't it fly away when you went to pick it up? And why is it just sitting here on my hand? It must be dead."

"On the contrary, it is very much alive," said Mr. Miyashita. "That is a luna moth, *Actias luna*, one of the Saturniidae, and it is simply too cold to move. It must warm its wings in the sun before it can fly."

"Then you've seen one before?" Charlie asked.

"Yes, I have. But not many. I am very surprised to come across a luna moth in this part of the world, especially one so large. The wing span must be at least four inches. Perhaps a fraction more."

"Looks tropical, doesn't it?" Charlie said. "Like it has no business being in Alberta. It should be in a jungle, somewhere up the Amazon."

"Very flamboyant, indeed," Mr. Miyashita agreed. "Especially in a landscape as muted as this. It is most certainly not native to the foothills."

"Then how did it get here?" I asked.

"Probably blown in on the wind," Charlie said. "Look. I think it's starting to move."

I felt one of the legs jerk and saw an antenna stir a fraction. Perhaps the warmth from my hand was helping.

"I believe the luna moth is primarily a nocturnal creature, and this one must have been chilled to immobility last night," said Mr. Miyashita. "We should put it back in a tree so it can continue warming its muscles."

"But, sir, a bird might get it," Charlie protested. "Can't we stay and make sure it's safe until it can fly."

"It is not our business to meddle with . . ." Mr. Miyashita stopped in mid-sentence. "By all means, Charles. It will give us an opportunity to make a photographic record of your *Actias luna*. I think you may have made a rare find this morning. However, the view camera will not do at all. Perhaps you would be so good as to fetch the Rolleiflex?" Charlie raced off to the car to collect the smaller camera.

I stood holding the moth. Soon its legs began to stir, and the big wings gave a faint flutter or two. By the time Charlie returned, the flutter had become a distinct twitch. He took the moth from me and placed it in the sun on the trunk of a poplar sapling. Mr. Miyashita snapped some photos. As he did, the wings began to beat, in spasms at first, but soon in a blur of green that lifted the furry body off the branch, up into the morning light. We stood and watched until it was lost from sight in the trees.

Mr. Miyashita was right about Charlie making a rare find. In fact, it was unique. When I was doing my master's at the University of Alberta, an entomologist I'd got to know took me to the biology department to see Dr. Strickland's famous insect collection. I told him about Charlie's luna moth. He was skeptical and informed me that *Actias luna* was an eastern species, that there was no record of it occurring west of the Alberta-Saskatchewan border. I know he didn't believe I'd seen one at Bragg Creek. He said that in order to verify a sighting for the official record, a specimen must be collected and preserved, and what a pity it was we hadn't done this. Moths were easy to kill, he added, especially big ones in a comatose state like Charlie's luna.

1940 WAS CHARLIE'S summer for parties. We had one for him in June when he graduated from high school and, as usual, another on his birthday. After we returned from Banff, Mum was busy kitting him out to start university in Edmonton that September. Nevertheless, she still found time to bake a cake and put up paper streamers in the backyard. Taking a cue from Mr. Miyashita and the root cellar, she even strung Christmas lights in the lilac bushes and plugged them into an extension cord that she ran from an outlet in the kitchen.

That Saturday night, Dad and Charlie built a bonfire from the last scraps of Naylor's shed. When the guests arrived, we roasted sausages over the coals on long-handled toasting forks that Dad had made with specially twisted tines to keep the sausages from falling off. After the candles and cake, Charlie plugged the gramophone into the extension cord, and we danced on the lawn.

Norman couldn't get leave, but Terps and her sisters came, and so did some of Charlie's school friends, and a few of our neighbours, including Porky Sanders, who popped over from next door to deliver his wife's complaints about the racket and then stayed on for cake and punch. The Miyashitas missed the sausages but arrived in time to watch Charlie blow out his candles. They didn't stay long and neither did Canon Giles, who had given Mr. Ledger a ride to our place. Mr. Ledger was crestfallen when Mrs. Miyashita told him she had to leave before the dancing began. However, as senior guest, it fell to him to give the birthday toast and that perked him right back up. He began by offering formal, but obviously heartfelt, congratulations to young Charles on the occasion of his eighteenth birthday, and ended by wishing him great success in his university studies and all his future endeavours.

On the Monday after the party, Charlie announced that he was joining the air force.

Assignment #9
DO YOU ENJOY TRAVELLING?

Assignment #10
WAS (OR IS) THERE A GREAT LOVE IN YOUR LIFE?

JANICE GAVE US TWO ASSIGNMENTS today—one for this week and the other to occupy us during the week she'll be on holiday. She is so excited about going to Mexico that she could hardly remember where she was this afternoon, let alone pay the rapt attention that's expected of her during our class readings. She and her latest boyfriend leave Saturday for a seven-day package holiday in Puerto Vallarta. He's a snow boarder she met on the slopes at Kananaskis over Christmas. All this great-love-of-your-life stuff led Meggie and me to conclude that poor Janice has fallen hard. We invited her for a bon voyage drink after class and, with hardly any prompting, heard all about the awesome Todd—looks to die for, fabulous athlete, really smart and funny and romantic. However, we suspect that he's broke (he'll pay me back), unemployed (he's going to look for a job as soon as we get home), and a womanizer (he's totally over Stephanie). Todd sounds more than a bit dodgy to both of us, but that's probably just the generation gap talking. Besides, you're only young and stupid once, so you might as well enjoy it. God knows, Meggie and I both did.

On the other hand, old and stupid seems to be a permanent condition. At least it does if I'm the example. I was making such progress and feeling so strong that I reckoned I didn't have to bother with my walker simply to get from my chair to the bathroom. Of course, I tripped and fell. Fortunately, I didn't break anything this time, but I did bang myself up pretty badly. The two black eyes I got when I hit my head on the end of the bed are especially fetching. I still look like a senile panda, and it happened more than a week ago. The upshot is that Valentine's Day at home is no longer possible. I don't know which is worse, not going home or knowing that it's my own damn fault.

I missed last week's memoir class because of my fall too. I can't remember what the assignment was, although I'm sure Meggie told me. It must not have been too thrilling because I decided to give it a miss and finish work on My Significant Year instead. Actually, I'm not paying all that much attention to Janice's topics these days. Janice says that's good because the exercises she gives us are only jumping-off points and that I should write what I want to write.

As usual, Meggie and I spent some time discussing our new assignment. Turns out, we've both done more than our share of travelling. Between us we've visited every continent except Antarctica and enjoyed ourselves immensely in the process. However, Meggie thinks that she wasn't really a traveller, she was only a tourist. According to her, a tourist goes on trips and returns home the same person, but a traveller is forever and fundamentally changed by the journey. I'm not sure I agree, but it is a view I hadn't considered, and one that puts my own travel in a very different perspective. By Meggie's definition, I've been a tourist too, more often than not. Perhaps the only time in my life I was a traveller was on a trip to Hong Kong in the autumn of 1941. That journey was so strange, so full of things beyond my experience, I sometimes have difficulty believing it happened. But I know that it did because it was beyond my imagination too.

If I'm to be honest, I have to admit my Hong Kong trip remains an unfinished chapter in my life, one I have avoided rereading. If I were wise, I'd probably close the book and leave it at that. Then again, if I were wise I wouldn't have fallen off a chair and ended up at Foothills Sunset with nothing better to do than rake through the past. All right, Kay—she gives herself one upside the head—stop this depressing rambling. You're about two moans and a sigh away from *Question Period*. So get on with it. Now.

SO MUCH HAPPENED in the year between Charlie's joining the air force and my trip that I suppose it's inevitable some of the details have become a bit muddled. On the other hand, the connections between the events that led me to Hong Kong are now much clearer than they were back then. In hindsight, the links seems so obvious that it is easy to trace how one led to another. But believe me, at the time, nothing was obvious, at least not to me.

Charlie was called up to Edmonton in September of 1940 to begin his basic training. The weeks preceding his departure had been grim, especially the one right after his birthday party. When he turned eighteen, Charlie became of legal age to sign up for the army. However, my brother had his heart set on becoming a pilot, and in order to join the air force, he either had to be twenty-one or have permission from his parents. Mum flatly refused to sign the consent papers and wouldn't be budged. Although not as intractable as Mum, Dad balked at signing too. But Charlie was determined. Their fights were long and loud and futile. The stony silences that followed were worse. Finally, Dad capitulated.

"Permission or no, he'll manage somehow," Dad said. "Charlie's dead keen and nothing we say will stop him. He'll get into the air force one way or another, so we'd best make up our minds to it and sign the damn papers."

In the end, Mum admitted the truth of what Dad said and signed too. She regretted her surrender until the day she died. I don't think she ever slept properly after Charlie left. If I woke in the middle of the night, I'd hear her prowling the house. Sometimes, I'd get out of bed and go downstairs to the living room, where I'd find her, sitting in the dark with a book on her lap, staring out at the empty street. She suffered from insomnia for the rest of her life.

By Christmas, the first shock of Charlie's absence had passed, but oh how we missed him, not just my family but the Miyashitas and all our other friends too. Especially Terps. We'd have missed him if he'd gone off to university, but this was different. We were afraid for him and rightly so. I know Mum prayed that he would not qualify for flight training, but he did. When he was sent to the Elementary Flying Training School in Lethbridge, she prayed he would wash out as a pilot and be sent to a safer job. When he turned out to have a special aptitude for flying, she prayed he would not be killed in training. An appalling number of student pilots died in training accidents. All the while, the war ground on, and no one was foolish enough to think that it would end before Charlie got his wings and was ready to join the fight. The news was grim that year. The papers carried regular tallies of the Allied ships sunk by German U-boats, as well as news of the Luftwaffe's bombing raids on Britain. The industrial areas in the midlands and the north were hard hit; even little Morpeth, Mum's hometown, did not escape.

Charlie got a week's Christmas leave, but he had to be back in Lethbridge on the thirtieth of December. There was no party for us that New Year's Eve. Not that there was much to celebrate. Wishes for a happy 1941 seemed more ironic than heartfelt. Later in January, he went on to the next stage of his training and was posted to the Service Flying Training School at Fort Macleod. He couldn't come home in February for my twenty-first birthday, so we decided to postpone the real party until late March when he was supposed to have a few days leave. As it turned out, he only got twenty-four hours. Still, Mum baked me an extra-fancy cake and put up the crepe paper streamers. Our friends came to cheer as I blew out the candles. Terps was there, and Charlie spent most of the evening at her side. It was pretty obvious that he'd begun to regard Terps as a lot more than a pal. She was with us the next afternoon when we took him to the train station. Dad couldn't come because he wasn't able to get time off. The Ogden shops, once idled by the Depression, were back working to full capacity building engines for the Canadian Navy's Corvettes.

It was three women who stood and waved Charlie on his way. There were plenty of other mothers and sisters and girlfriends on the platform with us, all waving to boys who were little more than children. But those children became the men who flew the bombers that reduced Germany's cities to rubble, men who learned their deadly skills over the Canadian prairie. By then, the British Commonwealth Air Training Plan was well underway and the Fort Macleod school was one of many facilities located in Alberta. Charlie was seldom far from home until he was sent overseas. Unfortunately, that didn't mean we saw much of him. Like other families, we had to make do with letters. Charlie's were full of news about his progress as a pilot, or at least as much of it as he was allowed to talk about. He was thrilled by the whole business of flying. It was almost as if he were living a story out of one of the *Boy's Own Annuals* that our grandmother used to send him every Christmas. I wish I had still had those letters, especially the one describing his first flight. I looked for them after Mum died, but I did not find them among her things.

Pilot Officer Charles Jeynes got his wings in February 1941. We all expected him to be shipped overseas immediately. Instead, he was sent to Ontario to be trained as a flight instructor, which did not please him at all. He qualified after two months and then went to teach at the flying school in Saskatoon. Amazing when you think of it. Until the previous September, Charlie had never been in an airplane. There he was seven months later, teaching other fellows to fly. But Charlie wanted to fight, not teach. He put in for overseas duty at every opportunity.

MY OWN ROUTINE was as ordinary as ever. I went to the office on weekdays. I spent time with my friends at the weekends. I wrote to Charlie and Norman every Sunday afternoon. I lived my life.

The Miyashitas invited me to accompany them to Banff again that summer, but I couldn't leave my parents on their own for a month to worry about Charlie. I did go, but only for a few days at the beginning of the trip. Nikkou and I spent the rest of July in Calgary with Mum and Dad and Charles Darwin. By the time Mr. Miyashita came back to the office, I had enough questions about *The Origin of Species* to occupy our coffee breaks past Christmas. He did his best to help me, but it was obvious his heart wasn't in our tutorials. Neither was his head. He wasn't able to concentrate on anything just then and neglected both the stock market and his photography. I don't think he'd enjoyed his Banff holiday much either because he and Mrs. Miyashita came home a week early.

Mr. Miyashita did not mention anything about my going to Hong Kong until late October, although I think he may have begun to consider the possibility much earlier. Right after Labour Day, he asked me to apply for a passport, saying it was customary for secretaries who worked for international companies to have current travel documents. Because our office did next to no business I failed to see his logic but did as I was told. This took place shortly after he received word of his uncle's death.

Uncle Nori had died in August and left Mr. Miyashita his collection of Sharaku woodblock prints. There were fifty of them altogether, including a complete set of the kabuki actor head and shoulder portraits like the one of Tokuji. Those prints would probably be worth a few million today. Even in 1941, they'd have fetched a pretty penny, but their monetary value was of no significance to Mr. Miyashita. For him, Uncle Nori's Sharakus represented a last connection to his mother and to the part of his Japanese past that he loved. His uncle's death grieved him, but so did the fact that there was little chance he would ever claim his inheritance. The Japanese government took a dim view of exporting the country's cultural treasures, and fifty Sharaku portraits would certainly have fallen into that category. There seemed to be no way for Mr. Miyashita to prevent his prints from remaining in a legal limbo in Japan. I think he also worried that somehow they'd end up going to his own family. However, even if he could have obtained official permission from the Japanese government to allow for the export of the prints, there still wouldn't have been a hope of getting them into Canada due to the near-complete collapse of relations between the two countries. Virtually all trade had stopped by 1941. In July, Ottawa had frozen Japan's Canadian assets, including those of Miyashita Industries.

Neither the trade ban nor the freeze of the company's assets made much difference to life at the office. Mr. Miyashita had the company name removed from the door, but that was it. Besides, Miyashita Industries' sole remaining Canadian asset, all that was left to freeze, was a single bank account, and although its balance was substantial, the money was irrelevant to my boss. I don't think he even noticed that the company funds had been frozen. They simply did not matter to him.

On the other hand, Ottawa's order-in-council requiring every Japanese Canadian over the age of sixteen to carry an official identification card did. That such a thing could happen in his beloved Canada shocked him profoundly. In March of 1941, the RCMP began the compulsory registration, photographing, and fingerprinting of every person of Japanese ancestry then living in Canada. Neither the Mounties nor the military authorities considered them a threat, but that did not deter Mackenzie King's government. The fact that many of those targeted had been born in Canada, as had their parents, counted for nothing. Even though their families had lived here far longer than my own English Johnny-come-latelies, the new law required them to carry an identity card with a photo and thumbprint on it. There were no exceptions.

Mr. Miyashita ignored the order. Neither he nor Mrs. Miyashita was photographed or fingerprinted until after Pearl Harbor. Perhaps the Mounties simply failed to notice one elderly couple living hundreds of miles inland. At that time, most Japanese lived on the West Coast and they were the focus of the prevailing hysteria. It was feared they might work as spies and saboteurs, especially the fishermen, who, rumour had it, were already secretly mapping the coast for the Imperial Navy. No one asked why the Imperial Navy would bother to do this when marine charts of both coasts had been available from the King's Printer for years. Common sense seemed to be in short supply and facts were conveniently ignored. For instance, Vancouver's Japanese community had been under covert surveillance by the RCMP since 1938, but the Mounties never discovered any Japanese engaged in subversive activity. Not a single person. That was a fact. It changed nothing.

The day compulsory registration went into effect, Canon Giles dropped by the office to offer support to his friend. A number of churches in Vancouver had protested the government's draconian measures. The Canon, along with a handful of colleagues from other denominations, made a similar stand in Calgary. A fat lot of good it did them. The gentlemanly protest of a few outraged clergymen was hardly noticed. If I hadn't known Canon Giles, I doubt that I'd have heard about it myself. Mr. Miyashita was angry too, but his anger was oddly detached. That morning he spoke as if he, personally, had nothing at stake.

"These people are Canadians," Mr. Miyashita said to the Canon. "How can we allow the government to do such a thing to our own citizens?"

Canon Giles had no answer.

THE TELEGRAM NOTIFYING Mr. Miyashita of Uncle Nori's death and his bequest was the first communication he'd had from Japan in months, and even that did not come directly from Hiroshima. A friend of Uncle Nori's, a Mr. Nakimura, sent the information to his cousin, a businessman living in Hong Kong. The cousin, in turn, forwarded the news to Calgary by telegram. We found out later that Uncle Nori knew he was dying and, sometime in the weeks before, had given the prints to his friend for safekeeping. We did not hear anything more about them until early October when a second telegram from the Hong Kong Nakimura brought the surprising news that the Sharakus were safe in his office. The message was short and cryptic—ACTORS ARRIVED THIS OFFICE STOP AWAIT INSTRUCTION STOP. Somehow, the prints must have been smuggled out of Japan and into Hong Kong, hence the telegram's cloak-and-dagger language. I never knew this for certain, but there was no way they could have got there legally.

Hong Kong or Hiroshima, it made no difference to Mr. Miyashita because he still could not collect his Sharakus. Attempting to import them might draw attention to the fact that he had not registered with the Mounties. Out of touch as he seemed to be at times, he had enough common sense to realize this.

He dismissed my suggestion that Mr. Nakimura could send them by mail. "Think of the newspapers, Miss Jeynes," he said. His foreign papers now arrived sporadically if at all. The mailman hadn't delivered a Japanese paper for months. "Think of the newspapers."

Mr. Miyashita also knew he could not travel to Hong Kong to collect them himself because once he crossed the border, he would not be allowed back into Canada. That afternoon he dictated a telegram for me to send to Hong Kong, thanking the cousin for his help and requesting him to continue sheltering the actors until further notice.

For the next week, Mr. Miyashita was restless and preoccupied. He became even more distracted with the arrival of another telegram from the Hong Kong Nakimura: ACTORS MUST LEAVE SOONEST STOP ADVISE STOP. He had me wire back immediately, requesting that Nakimura keep the prints until at least the beginning of the New Year. Nakimura replied the next day stating in terms that were no less blunt for being veiled that the actors must be gone before the end of November at the latest because he was closing his office and leaving

Hong Kong for good. After November 30, the actors would be left to fend for themselves. Mr. Miyashita read the telegram through twice, went into his office, and closed the door. I didn't see him for the rest of the afternoon.

One morning the week after Thanksgiving, he asked me to track down a phone number for an old school friend of his who had settled in San Francisco. Seiji Watanabe had immigrated to California the year before Mr. Miyashita was banished to Calgary. At first they kept in touch, but eventually their correspondence petered out, and they had not communicated in almost thirty years. Mr. Miyashita thought, or more likely hoped, that his friend might still be living in San Francisco, but he did not have an address to help narrow the search as he had always sent his letters care of General Delivery. Truth be told, after all those years he didn't know if Mr. Watanabe was even alive. Personally, I thought our chances of finding the man were slim to none. Nevertheless, a diligent telephone operator in San Francisco managed to track down listings for two S. Watanabes. Those were the days before direct dialing, so I got her to place a station-to-station call to the first number. I reached a woman who spoke no English but still managed to get very agitated when I said I was calling from Canada.

"Canada, no! No Canada! No no no! Canada, no!" she shouted. To this day I wonder why the mention of Canada, surely one of the world's most unalarming nations, roused such passion in her. While she ranted, I put Mr. Miyashita on the line. Speaking in Japanese, he quickly determined that the number did not belong to the S. Watanabe he knew. We were both relieved.

The other number listed was for an import-export business, S. Watanabe & Son. This time I got the operator to place a person-to-person call. A young man answered and asked the operator to wait while he called his father to the phone. Then, much to my amazement, Mr. Miyashita's old friend Seiji came on the line. The two of them talked in Japanese at the top of their lungs. I had no trouble hearing Mr. Watanabe's end of the conversation. It carried quite clearly from the phone in Mr. Miyashita's office all the way out the door to where I sat at my desk. I couldn't understand a word, but judging by the laughter at both ends of the line, their talk was a happy one and it lasted for almost an hour. This was unheard of in those days when long distance was pricey. Nevertheless, he called his friend every few days. Although the news still commanded Mr. Miyashita's attention to a degree, only those conversations with Mr. Watanabe fully engaged his interest. They always spoke Japanese, so I have no idea what they discussed.

As the month wore on, Mr. Miyashita began to seem worried as well as distracted. He started to fret about my passport, which still had not been sent from Ottawa. It finally arrived the week before Halloween. After that, his phone calls to Mr. Watanabe became a daily occurrence. Then one morning, in a reversal of the usual process, Mr. Watanabe phoned him. Afterwards, my boss emerged from his office looking happier than I'd seen him in months.

"Miss Jeynes, I have an important request to make of you," he said, sounding relaxed and almost like his old self. "Please note that it is a request and only a request. I am most assuredly not issuing an order as your employer. It is important that you make the distinction because you must feel free to say no. However, before you come to a decision, I would like you to consider what I have to say very carefully. Please do not give me an answer today. You must first go home and discuss my request with your parents. Will you do this?"

"Yes, sir," I said, wondering what could need such an elaborate introduction.

"Very well then. As you know, it is a matter of some urgency that my late uncle's Sharaku prints find their way to Calgary from Hong Kong before the first of December. For reasons we need not discuss, it is presently inconvenient for me to make the trip to collect them myself. That is why I am asking you to consider going in my place."

I was stunned. Hong Kong? Me? The Kay Jeynes who'd never been farther away from home than Revelstoke? I opened my mouth to speak, but no sound came out so I closed it again. I must have looked like a fish gasping its last.

"Time is running out for the prints, so it is important that you travel as quickly as possible," he said. "That is why you must go by air.

Pan American Airways operates a regular flying boat service from San Francisco to Hong Kong. The Clipper makes a number of overnight stops en route, but it is still much faster than going by sea."

"I've seen the Pan American flying boats in the news at the movies." I finally managed to stammer out a few words. "They're big."

"Yes, they are. Very big indeed," Mr. Miyashita agreed with a tolerant smile. "But more important, they are also very fast."

He could have added very expensive to the list. In those days, a trip to China by air cost a fortune. You had to be either stinking rich or a VIP to travel on the trans-Pacific Clippers. Business tycoons and movie stars frequently appeared in the news reels, walking up the gangplank to the flying boats moored at the Pan Am dock in San Francisco Bay. They smiled and waved at the camera as they embarked on their journeys to places that, for most of us in those days before Pearl Harbor, were no more than exotic names scattered across a map. Manila, Macao, Noumea, Honolulu—that airplane was a byword for glamorous travel. Claire Booth Luce, a Pan Am passenger herself, once wrote that flying across the Pacific on the Clipper would someday be regarded as the most romantic voyage of all time. The only aircraft in recent years that approached a similar legendary status was the Concorde, but it could not touch the old flying boats for sheer luxury of service and the lavishness of the space provided for passengers. A trip on the Concorde was cheaper too, at least in relative terms. As I remember, my return San Francisco–Hong Kong ticket on the Clipper cost around sixteen hundred American dollars. That was almost as much as I earned in two years at my job. You could buy a perfectly respectable small house back then for very little more.

"The speed of these new Boeing 314s stretches the bounds of credibility," Mr. Miyashita continued. "San Francisco to Hong Kong and back in less than half the time it takes the fastest steamship to sail one way. Is that not an amazing feat?" He shook his head in wonder. "But we will speak no more of this today. You must go home and discuss it with your father and mother."

"Before I discuss anything with them, sir, I really should know when I would be leaving."

Mr. Miyashita opened his desk drawer and took out a small notebook that he consulted.

"I have booked a drawing room for you on the train to Vancouver leaving this Saturday. From Vancouver you proceed directly to San Francisco, where you stay for a night before flying to Honolulu on Wednesday afternoon. The Clipper lands in Hawaii the following morning, November 13. From there you continue the next day to Hong Kong, arriving Wednesday afternoon, the nineteenth of November. Please note, that takes into account your crossing the International Date Line. I have notified Mr. Nakimura's cousin in Hong Kong of your arrival time, and he has agreed to meet the plane and bring the prints with him. That way you can complete your business in time to reboard the Clipper next morning and begin the return journey. You will be back in San Francisco by November 26 and home in Calgary by the end of the month." He closed the notebook.

"Think of it, Miss Jeynes. You will fly across the Pacific and back in less than two weeks. When I consider my own journeys to and from Japan, I find this astounding."

"You mean the whole trip is booked?"

"Please, do not let that concern you. Admittedly, reservations on the Clipper are difficult to obtain—without the help of my friend Seiji Watanabe and his son, Robert, I doubt we could have booked passage for you. I myself am still not certain exactly how they managed it. But you must not let any of this concern you. Should you choose not to go, the whole trip can be cancelled without difficulty. However, we must not proceed with this discussion until you consult your parents and come to a decision."

What was there to decide? Of course I wanted to go. How could a young woman with an ounce of adventure in her soul refuse such an offer? My only worry was that my parents might be reluctant to give their permission. I knew they would find the prospect of their daughter travelling halfway around the world on her own daunting. I did myself. That afternoon, as I sat at my desk unable to concentrate on the accounts payable file in front of me, I mustered all the arguments I could in support of my decision. I rehearsed them as I walked home. I wanted to sound reasonable and mature and responsible. I had to convince Mum and Dad that I was now a grown woman of twenty-one, capable of looking after herself on a long journey. I certainly thought I was. Well, almost certainly. After all, if Charlie could learn to fly an airplane at the age of eighteen, then surely his older sister could manage to sit in one.

My careful arguments proved unnecessary. Naturally Mum and Dad were taken aback when they heard my news, but Mum made us a pot of tea and we sat at the kitchen table discussing Mr. Miyashita's request in a surprisingly reasonable manner. The international situation did concern my parents, but their worries were focused on Europe, where Charlie would be sent to fight. Canada was still at peace with Japan. For most of us back then, it was unthinkable that Japan would launch a direct attack on the United States or on the British stronghold of Hong Kong. Everyone assumed that if the Japanese did make further moves to expand their empire, they would invade the resource-rich countries of Southeast Asia. We never dreamed they would bomb Pearl Harbor first.

"It's not a good time for a person to be so far away from home. The world being what it is right now, nothing's safe," said Mum. "What if something should happen while you're away?"

Perhaps she was talking about world politics, but I took her to mean what if something should happen to Charlie.

"I won't be away all that long. I only spend one night in Hong Kong and then leave for home the next morning."

"How long would you be away?" Dad asked. "Would you be back before Christmas?"

"By air, San Francisco to Hong Kong is less than a week there and a week back. Add on the return train trip from Calgary to San Francisco and it's still nowhere near a month. More like three weeks and a bit. I'll be home ages before Christmas." Right then, I believed it too.

"I guess we should try to look on it as a real opportunity, a trip like this, shouldn't we?" I knew Mum was not expecting an answer. She was convincing herself. "It's a once-in-a-lifetime chance to see the world and it would be a pity to let it slip away. But I still can't help worrying about you being off on your own on the other side of the world."

"Where would you be staying when you're not on this airplane?" Dad asked.

"Pan American puts you up all the way from San Francisco to Hong Kong and back. Accommodation, meals—they take care of everything."

"Well, I suppose that counts for something."

"After all, she'd be on an American airplane with a big American company looking out for her," Mum said. Now my parents were doing their best to reassure each other.

"You've got a point there," Dad said. "The Yanks may not be much for helping their friends, but they do look after their own."

"I've heard that those big new planes are very safe. At least that's what they say on the news at the pictures. Safest airplanes ever built, they call them. Still, it's an awful distance from home for a youngster to be travelling, especially a girl all on her own."

"I know it's hard, Judith, but we have to remember that Kay's gone twenty-one and earning her own way in the world. No matter what we think, she's going to make her own decisions."

Mum turned to me. "Your dad's right, Kay. When you get down to brass tacks, it is up to you. Go or not—that's something you have to decide for yourself. But you mustn't expect us to stop worrying about you, pet. You're still our Kay."

I don't know if I could have been so reasonable had one of my own children presented me with a similar situation. Probably not. Sometimes I think my mum and dad were far wiser parents than I ever was. However, I also think they knew that, like Charlie, I would have gone no matter what they said. By leaving the decision to me, they'd saved us all a lot of pointless grief.

Oddly enough, the one person who did voice strong objections was Mrs. Miyashita. She made no secret of the fact that she thought it reckless of her husband to put me at risk for something as inconsequential as mere material objects like the Sharaku prints. To be fair, Mr. Miyashita did inform me of his wife's opinion, although he neglected to mention the vehemence with which she held it. Mrs. Miyashita did that for herself. She marched into the office the next morning and insisted I put on my coat and hat because she was taking me out for tea. We had hardly settled into our chairs at Picardy's before she began to talk. She was so overwrought that I had more difficulty than usual understanding her. The rather embarrassing gist was that although Uncle Nori's prints were precious—and it was plain Mrs. Miyashita had her doubts on that score—their value could not begin to compare with mine. I was more precious than all the Sharakus in the world. It was the first and only time I heard her disagree with her husband. Except for this single instance, she always deferred to him, at least publicly. Her outburst was so out of character that it shocked me. But it did not convince me to stay home.

Once Mrs. Miyashita accepted that I could not be dissuaded, she was very helpful. That afternoon she took me to see Miss Peebles and had her whip up a couple of travelling outfits on a rush order. One was a tropical-weight navy blue suit that I'll never forget. It had a double-breasted jacket with padded shoulders, fitted waist, and a belt, worn over a straight skirt that stopped just below the knee. The redoubtable Miss P. copied it from a photo of a Schiaparelli model that caught my eye in a summer issue of *Vogue* in the stack of old fashion magazines she kept in her waiting room. She even added a flourish of her own, a secret pocket sewn into the lining above the waist directly under my left arm. It was big enough to hold my passport and some paper money without spoiling the line of the jacket. I've never felt smarter in my life than I did in that sort-of Schiaparelli suit. I splurged on a chic little hat and a pair of kid gloves to add the finishing touches. I may not have been a sophisticated world traveller, but, damn it, I sure looked like one. Back then, flying was far from the everyday chore it has become; people dressed up to travel on airplanes.

Luggage wasn't like it is today either, featherweight synthetics over alloy frames. Travellers regularly hauled their belongings in steamer trunks and heavy leather suitcases, all easily accommodated on ships and trains but totally inappropriate for airplanes. Meeting the Clipper's fifty-pound baggage limit could be a real challenge when your luggage alone could weigh that. Mrs. Miyashita solved the problem by buying me a cheap canvas suitcase and a leather strap to belt around it. She came to our house the afternoon before I left and packed it for me too.

Turned out, she was a packing genius, an absolute wizard at folding clothes so they occupied a minimum of space. I began to suspect her father had included a short course in suitcase management in his daughters' practical education. Or maybe it was all those years of origami.

After she finished, Mum made us a cup of tea, and I modelled my travelling outfit. I'd just picked up the suit from Miss Peebles that morning, so neither of them had seen the finished product. They both thought the secret pocket was brilliant and proceeded to lay down the law about how I absolutely must keep some money hidden in it for emergencies. They stopped just short of making me cross my heart and swear. I didn't tell either of them that I already had an envelope stuffed with bills, mostly American twenties and British five-pound notes, waiting to be tucked under my arm.

That morning, Mr. Miyashita had called me into the darkroom and opened a cupboard under the dry bench that I had always assumed held photographic paper. In reality, it hid a small safe with a combination lock. He showed me how to manipulate the dial.

"It is quite straightforward. The combination is 28-4-9. I chose those numbers because that is the date my wife and I arrived in Calgary to live, the twenty-eighth of April 1909. Now see if you can make it work."

It took me a few tries to get the hang of it, but finally the dial clicked into place, allowing me to pull the handle up and swing back the heavy door. I found myself staring at bundles of banknotes, all bound with paper bands and neatly stacked on two shelves. Canadian dollars, American dollars, British pounds—there must have been at least twenty-five thousand dollars in cash right in front of my nose. Dumbfounded doesn't cover it.

Mr. Miyashita closed the safe door and had me open and shut it three more times for practice. When I opened it for the last time, he removed a bundle of each currency and counted out a pile of bills.

"You will find that it is wise to carry cash in appropriate currencies when you travel," he said as he counted, "but you must not keep it all in one place. Some you may keep in your wallet where it will be readily accessible, but the lion's share is best hidden safely away. Even so, it is important that you keep it with you at all times." He replaced the remaining notes in the safe, closed the door, and spun the dial. "That is a cardinal rule for travellers, Miss Jeynes. Never be separated from your money. Never."

"Yes, sir," I said mostly because he seemed to expect a response. It was another of those cross-your-heart occasions.

"When I travelled to foreign places as a young man," he continued in a less emphatic manner, "I often wore a money belt under my clothing, and I have purchased one for you. However, my wife pointed out that this stratagem may not be convenient for young ladies. That is why I also took the liberty of calling Miss Peebles and asking her to construct a hidden pocket in the jacket of your new suit. You must keep enough money in it that, should your CPR travellers' cheques be stolen or you lose your documents or miss your airplane, you will still be able to pay your passage home."

"Stolen? You think I might be robbed?" At that moment, Hong Kong began to feel very far from home.

"Please, I mention these possibilities merely by way of example." Mr. Miyashita was quick to reassure. "I am certain that none of them is likely to occur. The chance of something so dire happening while you are with the CPR or Pan American is practically nil. But, as a traveller, you must always prepare for such remote contingencies. Then if something untoward should occur, you will be ready to take appropriate action, will you not?"

"I guess so," I said, sounding a bit wobbly. "At least I'll do my best."

"And I know that your best will be more than up to the occasion, Miss Jeynes. If I did not think you a highly intelligent and resourceful young person, I would never have asked you to undertake this task for me. I have every confidence that you will be a truly intrepid traveller."

I found it gratifying that Mr. Miyashita considered me intelligent and resourceful, although I knew that he was enjoying a bit of a joke at my expense with that last remark. As a matter of fact, it tickled him so much that from that afternoon on, he took to calling me his Intrepid Traveller. To a girl determined to regard herself as oh-so-sophisticated, this was wildly annoying.

Before we left the darkroom, he put the cash he had counted into an envelope. It added up to more than a thousand dollars, well over a year's salary for me, and would have paid my way back from Hong Kong by steamship ten times over.

"And by the way," he said as he handed it to me, "I do not think we need mention this extra bit of insurance outside the office, do we?"

"No, sir, we don't," I agreed.

And that is how Intrepid Traveller came to catch the CPR passenger train to Vancouver on Saturday morning, the eighth of November 1941.

MY GRANDDAUGHTER CAME to visit yesterday and brought my old snow-boot box with her. We had a grand time poking through the bits and pieces—a photo of Nikkou Mum had taken in our backyard, a ticket for the Clipper, a postcard I'd sent to Mum and Dad from Hong Kong that wasn't delivered until the summer of 1946. How ancient all of it must have looked from Sally's twenty-five-year-old perspective. She even told me I should leave my "papers" (AKA old junk) to the University of Calgary archives. I suppose she has reason to be a little cracked on the subject of historical preservation since she's in the middle of a PHD in archaeology. (I'm beginning to suspect there's a gene for history in our family.) I should ask her what a future archaeologist might make of Meggie's swizzle sticks. Speaking of which, Sally came with me to Meggie's room at drinks time. She lugged the boot box along, and the three of us continued sifting through the detritus of my life. Curiosity drove Meggie to wear her glasses. She came across a snapshot that Mum had taken of me all dressed up in my travelling suit the afternoon before I left for Hong Kong. It was a bit of a shock to see how young I was in that photo. Still, Sally thought I looked pretty dishy—at least that's what Meggie and I understood "Hey, Gran, you were really hot" to mean.

Janice was spot on about old odds and ends triggering memories. Until I saw myself in that photo, I didn't remember how it felt to stand there all those years ago on the brink of a journey that would take me halfway round the world. I know I didn't sleep much the night before I left. I was too excited to be tired.

Over the years, I've travelled by train many times in many parts of the world, but I've never felt the way I did that Saturday morning when

The Dominion steamed out of the CPR station, taking me to Vancouver on the first leg of my journey. I'm sure part of the exhilaration was sheer relief at finally being on my own, away from Mum and Dad and the Miyashitas. They'd all fussed over me so much in the last week that it was lovely to sit in my private drawing room with the door shut and nothing to do but watch the Rockies pass my window.

The Dominion pulled into Revelstoke around six that evening, bringing me to the outer limit of my previous travels. Everything beyond was terra incognita. Although it was snowing a little and almost dark, I got off the train and strolled along the platform to stretch my legs. There must have been a mill nearby because the air smelled of woodsmoke and fresh-sawn timber. The cold cut through my thin raincoat, but I walked the length of the train and back a couple of times before the conductor called the "all aboard" and I climbed up the steps to the warmth and my dinner. As I sat watching the waiters weave through the swaying dining car with their loaded trays, I had the feeling that the bonds tethering me to Calgary and the familiar were stretching thinner and thinner by the mile. I wondered if I would feel them snap, or if they would simply disappear. Either way, I knew I would leave the old Kay Jeynes behind, that I would be free to become a new Kay Jeynes, a Kay who could be whatever I chose. Then the waiter put a plate of salmon in front of me and broke the spell.

I'd packed away a good lunch, but I still made short work of that salmon. The CPR's Chinese cooks turned out superb meals in their rolling kitchens. The company prided itself on the freshness and quality of its cuisine; the dining car menu traditionally featured the specialty of the area that the train was passing through—Winnipeg goldeye in Manitoba, Alberta beef on the prairies, salmon in British Columbia. The railway set an elegant table too, with the same linens, china, and heavy silver plate familiar to me from the Banff Springs. Despite the motion of the train, nothing on a CPR dining car table dared to rattle except the ice in the water pitchers.

Intrepid Traveller was too shy to strike up a conversation with any of her fellow passengers. After dinner I took my overstuffed self back to my room and read until I felt sleepy. As I shook the folds out of my nightgown, an origami crane fell to the floor. Mrs. Miyashita must have slipped it in while she was packing. She'd written a message in tiny characters on the white wings, the Japanese equivalent of bon voyage, I assumed. Like many of my assumptions, that one proved false. Years later, I happened to come across the crane tucked away in an old passport case at the back of a drawer. I showed it to a friend of ours whose company had enrolled him in a Japanese language course for businessmen. He copied out the characters to take home for translation practice and later informed me that the message read, "May good fortune fly with you, my beautiful girl," or perhaps it was ". . . my beautiful daughter." His Japanese was still pretty basic so he couldn't say for certain. That night on The Dominion, I put the crane in my secret pocket, where it remained for the whole trip, my good luck talisman. Then, remembering Mr. Miyashita's cardinal rule for travellers, I folded my suit jacket, placed it under the covers between me and the window, and turned out the light. The last thing I remember is listening to the sound of the wheels change in timbre as the train passed over a trestle somewhere west of Kamloops. When the porter knocked on my door, it was seven-thirty in the morning, and we were an hour out of Vancouver.

In Vancouver, the CPR collected those of us who were going to the US and put us on the *Princess Marguerite*, one of their West Coast Steamers, bound for Seattle. It was a fine day, with sunlight glancing off the water and breeze enough to fill the canvas of the pleasure craft out for a Sunday sail in the Strait of Juan de Fuca. I'd never seen the ocean before, and although Mr. Miyashita had reserved a stateroom for me, I spent most of my time on deck. At one point, I spotted an ocean liner in white tropical livery steaming for Vancouver. The man standing next to me at the rail said it was the *Empress of Japan*, but the fellow next to him, who seemed to have made a hobby of the shipping news, thought it had to be the *Empress of Asia*. They asked me where I was headed, and when I answered Hong Kong, they immediately wanted to know what ship. I impressed them no end when I said I wasn't sailing, that I was flying on the Clipper.

That night I climbed aboard a Southern Pacific train in Seattle.

My day in the sea air had me in bed and asleep before it pulled out of the station.

MEMOIR CLASS MET today even though Janice is away. Getting together every Wednesday afternoon has become a habit. As usual, people read from what they'd written for last week's assignment. When it was his turn, Jim Leandros told us he had intended to write about being taken to Greece by his father back in 1928. He was five years old, and his father wanted to show him off to the relatives in the old country. However, Jim said that the minute he sat down to work on the assignment, he realized he hadn't a memory of his own for the telling. Everything he thought he knew about the trip had been told to him later by other people. He is certain of only one thing: he stood on a path and petted a baby donkey. That single memory is so vivid that, to this day, he can almost feel the tickle of whiskers as the tiny creature tried to suckle his fingers, and see its pink hooves, no bigger round than quarters, planted in the dust in front of his own scuffed, little boots. But, for the life of him, he cannot recall a single member of his father's family. He wondered why he has no recollection of his own grandfather when that baby donkey has stayed with him a lifetime.

This started quite the discussion. Dave's theory is that you remember the things that were most important to you at the time although you don't always remember why they were important. He said Jim was probably feeling lost among all those strange adults, and that a five-year-old boy would be missing his mother too. Because the baby donkey was his own size, stroking its warm little body probably comforted him just like cuddling a teddy bear might. Believe me, that's not the dumbest thing Dave has ever said. Even so, I'm sticking to my theory that memories, both the important and the trivial, are all stored away in your brain waiting for a trigger—a sound, a slant of light, a smell—to flash them into your conscious mind. Jim's grandfather just needs the right trigger and there he'll be.

Meggie says that sort of reminds her of the French guy who dunked a cookie in his tea and then wrote a zillion-page book about it. She's even willing to admit that it's a lovely theory, although for her it will remain only a theory until something flashes the present whereabouts of her missing television remote into her mind. Still, she thinks it's a waste of time to fret about gaps in your memory, especially if you are as old as we are. We should be happy we can remember anything, and even happier that we're still here to do it. After all, our memories are like everything else—they slip with age. As cheeks sag to jowls and chins droop to wattles, so the moorings of memory slacken and pieces of the past drift away on the currents of time.

Meggie added that we should consider ourselves two of the lucky ones because despite her stroke and my fractures, the pair of us are still the "got all her marbles" kind of old ladies. Neither of us shows any signs of being off with the fairies yet (or so we like to think), and for this we should be profoundly grateful. What could I say to that but amen?

As a matter of fact, Meggie and I have both found that in tackling Janice's weekly topics, we are constantly surprised by what we do recall. It's almost as if the more you remember, the more you can remember. What a very odd process this has turned out to be. Kind of like a mental version of my physio sessions—the farther I walk, the farther I can walk. No wonder Janice calls our writing assignments exercises.

Even so, I have to admit that one piece of my past has definitely drifted: the day I spent in San Francisco in 1941. Such a wonderful city, you'd think I couldn't possibly forget my first visit, but there's very little about it I'd swear to. I've been to San Francisco many times over the years, so it could be that the trips have become jumbled in my mind. Or perhaps what happened later in Honolulu and Hong Kong simply overshadowed everything else. Besides, I was only there for a night and part of the next day. It was a lovely day too, brisk and sunny with an ozone-fresh breeze off the sea. Either that or memory has once again triumphed over meteorology. I'm sure I went for a ride on a cable car but only because Mum kept the postcard I sent. I'd marked the place where I sat with an X.

I know for certain that I telephoned the Watanabes to deliver Mr. Miyashita's greetings and to thank them for booking my passage on the Clipper. I spoke to Robert, who informed me that my ticket was waiting for me at the Pan American terminal. He added that a good friend of his would be travelling on the same plane. He and Peyto Willis had known each other since their Stanford days, and Peyto would be happy to give me any assistance I might need. I told Robert that I'd be pleased to meet his friend, but that I didn't anticipate needing help.

"You probably won't," he agreed. Then he added that it might be best if I didn't mention the role that he and his father had played in securing my ticket. "I'm sorry to have to say this, but Japanese names don't make good references these days. To be honest, if Peyto hadn't dealt directly with Pan American for us, you probably wouldn't be going anywhere. That's why you would be wise to play it safe and not mention my father or me. Or Hero Miyashita, for that matter. Especially not that you're working for him on this trip. If anyone asks why you're travelling, tell them you're on a holiday. Not that there's anything to worry about. But on the off-chance you do run into trouble, Peyto will be there to give you a hand. He's flown to Hong Kong on the Clipper three or four times, so he knows the ropes. You can count on him."

"How will I recognize him?" I asked.

"He knows your name. He says he'll find you in the terminal."

"I'll look forward to meeting him," I said, more to be polite than to acknowledge any need for help.

"And by the way, I'd really appreciate it if you didn't tell Mr. Miyashita that Peyto is the one who got you your Clipper ticket. I haven't told my father because he's upset enough as it is about the way people are starting to treat us Japanese here in the States. I don't want him to know that there's no way either of us could have got you on that plane. He and Mr. Miyashita both think I'm the one who dealt with Pan Am, so if you would leave it at that, I'd be grateful."

Later in the morning, I went to a bank, where I exchanged some of my American dollars for Hong Kong dollars. I remember that very clearly too, mainly because the teller never batted an eye. If I'd done the same thing in a Calgary bank, I'd have been the topic of the day.

In the same way Jim knows he went to Greece when he was five, I know that Treasure Island is a man-made island in San Francisco Bay built as the site of the 1939 San Francisco World's Fair and as the centre of Pan American's flying boat operations on the West Coast. There wasn't much left of the fair by the autumn of 1941, but the sea plane port was busier than ever. The Pan American limo dropped me off in front of the terminal, and that's where my memories really begin.

The terminal had previously served as the fair's administration office. Pan American took it over when the exposition closed. It was a white, three-storey structure built in an imposing semicircle that I'm certain measured well over a hundred yards across. It really was longer than the proverbial football field. Aside from that one fundamental curve, the rest of the building, including the flight control tower on the top, was all angles and straight lines, a monument to art deco. A statue of Neptune clutching an airplane to his manly bosom stood near the front entrance. I recall not feeling all that heartened by its implications. I saw the terminal again last year when it turned up on television in a Hollywood movie, playing the role of Berlin Airport. They'd dressed it up in enormous Nazi flags, but it was instantly recognizable to someone who'd known the old place before it went into show biz.

I must admit I have a special affection for that building. It's where I met Peyto for the first time. He caught my eye the minute he walked through the door, or rather his panama suit did. Until then, I'd never seen a man in a white suit except in the movies. I suppose Peyto was what young Janice would call My Great Love. I fell in love with him on the flight to Honolulu. Or at least I felt the overwhelming sexual infatuation that someone as young as I was then can mistake for love. Who knows, maybe I wasn't mistaken. Maybe Peyto really was My Great Love. I never got a chance to find out. I do know for certain that he was My Great Romance. There I was, alone and far from home, off on a once-in-a-lifetime voyage to romantic places, a naive girl who fancied herself a woman of the world. The only thing needed to complete the scene was a dashing leading man. And along came Peyto.

That night, eight thousand feet above the Pacific, we sat and talked. It wasn't a particularly romantic conversation. He told me about his job, I told him about my family. We discovered we both liked dancing and Fred Astaire movies, so I told him about Charlie and me at talent night, and how worried we were about Charlie now that he was in the air force. That led us to talking about the war. Peyto thought that America would be in it pretty soon by the look of things. When that happened, he'd take leave from his job and join the navy if they'd have him. He had a good friend who was already serving on an aircraft carrier. It was all everyday stuff for the time, an ordinary conversation. But it did not feel ordinary to me. Finally, a weary steward interrupted. All the other passengers were in bed when, politely but firmly, he shepherded us to our separate berths.

My Great Romance and I didn't manage so much as a goodnight kiss. That first night, I lay alone between Pan American's pristine cotton sheets, awash in a sea of hormones. Peyto and I didn't make love until the day after we landed in Honolulu. We spent the next seven weeks doing our best to make up for lost time. He was my first and best lover. Sex with him was not merely a pleasure. Making love with Peyto was a joy. On a less romantic note, I would like to add that it was also one hell of a lot of fun.

But what an innocent I was back then. In some ways though, that innocence did have its advantages. Maybe I didn't know much about sex, but on the other hand, that meant I wasn't burdened with a lot of notions about what was proper behaviour in bed and what wasn't. To give Mum her due, when I began to menstruate, we did have the requisite talk about the birds and the bees, although our discussion dealt strictly with the theoretical, not the applied, aspects of the topic. "You'll find all that out when you're married," was as far as Mum's practical information went. As it turned out, ignorance was indeed bliss, at least it was for me. My lack of knowledge of what people actually did together when they made love allowed me to be a remarkably uninhibited learner. Enthusiastic too. At the beginning, I think I had a twinge of conscience about "going all the way," especially with a man I'd just met. I worried about getting pregnant, but the first time we had sex Peyto showed me how we could prevent that. So conscience stilled and worries quieted, I happily embarked on my life as a fallen woman. It was grand.

I was also naive enough to assume that what Peyto and I did in bed together was what everyone did. That might be true today when you consider that pretty much everything we got up to children can now watch on prime-time cable. But back then, it came as quite a shock when

I discovered that not all men were as uninhibited as Peyto. My husband, for one. I remember once, early in our marriage, when we were making love, I whispered to Ken that I had other lips besides the ones on my face and they would love to be kissed. The poor man was so shocked he couldn't speak. When he finally found his voice, he told me that oral sex, "that kind of perversion," as he called it, was something only whores did. He spent the rest of the night on the couch in the living room. (I wish I'd had the guts to ask him how he got to be such an expert on what whores did.) It was nearly a month before we had sex again.

Looking back, I don't think my husband's reaction was all that unusual, considering the time and place in which we both grew up. If anything, Ken had a fairly healthy attitude to sex. Believe me, back then plenty of men honestly believed that sex was something decent women simply endured in order to have children. I'm not sure they even realized that nice ladies like me could have orgasms or, come to think of it, that women had orgasms at all. Thank God, Ken wasn't one of them. Still, I don't suppose he could help being a bit of a prude any more than I could help comparing him with Peyto. Now I realize how unfair that comparison was. Peyto and I were together a matter of weeks—Ken and I were married almost fifty years and had three children. For all I know, if I'd spent fifty years with Peyto, he might not have lived up to my memory of him either. Still, pleasant as sex with Ken could be, it was nothing like the thrill of making love with Peyto. Affection cannot compete with passion.

NOW THERE'S A messy bit—a fistful of pages to rip out of my notebook. I cringe to think of my children and grandchildren reading that stuff. I don't care if they know I had a sex life—after all, how do they think they got here? But I do care about them reading what I wrote about Ken. Not because what I said about him isn't true but because it's disloyal. If Ken and I couldn't talk about our sex life when he was alive, then I can damn well keep my trap shut now he's dead. He was a good man and a good father and that's how his family should remember him. The rest is nobody's business but ours.

I won't rip out the pages about Peyto though. There is nothing to be ashamed of there and no one left to hurt except maybe me. Until now, I've never talked about him with anyone but Terps, and by the time of that conversation, we were both old women. It's time I told his story.

AT THE RATE I'm progressing, I'm not going to finish these notes before I go home. I promised myself that by the time I left Foothills Sunset I'd have them completed up to the end of the war, all ready to whip into shape for my real memoirs. Well, good luck to me. I've tried for an entire day and haven't managed to write a word about Peyto. I don't even know where to start—and that's not because my memory has failed me. Anything but. I can remember every day we were together, from my first glimpse of him in the Pan Am terminal to my last in the Seattle train station. Perhaps I can't get started because I do not want to consider what I lost when I got on that train back to Canada. At the time, I thought we would spend the rest of our lives together, that after the war we'd marry and live happily ever after. Maybe that dream could have turned into reality, although, looking back after all these years, I'm not so sure. But Peyto was killed at the Battle of Leyte Gulf and that was the end of it. Still, I would like someone besides me to know about him so that he won't die when I do. Even though we never got the chance to have children together, if I tell my own children and grandchildren about him perhaps, like Mum and Dad and Charlie and the Miyashitas, he can live a little longer in their memories. The Great Love in My Life or not, if Peyto hadn't been around to help me when I really needed it, I wouldn't be here today and neither would they.

Good God, I'm turning into a sentimental fool. Come on, Kay, you dreary old bag. Sharpen your pencil and get to work or you'll waste another day staring out the window. It's not like you have all that many days left. Just do as Janice says—begin at the beginning and carry on from there.

I remained true to my parents' principles and arrived at the Pan Am terminal so early I was the first person to check in. I showed the clerk at the counter my passport, and identity established, he handed me my ticket along with a small, zippered bag in which to pack my overnight things before my suitcase was weighed and whisked away. Everyone and everything that went aboard the Clipper was weighed and then stowed so that the plane's hull floated level in the water. Apparently this was especially important for takeoffs and landings. Thanks to Mrs. Miyashita's packing expertise, I was not one of those unfortunate souls forced to stand in public pawing through the contents of a bulging suitcase to extract a nightie and toothbrush. Mine were conveniently to hand at the top of the case. After that, I had nothing to do until boarding time, which was around four o'clock. The Clippers always took off and landed in daylight.

I was too excited to sit, so I strolled around the terminal. Its lofty ceiling and banks of tall windows gave the whole place a feeling of light and air. Everything was up-to-the-minute art deco, from the panelled walls and cylindrical chandeliers to the pattern of the bars in the wrought-iron guard rail that ran along a mezzanine above the main entrance. I stopped in front of an enormous globe with all of Pan American's routes marked on it and traced the one I would soon be flying: San Francisco to Honolulu, Honolulu to Midway, Midway to Wake Island, Wake to Guam, Guam to Manila, Manila to Macao, Macao to Hong Kong. My eyes followed the line of dots scattered across the vastness of the Pacific, no more than specks in the blue. Right then, Mum and Dad and Calgary felt very far away. A wave of homesickness washed over me. I would have burst into tears if I hadn't heard Mum's voice telling me to straighten my spine, show a bit of gumption, and get on with it. Slouching around mooning over some outsized map wasn't going to get Mr. M.'s pictures home from Hong Kong, was it?

Soon the terminal bustled with people, some of them passengers, others there to see them off. Newspaper and movie news photographers hung around the check-in counter waiting to see if anyone famous was boarding that day's flight. I found a place to sit nearby and did the same. All the time I wondered which one was Peyto Willis. It kept my mind off the Pacific Ocean.

There were no celebrities that day, at least none that I recognized. The majority of the passengers were men, many of them travelling alone. That's when I first saw Peyto and his white suit. At the time I didn't realize who he was, but I did notice that he seemed closer to my age than most of the other passengers. They looked old to me, Mum and Dad's age at least. I gave Peyto a surreptitious once-over as he stood at the counter. Suit aside, I suppose he was an average-looking man—late twenties, medium height, slim—nondescript really, except for his hair, which was even redder than Terps's. It truly was the colour of a new-minted penny. But, despite the hair and its accompanying boy-next-door freckles, I decided there was a whiff of danger about him too. Maybe he was a spy. A spy on the good guys' side but a spy nonetheless. (I really had seen far too many Mr. Moto movies.) Turned out Peyto was an engineer and worked for Continental Farm Implements. He spoke fluent Cantonese and was the company's chief representative in Southeast Asia and southern China, although, with the Japanese now occupying the mainland near Hong Kong, the Chinese part no longer amounted to much. I watched as he presented his passport to the clerk and collected his overnight bag. The clerk returned the passport and then, to my surprise, pointed at me. I looked away but not before Peyto turned and caught me staring. He said something to the clerk before he moved along to the scales. I tried to be a little more subtle as I watched him transfer pyjamas and shaving kit from his suitcase to the overnight bag. When he'd finished at the baggage counter, he turned and walked toward me. I pretended to be scrutinizing a chandelier and only looked down when he stopped directly in front of my chair.

"Miss Jeynes?"

"Yes, I'm Kay Jeynes."

"You're Kay Jeynes from Calgary?"

"The very one. At least that's what it says on my passport. You must be Robert Watanabe's friend."

"You'll have to forgive me, Miss Jeynes. It's just that I was expecting someone older. My name is Peyto Willis."

"I'm glad to meet you, Mr. Willis."

"Please, it's Peyto."

"I'm Kay." I stood, and we shook hands.

"And you're Bob's father's friend's secretary."

"You seem to know a lot about me."

"That's it, I'm afraid. Except from the way Bob talked, I was looking for a woman around his dad's age."

"Sorry to disappoint you."

"I guess I'll just have to live with it, won't I?" He smiled but not one of those little lip-twitchers that don't so much as show a tooth. Peyto's smile was a great big, let 'er rip, enamel-flashing delight. I realize now that he smiled the way he lived his life—full out and in the moment. I can feel myself smiling as I write this, just as I smiled back at him all those years ago. Today or 1941, how could I resist? I was attracted to him the minute he walked through the door, but that smile was the clincher.

"I understand this is your first flight on the Clipper, Kay."

"It's my first time in an airplane." I hadn't noticed until then that he was still holding my hand.

"Then we'd better make sure it's a good one. Come on, there's the first bell. They're getting ready to board." He tucked my arm in his, and we went to join the line of passengers beginning to form near a side door.

A second bell set off a flurry of last-minute goodbyes that ended when we were escorted out to a floating dock behind the terminal where the Clipper lay at its mooring. No one who travelled on it could ever forget their first sight of that enormous double-decked airplane bobbing on the water. Back then, the Clipper was the biggest commercial aircraft in the world. I looked up at wings that must have measured three times the length of our backyard. Four engines hung suspended from them, each bigger than our car, their propeller blades tall as a man. Rows of square windows, one above the other, swept along the fuselage to a tail that towered thirty feet above the dock. I could hardly believe that something so huge could actually get off the water, let alone fly.

Peyto and I stood arm in arm and watched as the all-male flight crew marched up the gangplank to an open door beneath the immense wing. (Pan American considered duty aboard its Pacific flights far too strenuous for women.) Their immaculate, naval-style uniforms were a reminder that the Clippers had been named in honour of the old sailing ships and were themselves ships as well as planes. The crew performed this ritual march before every voyage of every Clipper. Pan American rightly regarded its trans-oceanic flights as a very big deal and went to great lengths to make certain that passengers did too. The pilots led the way, followed by navigators, radio operators, engineers, and stewards. It began to look as if there would be more crew than paying customers on our flight. We outnumbered them by only four to one on that longest leg of the journey to Hong Kong. That was because of the sleeping berths. The flight from San Francisco to Honolulu took all night, and Pan American provided every passenger with a sleeping berth as spacious and comfortable as the ones on trains. However, because one berth occupied the space of two seats, the Clipper could accommodate only half the number of passengers on overnight flights as it could carry during the day.

Thirty-four of us, a full overnight load, followed the crew into the Honolulu Clipper that afternoon. Walking up that gangplank was one of the most exciting things I've ever done. My excitement was tinged with a touch of anxiety too: I knew that once the steward closed the door, there would be no going back. I would be trapped in that plane until we either crashed in the sea or landed in Hawaii. Melodramatic of me, I suppose, but, truth be told, I've experienced a twinge of that same claustrophobic uneasiness every time I fly. Fortunately, it goes away as soon as I'm buckled into my seat—just as it did that first time.

I wish I could pretend that I actually remembered for myself all that stuff about the number of passengers and only taking off and landing in daylight, but I'm going to come clean and admit that I got Jerome to look up the Pan American Clipper for me. He brought me stacks of information. He says it's a piece of cake to look things up on the Web. According to his printouts, my plane was a Boeing 314, and it could carry seventy-four passengers during the day but only thirty-four on overnight flights. Then again, another printout says it could carry seventy-six during the day and still another maintains it was sixty-eight. I'm beginning to suspect that this Internet research business may be a little more challenging than Jerome led me to believe. Nevertheless, without his contribution, I couldn't have told you that the plane's ceiling was 13,400 feet, or that because its cabin wasn't pressurized, the Clipper usually flew around 8,000 feet at a stately cruising speed of 180 miles an hour. Even so, I was pretty much spot on about its size, though for all its bulk the Clipper didn't weigh nearly as much as a modern jet. Still, at forty-two tons fully loaded and ready for takeoff, it was no feather-weight. Small wonder it needed such enormous wings. Those wings were so big that the engineer could get inside them while the plane was in flight and crawl all the way out to the engines to make repairs.

This afternoon at martini time, I read that last paragraph to Meggie. I thought it was fascinating myself, but I guess I'm more scientifically minded than she is. Meggie says all this technical stuff is a colossal bore and pointed out that if my grandchildren are at all interested in an old airplane (which she doubts) they can look up the Clipper's statistics on the Internet for themselves. Her suggestion: forget all that mechanical bumpf and stick a famous movie star on board to liven things up. Clark Gable maybe.

"Why would I tell them that Clark Gable flew on my Clipper when he didn't?"

"Why not?" Meggie said. "What does it matter? And who says he didn't? We'll never know for sure because he was travelling incognito."

"On important government work with his sidekick Cary Grant?"

"Now you're getting the idea. Cary really was a Clipper kind of man, wasn't he? Suave, sophisticated . . ."

"Okay, okay, make it Clark and Cary."

"See, that paragraph's already more interesting." I must have looked doubtful. "C'mon, Kay, you gotta remember these are your memoirs. You can put any damn thing you want in them."

Sometimes I get the feeling that Meggie has not fully embraced the true memoir spirit. Besides, the any damn thing I really do want to put in is that airplane. However, she may have a point about Jerome's engineering statistics being a little on the dull side, at least to people who never flew on the Clipper. Good thing I haven't told her about Peyto—she'd think I was crazy to be putting in stuff about an airplane when I could be telling about a man. Trouble is, I'm finding that after all these years, the memories of him still hurt. Even the happy ones. Odd, that. You'd think that memories of emotions felt that long ago would slip away along with everything else, wouldn't you? But they don't. Places you lived, things you did, even the faces of friends may fade, but emotions last a lifetime, their intensity undiminished by the years. I understand all too well why so many war veterans, the old men you see interviewed on History Channel documentaries, choke up when they talk about their buddies who didn't make it.

But I'm too weary to think about any of that right now. It's late—that's after ten here at The Alzheimer's Arms—and I have physio tomorrow morning so I'd better close down and get some sleep. Meggie maintains that you mustn't nod off thinking gloomy thoughts, so she never listens to the news or reads Canadian novels in bed. To ensure pleasant dreams, she recommends tuning the radio to some late-night jazz and letting memories of a happy day float through your mind. Lately, she and Hersh have been golfing the old course at High River on a sunny June morning. Meggie usually drifts off around the third or fourth green, although on good nights, she thinks they probably play a few more holes in her dreams. Who knows, maybe tonight I'll treat myself to a nice romantic dream about Peyto.

I SHOULD LEARN not to say stupid things like that, even as a joke. I did dream about Peyto last night, and it was horrible. Everything started out fine. We were having a lovely time swimming side by side off the little beach in front of Marilyn's house on Oahu when I noticed we had become separated. Then I saw that the water was full of sharks. There were dozens of them, black shapes circling under me. I tried to swim back to Peyto, but the sharks blocked my way. It was a relief to wake up, racing heart and all. I'm way too old for that kind of crap. No wonder old people die in their sleep. I'll say one thing for my subconscious though—it doesn't mess around with subtleties. Whacks me over the head with an obvious symbol or two, and then wakes me up so I'll be sure to remember them.

PEYTO HAD ARRANGED for us to sit together. He had flown across the Pacific on the Clipper four times, so I wasn't surprised when the steward greeted him by name before leading us to a compartment in front of the port wing. The passenger cabin occupied the whole lower deck, but unlike modern jets with their rows of forward-facing seats stretching down the length of the plane, the Clipper was divided into a series of large, luxuriously appointed compartments on either side of a central aisle in which half the seats faced forward, the others aft. This was an overnight flight, so there were only the two of us in our compartment. Peyto gave me the forward-facing window seat because he said it had the best view. I sat down in what was a large, comfortable armchair with a seat belt. Peyto took the seat next to me and showed me how to buckle myself in while the stewards settled the other passengers and stowed the overnight bags for takeoff. Despite the staff's cool professionalism, an air of excitement pervaded the whole operation. I can't believe there was ever a traveller so jaded that taking off in the Clipper was a bore.

With cabin and passengers secure and the outer door sealed, we were ready to go. The pilot started the engines, the ground crew cast off the mooring lines, and we began the taxi from Clipper Cove out into San Francisco Bay. Backwash from the propellers shimmered over the surface of the water. I saw a line of people along the shore waiting to watch us take off. A Clipper flight was an event and, no matter where in the world they travelled, Pan Am's flying boats always had an audience.

"Airplanes take off into the wind," Peyto informed me, "so we'll see the Golden Gate Bridge today. Alcatraz, too, maybe. You can wave to Machine Gun Kelly."

I did see the bridge, but I don't recall a prison, so I guess I didn't get to wave to Mr. Kelly. What I do remember with absolute clarity is the takeoff itself. The pilot turned the Clipper into the wind and opened the throttles. The engines roared, and the whole great machine vibrated. It took ages to reach lift-off speed, so long that I began to think we might be sailing to Hawaii. There were a few whitecaps out in the bay, minor stuff really, but even so, they made for a bit of a rocky ride. The Clipper bumped its way over each passing wave. As we gained speed, the bumps came faster and faster and faster until it felt as if we were skimming over a giant washboard. After what seemed like miles, the hull broke free of the water, and our boat became an airplane. Nowadays, the Clipper's climb to cruising altitude would feel pretty tame to someone used to flying in modern jets where it's zoom down the runway and up like a rocket. We rose very sedately—none of this pinning you to your seat stuff. I sat with my nose pressed to the window, watching the waves recede as we climbed. Then the Clipper dipped a wing, banked southwest, and aimed its nose into the late afternoon sun. We were officially on our way to Hawaii.

"This is absolutely fantastic!" I said. "It's amazing! I've never felt anything like it in my life." At that moment, I understood why Charlie loved flying.

"I thought you must be enjoying yourself—you were laughing out loud. And you clapped when we lifted off the water."

"I did? Really?" Well, there went my sophisticated world traveller image, lost in a spray of salt water and a thousand feet of air.

"Yes, Miss Kay Jeynes from Calgary, you really did." He beamed that wonderful smile at me again.

"Well, Mr. Peyto Willis, I'm a simple soul. I laugh when I'm happy, I cry when I'm sad, and I just found out that I applaud when something thrills me." I turned back to the window. "Look at the people on that sailboat. They're waving to us." I proceeded to tarnish my image still more by waving back.

"Keep your eyes peeled for an ocean liner. The passengers all come out on deck to watch us fly over."

Shortly after sunset, we did spot an ocean liner, but by then it was too dark to see any passengers. The ship's lights were the only thing visible from the air. The steward informed us that we were looking down on the *Monterey*, a Matson liner bound for Honolulu, and that we would be in Manila before she reached port. As we flew over, the *Monterey* beamed a search light into the sky. The Clipper returned the greeting by flashing her landing lights.

Later that evening, interested passengers were invited to visit the flight deck. It was on the upper deck along with the crew's quarters and the baggage compartment. When it was our turn, Peyto and I followed the steward up a curved staircase to a room near the front of the plane where he introduced us to the crew on duty at the work stations. We didn't get to meet the pilots because the cockpit was blocked off by heavy curtains closed tight to protect their night vision from the cabin lights. Fortunately, the navigator had a few minutes to spare. He led us through a door into a cramped space between the flight deck and the baggage compartment where a narrow ladder sat directly beneath a glass dome set into the roof of the plane. As we stood waiting for our eyes to adjust to the dark, he explained that the dome was a navigational observatory where, on clear nights, he used a sextant to shoot the stars. He added that you got quite the view from up there, and we were welcome to go take a look if we wanted. He didn't have to ask twice.

Peyto flipped a coin, and I won first turn. I climbed to a small platform at the top of the ladder where I sat and peered out of the dome into a night deep with stars. In all my life I have never seen such stars—stars in numbers that rendered number meaningless, drifts of stars to the reaches of the galaxy and beyond to the faint clouds of distant nebulae, each ghostly wisp another great galaxy of stars. With no markers against which to judge our speed and the air free of turbulence, it felt as if the Clipper were suspended in space, and that I was above it drifting free. That night over the Pacific, for a few giddy moments, I floated in the stars.

"Miss Jeynes, it's time to come down. Miss Jeynes!" I was vaguely aware of someone calling to me. Then I felt an impatient tug at the hem of my skirt. "I'm sorry, Miss Jeynes," the navigator said, "but I've got to report our position soon, so if you want your friend to have a look-see, you'd better come on down."

While Peyto took his turn in the dome, the navigator told me that we were lucky to have such a grand night for flying, that this was the clearest sky he'd ever seen over the Pacific.

And there I go, getting ahead of myself again. I didn't go up to the flight deck until after dinner. Before that, I'd flown into a sunset, drunk my first cocktail (a "Clipper" bought by Peyto to celebrate my first takeoff), and eaten my first airplane meal. Pan American did not expect its passengers to consume unpleasant food off plastic dishes delivered to their seats on little plastic trays. We sat at linen-draped tables in a real dining room, ate filet mignon from china decorated with the Pan American logo, and drank California wine from proper stemware. It was like The Dominion's dining car with wings.

JANICE IS BACK from Mexico. No mention of Todd though. Even Meggie couldn't coax a word out of her, and Meggie at her most persuasive could make James Bond babble. But Janice was all business. Her topic for this week's assignment is "Your Creative Side: Has Any Art (or Craft) Been a Part of Your Life?" I think I'll have to give it a miss because I'm nowhere near finished "Travelling," but Meggie's going to give it a whirl. She used to be an embroiderer before her sight went.

And speaking of Meggie, I have to admit that she did get up my nose a bit when she said that the reason I'm behind on our Travel assignment is because I spent so much time on "that old airplane." In an attempt to prove to her that not everyone will find my memories of the Clipper as boring as she does, I read some of my notes on it aloud in class this afternoon. It was a first for me, my reading-aloud maiden voyage. Now I know how the *Titanic* felt. Afterwards nobody said a thing except for Janice. Even she just made her standard encourage-the-troops noises. (I think she's soured on travelling these days.) Then Meggie came through, staunch pal that she is, and said that listening to me read made her wish she'd had a chance to fly on the Clipper too. I don't know if she meant it, but I appreciated the moral support. After class, she put a couple of extra olives in my martini by way of consolation and told me I shouldn't worry about the reception the Clipper got.

"How many times do I have to say it, Kay? These are your memoirs. If you want to write about your airplane, then do it. Besides, I think I was probably a little hard on you when you read that part to me the other day. On second hearing it's much more interesting."

Well, so much for reading aloud. I guess I asked for it. No matter—the Clipper pages stay in and that's that. I loved that beautiful airplane, and I mourn the fact that not a single one of them still exists. Boeing made only twelve 314s. Some were destroyed in the war, some crashed, and some were scrapped. By the war's end they were no longer needed. The Americans had bulldozed runways on every hunk of coral in the Pacific that called itself an island, and new, long-range aircraft could manage the distances between them with ease. The golden age of the flying boat had ended.

"And exactly who is this Peyto person?" Meggie asked.

"Was," I said. "He died in the war."

"Were you in love with him?"

"I certainly thought I was."

PEYTO AND I made our way back down the stairs to our compartment. I put my face to the window and cupped my hands around my eyes to block the reflection of the cabin lights. I looked up at the part of the sky that wasn't masked by the wing, but it held nothing like the sight I'd seen from the dome.

"I envy you. I'll bet you've looked out the dome lots of times on your other flights." I settled back in my seat.

"Nope. Tonight was a first for me too," Peyto said. "I've been to the flight deck before, but I've never been invited up to the dome. My guess is I have you to thank for that. The navigator couldn't resist showing off his stars to a lovely woman."

"I didn't know it was possible to see that many stars. Not without a telescope," I said, mostly to cover my confusion. Fellows had told me I was pretty before, but none of them had ever called me a woman.

"I saw a falling star when I was up there. It looked so close I caught myself ducking. Guess I should have given it a round of applause, shouldn't I?" he said. I was at a loss for a suitably clever reply to this gentle teasing. "But you're right—that view was really something. I've never seen a sky to beat it, not even from the top of Haleakala."

"What's Haleakala?" I asked, happy to be on steadier conversational ground. "Or should that be where?"

"It's a dormant volcano on Maui," he said. I must have looked blank. "Maui is one of the Hawaiian Islands. It's south of Oahu." Still blank. "North of the Big Island."

"I'm afraid my Hawaiian geography is pretty shaky," I said.

"If you were going to spend more than one night in Honolulu, we'd fix that. We could sail to Maui and see how Haleakala's stars stack up to the Clipper's."

"You seem to know Hawaii well."

"I went to school there. My parents were missionaries in China. I grew up in a little place near Canton, but when I turned fourteen they packed me off to high school in Honolulu."

I couldn't imagine living thousands of miles away from Mum and Dad and Charlie, especially not at the age of fourteen. "Weren't you homesick?"

"I don't remember," he said. "If you were a missionary's kid, you went away to school. That's just the way things were, so I guess I didn't think about it much. Besides, most of the other mission children were sent back to the States to a Baptist boarding school in Ohio. I was lucky. I got Honolulu."

"Did you know anybody there?"

"Not at first. My parents made arrangements for me to board with some other missionaries who were living in Honolulu at the time. They left for a post in India at the end of my first year, but by then it didn't matter because I'd made friends of my own."

"Where did you live after they left?"

"With a buddy of mine from school and his mother. When I told John that pretty soon I wouldn't have a place to stay, his mom wrote to my parents and asked if I could come live with them. I spent most of my time at the Margolises' house anyway, so it wasn't like moving in with strangers. I lived at Marilyn's for the next three years, until John and I left for Stanford."

I knew for certain that Mum and Dad would never have sent Charlie or me to live with people they didn't know and had never even met, especially not at the age of fifteen. I guess that's why I assumed that Marilyn Margolis must have had some pretty impressive Baptist credentials going for her. It did seem a bit odd though. Peyto didn't strike me as the religious type, but maybe American Baptists were different from Canadian Baptists. I'd certainly never met a Calgary Baptist who drank cocktails and smoked Camels, at least not in public.

"Marilyn is like my second mother," he continued. "You know, I bet the two of you would really hit it off."

In my long experience, that particular prediction is frequently the harbinger of its own doom.

"Is Marilyn a missionary too?"

"Nope. And that's only one of her good qualities. But you'll see for yourself tomorrow. She's driving out to Pearl to meet the plane. You know, it really is too bad you can't stay longer in Honolulu."

"I don't stay long anywhere on this trip. But you already know that since you're the one who got me my ticket."

"I thought it was a pretty rushed trip when I booked it. As a matter of fact, I double-checked the dates with Bob just to make sure I got them right. He told me that you're going to Hong Kong to collect a painting or a drawing or something. Must be a pretty important piece of art to rate courier service by Clipper."

"It's pieces of art, and they are important, at least to my boss."

"Are they top secret or are you allowed to talk about them?"

"They're no big secret," I said. "Except maybe from the Japanese government, and it seems to be occupied with more important things at the moment." I told him about the Sharaku prints.

"What do you know about this Nakimura?" he asked when I had finished.

"Only that his cousin in Japan was a good friend of Mr. Miyashita's uncle."

"I'm surprised the man's still living in Hong Kong, considering the way the Chinese feel about Japs these days. Can't be very comfortable living in the middle of a million and a half people who hate you."

"Maybe that's why he's leaving at the end of the month."

"Do you know anybody who can help you while you're there?"

"No. But I don't see myself needing help. It's all pretty straightforward. Mr. Nakimura is going to meet the plane and give me the prints. Then I spend the night at the Peninsula Hotel and leave for home the next morning."

"May I ask how much he's charging for all his time and trouble?"

"Nothing. Mr. Nakimura never mentioned money in his telegrams, so I guess it's what you call a gentleman's agreement. Mr. Miyashita did send him some money back in September, but that was only to cover expenses."

Peyto looked skeptical but didn't say anything. Instead, he rang for the steward and ordered coffee and cognac. When it came, I followed his lead and swirled my cognac around the balloon glass before taking a tentative sip. I decided its slightly astringent taste was much more to my liking than the grenadine-laced sweetness of the Clipper Cocktail.

"So cognac's a kind of brandy," I said. The Clipper's brandy didn't bear much resemblance to the stuff Mum sprinkled on the Christmas cakes. "It's really good." I seemed to be catching on to this liquor-drinking business.

Peyto responded with an absent-minded smile. He hesitated before he spoke as if he were making up his mind about something. "Kay, if it's all right with you, when we get to Hawaii, I'd like to send a telegram to a friend of mine in Hong Kong. His name is Sam Leong and he's the assistant manager of the Continental Implements office there. I'd like him to meet you at the plane and help you out with Mr. Nakimura."

"That's very kind of you, but it's really not necessary."

"It probably isn't," he agreed. "But it's always good to have someone you can count on when you're doing business in a foreign place, especially a girl all on her own who hasn't travelled much."

I tell you, Peyto managed to raise Intrepid Traveller's dander more than a little with that remark. Back in the terminal he'd assumed I was an old lady. Now he was treating me as if I were some helpless bit of fluff.

"This girl on her own seems to have got herself halfway to Honolulu without any problems." I must have sounded pretty huffy because he changed tack immediately.

"I apologize if that came out wrong, Kay. I don't mean to imply that you're anything but a very capable woman. If you weren't, your boss would never have sent you on this trip. But Hong Kong is a whole different kettle of fish."

"I'm only going to pick up some art and spend one night in a hotel. That's it. Besides, Hong Kong is British." Ah yes, I was my parents' daughter. "What can happen to me in the lobby of the Peninsula Hotel?" Cocky stuff. Maybe it was the brandy talking.

"Well, for starters, you don't speak Cantonese and you're probably not fluent in Japanese either. What if Nakimura gets delayed? Or what if he's sick and can't make it? Or maybe he decides he wants to meet you somewhere else?"

Those were contingencies I'd not considered. "Then I suppose he'd call me or leave a message at the hotel."

"You're assuming Nakimura speaks English."

"All his telegrams were in English."

"Maybe he got someone to send them for him. Believe me, Kay, even simple things can get complicated when you don't understand what people are saying to you. I know because it's happened to me."

It had never occurred to me that language might be a problem.

"I wish I could be there to help you myself. But since I can't, I think you should let me wire Sam. Just in case."

"I thought you were coming to Hong Kong too?"

"I am, but not for two weeks. I'm staying in Hawaii for a while. Didn't Bob tell you? I'm only going as far as Honolulu on this plane. I'm booked to fly on to Hong Kong two weeks from Friday."

Well, that was a blow. Not because I was really convinced I'd need help with Mr. Nakimura but because I realized Peyto and I only had a few more hours together.

"If Bob had told me exactly what you were up to in Hong Kong," he continued, "I'd have arranged to spend time in Hawaii at the end of my trip, not the beginning. Then I could have been in Hong Kong with you. There's not a hope of that now. The Clipper is so booked these days, you're lucky to get a seat, never mind change your reservation."

"What you said about not speaking Chinese does make sense," I admitted. Perhaps I had been a bit churlish about his offer. After all, it was kindly meant. "So if you'd like to send a telegram to your friend, that would be fine with me." Not exactly a graceful acceptance.

"Good. I'll do it as soon as we land. And maybe we could get together when you're back in Honolulu, so you can tell me how things went."

"I get back on a Monday. That's November 24, I think." Think, my eye. I knew to the hour when the Clipper was scheduled to land. I had the whole timetable memorized, but I didn't want to look too eager. Talk about coy. My God, girls can be silly. "So you'll be in Honolulu then?" I continued very offhand, although I knew the answer to that one as well.

"For sure," he said. "I'll be standing on the dock waiting for you."

WE LANDED IN Honolulu shortly after dawn. On the way in, Peyto hung over my shoulder pointing out places he would take me if only I weren't leaving the next morning. I don't remember any of them. Since the day Captain Cook sailed into Waimea Harbor, travellers have been mesmerized by their first sight of the Hawaiian Islands, and I was no exception. Like Cook in 1778, most people arrived in the islands by boat in 1941, so the Clipper provided me with a rare view for the time. We flew in from the northeast. Oahu first appeared as a distant patch of haze on the horizon but, as we approached, a solid shape began to emerge from the mist, its contours defined by the outline of green mountains against the blues of sky and sea. Near the island, the ocean itself changed colour. The dark of deep water gave way to the lucent turquoise of the coastal shallows. The mountains began at the shore, ranges born of ancient lava flows long-weathered to sharp ridges. All but the highest peaks were covered in lush vegetation.

Soon the Clipper banked south and began to descend, following the path of a broad interior valley. We flew over what I thought might be sugar cane and pineapple plantations, although, at the time, I did not know what either crop looked like. By then, we were low enough to see people already at work in the fields look up and wave to us. A woman on a white horse trotting past a palm grove stopped and waved too. So did the sailors on the decks of the navy ships lying at anchor near the Clipper's landing area. I waved back to all of them from my chair high in the bright morning sky. For me, everything that passed beneath the Clipper was new and exotic and lovely to behold. It was too rich a feast for a prairie kid's eye. I could not believe it was real. I began to feel a little unreal myself.

The Clipper touched down so gently I hardly realized we were no longer flying but floating on the gentle swells of Pearl Harbor. At the dock, the steward opened the door, and I followed the line of passengers down the gangplank into sunlight and fresh air. I tell you, Hawaiian air was a revelation, warm and soft with moisture, a balm to my dry winter soul. And right there in front of me, just off the dock, not five feet away, a school of impossible canary-yellow fish hovered near the surface of the water. They darted off when a branch, fallen from one of the coconut palms lining the shore, floated over them. Light danced on the water, and I swear my heart danced too. What wouldn't I give to feel like that just one more time?

I remember telling myself that this perfect morning was real and that I was actually standing on a dock in Honolulu. I wasn't aware that I had spoken out loud until I heard Peyto's voice.

"Every morning in Hawaii is perfect," he said. "And then the day gets better."

We walked to the end of the dock, where beautiful young Hawaiian women stood, their arms loaded with flowers. Not a word of a lie, they really did drape leis around our necks and welcome us to the islands. I know the whole thing probably sounds pretty hokey now, but, in my memory, that little aloha ceremony made a perfect ending to the loveliest flight of my life. I realize that these days "lovely flight" is an oxymoron. As you trudge through modern mega-airports with their security checks and X-ray machines, their sniffer dogs and cold-eyed guards, it's almost impossible to believe that flying was ever such a pleasure. You're lucky if someone tosses your luggage at you when you land, never mind a garland of flowers. Sadly enough, that's now as true in Hawaii as it is anywhere else. But, once upon a time, you were welcomed with orchids and *Plumeria*.

At the florist's down the street from my condo they call *Plumeria* by its common name, so when I need cheering up on a grey winter day, I pop in and ask for a little bouquet of frangipani. A single one of its sweet-scented blooms is magic enough to conjure up my real and perfect morning on the Pan Am dock in Honolulu all those years ago.

TO MY GREAT surprise, Peyto's prediction that Marilyn Margolis and I would hit it off came true. The two of us were friends from the moment we met until she died forty-five years later at the age of ninety. At first, our friendship revolved around Peyto, but after he was killed, it was a comfort to us both to be able to talk about him. For me, this was especially true since there was no one else in my life who knew what he had meant to me. We mostly carried on our friendship by letter, but on the occasions when we did get together, it felt as if we'd seen each other only the day before.

Marilyn stood waiting for Peyto just beyond the dock. As soon as she saw him, she waved and let out a whoop.

"Peyto, darlin'! Over here!"

Marilyn was a Texan, born and raised. Like her home state, everything about her was larger than life. For starters, she was a big woman—lean, long-limbed, taller than Peyto—and she never made any effort to minimize her size. That morning she wore a white linen suit trimmed with red piping that, if anything, accentuated her broad shoulders. A pair of red, wedge-heeled espadrilles and a big, floppy-brimmed panama hat added a few more inches to her height. I held back as she enveloped Peyto in a bear hug that sent the hat flying, uncovering a head of thick, curly hair, blond as a palomino's tail. I thought for certain hair that colour had to come out of a bottle, but in Marilyn's case, salt water and sunshine had done the trick. She loved the water and not a day went by that she didn't swim in the ocean at least once. She continued to swim for the rest of her life, right up until the year before she died.

"It sure is good to see you, you red-headed rascal!" She put her hands on Peyto's shoulders and held him at arm's length for inspection. "Everyone's been asking for you. When's Peyto coming home? When's Peyto coming home? That's all I've been hearing for a month!"

Her accent was pure Texas. I'd only ever heard people talk like that in the movies.

Peyto retrieved the hat and introduced us. He told Marilyn that this was my first visit to Hawaii.

"Aloha, Kay, honey." Marilyn whacked the hat against her skirt a couple of times in a not-entirely-successful effort to shake the dust off its brim, then plunked it back on her head. "I'm real pleased to meet you. And I know you're going love it here."

Like the well-brought-up Canadian girl that I was, I held out my hand to her. Marilyn ignored it. Instead, she stepped forward and gave me a hug almost as big as the one she'd given Peyto. Off went the hat again. This time I was the one who scrambled to pick it up.

"That'll teach me to try looking like a glamour gal before breakfast." She laughed and winked at me as she rolled up the hat and stuck it under her arm. She had a smile just like Peyto's.

"Kay, we're having a luau out at our place tonight to welcome this character home, and I hope you'll do us the honour of coming."

"*Luau* is the Hawaiian word for feast," Peyto explained.

"And this one's going to be a feast for sure," Marilyn added. "David was busy putting the pig in the imu pit when I left the house."

"You will come, won't you, Kay?"

"Peyto'll pick you up at the hotel at three." Marilyn didn't bother to wait for my yes.

"Then we can all have a swim before the luau starts. But say, now that I think on it, it might work better if he picked you up earlier. Then the pair of you could get in some sightseeing before we swim. You could even hike up Diamond Head. I'm telling you, Kay, the view is worth the climb. You can see just about all of Honolulu from up there. And then tomorrow you can take a drive up past Koko Head and—"

"I wish we could do even some of that," Peyto interrupted. "But Kay's leaving for Hong Kong on tomorrow's Clipper."

"You mean you've only got one day in Honolulu? Now that is a real shame." Marilyn was genuinely disappointed. "Well, I guess we'll just have to cram as much into today as we can. How about we start by driving you into Honolulu and showing you the sights between here and the Royal Hawaiian?"

AS THINGS TURNED out, I remained in Honolulu for two more weeks. I learned about my unexpected change of plans when Marilyn and Peyto and I arrived at the Royal Hawaiian Hotel and found the manager of Pan American's Honolulu office waiting for me in the lobby. With many apologies, he explained that some army bigwig had claimed my place on the next morning's flight to Midway. In those days, the military had priority on all forms of transportation. I was the last passenger booked, so that made me the first passenger bumped. The manager presented me with three choices. First, I could leave for San Francisco on a P&O liner scheduled to depart Honolulu on Monday morning. Second, I could secure the last seat available on the next east-bound Clipper scheduled to leave Honolulu for San Francisco in one week. Or third, I could wait two weeks in Honolulu and carry on to Hong Kong by Clipper. Whatever I chose to do, it would be at Pan Am's expense, including accommodation at the Royal Hawaiian. If I would be so kind as to let him know my decision by Sunday afternoon at the latest, he would make the necessary arrangements.

"When would I get to Hong Kong?" I asked.

"The third of December," Peyto answered for him. "Remember, that's the Clipper I'm going on."

"But December is too late. I have to be in Hong Kong before the end of November or Mr. Nakimura will have left."

The manager apologized again but said there was absolutely nothing more he could do.

"Isn't there a boat I could catch?"

The manager shook his head; he had already checked. There were no passenger ships leaving Honolulu that would get me to Hong Kong any sooner than the Clipper. November was out of the question and that was that. Then he gave me his business card and with one last apology left us standing in the lobby.

"There's gotta be something we can do," Marilyn said. "Maybe some other passenger would like two free weeks in Honolulu. Even rich folks like to get things for free. It can't hurt to ask."

"I doubt it would be worth the trouble," Peyto said. "Everyone on tomorrow's plane will have an important reason for making the trip or they wouldn't have come by Clipper. You can bet they all want to get to Hong Kong just as much as Kay." Then he told Marilyn the purpose of my trip.

"Why can't your Hong Kong office help her?" Marilyn asked him. "Maybe this Nakimura fella would let them keep Kay's pictures safe until she can get there?"

"Kay, with your permission, I'd like to send a telegram to Sam Leong to see what he can do," Peyto said. "He might be able to sort something out before we get there."

"Thanks. I'd appreciate that." This time, Intrepid Traveller didn't climb on her high horse and proclaim her independence. And she sure liked the sound of that "we."

NICKNAMED THE PINK Palace because of its bright pink stucco exterior, the Royal Hawaiian Hotel has been one of Honolulu's most recognizable landmarks since it opened in 1929. I remember thinking that it was a pleasant place, although, in my snooty young opinion, not a patch on the Banff Springs. When it came to hotels, my brief acquaintance with the Castle in the Rockies had given me a distinctly elevated set of standards. May I add that they fell fast and far when I began to travel on my own nickel.

My fourth-floor room had a glorious view of Waikiki Beach and a bathroom that I had to admit was the equal in every way of my white-tiled sanctum sanctorum in Banff. My suitcase was waiting for me on the luggage rack at the end of the bed. After I unpacked, I settled down at a little desk in front of the window, alternately gazing out over the palm trees to the ocean and writing a letter to Mum and Dad on Royal Hawaiian stationery. I neglected to mention that I'd been bumped from the Clipper. I'd write them again when I had decided what to do. I'd wire Mr. Miyashita then as well. After all, what would be the point of sending him a telegram before Peyto had contacted Sam Leong? Until we heard from Hong Kong and knew all the facts, I couldn't possibly make a sensible decision about what to do, could I? At least that's what I told myself although, at some level, I must have been aware that I was simply spinning justifications after the fact. From the moment Pan Am offered me the choice, I knew I would be on the Clipper with Peyto.

THE TWO WEEKS that followed were probably the happiest of my life. Meggie laughed when I told her this.

"Now isn't that a surprise. You were twenty-one and in love. Not to mention you'd just discovered sex. All of that on a beautiful tropical island thousands of miles away from Home and Conscience. What's not to be happy about?"

Meggie was spot on with that last shot. I'd deserted my Calgary conscience somewhere in the middle of the Pacific Ocean without so much as a backward glance. If I hadn't, I would certainly have contacted Mr. Miyashita that morning and then obeyed what I knew would be his order: catch the first boat home. Instead, I sent my travelling suit to be cleaned, deposited my passport and money in the hotel safe, and bought a bathing suit, a daring two-piece number, in a shop down the street. I wandered around Waikiki, even then a tourist ghetto, albeit a much quieter and slower-paced one than it is today, and treated myself to lunch under the famous banyan tree at the Moana Hotel.

Peyto picked me up around two, and we drove along the coast out past Diamond Head to Marilyn's place. We turned off the main road through an open gate and down a driveway flanked by a hibiscus hedge covered in blooms. I had no idea that hibiscus grew that big. Until then, I'd only seen single plants in little pots that Whitburn's Florist Shop occasionally brought in during the winter. After a hundred winding yards, the hedge opened out to a lawn that sloped down to the sea and a sprawling white-washed bungalow. Marilyn's house stood thirty feet above the water at the beginning of a rocky spit of land that jutted out into a small, sheltered bay. A verandah, which Peyto informed me is called a lanai in Hawaii, ran around three of its sides, providing both shade and spectacular views. Double doors leading from almost every room in the house onto the lanai stood open, erasing the boundary between indoors and out. There were no screens on any of the windows, but a light breeze from the ocean kept the house cool and relatively bug free.

As soon as we got out of the car, an enormous black dog that owed a lot to Newfoundland ran down the steps from where it had been sleeping and flung itself at Peyto's feet in a big-dog version of one of Nikkou's greetings that was no less enthusiastic for being a little ponderous. Marilyn and a tall Hawaiian man followed at a more sedate pace. Both of them were in bathing suits, towels slung over their shoulders.

"That's the only time you'll ever see Lucy do that," Marilyn laughed. "She's usually such a dignified girl, but she makes a real fool of herself every time Peyto comes home."

Marilyn gave me another of her hugs and then introduced me to David Kamaka, her business manager. Until then I hadn't known that Marilyn had a business to manage. Turned out, she owned a thriving market garden a few miles up the road from her house and did a brisk trade supplying fresh produce to local hotels and markets. It took me a while to catch on to the fact that David and Marilyn were lovers. I think

211

it shocked me a little to realize people that old were still interested in sex. After all, Marilyn was older than my mother. That led me to wonder if perhaps Mum and Dad still . . . I hopped off that uncomfortable train of thought pretty quickly.

Officially, David didn't live at Marilyn's house, but in every other way the two of them might as well have been married. As a matter of fact, I never did understand why they didn't marry. Marilyn said it was because they'd both been married once already and neither felt the need to do it again. No matter, they were happy with their arrangement for more than thirty years, until David's death. The four of us frequently had breakfast together out on the lanai over the next weeks. The old Calgary me could not have imagined that I would be eating breakfast with my lover and a woman I'd met just days before and her lover. I preferred not to dwell on what Mum and Dad would have to say on the subject of breakfast at Marilyn's.

"Hurry and get changed, you two," Marilyn said. "We'll meet you on the beach." She whistled, and Lucy, regaining her feet and her dignity, trotted to her side. "Kay, you don't have to worry about Lucy. She's a big girl, but she's gentle as a lamb." As if to prove the truth of Marilyn's words, the dog ambled over and licked my hand. Believe me, when Lucy licked your hand, you knew you'd been licked.

"You have to keep an eye on her when you're swimming," David cautioned. "Lucy likes to rescue people."

For a place about to host a big party, it was remarkably quiet inside the house. Peyto and I seemed to be the only people around. He showed me to a bedroom where I changed into my new bathing suit. I followed the lanai to the front of the house and found him already changed and sitting on the steps, smoking a cigarette as he waited for me. We wandered down a rocky path to a gazebo near the end of the spit of land. A set of wooden steps built over the rock took us down the last few feet to the little beach, ten yards of fine sand sheltered from the waves in the bay by the spit itself. Marilyn and David and the dog were already in the water. Peyto ran in and swam over to join them. After a little hesitation, I did the same. What a glorious feeling it was to swim in the ocean for the first time. The buoyancy of the salt water made it seem effortless. As soon as she saw me in the water, Lucy swam to my side. For some unfathomable doggy reason, she had decided that I needed looking after and kept trying to nudge me toward shore. Marilyn would call her away but, a few minutes later, there she'd be, paddling along beside me with her powerful webbed paws, doing her best to herd me back to safety. The five of us swam along the coast for a good fifteen minutes, then turned around and swam back.

"You're starting to sunburn. It's time to find you some shade," Peyto said as we reached shore and splashed our way up onto the sand. Water streamed off his back and legs, and the downy red-gold hair that covered his body glistened in the sun. I can still see him standing there on the beach, one hand shading his eyes against the glare off the water and the other reaching out to me. Oh Peyto, you truly were my golden lad, and I have missed you all my life.

Marilyn and David went back to the house. After making sure I was safe on dry land, Lucy shook herself and trotted after them. Peyto and I climbed the steps to the gazebo, where a pitcher of iced pineapple juice had materialized during our swim. I stretched out on the big, padded chaise. Peyto pulled up a chair and sat with his feet resting on the end of it. We didn't talk. We just sat and looked at each other. I remember dozing off to the sound of little waves slapping against the rocks on the seaward side of the spit. I woke to find Peyto still in his chair, still looking at me. We went for another quick swim before we walked up to the house to shower and change back into our clothes.

I volunteered to help with the luau preparations and was put to work as Marilyn's step-and-fetch-it. We found her busy in the kitchen mixing up a huge bowl of fruit punch. She looked wonderful in a royal blue, floor-length silk shift patterned in pink peonies. She had white orchids pinned in her hair and an orchid lei around her neck. She leaned over the bowl, a spoon in one hand to sample the punch, her lei held up in the other to prevent its petals from trailing in the drink.

I hadn't brought any party clothes with me. I was stuck with Miss Peebles's other rush creation, a tailored, navy blue linen dress with white trim. (Miss Peebles regarded navy as the only serviceable colour for travel.) It looked very stiff and proper-Canadian-afternoon next to Marilyn's flowing shift, and I told her as much.

"I think you look real smart in that dress, Kay," she said. "But if you like, I'd be happy to lend you a mumu."

Peyto laughed. "And then Kay can spend the whole night tripping over it."

"Well I'll be darned if that's not the truth. You know, I sometimes forget I'm ten feet tall. Never mind, Kay, honey, we can still have you looking as Hawaiian as all get out. All's we need is a few flowers."

That was my first task of the evening, cutting blooms from the hibiscus hedge that Marilyn bound together with thread and pinned in my hair. "Not bad, but you need more flowers." She took off her own lei and draped it around my neck.

"How's that for Hawaiian?" She stood back to inspect her handiwork. "What do you think, Peyto?" He simply stood and stared at me, lost in a world of his own.

"Peyto?" Marilyn gently called him back to earth. She looked at him and then at me and smiled. "C'mon, you two. We gotta get back to work. Peyto, you can set up the torches on the lawn, and Kay, you and me will go round us up some cups for this punch."

I hurried to keep up as she strode down the hall on her ridiculous sandals, the ones with white orchids embedded in their high lucite heels.

Last night after dinner, I told Meggie about Marilyn's sandals.

"I didn't know they made hooker heels back then," she said.

"Hooker heels? That's what they're called?" I have to admit I was crushed. Back in 1941, I had yet to hear the word *kitsch*. I thought Marilyn's frivolous sandals were lovely and pretty darn sexy too. I desperately wanted a pair of my own.

"I had a pair myself, back in the fifties." Meggie smiled at the memory. "Mine had red roses in them—thorns and all. They were great."

By five-thirty Marilyn's place was alive with people and preparations. By six, the last of the guests had arrived and it was time for the luau to begin. It looked like half of Hawaii had come to Peyto's party and brought their families with them. I was introduced to every single person, including the children. I couldn't begin to remember all their names or their relationship to Peyto. I know some were former school-mates; others were neighbours or people who worked for Marilyn, and in some cases, all of these. Not that it mattered. It was obvious that everyone there considered Peyto a friend and held him in high regard. Many of them came bearing gifts of food just like guests did back home. However, I'd never been to a party in Calgary with so many differ-ent kinds of people. That night I met Hawaiians, Japanese, Chinese, Portuguese, Americans, even one lone Englishman. They made me feel very welcome and asked all sorts of polite questions about Canada. I don't think they really believed me when I told them how cold it would be in Calgary right then, except for one of the Americans and she came from North Dakota. All the while Lucy, a hibiscus lei around her furry neck, padded her genial way through the crowd wagging her tail and greeting the guests. She was especially gentle with the children, although I noticed that she didn't allow any of them within shouting distance of the water.

And then the feast began. I remember every dish I tried that night. Even now, as I sit here writing, my mouth is watering at the memory of sweet potatoes fresh from the fire pit in their ti leaf wrappings, the steam rising off them redolent of damp earth and honey. I tried poi that night too. Not that poi ever made my mouth water. Neither did the roast pig, although everyone said it was delicious. Probably it was, but the sight of that whole carcass, with the pig's head still attached, being lifted from the fire pit and hacked into hunks was revolting. It made a lasting and unpleasant impression, which I suppose is more a comment on my own carnivorous hypocrisy than a reflection on the quality of the meat.

It was well after dark and the torches were burning brightly by the time we finished eating. Some of the guests brought out musical instru-ments and played while the rest of us danced on the lawn just like at Charlie's birthday party. There were plenty of traditional dances too. I remember David performing a very dramatic hula in honour of Peyto's return. Toward the end of the evening, a large Hawaiian woman sang a hymn asking God to watch over those in peril on the sea. Lily Pahia had been Marilyn's housekeeper for years, and she dedicated her hymn to Marilyn's son, an officer on the aircraft carrier *Yorktown* then out at sea. The luau ended shortly after that, and Peyto drove me, a Chinese grocer, his wife, and their four little daughters back to Honolulu. I sat in the front seat next to Peyto with the youngest sound asleep on my lap. He dropped me off at the hotel with a quick kiss and the promise of a late breakfast and a swim the next morning. I waved as he drove off with his carload of sleeping children. Their parents smiled and waved back to me through the rear window.

There was a telegram from Mr. Miyashita waiting for me at the hotel: TRUST JOURNEY HAS BEEN PLEASANT THUS FAR STOP CONFIDENT INTREPID TRAVELLER WILL HAVE GREAT SUC-CESS HONG KONG STOP ALL WELL AT HOME STOP PARENTS SEND LOVE STOP ALL LOOK FORWARD TO YOUR SAFE RETURN STOP H MIYASHITA.

Any other time, I'd have been cheered by hearing from home and recognized Mr. Miyashita's extravagantly wordy cable for what it was—a thoughtful message designed to buck me up in case I was feeling homesick. As things stood, it only made me feel guilty.

The next morning at ten, Peyto met me for breakfast as promised. By then, I'd already been up and out for a swim. He changed into his trunks in my room and joined me on the beach. We swam and then had coffee and rolls and fresh pineapple at a little table on a terrace overlooking the ocean. Peyto told me that Marilyn had invited me to her place for dinner that evening and, if I wanted, we could spend the rest of the day sightseeing. I agreed and we went back to my room to change out of our bathing suits. That's as far as we got. Out of our bathing suits, I mean. As we both knew would happen, we ended up making love. Word among the Greer & Western girls had it that your first time was supposed to hurt and could be very messy. I found that to be about as unreliable as every other bit of G&W folk wisdom. For the record, my first time was a revelation. I never imagined anything could feel so wonderful.

Afterwards, as we lay in my bed, me marvelling at what my body had just discovered, Peyto propped himself up on one elbow and traced the line of my lips with his fingers.

"Well, at least you're smiling," he said. "Although I was kind of hoping for a round of applause."

"You want applause, mister, you'd better try again."

We never did see any tourist sights that day. We swam. We made love. I think I even remembered to applaud once or twice. Looking back, I can hardly believe that there was ever a man as indefatigable as Peyto or that I was ever that young and full of energy. And perhaps we weren't. Quite so indefatigable and full of energy, that is. I admit that time may have enhanced my memory of our stamina just a little because I also recall that Peyto fell asleep for an hour in the afternoon. This time it was my turn to look at him as he slept in the tangled sheets. The afternoon sun filtered through the slats of the bamboo window awnings, covering his naked body with stripes of light and shadow. And there I lay, in love with the sight of him, the smell of him, the feel of him. I was in love. I was in love.

THAT EVENING AT dinner, Marilyn invited me to stay at her house for the remainder of my time in Honolulu.

"Since you and Peyto will be out seeing the sights every day, staying here just makes a lotta practical sense. Besides, you can get mighty lonesome rattling around a hotel all by yourself."

It made sense to me too. Nevertheless, I did keep my room at the Royal Hawaiian, and that's the address I used in all my communications with Mr. Miyashita and my parents. Peyto and I stopped at the hotel most afternoons, ostensibly to check for messages but mostly to make love. We didn't miss an opportunity. At Marilyn's house, I had the room next to his so, at night, my bed was only a short commute along the lanai. Sometimes after dark, we'd go for a swim off the little beach down from the house. It always seemed to end with the two of us on the chaise in the gazebo. Once, we only got as far as the beach, where we threw caution and our bathing suits to the wind and made love on the wet sand as the waves lapped at our feet. Doesn't that sound romantic? Well, I assure you that it wasn't. I would strongly discourage you from even thinking about indulging in sex on beaches. Afterwards, I found sand in places I didn't know I had places.

Years later, Ken and I went to see *From Here to Eternity*. Remember the famous beach scene where Burt Lancaster makes mad, passionate love to Deborah Kerr as the waves crash over them? The minute it started, I burst out laughing. I laughed so hard I had to go out to the lobby to get myself under control. Ken thought I'd lost my mind, but how could I have explained?

Peyto heard back from Sam Leong on Sunday morning. His cable brought the news that Mr. Nakimura had already gone back to Japan. However, he had left the Sharakus in Hong Kong with an English businessman named Merridew. Sam would let us know what arrangements he could make with Merridew for their return.

"Well, that sounds hopeful," Marilyn said. "At least your pictures are still in Hong Kong."

"I wonder why Mr. Nakimura left early?" I said. "And why didn't he let Mr. Miyashita know?"

"People in Hong Kong hate the Japs so much that I'm surprised Nakimura didn't hightail it for home long ago. And besides, all Japanese assets in Hong Kong have been frozen since July," Peyto said. "I have a feeling that Nakimura had to leave in a hurry and, if I'm right, then your boss's art wouldn't be his biggest concern. Matter of fact, he'd probably try to dump the prints fast and realize some cash while he could. My guess is he sold the whole lot to Merridew, along with the information about when and where you'd be in Hong Kong."

"But the prints weren't his to sell," I said.

Peyto gave me the pitying look my remark deserved. "Kay, forget about Nakimura," he said. "You've heard the last of him."

At least Sam's telegram settled the question of what to do next. If there were any chance at all of recovering the prints, then Intrepid Traveller would do her best. After all, I had come this far. It would be a pity to abandon the Sharakus now. That afternoon, I phoned Pan American to let them know I would be continuing on to Hong Kong by the next Clipper, Peyto's Clipper, as I had begun to think of it. That part was straightforward enough. It was the return trip that got complicated. At the time, we couldn't be certain of what, if anything, Sam Leong might manage to arrange with Merridew.

"You'll be cutting things pretty fine if you're booked to arrive in Hong Kong one day and then turn around and leave for home the next," Peyto said. "The timing was tight on that plan, even when Nakimura was still in the picture."

As it was, after many telephone conversations and much checking of schedules and bookings, Pan American managed to secure me a return ticket on a flight scheduled to leave Hong Kong for Manila a week later, on December 11. There, I'd connect with another Clipper on its way back to the States from New Zealand. That flight would cross the Pacific in the usual five days and have me back in San Francisco by December 16. Would that do, Miss Jeynes?

Yes, thank you, that would do. I would have three more weeks with Peyto. That would do Miss Jeynes very well.

I decided not to cable Mr. Miyashita about my change in schedule until after we had heard from Hong Kong again. A day later, Sam Leong's second telegram arrived.

"Sam asked around. Apparently this Merridew is a pretty shady character," Peyto reported. "Calls himself a businessman, but the Hong Kong police probably have another name for it."

"Then why on earth would Mr. Nakimura trust a man like that with the Sharakus?"

"He probably knew him, at least by reputation, which meant that he could be pretty sure Merridew would still do business with a Jap."

"Business?"

"Well, he isn't doing this for free," Peyto replied. "According to Sam, Merridew wants a hundred British pounds to deliver the prints to you at the Peninsula Hotel."

"A hundred pounds!"

"Considering how much you say those things are worth, it's a bargain. Sounds to me like the shady Mr. Merridew is in need of some quick cash. Otherwise, he'd keep the Sharakus and sell them himself."

"But a hundred pounds? That's five hundred dollars!"

"We can always try to bargain him down, but right now, he's the one with the goods. It all depends on how much your boss wants his art, and how badly Merridew needs the money, doesn't it?"

A SAD DAY here at Foothills Sunset. Dave died last night. He seemed fine at dinner. Just went to bed and didn't wake up. Meggie says that's the way to do it: pop off in your sleep—no lying there unable to move or speak, trapped inside your worn-out old body like a prisoner in solitary confinement. Having that stroke has given Meggie a real horror of ending her days as a human vegetable.

Janice was very upset when she heard the news. I think she's become fond of all us old crocks in her writing class. Not a very smart thing to do if you work at a place like Foothills Sunset. But look who's talking. Meggie and I have become pretty fond of each other. To be honest, if you'd asked me last year, I'd have said it was impossible to forge such a wonderful new friendship at this time of my life and especially unlikely in a place like this.

Today Janice gave us an assignment on friendship. She says it's in memory of our friend Dave. I don't know as I'd count Dave as a friend, but he was a decent enough old codger in his own loony way. Our class certainly won't be the same without him. Anyway, Janice's assignment for this week is "Recall a Significant Friendship in Your Life." I'm going to have a crack at this one mainly because it will give me the perfect opportunity to tell more about Marilyn.

Most of what I can tell you about her background, I learned in one afternoon. I think we both realized that we weren't going to have the luxury of time when it came to getting to know each other. We had two weeks to cement the bonds of our friendship and that was it.

A few days after the luau, Peyto and David and a few of their friends went surfing. They planned to spend the whole day on the north shore of the island. After an early breakfast, they loaded their heavy wooden boards onto the market garden's delivery truck and left for the day. Without Peyto, I felt at loose ends and, I have to admit, just the tiniest bit miffed that he would sooner surf with his pals than spend the day with me. I got over my hurt feelings pretty quickly when, after our morning swim, Marilyn announced that we had to hurry and change because she was treating me to lunch at her favourite restaurant in Honolulu. It seemed a little early to be thinking about lunch, but I went and put on my navy blue suit and my little goes-with-everything travelling hat. Marilyn looked very smart in a red, shirt-waisted, linen dress. She complimented me on my hat.

"I decided not to wear that fancy panama of mine," she said. "Figured it was a little too Mata Hari for the Wai'oli Tea Room. Besides, I don't seem to be able to keep the darn thing on my head for more than two minutes at a stretch."

We didn't take the car. Marilyn led me down a path through the trees to where a battered old pickup truck sat parked near the road. We climbed in and proceeded to rattle along the five miles to her market garden, where we picked up a load of vegetables and a crate of papayas. Boxes stowed, we headed for Honolulu, where I assumed we'd be delivering the produce to one of the hotels on Waikiki. Instead, once we reached the city, we turned north past the university and on up the Manoa Valley. We arrived at the Wai'oli Tea Room shortly before noon. It stood hidden from the road in a grove of trees, a single-storey timber and stone building with big shuttered windows wide open to a manicured garden. Across the garden from the restaurant was a pretty little church built of dressed blocks of lava.

"Whole place belongs to the Salvation Army," Marilyn explained. "They built the tea room to give the older kids at their orphanage some training so's they'll be able to get jobs in the tourist trade. The Sally Ann reckons that tourists are going to be a huge part of Hawaii's future, and I think they're right. They're a big enough part of business here now. Anyway, the girls learn how to cook and wait tables and run a restaurant, and a darned good restaurant too."

"And the church?" I said.

"Kay, darlin', it's the Salvation Army. There's always a chapel somewhere in the picture."

We pulled up to the back door of the tea room, where a couple of the older girls hauled our load of produce off to the kitchen. I assumed the restaurant was a customer of Marilyn's market garden but was quickly disabused of that notion by the woman who managed the place.

"God bless you, Mrs. Margolis," she said. "These donations of yours are a real big help to us."

"Any chance of a table for two today, Captain Brown?" Marilyn asked.

"No need to ask," the Captain replied. "There is always a place for you at our table."

After we finished our lunch of fresh fruit and scones still warm from the oven, the young waitress brought us tea in a proper brown pot that would have earned my mother's stamp of approval. While the tea steeped, we sat back in our chairs and watched a boy push a lawn mower back and forth between the flower beds, filling the air with the smell of freshly cut grass. Then Marilyn poured the tea and we talked. Or, rather, she asked me all sorts of questions, and I talked about Mum and Dad and Charlie and the Miyashitas and how I'd wanted to study history but had become a secretary instead and gone to work for Mr. Miyashita. To me, my story sounded ordinary, but Marilyn seemed genuinely interested in every detail. The waitress brought more hot water for the teapot, and, cups refilled, it was my turn to ask the questions.

Marilyn's story was not ordinary at all, at least not by my standards. She had been orphaned at the age of four when the great hurricane of 1900 destroyed Galveston, killing more than six thousand of its citizens, her parents among them. That's when she was sent to live with an aunt and uncle straight out of *Grimm's Fairy Tales*. The day she turned fourteen she packed a few clothes and her only photo of her parents and left Galveston for good. She caught a Greyhound bus to Houston, where she got herself a job waiting tables in a diner. No one ever came after her or tried to find her.

"I was tall for my age," she explained. "And I looked a lot older than I was, so nobody asked any questions."

At sixteen she fell for one of the customers, a handsome young roughneck who worked in the local oilfields.

"He was a nice enough kid but gutless. The little skunk knocked me up and left me flat."

After a stint in a Salvation Army home for unwed mothers, she found herself, at the age of seventeen, back at the diner supporting herself and her son, John. I was impressed. In those days, girls who produced illegitimate children were strongly encouraged to give them up for adoption. As a matter of fact, in many of the homes and shelters for unwed mothers, that encouragement often amounted to coercion. It was a tough-minded young woman who raised a child all on her own. Still is.

"That's when I got a whole great big bucket of luck dumped right in my lap," Marilyn continued. "There was this older guy used to come in for breakfast every morning. Had the look of a man who'd worked outdoors most of his life, but he didn't dress like one. Always wore a nice pressed suit and polished boots. He was a gentleman too—took his hat off soon as he stepped in the door. When he found out about John, he took to leaving me extra-big tips. 'That's to buy your little fella a quart of milk,' he'd say, but with the money he put down, pretty soon I could've got Johnny his own cow. I tell you, those tips were a lifesaver to me. And he never asked for anything back either, though I knew he was sweet on me by then. Ed Margolis was a good, kind man. I married him when I was eighteen and he was forty-two. That was a couple a years younger than I am now, but back then forty seemed ancient to me. Kinda funny that, how your way of seeing the world changes as you get older."

"So you fell in love with him." I had a galloping case of romance on the brain.

"Well, I'd tried that falling-in-love stuff once, and it didn't seem to work out too good for me," she said. "I don't suppose I was what you'd call 'in love' with Ed, but I sure did love him and I know he loved me and he loved my boy. Called Johnny 'son' from the day we were married. Ed was rich too, and that was sure a surprise. I thought he worked for a drilling supply outfit. Turned out he owned the whole darn company. Probably a good thing I didn't know"—she laughed—"or I might've gone and married him for his money."

"How did you come to live in Hawaii?" I asked.

"That's a whole other story." Marilyn poured us each another cup of tea. By then I was practically sloshing in the stuff. "We'd been married a couple of years when one morning Ed got out of bed and collapsed on the floor. Turns out his heart had never been right from the time he had rheumatic fever as a kid, but he'd managed okay until then. The doctor said it was an enlarged heart. He couldn't work any more. That's when we decided to sell up and take a nice long vacation so's Ed could have a rest while we thought about what to do next. He'd always wanted to see Hawaii, and Johnny was all for it too, so away we went. When we got to Honolulu, the three of us took one look at the place and never wanted to leave. We sure weren't hurting for money, so there was no reason why we couldn't stay here forever if we wanted. We bought us a house, found a school for John, and felt like we'd come home. That was back in '25. I remember Ed saying that he didn't have to bother going to heaven because he was already living there. He died two years later. Just about broke Johnny's heart. That's why I was so glad to have Peyto come live with us. He was a real big help to John. And me too. Gave us something to think about besides how much we missed Ed. You can't be miserable for long with Peyto around."

I asked Marilyn if she'd ever met Peyto's parents. No matter how well the arrangement had worked out, the fact that they had sent their fourteen-year-old son to live with a stranger still bothered me.

"Met 'em once. They were on their way back to the States from China and stopped off in Honolulu for a few days. That was right before John and Peyto left for Stanford."

"You mean they hadn't seen him since they sent him away to school?"

"Nope. Too busy saving souls, I guess. China's a real big place, you know. A lotta souls there."

"What were they like?"

"Peyto's folks?" Marilyn leaned back in her chair. "Well, if I were to speak in my usual refined and ladylike manner, all's I could tell you is that one meeting was enough."

"And if you weren't?" I asked.

"Well, then I'd probably say that the Reverend Wilbur Willis and his missus were a couple of Pious Petes and about as warm and friendly as an icebox full of rattlesnakes."

"Peyto managed to find you and John, so things worked out for him. But his parents couldn't have known that when they sent him away. They left him with a total stranger. How could they do that to their own child? I don't understand."

"Me neither," Marilyn said. "Least I didn't until I met them. They pretended they'd been real worried about sending Peyto to school in Honolulu, but honestly, they didn't give two hoots what he did or where he went as long as it was away from them and their religious pals. That's why they shipped him here in the first place instead of back to the States with the rest of the missionary brats. After all, old Windbag Wilbur was a big noise in the missionary trade—still is, as far as I know. He couldn't have some wild child of his messing all that up, could he?" Marilyn paused but only for breath.

"And as for Ma Willis, she was even worse. A galloping old snob with nothing to be snobby about, least nothing that I could see. It took her about two minutes to let me know that she was one of *the* Peytos of Dayton, Ohio—whoever they were when they were at home. She was so damn ladylike, she wouldn't've said shit if you dumped her in a manure pile. How those two ever produced Peyto beats me. Gotta be one of the mysteries of nature. They're back in the States now, high-hattin' it around Dayton at last report. Lucky old Dayton."

"Was Peyto really such a wild child?" I asked.

"Depends whose notion of wild you go for. I know he mostly palled around with the Chinese kids, and one time him and Sam Leong got drunk on rice wine. The two of them liked chasing after girls too. In my books that makes them pretty much average boys. In Wilbur Willis's books, it made them sinners."

"Were the girls Peyto and Sam chased after Chinese?"

"Well, those are the kind of girls you generally find in China." Marilyn laughed. "Chinese ones."

"Then I'll bet his parents didn't like that much either." I knew how my own parents would react if I brought home a Chinese boyfriend or, for that matter, how they would view Marilyn and David's relationship. And I think my parents were a lot more tolerant than Peyto's sounded.

"You got that one right. The good Reverend Mr. Willis earned his living saving Chinese souls, but he sure wasn't going to stand for his son getting cozy with a Chinese girl. And they called themselves Christians." Marilyn shook her head. "You got the time, Kay? Couldn't find my watch this morning."

"It's two-thirty."

"Lordy! I promised Lily we'd be back by three. We gotta get a move on."

Marilyn paid the lunch bill. She left a very big tip for our orphan waitress.

CLIPPER OVER BOOKED STOP DELAYED HONOLULU GUEST OF PAN AM STOP DUE HK DEC THREE BY CLIPPER STOP NEW PLAN COLLECT ACTORS STOP RETURN SAN FRANCISCO BY CLIPPER DECEMBER EIGHTEEN STOP ALL IS WELL STOP INTREPID TRAVELLER.

I thought for a whole day about how to word that telegram to Mr. Miyashita. It cost a fortune to send, but I decided that I had to cover all the bases—the reason for my delay in Honolulu, the fact that I was still being looked after by Pan Am, the new plan I'd made to continue on to Hong Kong and collect the Sharakus, and, most important, the date of my return home, or at least my arrival in San Francisco. I signed it Intrepid Traveller because I decided that sharing in his little joke would let Mr. Miyashita know better than anything that I was safe, secure, and confident. It would convince him I had everything in hand despite the setback. From then on, I signed all my telegrams to him Intrepid Traveller, and he addressed all his wires to me the same way. I had no way of knowing how much trouble that would cause him down the road.

As I had expected, Mr. Miyashita fired back a telegram the next day. Its meaning was unambiguous. DO NOT CONTINUE HONG KONG STOP IMPERATIVE INTREPID TRAVELLER RETURN HOME SOONEST STOP H MIYASHITA.

For a minute or two, I thought about pretending I hadn't received the telegram, but I knew I couldn't be that dishonest. On the other hand, I didn't have the slightest intention of cutting short my time with Peyto no matter what the boss ordered. I came to a compromise—at least it seemed like a compromise to me. I waited two more days before I sent a reply stating that I had investigated the possibility of returning immediately but the first east-bound Clipper was already fully booked. It could have been the truth. After all, hadn't the Pan American station manager himself told me on the day I landed in Honolulu that there was only one seat left on the next Clipper flight to San Francisco? Surely it was reasonable to assume that seat, too, would be booked by now. At least that's what I told myself. I intentionally did not mention the possibility of going home by ship. Once again Intrepid Traveller assured Mr. Miyashita that all was well. I did not send a separate wire to my parents because I knew that he would call them and pass on the news. Besides, it was easier to tell my sort-of-truths to him than to them.

The next day I got two telegrams, one from Mum and Dad (BOAT HOME NOW) and the other from Mr. Miyashita informing Intrepid Traveller that he had booked her a passage on a ship leaving Honolulu for San Francisco the next morning. This time Intrepid Traveller did out-and-out lie. I pretended I hadn't got the wire until after the ship sailed. In my hormone-addled mind, delaying a telegram's arrival time didn't seem nearly as dishonest as pretending I hadn't got it at all. After all, it was only a matter of a few hours, half a day at most. In any case, the upshot of this flurry of telegrams was that nothing changed. I would fly to Hong Kong with Peyto just as I had intended all along.

During those two weeks in Hawaii, I did not simply visit an island in the Pacific but an island in time as well. At least that's how it feels to me now. I drifted through those fourteen days suspended in a haze of happiness, but inevitably, the clock began to tick again. Early in the morning on the last Friday in November, Marilyn drove Peyto and me to Pearl to board the Clipper for Hong Kong. She cried when it came time to say goodbye, and I know I shed a few tears myself. I promised to visit her again as soon as I could, a promise it took me far too long to keep.

SOME VERY GOOD news this morning. I'm going home at the end of the month. Two weeks and five days and I'll be sleeping in my own bed. I'll have to put on my writing skates if I'm going to reach the end of the war before I leave Foothills Sunset. To help speed things up now, I've decided to include some of the letters I wrote to Mum and Dad while I was on my trip. Mum saved every letter and postcard I sent and put them in a brown envelope labelled "Kay's Big Trip." I found it when I was clearing out the old house after she died. Fortunately, I had the good sense to toss it into my snow-boot box, and now, almost fifty years later, I've finally got around to opening it.

Reading the letters has been great fun. I think I'll just chuck them in as is when I go home and start to put my real memoirs together. For one thing, they will undoubtedly be more accurate than my old lady's memory. Well, at least they'll be more accurate as far as they go. Turns out I was quite the little virtuoso in the art of telling selective truths. I should have gone into politics. For instance, the letters from Honolulu don't say much about Peyto; they don't even mention him by name. I told Mum and Dad that I'd sat next to a nice businessman on the Clipper whose parents were Baptist missionaries and that he had introduced me to a good friend of his in Honolulu. My well-groomed narrative describes the friend as an older woman, a widow with a grown son. I reported that Mrs. Margolis had kindly taken me under her wing during my involuntary stay in Hawaii. An account of how I helped her deliver a donation of fruit and vegetables from her garden to the Salvation Army orphans features prominently. All things considered though, I'd have to say that the letter describing the remainder of my journey across the Pacific is the masterpiece of the lot. It makes no mention of Peyto whatsoever. Since I spent every minute of every day and every night with him, this was quite an accomplishment.

In truth, reading that letter now is like reading a travel diary written by a stranger. My tiny handwriting covers both sides of ten sheets of the stationery provided by Pan Am's hotels along the route. There are some pretty good descriptions of those hotels, particularly the ones the airline built on Midway and Wake Islands expressly for its Clipper passengers. Midway and Wake were so far off the beaten path that no civilian facilities existed on either until Pan Am decided to use them as fuelling stops. Midway had been the site of an old cable station and did have a military base, but Wake was not much more than a mile or two of sand and sea birds. Pan Am shipped in and built everything needed to run its seaplane ports—docks, fuel dumps, weather stations, maintenance facilities, the hotels themselves. While they may not have risen to the same class of luxury as the Royal Hawaiian, those tidy, one-storey buildings did provide comfortable, small rooms and excellent meals. I remember that the airline really blew the trumpet in its advertising about how the hotels served guests fresh produce flown in with them on the Clipper. The plane I was on also carried a box of library books from the Honolulu Public Library for the Pan American staff. I think the books were even more welcome than fresh vegetables in those isolated workplaces.

The letter goes on at great length about Midway's gooney birds, the Laysan Albatrosses, great seafaring birds with wingspans over six feet and a complete lack of fear of human beings that had earned them their nickname. I'll stick those pages in for sure. Amazing creatures, the goonies. There were scores of them nesting on the ground near the hotel. Late in the afternoon of our arrival, Peyto and I went for a swim to stretch our legs after the nine-hour flight from Honolulu. On our stroll down to the beach, we passed within a few feet of a huge adult gooney sitting on its nest. It took no notice of us. We could have walked right up and patted it, but the Laysan was a protected species back then, just as it is now, and pestering them was frowned upon. Many of the goonies nested in the area of Midway controlled by the military, which, in those uneasy days leading up to the war with Japan, was fenced, guarded, and strictly off-limits to civilians. We were only permitted in the tiny area directly surrounding the Pan Am base. I wonder how the poor phlegmatic goonies fared during the Battle of Midway? Probably sat on their nests and watched while Japanese bombers dropped explosive eggs all around them. At least they survived the war, which is more than the Pan American bases did.

I have another bird memory of Midway. This one didn't make it into the letter, and I had forgotten all about it until last night when I was telling Meggie about the goonies. I remembered that Peyto and I had been awakened at dawn by a canary singing outside my window. That morning at breakfast, Peyto asked the station manager about it and was told that a long-departed employee of the island's old cable station had released a dozen of his pet canaries shortly before the First World War. By the time my Clipper touched down, nearly thirty years later, there were flocks of their descendants everywhere. It's a wonderful memory that—making love with Peyto in my little room at the Pan Am hotel while the canaries made music at the window. I don't know how I could have forgotten it so completely. I wonder if the canaries are still there?

Mostly, those letters and postcards seem funny to me now. Prim little travelogues, often written as I sat beside Peyto on the long flights over water when there was nothing to see but ocean meeting sky along an endless horizon. I read a few of the postcards to Meggie last night, and we had a good laugh.

"Well, honestly, what else could you have said?" Meggie asked. "'Dear Mum and Dad, Having a swell time,'" she began in imitation of my style. "'Lost my seat on the Clipper one day and my virginity the next. Weather's grand. Love, Kay.'"

This sent us off into more gales.

"If there's one thing I have learned in a very long life, it's that there are times when honesty is not the best policy," Meggie continued when she had collected herself.

I didn't like to spoil the moment by mentioning that it was just that kind of dishonesty, my little sins of omission, that got me into the worst mess of my life.

I MAILED MY letter to Mum and Dad the day we landed in Manila. The next morning we changed planes and boarded the China Clipper, the smaller and slower-flying boat that Pan Am used as a shuttle between the Philippines and Hong Kong, the shortest leg of the trip. The big Boeing that brought me from Hawaii only went as far as Manila, then turned around and started back to San Francisco. My letter must have been on that return flight because it got to Canada long before I did.

The letter I wrote from Hong Kong never did make it home. I posted it in the lobby of the Peninsula Hotel on Sunday, December 7. On that side of the International Dateline, December 7 was the day before Pearl Harbor. It was also the day before I stood at the window of my hotel room and watched the Japanese bomb Hong Kong harbour. That Monday, when I saw planes flying low over the water and heard the boom of explosions, I thought the British air force must be out for a morning practice. I was surprised they had so many aircraft and such modern ones stationed in Hong Kong, and shocked that they would use real bombs in the crowded harbour. It wasn't until Peyto rushed into my room shouting at me to grab my things and run that I fully grasped what was happening. When he told me the China Clipper had been sunk, strafed, and burned at her mooring, I realized I no longer had a way to get home.

I WISH I had my missing letter now. I know that the Hong Kong I saw in 1941 was very different from the modern city bristling with skyscrapers that is its descendant today, but without that letter, the bombing raid will remain my most vivid memory of it. I found that out this afternoon when I began to write about the sights I saw from the Clipper as we landed in Hong Kong harbour. After a sentence or two I realized I was jotting down what I imagined I must have seen, not what I knew for a fact that I did see. Now I understand how Jim Leandros felt when he tried to write about his childhood trip to Greece. I guess my memoirs won't be going on about junks and sampans and ferries and floating restaurants. I talked to Meggie about my spotty Hong Kong memories. She says so what? If my grandchildren want a travel guide to the Hong Kong of 1941, they can buy themselves an old Baedeker on eBay. She thinks I should cut to the chase and get on with telling about Mr. Merridew and the Sharakus.

WE LANDED IN Hong Kong the afternoon of Wednesday, December 3. Peyto's friend Sam Leong stood waiting for us on the Pan American dock at Kai Tak airport. He took us straight to the Peninsula Hotel, where the airline had booked me a room. The Peninsula is in Kowloon near the harbour so it wasn't far to go, but even in that short distance, I knew I had arrived in a place so different as to be completely beyond my ken. Everything was foreign—the faces, the signs, the clothes, the voices, the smells. Most foreign of all was the sheer mass of people cramming the streets. Perhaps my memory has exaggerated their numbers, but I can still see narrow, winding pavements choked with people, all shoving their way in and out of shabby little shops. To this day, I can almost feel them surging by me, churning their way through the jumble of food stalls and street vendors' rickety barrows. People on foot, people on bicycles, people pulling rickshaws, all of them jostling for space, oblivious to the blaring horns of the taxis edging past. Since the Japanese invasion of China in 1937, the population of Hong Kong had doubled. That afternoon it felt as if every one of the city's million and a half inhabitants was out on the streets. And there I was, a kid from the underpopulated Canadian prairie, dropped into the crush. Compared with Hong Kong, Calgary was empty. Even on Stampede Monday, when everyone and his neighbour gathered downtown to watch the parade, I'd never seen crowds like the ones I saw on that average Wednesday afternoon in Hong Kong. But it wasn't only the sheer number of people that overwhelmed me. Before then, I had never experienced how it felt to be in either the racial or linguistic minority. It came as a shock. I was very glad to be with Peyto and Sam.

"Refugees," Sam said as he saw me staring out the taxi window at a woman and her three small children begging on a street corner. "Thousands of them have come here from China to escape the Japs. So many that there's no way for them to earn a living, and nowhere for them to live but the streets."

Even in the worst of the Depression, I'd never seen people living on the streets of Calgary, though in the summer, hobos passing through town often bedded down for the night on the north bank of the Bow River across from St. George's Island. Sometimes, when Mum and I went for an evening stroll along the river, we'd see the flicker of their bonfires across the water.

When he was in Hong Kong, Peyto usually stayed at a little Chinese hotel near the apartment where Sam lived with his wife and son, but this time he'd had Pan Am book him a room at the Peninsula. He couldn't get one next to mine, but he was on the same floor. Ridiculous when I think back on it, paying for two expensive rooms, one of which would be empty most of the time. All because we felt the need to maintain a facade of respectability for the benefit of strangers neither of us would ever see again. Peyto was insistent about our maintaining separate rooms. Not that we fooled anyone, least of all the staff of the Peninsula. I think he regarded it as his gentlemanly duty to protect my reputation.

I wasn't surprised to find a telegram from Mr. Miyashita waiting for me at the hotel. What did surprise me was that there was only one. IMPERATIVE INTREPID TRAVELLER LEAVE HONG KONG IMMEDIATELY STOP MISSION TOO DANGEROUS STOP RETURN SOONEST STOP THIS IS AN ORDER STOP H MIYASHITA. Even in the truncated language of that single cable, I should have been able to hear his distress. Instead, Intrepid Traveller sent a reply that afternoon blithely repeating the Clipper itinerary I'd outlined in my previous telegram and telling him that all was well with me in Hong Kong. What an idiot I was, an idiot blinded by the know-it-all arrogance born of ignorance that allows the young to assume they are immune to hurt and danger and even death. Good thing I was a lucky idiot or I wouldn't be sitting here writing this.

That night we ate dinner with Sam and his wife at a little restaurant near their house. Thanks to the school at Peyto's parents' mission, Sam spoke excellent English. On the other hand, his wife's English was on a par with my Cantonese, so Sam and Peyto spent a good part of the evening serving as interpreters. Mrs. Sam (whose name I am ashamed to say I have forgotten) was very kind to me. She was the one who took me shopping.

My meat-and-potatoes Canadian palate got a real workout that night. I tried all sorts of food for the first time—eel (excellent), squid (not bad but a little bouncy), chicken feet (grim)—and did it with chopsticks too. I didn't recognize much of what was set in front of me. Each time a new dish appeared, Peyto and Sam would watch my reaction as I took a first bite, then ask me to guess what it was. I didn't need to taste a chicken foot in order to identify it, but the look on my face when I took my first nibble of toe reduced them both to fits of laughter. Even Mrs. Sam couldn't help smiling, although, at the same time, she chided both her husband and his friend for being rude to a guest. Her tone of voice made translation unnecessary.

What a lovely evening we had in that little restaurant. The pleasure Peyto and Sam took in each other's company was obvious. That was the last evening they would ever spend together. After the war, with the help of Continental Implements, I managed to get an address and write to Sam. In his reply he told me that his son survived the occupation, but that Mrs. Sam had not. She died of an infection a month before the Japanese surrender. I saw Sam again in 1986 when Ken and I spent a few days in Hong Kong on our way home from a package tour to China. I couldn't bring myself to do all the explaining that honesty would require, so I told Ken I was going shopping when, really, I went to see Sam. He had remarried and, like me, was enjoying grandchildren and a good life. As we said goodbye, he told me that not a day passed that he didn't think of Peyto.

Before we left the restaurant, Sam brought Peyto and me up to date on Mr. Merridew and the Sharakus.

"Merridew sent a messenger to the office yesterday," he said. "A Chinese woman. She told me that he will meet Kay on Sunday afternoon at two o'clock in front of the temple in Tai O."

"That's miles away," Peyto said. "Why can't he meet her here in the city?"

"I asked that same question," Sam replied. "But she would give me no answer except Sunday at two o'clock in Tai O."

"And not until Sunday?" I asked. "Why the delay, I wonder?"

"Could be our Mr. Merridew is reluctant to show his face in town," Peyto said. "Or at the very least, he wants the home field advantage."

"Perhaps he thinks that Kay is a representative of Miyashita Industries and does not want to be seen doing business with her. Now that all Japanese assets in Hong Kong are frozen, such a transaction would be illegal."

"No one here knows who Kay works for. As far as anyone but us is concerned, she's in Hong Kong on vacation," Peyto said.

"Mr. Merridew must know who the prints belong to," Sam pointed out. "Nakimura would certainly have told him that. He would have to."

"Maybe," Peyto said. "But practically speaking, Kay's prints don't belong to anybody at the moment, do they? Unless you consider that possession really is nine-tenths of the law, in which case they're Merridew's. So what difference does it make where he collects his money?"

"Where is Tai O?" I asked, more to put an end to their depressing speculations than anything else.

"A good twenty-five miles from here," Peyto replied.

"Well that's not so far."

"It is by water. Tai O is on the east coast of Lantau island."

I must have looked dismayed.

"You must not let that worry you, Kay," Sam said. "I have already made arrangements with my cousin Chen to take us there in his motor launch. It is the fastest water limousine in Hong Kong. And the most beautiful."

"It's a Hacker-Craft." Peyto tossed off the name of the legendary maker of hand-crafted wooden pleasure boats. Being a nice polite Canadian, I nodded as if it meant something to me.

PEYTO WAS BUSY for the next few days, completing arrangements for shipping his farm machines to various small ports in Southeast Asia. He took me with him one day. That's how I first met the captain of the *Daisy Flanders*, the American freighter that had brought the Continental Implements' cargo from the States to Hong Kong. Captain Fraser invited us to lunch with him in the Officers' Mess, which sounds very grand but was baked beans on toast that we ate off blue willow china. The rim of my plate was chipped. Why I happen to remember that detail I do not know—shades of Sir Dudley North and the *Empress of Australia*. However, I do have good reason to remember Captain Fraser. If it weren't for him and the *Daisy Flanders*, I'd never have made it home from Hong Kong.

I did manage a little sightseeing. I know I rode the Victoria Peak tram because I bought and mailed the postcard to Mum and Dad at the upper station. Then I walked the rest of the way to the top of the mountain, where I looked through the bars of the wrought-iron fence that surrounded the Governor's Summer Residence. On the way back down to the station, I remember stopping to gaze out across the South China Sea. The alchemy of the late-afternoon sun had transformed its surface to liquid gold.

I went shopping too. I got Charlie a white silk scarf, thinking it would be a perfect present for a new pilot. I could never have bought him one at home because silk had become almost impossible to find. Probably all going to make parachutes. I found some green tea for Mrs. Miyashita, although I didn't manage to bring it home. It was in my suitcase along with Charlie's scarf and some little gifts I'd picked up for Mum and Dad. I deserted the whole lot in my room at the Peninsula. I left with nothing but the clothes on my back and the Sharakus.

Those Hong Kong days and nights with Peyto passed all too quickly. Suddenly it was Sunday, and time to meet with Mr. Merridew. Peyto and I stood in the morning sunshine on a little pier near the hotel, waiting for Sam and his cousin Chen. (I never did know whether Chen was his first or last name.) They pulled up in the most elegant boat I have ever seen, a thirty-foot motor launch, all sleek lines and polished mahogany, with an open cockpit that could seat half a dozen passengers in the lap of marine luxury. Peyto and Chen greeted each other like the old friends they were, then Sam introduced us. With Peyto translating, I complimented Chen on his beautiful boat. He replied to my praise with some suitably self-deprecating comments, but it was obvious that he was proud of the launch. I know it had a name—*The Speedy and Sumptuous Sampan of a Thousand Damp Delights* or something—one of those flowery Chinese names that sound so goofy translated into English. Peyto always referred to it as the Hacker-Craft, and so did I.

Peyto sat up front with Chen while Sam and I settled comfortably into the big padded seats directly behind them. Apparently Chen wanted to discuss a business deal he was contemplating with Peyto, but how they expected to carry on any kind of conversation over the noise of the big twin motors and the wind rushing past the open cockpit was beyond me. However, they seemed to manage. So did Sam and I, but it was a struggle.

"My cousin's business is doing so well that he wants to add another boat to his fleet," Sam leaned over and shouted in my ear as we roared off through the harbour.

"Well, this one is certainly a beauty," I bellowed back.

"It was not always so beautiful. Were it not for my cousin's timely intervention, it would now be on a scrap heap."

He told me how Chen had purchased the boat's remains for next to nothing from a wealthy merchant whose son had smashed it into a concrete pier on a whisky-fuelled joy ride.

"The drunken son was unhurt, not a scratch," Sam continued. "But the beautiful Hacker-Craft was in ruins." He shook his head at the unfairness of life.

Thanks to Peyto, Chen was able to have the launch restored to its full glory. It was now the flagship (and only ship) of his water-limousine business. The business had only been in operation for two years but was already such a success that he was looking to expand. Sam told me that Chen owed his success to Peyto, who had been willing to invest in him and his wrecked boat when no one else would take the risk. As a consequence, the grateful Chen's water limousine was at his silent partner's disposal whenever Peyto was in Hong Kong.

"But, Sam, we aren't making this trip for Peyto," I said. "I'm the one who has to go to Tai O, so you must ask your cousin how much I owe him for his service."

"I cannot do that." Sam was shocked. "My cousin would be deeply insulted if I did. You are Peyto's . . ." He hesitated for a moment. "You are Peyto's dear friend. Chen will do for you what he would do for Peyto." And that was the end of that discussion.

Sam and I didn't talk again for the remainder of the trip. We sat in companionable silence enjoying the ride. I began to count the ships we passed in the harbour but lost track when I caught sight of the *Daisy Flanders* lying at anchor. I tapped Peyto on the shoulder and pointed.

"Peyto, look over there!" I shouted into the wind. "It's the *Daisy*."

He turned around in his seat and cupped his hands around his mouth. "She's sailing tomorrow afternoon," he shouted back to me. "Bound for Manila, then back to the States."

CHEN DROPPED THE three of us off at a wooden dock a few minutes walk from the village, then immediately took his beautiful boat back out into the channel to wait for our return. Chen had been to Tai O before and made no secret of the fact that he did not like the place or its inhabitants. I soon began to see his point. There were at least a dozen people busy on the little fishing boats tied up at the dock, but none of them acknowledged our presence with so much as a nod. Any glances we got were not friendly ones.

"Looks like *gweilos* in fancy boats aren't the rage in Tai O," Peyto said. The welcome didn't get any warmer as we walked into the village. News of our arrival had travelled fast. People stood in doorways staring out with hostile eyes as we passed. I began to feel more than a little uneasy.

"Take heart, my round-eyed barbarian friends," Sam said with a grin in an obvious attempt to reassure me. "I promise to protect you."

"Fat chance," Peyto countered. "They don't like you any better than us."

"Alas, I fear that is so," Sam agreed.

I've heard people refer to Tai O as the Venice of the Orient, which makes about as much sense as calling Beiseker the Paris of the Prairies. Tai O was a poor, rural fishing village situated at the mouth of a little river. Most of its houses and shops were built over the water on stilts, hence the Venice comparison. And ramshackle affairs they were, as I remember. Nowadays, the place is a tourist destination, and that has replaced fishing as the number-one source of income. However, when I first saw it, Tai O was small, smelly, and remote—the Hong Kong back of beyond.

A seedy version of my old boss at Greer & Western stood waiting for us in front of the temple. Mr. Merridew was every bit as tubby as Mr. Calthorpe and had the same dew of nervous sweat on his forehead. However, for a portly man, the face under the black, slicked-back hair was incongruously thin and pointy. He looked like a fat ferret, and a grubby ferret at that. The grey dinge of his once-white suit was relieved only by the gravy stain on its lapel. The gravy motif continued on his necktie, a striped imposter doing its best to pass as English public school. Still, I could see that he had made an effort to spruce himself up. His face was nicked with shaving cuts and his down-at-heels shoes gleamed with new polish. I think he'd had a go at the gravy too, but all he managed to do was spread it around.

That's when I decided that Mr. Merridew was a man in need of cash, up front and right this minute. Although he probably did not realize just how valuable the Sharakus were, he must have at least suspected that he could make more than a hundred pounds by selling them himself. Except that would mean taking a risk. A big risk. What if he could not find a buyer? Then he'd be stuck with a stack of worthless paper and out whatever money he'd paid to Nakimura. No. Better a hundred pounds in hand than a thousand that might never come. Poor, desperate, sleazy Mr. Merridew. How could he know that a few days later in Hong Kong his safe British pounds would themselves become a stack of worthless paper?

"Miss Jeynes, I presume." He doffed a hat of the same colour and condition as his suit. "Allow me to welcome you to Tai O, dear lady." He gave Peyto and Sam the once-over as I introduced them. "I was not aware that you planned to bring associates with you. Gentlemen, this is indeed an unexpected pleasure."

Mr. Merridew was not at all pleased to see them. Clearly, he had assumed that, on my own, I would be much easier to intimidate. I have to admit that his assumption was correct because even with Peyto and Sam by my side, I still found him a little frightening. In light of that, I'm very proud of the way I stood up to him. We played a game that afternoon, and I won. Granted, he was nothing but a two-bit crook, strapped for cash and desperate, but on the other hand, there I was, a new-laid egg just rolled in from Calgary. My canny businessman grandfather, the Morpeth grocer, would have been proud of me.

"Unfortunately, it is not yet the hour of tiffin," Merridew continued. "But may I at least give you some tea? There is a small tea house nearby that brews an excellent cup. They keep a supply of Fortnum & Mason's best Assam on hand especially for me." All the tea in China and Mr. Merridew drank Indian.

The tea house perched above the water on long, spindly poles. The only light in its dim interior came from a small window that looked out over the channel. Mr. Merridew greeted the landlord in fluent Cantonese, and we settled ourselves around a bare wooden table under the window. The chairs were the spiritual kin of the ones in Greer & Western's lunchroom. The landlord's wife brought the tea. Sam told us later that the she was the woman who had delivered Mr. Merridew's message to him in Hong Kong.

Before the first cup had been poured, Mr. Merridew began asking me chatty questions. Had my journey on the Clipper been a pleasant one? How long I did I intend to stay in Hong Kong or, as he put it, "grace our fair city"?

"Mr. Merridew, I apologize for being in such a rush, but my time in Hong Kong is limited, and I must get back to the city as soon as possible. I have an important meeting there later today." My spur-of-the-moment fictional appointment came as news to Peyto and Sam, but they played right along. "So getting down to the matter at hand, I believe the agreed price for your services is a hundred pounds."

"Alas, dear lady, I regret to report that circumstances have changed."

"What circumstances are those?"

"A business associate of mine who is something of a collector has expressed an interest in purchasing the prints. He has made a preliminary offer of two hundred and fifty pounds."

"But the prints don't belong to you," I pointed out.

Mr. Merridew continued as if I had not spoken. "Of course, I told my associate that I would have to wait and discuss terms with you. After all, you have made a long and costly journey for the express purpose of collecting these works of art. I understand they are an inheritance and very precious to your employer. That is why I felt obliged to provide you with the chance to reply to my associate's offer."

We had come to the crunch. Did Mr. Merridew really have a buyer or was he simply doing his best to jack up the price? I put my money on the latter, reasoning that if he'd actually been offered two hundred and fifty pounds, the Sharakus would be long gone. Besides, a real collector would have offered a lot more. By then I was certain that Mr. Merridew had no idea of their real value. Because of his ignorance, I now had the upper hand.

"Where did you get the idea that collecting the prints was the sole purpose of my trip?" I did my best to mix condescension with incredulity. The incredulity part was easy, but it's hard to pull off condescension if you're a twenty-one-year-old girl dealing with a middle-aged man. I must have managed though because my words seemed to knock Merridew off his game.

"But, dear lady, I was led to believe that . . ."

"Then whoever did the leading was sorely mistaken." I shook my head, dismayed that he could actually believe such a ridiculous notion. "Mr. Merridew, my employer is a businessman," I continued. "He does not send his employees halfway round the world on a sentimental whim."

The pink tip of Merridew's tongue slid rapidly over his ferret lips. "I thought at the time it sounded rather far-fetched." He smiled as if we were enjoying a good joke together and then busied himself checking the level of the water in the teapot, buying time while he did his best to regroup. "However, I don't see that it changes anything. My associate's offer still stands."

"Then I think you should accept it," I told him. "Because I can't possibly match two hundred and fifty pounds. My boss has authorized me to pay you one hundred, and that's it." I stood and held out a friendly but final hand. Peyto and Sam stood too. "I'm sorry we could not do business together, Mr. Merridew."

"Now, now, dear lady. Let's not be hasty. Please sit and finish your tea. Do hear me out."

I withdrew my hand but remained standing.

"I have no wish to alter the basic elements of our previous agreement," he continued. "So perhaps we might come to a new accommodation, one that would suit us both. In all honesty, I confess that I would much sooner release such beautiful art to you than to my business associate. Now that I have had the pleasure of meeting you, I might even see my way to taking a small loss in order to do so."

The three of us sat down again.

"Since you have been so honest with me, Mr. Merridew, I will be equally forthright with you," I said after some consideration. "Perhaps I could raise the agreed amount by another twenty pounds. However, you must appreciate that this extra money will come from my own purse because, as I told you, my boss has allowed me exactly one hundred pounds to complete our transaction. I'm fairly certain he will reimburse me for an additional twenty when I return with his prints and explain your dilemma to him, but I know for a fact that he will not repay me for anything over that. So one hundred and twenty pounds is absolutely all I can offer, and it's twenty pounds more than I should."

"But that is more than fair of you," he said. "I knew we would find common ground."

I was not about to let Mr. Merridew get the idea I was carrying a lot of extra cash. All those Mr. Moto movies had taught me something. "I have to be frank though. I'm not carrying enough sterling with me to cover the extra twenty. I'm short on Hong Kong dollars too, but I think I can make up the difference in American money. I hope that's acceptable."

"More than acceptable," he replied. "In my business I have occasion to deal in many currencies. So may I conclude that we now have an agreement?"

"Where are the prints?"

"Right here, safe with Mr. Lee."

He called to the landlord. Mr. Lee emerged from a back room carrying a bulky oilcloth parcel secured by tasseled cords. His wife cleared away the tea things, and he placed it on the table in front of me. There it sat—six inches high, a foot and a half wide, and two feet long—the parcel I had travelled from the other side of the world to collect. I untied the cords and peeled back the oilcloth. Under it were layers of heavy silk, and under them, thick layers of soft white cotton. Beneath the last of the cotton nested a polished wooden box with Japanese characters brushed on its lid. It had obviously been specially made to store the Sharakus. I lifted the lid and there they lay, all carefully interleaved with sheets of rice paper. The portrait of Tokuji was third from the top. I took it from the box and held it up for Peyto and Sam. Even in the tea shop's dim light, the powdered mica background shone with the lustre of polished pewter, and Tokuji looked out at me just as he did every day at work. I placed him back with his fellows and quickly checked a few of the other prints at random. I recognized them all, thanks to my well-studied copy of Henderson and Ledoux. I counted the whole stack and then had Peyto do the same.

"All fifty are here and they seem to be in good order," I said as I began to rewrap the bundle. "But I'm no authority on *ukiyo-e*, so I've arranged to have them checked by an expert back in Kowloon." I hadn't done anything of the kind, but Mr. Merridew wasn't to know that.

"That is very sensible of you and I would expect no less," he said, looking mightily relieved. "And you must contact me should you have any concerns. You can always find me here in Tai O." Oh well, if I could lie like a rug then the least I could do was smile while Mr. Merridew did the same. "But I assure you, dear lady, your lovely works of art are exactly as they came to me."

It didn't occur to me until later that he might be worried about the number and authenticity of the prints. After all, he had no way of knowing how many were supposed to be in the bundle or if the ones in it were genuine. The Sharakus had passed through many hands before they arrived at his door. If I had discovered that some were missing or, even worse, decided that they were fakes, then he would have paid Nakimura for nothing.

I finished tying the canvas straps back around the oilcloth before I opened my purse and handed over one hundred pounds in crisp five-pound notes that I'd taken from the stash in my secret pocket that morning at the hotel. Then I rummaged in the purse, making a show of coming up with seventeen more pounds, five rather rumpled American dollar bills, and a scattering of loose coin. I stopped short of turning the purse upside down and shaking it. Instead, I asked Peyto and Sam if they could help with the remaining amount. They obligingly searched their pockets and, between them, found enough Hong Kong and American dollars to do the trick. Mr. Merridew counted all of it. He seemed to be well up on current rates of exchange. We were twenty-five cents over. He scrupulously returned the quarter.

I don't know who was more anxious to see us on our way, me or Mr. Merridew. He set a quick pace as he escorted us to the dock. Peyto carried the prints, and our silent foursome made its way back past the same villagers' malevolent glances. Chen saw us coming and pulled the Hacker-Craft up to the dock, ready to board. In the time it took him to collect the Sharakus from Peyto and stow them in the luggage hold, Mr. Merridew had made it halfway back to the village. He'd left us without so much as a bon voyage to dear lady or her associates.

As soon as we cleared the channel Chen opened the throttles and the launch surged forward, pressing us back against our seats. Personally, I couldn't get away from Tai O fast enough. We sped across the water, my heart pounding in an adrenalin-fuelled rush of elation and relief. I was giddy with triumph, drunk on my own success. Rainbows danced in the spray from the bow. The wind blew salt mist in my face. I wanted to laugh and dance and sing all at the same time. Instead, I threw back my head and let out the biggest, wildest, loudest yell of my life—a yahhhoooo to make a Calgary cowboy proud. It turned Peyto round in his seat. He looked back at me and began to laugh. Then he cheered too and clapped. So did Sam. Even Chen joined in the noise, although I don't think he understood what it was all about. We rode the rest of the way with big, silly grins on our faces. In light of what was to come, I suppose we were a little ship of fools. But at least we were happy fools on that last night of peace in Hong Kong.

The sun had almost set by the time we made it back to the pier near the hotel. While Chen and Peyto unloaded the Sharakus, I paid Sam back his money. He was reluctant to take it.

"But you will need this on your travels," he said.

"I'll be fine, Sam. I have plenty of money to get me home."

"Then this afternoon in Tai O with Mr. Merridew, all that was a deception? A bluff?"

"Absolutely."

"Who would believe an American could bluff so well? You had me fooled."

"I'm a Canadian."

"Canadian, American, what does it matter? You are clever enough to be Chinese."

THAT NIGHT IN my room, Peyto and I unwrapped the oilcloth bundle and lifted the prints from their box. We examined each in turn by the light of a small desk lamp. There they were, the faces from my book. Tomisaburo of the long, angular features made the first appearance on our stage, acting the role of a grand lady whispering malice into the ear of her servant girl, a fat-cheeked little fellow named Manyo. Next came Ebizo, the bulky-bodied actor with the pointy nose and worried eyebrows, who made a specialty of playing low-class villains. I remember Peyto remarking on his uncanny resemblance to Mr. Merridew. Then

Tomisaburo appeared again, this time at his vituperative best, thin lips pursed in a spiteful little simper that left no doubt as to how he earned his nickname, Nasty Tomi. He reminded me of Miss Bayliss, my old supervisor back at Greer & Western.

The illustrations in my Henderson and Ledoux were all in black and white. This was the first time I had seen the Sharakus' colours. The transformation took my breath away. After a hundred and fifty years, their pigments were still fresh and lively, so vivid they might have been pulled from the printing blocks the day before.

We looked at the portrait of Tokuji for a long time. It gave me an odd feeling to see him there on the desk, as if a dear friend from home had suddenly appeared in the room. I told Peyto about the print that hung in Mr. Miyashita's office. I tried to explain my attachment to Tokuji but couldn't find the words. Perhaps I didn't know the reason. Can't say that I do now.

"The others are beautiful, but I'll always love Tokuji best."

"Then I guess I'd better find you a Tokuji portrait for a wedding present," Peyto said.

"A wedding present?"

"Oh, I know it's traditional for the groom to give the bride a fancy piece of jewellery on their wedding day, but why can't we break with tradition?"

"Did you just ask me to marry you?"

"No, I certainly did not. I'm taking that for granted. After all, I assume you plan on making an honest man of me," he said. "Say, you're not some vile, seducing hussy who's been taking advantage of me for her own selfish pleasure, are you? I warn you, Kay. If you've been trifling with my affections, I'll be heartbroken."

That night we fell asleep planning our future.

PEYTO WAS UP and out of the hotel the next morning shortly after seven, off to meet Sam and Chen. Chen had his eye on a boat in Aberdeen and wanted his silent partner to inspect it with him. They had invited me along for the ride, but I declined, thinking that Peyto might like some time alone with his friends, free from his role as my personal translator. Instead, I took a leisurely bath, dressed in my newly cleaned suit, and ordered bacon and eggs from room service. I had just finished eating when I heard the booms from the harbour. I was standing at the window watching the planes when Peyto came barrelling back with the news that the Japanese were bombing Hong Kong.

"Come on, Kay, we've got to get out of here! Grab what you can carry. Come on, let's go."

All I took was my raincoat and purse. Peyto carried the Sharakus. We ran down the stairs and out of the hotel. I did not know where we were headed. I simply followed him. We ran all the way to the harbour, where Sam and Chen were waiting with the Hacker-Craft. Thick, black clouds of smoke hung over the city. The explosions of bombs falling near the airport punctuated the staccato din of anti-aircraft fire. Japanese fighter-bombers roared overhead, flying low, strafing the water on their way to Kai Tak. Everywhere, little boats scurried to escape. Chen swerved his way around them as we headed out of Hong Kong along the same route we'd taken the day before.

"Where are we going?" I shouted to Peyto.

"To the *Daisy Flanders*," he shouted back. "I hope to God we can catch her before she sails."

PEYTO AND I were hauled up onto the cargo ship in a big, canvas sling, like pieces of freight. We stood on her deck watching the Hacker-Craft carry Sam and Chen back to the city and the smoke. Peyto did not look away, even after his friends had disappeared from view. He continued to stare out over the water until I took his hand in mine.

"I forgot to say goodbye." He turned to me with a puzzled frown. "I forgot to say goodbye to them, didn't I?"

THE NEXT THREE weeks were not a nightmare, they just felt like one. Nightmares end when you wake up. This one got worse. Shortly after we'd been taken on board, Captain Fraser told us that Pearl Harbor and the Philippines had been attacked too. The United States was at war, and every American ship and sailor would be needed. The *Daisy Flanders* was bound for Seattle at top speed.

I was desperate to contact Mum and Dad, to tell them that I was alive and on my way home, but Captain Fraser had ordered complete radio silence.

"Don't want to broadcast our position to every Jap sub in the Pacific," he said. "If the Japs want the *Daisy*, they'll have to come looking."

Peyto and I shared the tiny cabin usually occupied by the ship's first mate. He kindly volunteered his space and bunked in with a couple of the other officers, saying that he probably wouldn't get much sleep on this trip anyway. As it turned out, none of us got much sleep. Not a night went by that we weren't summoned on deck by the lifeboat alarm because someone thought he'd seen a submarine. I took to sleeping with my lifejacket on. To add to the misery, the Pacific was anything but pacific, and Peyto and I were both seasick. He got over it quicker than I did. A week later, I was still lying in the first mate's bunk, wishing I were dead. When I was finally able to eat, all that seemed to be on offer were canned baked beans and kippers. I swear to God the *Daisy*'s cook could have written a book on a thousand and one ways to serve smoked herring, all of them disgusting. I felt nauseated on and off for the rest of the trip. Still can't look a kipper in the eye.

The crew were kind to both of us. My tropical travelling suit was no match for North Pacific winds, so they scrounged up a thick wool sweater and some warm pants for me. The pants were so big I had to hold them up with a length of cord. They found a sweater for Peyto too, and when the weather turned really foul and wet, they provided us both with slickers and rubber boots. No one gave a damn that Peyto and I were sharing one narrow bunk, although I noticed they all called me missus. I did not correct them.

We celebrated Christmas aboard the *Daisy Flanders*. It was a pretty glum affair, although a couple of the men tried to make the best of it and put up some makeshift decorations in the mess. After dinner, someone produced an accordion, and we sang Christmas carols until the lifeboat alarm sounded. We all ran up on deck to stand in the driving rain and wait for a submarine to torpedo us.

I spent those weeks longing to reach Seattle, so I could contact Mum and Dad. At the same time, I wanted the voyage to last forever so I could stay with Peyto. I had a wretched time on that trip, but considering the carnage I'd left behind in Hong Kong, I knew my little miseries were nothing. I was incredibly lucky to be on my way home. To this day, I bless the *Daisy Flanders* and her crew for rescuing me. In 1943 she was sunk by a Japanese submarine one day out of Honolulu. There were three survivors. Captain Fraser was not among them.

We arrived in Seattle early on the morning of December 30. I remember it was rainy and cold. I could have used my borrowed sweater and thick serge trousers, but I had returned them to their owners before I left the ship. Peyto and I took a taxi from the dock to the train station, where I immediately found a phone and placed a collect call to Mum and Dad. It was all I could do not to burst into tears when I heard Mum tell the operator in a shaky voice that she'd accept the charges. As soon as I said hello, Mum began to ask over and over if it was really me, where was I, was I all right? Her Geordie got so broad and her words came so fast that even I had trouble understanding her. Slow down, Mum, I begged her, slow down. I might as well have tried to stop an avalanche. I told her I'd be home as soon as I could get a train reservation, but I'm not sure she heard me. I promised to call again when I got to Vancouver. It was past ten in Calgary, so Dad was at work and I didn't get a chance to speak to him. I asked Mum to let the Miyashitas know I was safe. I repeated for the tenth time that yes, it was really me and I was in Seattle.

Peyto came with me while I booked tickets on that morning's Southern Pacific train to Vancouver and the next evening's Dominion from Vancouver to home. The Seattle-Vancouver leg was no problem, but The Dominion was heavily booked. The clerk informed me that there were no drawing rooms or berths available. It was either coach or wait until the third of January. By then, where I sat on a train seemed so trivial a detail that I couldn't think why the clerk even bothered to mention it. I'd happily have ridden in the baggage car.

The train for Vancouver left Seattle around eleven, so Peyto and I had another hour together. If I were a real memoir writer I'd tell what we did for that last bit of time and write about how we said goodbye. But I don't want to do that. It would serve no purpose except to bring all the old feelings back again. There's no point in tormenting myself now. I did enough of that at the time. Besides, there's really nothing much to tell. We said our goodbyes. I got on the train to Canada and came home. Peyto went to the Seattle recruiting office and joined the navy.

RAIN FELL IN wind-lashed sheets all the way to Vancouver. Dense, low-lying clouds made noon feel like late evening. In my memory, it is always night on that last leg of my journey home. I arrived in Vancouver in the evening and went straight to a hotel, where I phoned Mum and Dad again. Then I soaked in my first hot bath since Hong Kong. I spent most of the next day asleep in my room before I caught the New Year's Eve train to Calgary.

It was still raining when we pulled out of Vancouver, but as The Dominion climbed into the mountains and the temperature dropped, the rain turned to snow. Freezing drafts blew through the coach every time someone opened one of the heavy doors at either end. I sat in a window seat, shivering in my light suit and raincoat, my feet resting on the bundle of Sharakus. The farther east we travelled, the more it felt like a block of ice. I stared out at the snowflakes swirling past the window. Reflected in the light from the car, they glittered for an instant, then disappeared into the dark. At midnight, a woman near the front of the car began to sing "Auld Lang Syne," and the rest of us joined her in a dispirited chorus before the conductor turned down the lights for the night. Feet of new snow high in the Selkirks slowed the train to a crawl, and a slide on the track near the Connaught Tunnel stopped it completely. It took the section crew hours to clear the line. We arrived in Calgary eleven hours late, at half past six in the morning on the second of January 1942.

Mum and Dad were both at the station to meet me. Mum burst into tears as soon as she saw me waving from the train window. The second my feet touched the platform, she and Dad took turns holding me so tightly I could hardly breathe. It wasn't until I had children of my own that I could even begin to imagine the relief they must have felt. They'd brought my winter boots and overcoat to the station.

Mum only stopped hugging me long enough to stuff me into them. Dad carried the Sharakus, and we walked to the car, where Mum bundled me into the backseat, tucked a blanket around my legs, and climbed in next to me. As Dad drove us home through the familiar streets, she put her arm around my shoulders. I leaned against her and breathed in the old car's friendly pong. Thinking back on that morning, my clearest memories are of warmth, my parents' love, and the stink of mice.

Assignment #11
IS THERE ANYTHING IN YOUR LIFE THAT YOU REGRET?

AND HOW'S THAT FOR A depressing assignment? No wonder
Meggie and I are worried about Janice. For the past few weeks, she's
been giving us topics that could get Up with People singing the blues.
We figure it's delayed fallout from her trip with Todd. But no matter
what the cause, the kid has come up with some real lulus—"Is It Really
Better to Have Loved and Lost Than Never to Have Loved at All?"
"What Was the Deepest Sorrow of Your Life?" "What Was the Most
Difficult Goodbye You Ever Said?" Now isn't that a question to be
asking a bunch of old crocks like us? Our lives are one goodbye after
another—goodbye people you love, goodbye health, goodbye indepen-
dence, goodbye home, goodbye memory, goodbye, goodbye, goodbye.
And that's not whining, Mr. Peele, that's reporting.

Meggie didn't even bother to start work on the Deepest Sorrow
business. Just the thought of sifting through the contenders for that
particular prize was enough to depress her for the rest of the day.
Fortunately, I was still busy with "Travelling" so I didn't get around
to any of them. But you can see why we're worried about Janice.
Shedding a tear or two over your broken heart is one thing; wallowing in the Slough of Despond is another. And over a little shit
like Todd.

Meggie told me that I'm not being fair about Todd, that one
person's Little Shit can be another person's Great Love. She says she
understands how Janice feels because her own life was a series of Todds
until she hooked up with Hersh. Before she met Hersh, she was miserable; after they got together, she was happy until the day he died. I wish
I could say the same, but, except for my weeks with Peyto, I don't think
I ever had such a clearly defined period of happiness. And lo, I digress
for the millionth time. I've come to the conclusion that, in my case,
digress is the fifty-cent word for wool gathering. By the way, that's one
more thing you say goodbye to, the ability to focus on the task at hand.

And me with stacks of notes to finish before I go home. Six more days to make it to the end of the war.

AS I STARTED up the walk, I heard a dog barking inside the house.

"Is that Nikkou?"

"That's Nikky, all right. We're keeping her for a bit," Mum said. "Just until things get settled."

"What things?" I asked, but by then Dad had opened the front door and the little dog's whirling welcome put a temporary end to talk.

"Time for a nice cup of tea and a bite to eat," Mum said after Nikkou finally calmed down and we had taken off our overcoats and boots. "I'll bet you didn't bother with breakfast this morning, did you?"

"But, Mum, it's still early. I haven't had a chance to eat."

"Just look at you." She shook her head. "Nothing but skin and bone. That suit is hanging off you."

"I was seasick," I said.

"All peely-wally and eyes like two burnt holes in a blanket."

"Quit your clucking, Mother Hen, and leave the girl be," Dad said. "Can't you see she's weary? She's travelled half the world to get home. What she needs now is a cup of tea and her bed."

Mum went to the kitchen to make the tea, and I sat in her easy chair with Nikkou cuddled on my lap. Her soft little body worked like a furry hot water bottle. I wished I'd had her with me on the train.

"So you're feeling fitter now, are you?" Dad asked.

I looked at him.

"You're over that seasickness?"

"I'm fine. I feel like I'm still riding on the train, but I don't feel sick." Not right then I didn't, but I'd vomited at least once almost every day since I left Hong Kong.

"Well, that's good. Because your mother's right. You are looking peaked."

"I'm fine," I repeated with a little more snap than I'd intended.

"Steady on, pet. No need to bite my head off."

"Sorry, Dad. Guess I'm tired and a bit cranky."

Mum served us our tea at the kitchen table. She'd made porridge too, steaming bowls of Red River mix that cried out for a big dollop of cream. That morning it was real cream, not just top of the milk. Ever the optimist when food was involved, Nikkou sat near the table, her gimlet gaze fixed on me as I ate.

"Why is Nikkou here?" I asked.

"Well, you see, things aren't quite what they were before you left. So Tose thought that Nikky might be happier with us for a wee bit, until things settle down." My mother was not one to dance around a topic, but right then she might as well have been wearing Charlie's tap shoes.

"What things?"

"You know. Things," she said vaguely. "Another spoon of porridge?"

"For God's sake, Judith, Kay's a grown woman. Tell her the truth." Dad turned to me. "Kay, Nikky is here with us because Mrs. Miyashita is afraid someone will hurt her if she stays at their house. Feelings have been running pretty high since Pearl Harbor, and there are those who aren't above taking it out on a little dog because her owners are Japs."

"And after we heard about what happened to those poor Winnipeg lads in Hong Kong, things got even worse," Mum said.

"The papers were full of Hong Kong," Dad added. "So many of our fellows killed and the rest of them prisoners. People are wanting to pay the Japs back for that."

"Oh, Kay, it's been dreadful for Tose. They throw garbage at her house at night—rotten vegetables and old eggs. Mr. M. had to hire a man to come round of a morning and clean the mess away."

"It's a bad business, all right," Dad agreed.

"And last week someone emptied a great big pail of . . . Somebody emptied . . ."

"Some filthy bugger threw a bucket of shit into the root cellar," Dad finished.

"The next day, Mr. M. had the whole thing filled in with sand," Mum said when she found her voice again. "Buried everything inside it—Tose's vegetables, the Christmas lights, all those lovely shelves your dad made. Everything."

"I'd have done the same," Dad stated. "The man did what had to be done."

"That's when Tose asked us to keep her dog. I know she misses Nikky so I take her with me when I go to visit. I promised Tose we'd be over this afternoon. She'll be that glad to see you, Kay, and so will he. The poor souls have been worried sick."

I had a warm bath and then crawled into bed and slept until noon. Nikkou hopped up on the bed and snoozed beside me. Normally, Mum wouldn't have allowed a dog within ten feet of her freshly laundered sheets, but that morning she made an exception. I woke once and couldn't remember where I was. I reached out for Peyto and saw Mum sitting near the foot of the bed on a little chair she'd brought in from Charlie's room.

"It's all right, pet," she said. "Only me. Go back to sleep."

I don't know how long Mum sat there, but she and the chair were gone by the time the noon whistle woke me. I dressed in my warmest clothes and went downstairs, where she had my favourite lunch waiting on the table—Cornish pasties. I did my best and ate half of one, but by then my stomach was feeling uncertain again and I couldn't finish it.

"You're not well. It's plain as the nose on your face. I can tell by looking at you. And don't give me that guff about being seasick again."

"I have been a little off," I admitted. "But I'll be okay now that I'm home."

"Maybe you caught a bug on the ship. Not that I'll ever have a bad word to say about those that brought you home. Like as not you caught whatever it is before you got on their boat." Mum considered this theory for a moment. "Probably sick from eating all that foreign food. God only knows what found its way into that muck."

"Could be," I agreed, taking the line of least resistance. I wouldn't be telling her about the chicken feet any time soon. "But I'm sure it's nothing. A day or two at home and I'll be fine."

"How did you get yourself on that freighter anyway?" she asked. "Getting on a ship's not like popping down the road to catch the streetcar."

I was saved by the bell. Dad telephoned from work on his dinner break to see how I was doing. When we'd finished talking, it was time to collect Nikkou and the Sharakus and leave for the Miyashitas' house.

IN THE EIGHT weeks I'd been away, the Miyashitas had grown older and greyer and smaller. Mr. Miyashita looked as if he had shrunk inside his clothes—the collar of his shirt gaped and his suit was too wide for his shoulders. Mrs. Miyashita had lost weight too, and her face was drawn and more lined than I remembered. Mr. Miyashita welcomed Intrepid Traveller home with his usual courteous reserve, but Mrs. Miyashita, in a very un-Japanese gesture, opened her arms to me. I leaned down and returned her embrace. She was so small and thin, her bones so delicate, it was like holding a child.

"Dear Kay. We worried about you very much. We were afraid." She finally let go and took a step back. "Now I see you safe in my house and I am filled with happiness."

Mum said the Miyashitas had worried themselves sick over me, but until I saw them that afternoon, I hadn't realized she meant it literally. In Mr. Miyashita's case, the worry was compounded by guilt at having sent me into harm's way. I'm sure he felt responsible for my close call in Hong Kong. He did not know that I had brought most of my troubles on myself. If I had obeyed his cabled order and left Honolulu when he told me to, I would have been home and safe weeks earlier. That afternoon back in Calgary, I could not tell him the truth so I said nothing.

By this time, Nikkou was beside herself, twirling and bouncing at the end of her leash like a canine paddleball. Mum unsnapped the lead from her collar, and the little dog rushed over to Mrs. Miyashita. She lay shivering and whimpering at her mistress's feet. Mrs. Miyashita knelt down and murmured soothing things in Japanese as she stroked the golden fur. When Nikkou finally stopped trembling, Mrs. Miyashita looked up at Mum.

"Right you are, Tose," Mum agreed, although her friend had not spoken a word. "High time Nikky took a little turn in the backyard or we'll be in for a repeat of that last performance. Though I must say the rug cleaned up a treat, didn't it?"

"I'll let her out," I volunteered.

"No, no. Nikkou must not be outside alone," Mrs. Miyashita said. "I go with her."

"I'll take her. Don't worry, she'll be safe with me." I put my overcoat back on. "C'mon, Nikkou."

I stood and watched while the dog tore around the Miyashitas' backyard, alternately rolling in the snowdrifts and annotating her favourite places. She gave the area where the root cellar had been a particularly careful going over, urinating furiously to re-establish it as part of her territory. There was nothing left of the cellar. The door, its wooden frame, the electrical wires—all gone. In their place was a mound of sand surrounded by dirty snow covered in boot prints left by the workmen as they filled in the hole Dad had worked so hard to dig. The mounded sand make it look like a new grave.

Back in the house, I found Mum and Mrs. Miyashita in the kitchen making tea. Nikkou deserted me as soon as she got a whiff of digestive biscuit. I went to hang up my coat and saw Mr. Miyashita sitting in the living room, staring out the window. I collected the prints, still wrapped in their oilcloth, from where I'd left them in the entrance hall and gave them to him. He thanked me politely and set the bundle down beside his chair.

"Don't you want to unwrap the box and check them, sir?"

"There will be time enough for that, Miss Jeynes," he said. "Right now we must join your mother and my wife for tea."

I never saw the Sharakus again.

THAT EVENING AT dinner I could no longer avoid telling Mum and Dad how I had managed to board the *Daisy Flanders*. "An American man helped me out. He was staying at the Peninsula too. He works for a big farm equipment company, and they had shipped some tractors and rice harvesters to Hong Kong on the *Daisy*. The captain is a friend of his."

"How did you meet this American?" Mum asked.

"Our rooms were on the same floor of the hotel. Sometimes I'd see him in the dining room. Matter of fact, I'd just finished eating breakfast when the bombing started. That's when he told me to grab my things and come with him." I told them about running down to the harbour and riding out to the *Daisy* in his friend's launch.

"How old a fellow is he?" Mum asked.

"Almost thirty, I guess. Anyway, quite a bit older than me."

"Sounds like a decent chap," Dad said. "It's a good man who'll look out for a stranger when he's in trouble himself. More Yanks like him and we wouldn't have been fighting Hitler alone all these years."

"Peyto is a good man," I said. "He was going to join the American navy the day we landed in Seattle."

"Plato," Mum said. "His people must be Greek."

"Not Plato, Mum. Peyto." I spelled it for her.

"Peyto. That's an odd name, isn't it?"

"Peyto Willis." It was a pleasure just to say his name. I missed him so much it felt almost like a physical pain. This astonished me. Up to then I had no idea that the old cliché about aching with longing was anything but a figure of speech. "His name is Peyto Willis," I repeated. I wanted to tell Mum and Dad about him, but what could I say? How could I explain to my parents that I had put them and the Miyashitas through hell so I could have a romantic fling with a man I hardly knew, or that given a second chance, I would do it again in a heartbeat?

"Well, Americans do have funny names sometimes, don't they?" Mum said. "Like Mrs. Simpson. Who ever heard of a girl called Wallace?"

I WENT TO work at my usual time on Monday morning. Mr. Miyashita did not arrive until after eleven. I made coffee and carried the cups into his office. I noticed that he had taken Tokuji's portrait down from the wall and set it on his desk.

"Our time together will be short this morning, Miss Jeynes. My wife becomes anxious when I am away, so I must return home as soon as possible."

Later Mum told me that Mrs. Miyashita had not been past the gate of her own yard since Pearl Harbor, not even to go on their grocery shopping expeditions. Mum now bought and delivered the food. Mr. Miyashita had continued to come to the office a couple of mornings a week, but he always took a taxi. However, this was the first time he had left his house since Christmas, the day Hong Kong fell to the Japanese.

"Then maybe we should go over the receipts from my trip first thing," I said. "I've brought the money from the emergency fund and all the travellers' cheques I didn't use."

"Thank you, but we do not have time right now. We will leave that for another day."

"I should put it all in the safe then. At least the cheques and the cash."

"I would prefer you to keep the money with you. It will be perfectly secure at your house. However, in future, you must use cash from the safe to pay all the office expenses, including your wages. I trust you remember the combination."

"The date you and Mrs. Miyashita came here to live." I recited it to him.

"Yes. Our first day in Calgary." He stood and took Tokuji's portrait from his desk.

"Miss Jeynes, I would like you to have this," he said. "Please consider it my thanks for your fine work in bringing my uncle's Sharakus home for me. As you know, there is another copy of the Tokuji portrait among them, and I think you will agree that no one needs two heads, do they?" He smiled at his little joke and for that moment was almost his old self. "At least that is what Uncle Nori said when he gave this one into my safekeeping. And today, I am giving it into yours." He held the portrait out, and I took it from him. "Tokuji now belongs to you, Miss Jeynes. It is a great pleasure for me to know that our mutual friend has found a good home."

Looking back, I can see that in his own odd way, Mr. Miyashita was saying goodbye to me, or at least to the me who was his employee. I did not understand this at the time and was surprised when he did not come to work the next day. As it turned out, he never set foot in our office again.

That evening, Dad helped me hang Tokuji's portrait in my room.

OUTWARDLY MY LIFE soon returned to its old Calgary rhythms, but nothing was really the same. I'd arrive at the office at seven-thirty every morning, just like I always had, but now there was almost no work to do. I still made coffee at ten, but Mr. Miyashita was never there to drink it with me. Occasionally, I'd leaf through a few of the photo files, but I had finished all the real work on them. Most of my mornings I spent writing letters to Peyto and reading. In the afternoon, I'd often walk to the Miyashitas' house to see if they needed anything or, on snowy days, to shovel their sidewalks. The odd-job man who used to do this had long since departed. Mrs. Miyashita and I would have a cup of tea together, but Mr. Miyashita never joined us. I have no idea what he did to occupy his time. Mrs. Miyashita always said that he was upstairs working in his study and might join us later, but he never did. I think he sat staring out the window for most of the day. I seldom saw him, and when we did meet, he hardly spoke.

Sometimes I'd help Mum shop for their groceries, although that didn't take any time to speak of. Two small, elderly people don't eat much. Mum stopped taking Nikkou when she visited. She told me Mrs. Miyashita had decided that Nikkou found going back and forth between houses too upsetting. In reality, I think that it was Mrs. Miyashita who found it too upsetting. She could not bear saying goodbye to her little dog over and over.

I'd been back in Calgary for almost two weeks. I still felt pretty seedy and continued to vomit regularly. Naive as I may have been, I wasn't a complete idiot. I'd missed a menstrual period when I was on the *Daisy Flanders* but had optimistically put that down to seasickness and stress. By the time another month had passed and still no period, I knew I was pregnant. I suspected it had happened on the one occasion we had not bothered with birth control—another reason you shouldn't make love on beaches. I looked in the phone book and found a doctor with offices down the block from the Grain Exchange Building. Mrs. Kay Willis made an appointment to see him. I've long since forgotten his name, but I certainly do remember him confirming that I was pregnant. I probably should have been dismayed by the prospect of unwed motherhood, but I was overjoyed that Peyto and I were having a child. Perhaps Marilyn's example had something to do with that. Because of her, I knew I could raise a child on my own if I had to. But, of course, I wouldn't have to. Peyto and I were going to be married. The future we had planned our last night in Hong Kong had included children. All we'd done was start on that part of the plan a little earlier than intended.

I didn't tell Peyto or anyone else that I was pregnant. Right then, I didn't want to share her. I wanted her to be all mine for just a little longer. Somehow I knew she was a girl, and that I would love her all my life. Two days later, I lost her. I went back to the doctor, but all he could do was confirm that I had miscarried. He told me to call him if I started to bleed again, and warned me that I might find myself feeling a little blue, that this was a common reaction to miscarriage. He also said that perhaps I should wait a while before resuming what he referred to as "relations" with my husband.

He may have been mistaken about my marital status, but he was spot on about the blues. For the first and thankfully the last time in my life, I sank into what I now realize was a clinical depression. Back then, I didn't know such a thing existed. I only knew I felt miserable, especially in the mornings, and that hanging around the office doing nothing made me feel worse. All that seemed to help was physical exercise. A blizzard at the beginning of February led me to that discovery. After I had finished shovelling the packed drifts from the Miyashitas' sidewalks, I realized that my melancholy had lifted a little. I also slept better that night. That's when I took to going for long walks.

A few weeks later, we had a chinook. One fifty-degree afternoon, my walk took me over the bridge to St. George's Island. Many of the zoo animals were out enjoying the mild weather, basking on the sun-warmed concrete floors of their cages. I saw Dad near the polar bear enclosure, busy mending the outer fence, the one that kept patrons at a safe distance from the huge paws and their long, sharp claws. The Ogden shops were working overtime, but Dad still managed to find a few hours every month to help out at the zoo. He didn't bother to ask me why I wasn't at work. We talked a little about the weather and about the polar bear who was pacing back and forth along the bars of his cage, his fur yellowish and matted, his eyes blank.

"Poor old chap. Big fellow like him shouldn't be cooped up in a little cage like this," Dad said. "I read that these bears walk hundreds and hundreds of miles every year. Well, there's no walking back to the North Pole for you, my lad, so you'll have to make the best of a bad job."

Arms resting on the top rail of the half-repaired fence, we stood side by side and watched the bear. Finally, Dad broke the silence.

"How are you feeling, pet?"

"I'm fine." His question surprised me.

"Well, you don't seem yourself these days. Not by half."

"Really, Dad, I'm okay. I guess it's taking me a little time to get used to being back in Calgary."

"Your mother and I were thinking that you might go see Dr. Jackson. Maybe he could give you a tonic. Something to pep you up a bit."

"I don't need a tonic," I said. "At least, not one Dr. Jackson could give me." And then, much to my horror, I burst into tears. I leaned against the fence and wept. Dad put his arm around me. All the while the polar bear continued back and forth in front of us—five paces to the right and turn, five paces to the left and turn.

"Sorry, Dad," I said when I could talk again. "I don't know why I'm crying. I can't help it." I wiped my eyes and blew my nose. Self-pity was given short shrift at our house, so I half expected him to tell me to pull up my socks and make the best of things, like the polar bear. I know Mum would have. Instead, he stood quietly and listened to me. "It's just that I feel . . . I don't know what I feel. I sometimes wonder why I bother to get out of bed." The tears began to trickle down my cheeks again. It never entered my head to tell Dad about my baby. Looking back, I think that he and Mum may have known, or at least suspected. "It sounds so stupid. I wish I could explain it better."

"That's all right, pet. You don't have to explain anything to me," he said. "Ah, Kay, I'm sorry you're feeling like this. It's a bad business. I know because I felt the same way myself after I came home from the war. The world was a pretty bleak place for me then. It was for a lot of folk in those days. I felt like a great black fog had settled over me, and I couldn't find my way out of it. I only started to feel like myself after I met your mother."

He didn't speak again until my tears had stopped. "And you're going to feel yourself again too. You might not be able to believe that right now, but you won't be this way forever. Probably take a bit of time, but you'll come out of it. I know you will. And when you do, you'll be a wiser woman for it. I'm telling you the truth, Kay. You're going to be all right."

"I want to believe you, Dad. I don't know if I can, but I'll try."

"Well, pet, here's something you can believe with no trying at all. Your mother and I love you, and we always will. Nothing in the world will ever change that. Nothing."

If I hadn't been feeling so miserable, I would have been astounded to hear Dad talk like this. My dad never discussed emotions, his own or other people's, at least not when I was around.

"Now let's have a cup of tea," he said. "Your mother packed me a thermos and some ginger biscuits. We'll toss one in the cage for His Nibs here if you promise not to tell his keeper."

I'VE BEEN WONDERING why I'm writing about Peyto's baby now after keeping silent all these years; why I feel such a need to tell about her. Maybe I simply want to record that she existed and that she was loved. Not much of an explanation, is it? But it'll have to do because I can't think of any other. In retrospect, I wish I had written to Peyto about his child. The only person I ever told was Terps. We were both old by then, and Terps was dying in the Foothills Hospital. I went to visit her every day. The last afternoon we spoke, she told me that she and Charlie had made love during the week of leave he spent at home before he was shipped overseas. She said it had been a lifelong regret that she did not get pregnant. That's when I told her about Peyto's baby. Then the pair of us had a little weep together for good men who died too soon and children who never were, and maybe for ourselves too, because we both knew our friendship would soon be at its end.

I COULDN'T WORK on my notes yesterday. Too upsetting. I don't know how I'm going to finish if it keeps up like this. I asked Meggie what I should do.

"Quit writing if it upsets you." She said this as if it were the most obvious thing in the world, which I suppose it is. "Nobody says you have to finish. They'll still let you go home."

"But I can't quit. I've come so far that stopping now would be like giving in."

"So?" Meggie shrugged. "Give in. For God's sake, Kay, this memoir class was supposed to keep us sane, not drive us crazy."

"But it will drive me crazy if I don't finish. I'll keep thinking about all the things I didn't have the guts to tell."

"Damned if you do, damned if you don't, eh?"

"Probably worse if I don't."

"Then get through it as fast as you can. Don't stop to think. Scribble down the most important stuff and fill in the blanks after you go home. You'll be happier when you're back in your own place."

Sounds like a good plan to me.

IN MARCH OF 1942, Charlie's request for overseas duty was granted. Before he left for England, he was given a week's leave to spend with his family. The world always seemed brighter when Charlie was around, and that week was no exception. Although we knew we probably wouldn't see him again for a long time, those few days still stand out in my mind as happy ones. We even had a party, so he could see all our friends before he left. Mum tried her best to make the party as cheerful as she could, but I know her heart wasn't in it. Still, she put up the streamers, baked Charlie's favourite chocolate cake, and issued the invitations. Mr. Ledger was there and so were Canon Giles and his wife and children. Terps had practically lived at our place for the week, and that evening she brought her sisters with her. I think most of the neighbourhood crammed into our little house to say goodbye to Charlie. As my parents' parties always were, it was a happy evening, with punch and dancing and lots of laughter. Only the Miyashitas were missing. Mrs. Miyashita had telephoned in the morning to say that Mr. Miyashita had a slight cold and could not leave the house. The next day, Charlie and I went to visit. He was as shocked as I had been by the change in them.

It seemed no time at all until, once again, we were standing in the CPR station, waving goodbye to Charlie. That afternoon Dad was with us, and afterwards he drove Mum and Terps and me back to a house that felt empty and far too quiet. Terps stayed for supper. After we had eaten, Dad turned on the radio, and we all listened to Jack Benny. Then Nikkou and I walked Terps home.

CHARLIE SURVIVED THE war. As a matter of fact, he got a medal for surviving. He was a bomber pilot, and they gave him the Distinguished Flying Cross for coming back alive from fifty-one missions. He had flown almost two full tours of duty by the war's end. He came home in September of 1945. At that time I was working in Ottawa. Charlie's train was scheduled to stop there for an hour, so I took some time off work to go meet him. Some of the saddest moments of my life have occurred in train stations.

It took me a moment to recognize the man who stood waiting for me on the platform. He seemed much bigger than I remembered my brother, more filled out and muscular. It did not take me any time to realize that he was drunk. Charlie was not politely tipsy. Charlie was slurred-word, stumbled-walk, slack-jawed pissed—so drunk he could hardly stand up. If it hadn't been for two of his fellow officers propping him up, he probably would have fallen over. They had all been drinking, and although his companions were feeling no pain, they were models of sobriety compared with my brother. In those days you needed a special permit to buy liquor from provincial government liquor stores, so God knows how the three of them had managed to get their hands on enough booze to drink themselves into this state, especially Charlie. However, I guess that anyone resourceful enough to find his way back from fifty-one bombing missions was resourceful enough to find himself a bootlegger.

The four of us went for coffee in the station's café. Charlie didn't touch his. He didn't talk either. He looked at me with glassy eyes and mumbled my name a few times, but that was it. I asked his friends if they would try to have him sober when he got off the train in Calgary. Then I went back to work. I'd be surprised if Charlie remembered our meeting.

Because I was still living in Ottawa at the time, what little I do know about Charlie's life in Calgary after the war I pieced together from talks with Mum and Terps. According to Terps, when she and my parents met him at the Calgary station, he was only a little the worse for drink—just drunk enough to pass it off as a final celebration with his pals. From then on, he swung between slightly under the influence to totally plastered, depending on the time of day. However, no matter what his degree of inebriation, Charlie was a polite drunk. Terps said that he was always courteous and agreeable whenever they met, although he treated her like a total stranger. He never called her. He never acknowledged that they had been in love or had made plans for the future. He never talked about the war. She said it was as if the Charlie we knew no longer existed. And she was right. He didn't.

Charlie's days never varied. He'd get up late, toy with the lunch Mum cooked for him, and then go out. Sometimes he'd tell her he was off to the movies or the library; other times he didn't bother to invent a destination. He never came home until after the bars closed. According to Mum, Charlie was having a little holiday, letting off a bit of steam before he decided what to do with his life. She wanted him to go to university and resume his interrupted education. Charlie agreed that this was a fine idea, then carried on drinking. One bitterly cold night in late November, he was struck and killed by a train as he crossed the tracks on his drunken walk home to east Calgary. Mum and Dad always maintained it was a terrible accident, but I believe my brother walked into that train on purpose. I know that he was a casualty of war as surely as if his airplane had been shot out of the sky.

MUM BAKED PEYTO a fruitcake. She decorated the top with two flags—a Union Jack and a Stars and Stripes—that she made from coloured icing. That cake was the first of many. Mum often baked for Charlie and Norman, and shortly after I got home from Hong Kong, she added Peyto to her care package list. This came about after I received five letters from him in one week.

"That's the fifth this week, and it's only Thursday." She handed Peyto's latest letter to me when I got home from work.

"I don't think Peyto has much family," I said. "When I told him that I wrote to Charlie and Norman every Sunday, he asked if I'd add him to my list."

"Must be a lonely business, off training to fight and no family at home to worry about you," she said. "Well, I'm baking fruitcakes for Charlie and Norman this week, so I'll bake him one too. Though a fruitcake's a pretty paltry thing when you consider what he did for us. There's not enough thanks in the world for that."

"I know he'll really appreciate the cake. Just the thought that you baked it for him will be something." Both Mum and Dad had already written to Peyto to thank him for rescuing me.

Peyto did appreciate the cake. As a matter of fact, he and Mum struck up quite a correspondence. Every time she mailed a care package to him, she included a letter that he always answered. Peyto never let on that we had met on the Clipper and spent all those weeks together in Hawaii. I wrote and asked him not to tell Mum about anything before Hong Kong, that I would tell her and Dad about our relationship myself when the time was right. Not that my parents didn't know Peyto was in love with me—the sheer volume of his letters told them that. Odd as he must have found it, Peyto honoured my request.

Back in those days the phrase *loose lips sink ships* was taken very seriously, so most of the time during Peyto's training, and afterwards when he went on active duty, I didn't know where he was. That was classified information. I sent my daily letters and Mum her care parcels to an address in California, where they were forwarded to him. The system actually worked quite well, and Peyto got most of the mail we sent him. We received most of his letters too, although sometimes they arrived in big batches and not always in the order he wrote them. His letters were full of funny stories about the men he was training with and life in the navy. He was allowed to say very little about his work, only that he was being trained to supervise the storage and mainte-nance of airplanes on aircraft carriers. Peyto's degree in engineering and the fact that he had worked with heavy machinery at Continental

Implements prompted the navy, in a moment of good sense, to train him for something that would use this education and experience. Eventually, Lieutenant Peyto Willis was assigned to the light carrier USS *Princeton*. He got a big kick out of that—a Stanford man serving on board a ship named for Princeton. The *Princeton* fought in the Battle of Leyte Gulf. She was sunk by a Japanese bomb on the twenty-fourth of October 1944.

NOT LONG AFTER Peyto died, Marilyn wrote and asked me to join her in Hawaii after the war. She wanted me to come work with her and David in running the market garden business. Believe me, I was tempted. I was living in Ottawa in August of 1945 when the atom bomb ended the fighting in the Pacific. I came back to Calgary in late autumn for Charlie's funeral. After that, I knew I couldn't leave Mum and Dad, at least not for a while. So I stayed home and married Ken and had children and got on with my life. Over the years, I've wondered what that life might have been if I'd accepted Marilyn's invitation, although, after my children were born, it became impossible for me to imagine any life that did not include them. Probably I'd have met someone else in Honolulu and had other children, but they would not be Sean and Thomas and Lauren. From the first moment I held my babies, a world without them was unthinkable.

BY THE TIME Charlie left for England, the evacuation of Japanese Canadians to detention camps was already underway. Sometimes they were given only twenty-four hours' notice. Each person was allowed to take one suitcase and the clothes they were wearing. A government order forced them to turn over the remainder of their property and personal belongings to the Custodian of Enemy Alien Property. Some custodian. A year later the government passed an order-in-council that granted the Custodian the right to dispose of Japanese Canadians' goods and property without the consent of the owners. And so the Custodian did. Fishing boats, farms, houses, businesses, possessions of all kinds were sold at knockdown prices. It was not until 1988 that the Canadian government announced a redress settlement that included compensation for individuals and an official apology for wrongful incarceration and seizure of property. Many of those who had suffered under the laws did not live long enough to benefit. The Miyashitas didn't.

As it had with the issuing of identity cards the year before, the official arm of the law took a lot longer to catch up with the Miyashitas than it had with the West Coast Japanese. I've always thought they might have been overlooked completely had it not been for those stupid Intrepid Traveller telegrams. A diligent telegrapher in the CPR office remembered the old Jap who'd sent a suspicious cable to Hong Kong to somebody called Intrepid Traveller, and he reported it to the police. Like all CPR telegraph offices, the one in Calgary kept careful records of messages sent and received. Unfortunately, when the police went to investigate, all the Intrepid Traveller messages had mysteriously disappeared except for the one in which Mr. Miyashita ordered Intrepid Traveller to leave Hong Kong immediately as the mission was now too dangerous. Even that message was incomplete. In an astounding coincidence, the line with my real name and my address at the Peninsula had been torn off. All that remained were the last words: *Hong Kong*. In those jittery days, it was all too easy to jump to the conclusion, on the basis of such flimsy evidence, that Mr. Miyashita and Intrepid Traveller were spies. It was only another short hop to believing that Mr. Miyashita must have had foreknowledge of the bombing of Pearl Harbor and Hong Kong, otherwise why would he have ordered Intrepid Traveller to flee just days before the Japanese attack. And those were the tamest of the interpretations. The whole thing was insane. Later, Canon Giles told me that the telegrapher who had informed on my boss had a brother serving with the Winnipeg Grenadiers. The brother had been killed in the Battle of Hong Kong, and blowing the whistle on Mr. Miyashita was the telegrapher's crazy way of avenging his death.

I first found out about the whole preposterous business two days after Charlie left. It snowed during the night, and the next morning I walked over to the Miyashitas' to shovel the sidewalks. Canon Giles's car was parked outside the house. I found the three of them sitting in the living room. The Canon immediately told me what had happened and that Mr. Miyashita was in danger of being arrested as a spy. The Miyashitas remained silent. I think they were both in shock.

"But that's ridiculous," I said. "I'm Intrepid Traveller. Mr. Miyashita sent that telegram to me. Calling me Intrepid Traveller was only a joke."

"Well, the police are checking it out," Canon Giles said. "They're calling in the Mounties."

"They don't need the Mounties, they need to talk to me. Intrepid Traveller is me. I'm the one who was in Hong Kong. Everybody knows that. You know, Terps knows, Mr. Ledger knows. For cripes sake, everybody at St. Chad's knows!"

"Calm down, Kay," he said. "The police don't know you were there."

"Then they should ask. Some spy. Intrepid Traveller was one big blabbermouth. I told everyone where I was going. I sent postcards to half the neighbourhood." At that moment, I did not remember that Mum and Dad had not yet received the one I mailed to them the day before the bombing. "Why don't the police stop and ask instead of jumping to conclusions?"

"I'm afraid it's a little more complicated than that," Canon Giles said.

"How can it be? I'm going down to the police station this minute. I'll give them Intrepid Traveller, all right," I said, sounding remarkably like my mother.

"No, Miss Jeynes, you will not go to the police station." Mr. Miyashita spoke for the first time that morning. "And you will say nothing about this business to anyone. Remember, you are my secretary, my keeper of secrets."

"But, sir," I said. "All I have to do is tell them that I'm Intrepid Traveller and everything will be all right again."

"No," he said. "It will not."

"But honestly, sir, if I tell them that I'm Intrepid Traveller then . . ."

"That is enough, Miss Jeynes," he said curtly. "I forbid you to speak of this to anyone." He was now as cold and aloof and distant as he had been the morning when I unthinkingly referred to Japan as his home. "You will remain silent. That is my order, and you will obey it."

"Dear Kay, please do as my husband asks," Mrs. Miyashita said quietly. I knew there would be no more discussion of Intrepid Traveller.

"It's time for us to be going, Kay," Canon Giles said. "I'll drive you home."

Mr. Miyashita did not say goodbye. He sat stone-faced and silent while Mrs. Miyashita followed us to the door.

THE CANON PULLED up in front of a coffee shop on 17th Avenue not far from the Stampede grounds.

"Let's have a cup of coffee," he said. "I think we could both use one about now."

I had been in tears since we left the Miyashitas' house. I was angry with Mr. Miyashita and hurt. I dried my eyes and followed the Canon into the coffee shop, where he ordered us each coffee and a piece of apple pie.

"Margery thinks I'm putting on weight, so we don't have pie at home anymore. Come on, Kay. Buck up and have a bite. It's excellent."

"I don't care what Mr. Miyashita says," I blurted out. "I have to tell the police that I'm Intrepid Traveller. Mr. Miyashita loves Canada. He thinks he is a Canadian. You know that as well as I do. He'd never do anything to hurt Canada."

"You should do as he asks," the Canon replied.

"I can't stand by like some spineless little coward and let them accuse him of spying. I have to stand up for him."

"Kay, you are not Mr. Miyashita's only friend. I assure you that you will be doing him no favours if you speak to the police."

"They'll arrest him if I don't."

"It hasn't come to that yet, and I don't think it will. But right now, your marching off to tell the authorities that you are Intrepid Traveller will do nothing but harm."

I began to protest again, but the Canon held up his hands to silence me. "Please. You've made your point. Now calm down and listen carefully to what I am going to tell you."

"All right, I'm listening," I said in a tone so surly it would have earned me a sharp reprimand from my parents. "But I still don't see why he won't let me stand up for him. I'm not afraid."

"Kay, Kay, Kay. Stop and think for a moment. This is not about your courage; it is about Mr. Miyashita's. Can't you see that he is doing his best to protect you?"

"Protect me?"

"Yes, you. You could be in very serious trouble. What if the police suspect you of being Mr. Miyashita's dupe, that he used you to spy for him?"

"Me? A spy? That's a laugh. Who'd ever believe I'm a spy?"

"Maybe no one. But suppose the police do? Then what would your rushing to tell them that you are Intrepid Traveller have accomplished?"

"It would get Mr. Miyashita off the hook, that's what."

"Or it could put you on the hook with him."

"You don't know that for certain."

"No, you're right, I don't. But there is one thing I do know for certain. If you go to the police, then Mr. Miyashita will be left with nothing. As things stand now, he can't protect his wife, he can't protect his home, he can't protect himself, he can't even protect their little dog. He no longer has money or property. All he has left is the power to protect you, and if you insist on going to the police, you'll have taken that from him too. Can you understand that, Kay?"

"I understand that if he is arrested and charged with spying that he could be executed. They hang spies, you know."

"Mr. Miyashita is well aware of the gravity of his situation, but he would sooner take that risk than put you in jeopardy. Please, let the man do this for you, Kay. You are all he has left."

"What about Mrs. Miyashita? I have to stand up for her sake too."

"You heard Mrs. Miyashita yourself. She asked you to obey his order."

"And if I do, that'll be it. They'll arrest him for sure."

"I don't think so. As a matter of fact, I'm almost certain they won't. I'll tell the police about Intrepid Traveller myself. I also have some information about the man from the telegraph office, the one who told them about the Hong Kong cable. I think with that and the help of some of my colleagues, we can put things right for Mr. Miyashita."

"What if you can't?"

"Then you may go and tell the police your story. But, please, don't rush in now. Give us a chance first."

I did wait, and Canon Giles did put things right—or at least as right as they could ever be. He explained to the police about Intrepid Traveller and told them that the brother of their informer in the telegraph office had been killed in the Battle of Hong Kong. Under questioning by the police, the poor fellow confessed to destroying the other telegrams and removing my name from the one that remained. The big Intrepid Traveller spy case collapsed to nothing more than a grieving brother bent on revenge. Still, the upshot of this unpleasant episode was that it brought the Miyashitas to official notice. They were immediately photographed and fingerprinted and issued with identity cards. By then, it was almost certain they would be sent to one of the British Columbia detention camps, although that did not happen until mid-May.

For those next two months, life went on as usual, or as usual as it could be in those unsettled years. I continued to go for long walks, and gradually, as the sun rose higher in the sky and the days lengthened, I began to feel better—just as Dad said I would. With the coming of spring, my depression slowly lifted, and although I was still plagued with worries about Peyto and Charlie and Norman too, I was no longer lost in the black fog. When the last of the snow melted, I bought myself a second-hand bicycle and began to go for long rides. I remember one sunny afternoon pedalling up the 10th Street hill (a real challenge on that old rattletrap of mine) and on out into the country, all the way to where Centennial Park is now. Back then, it was still prairie. The hillside north of the creek was covered with crocuses, great clumps growing so close together that the whole slope was purple with them. I'd never seen wild crocuses in such profusion before and I never have since. Sad to say, it's been a long time since I've seen a prairie crocus at all.

I still went to the office every morning, although I often left early to go biking. Most afternoons, I visited the Miyashitas. By this time Mr. Miyashita hardly spoke to me or, for that matter, to anyone else.

Since the Intrepid Traveller incident, he seemed a little more remote every time I saw him, as if he were retreating deep inside himself. As the weeks passed, I began to hope that the authorities had overlooked the Miyashitas, and that once again, they had fallen through the bureaucratic cracks. I guess I never really believed it though, because I spent the whole time in a constant state of apprehension, forever waiting for the other shoe to drop.

And drop it did on the Thursday before Victoria Day. It landed with a thud in the form of a policeman knocking on the Miyashitas' door to inform them that they had forty-eight hours to ready themselves for transportation to the Slocan Valley. There they would be detained at the New Denver internment camp in a special section reserved for women, children, and elderly men. In the meantime, they were under house arrest: a guard would immediately be posted outside their door. This last insult was particularly gratuitous because, after Pearl Harbor, the Miyashitas had essentially put themselves under house arrest. Nevertheless, the policeman posted himself at the top of the front steps and stood guard right under Buffalo Bill. As soon as Mrs. Miyashita closed the door behind him, she called Mum. No one in authority had thought to have the prisoners' telephone disconnected.

Mum and Mrs. Miyashita said their goodbyes the evening before the Miyashitas were taken away. Mum gave her friend a photo of Charlie and me at the Millarville Races and another of Nikkou that she'd taken the summer before. Mrs. Miyashita presented her with a silk kimono that Mum greatly admired, the plum-coloured one with the dragon-flies. Mum showed me the kimono when she got home. Then, although it was only eight-thirty, she went to bed. Dad and I heard her crying. I immediately started up the stairs to comfort her, but Dad told me to leave her be, that right then there was nothing either of us could do.

THE MIYASHITAS WERE sent to New Denver on the morning of Saturday, May 23, 1942. It was a beautiful spring morning—sunny, trees in leaf, tulips in bloom, and a sky so clear you'd swear you could see all the way to Banff. The air even smelled of the mountains. Close your eyes and you were not in the middle of a city, you were on top of the Rockies. I walked downtown to the CPR station and found the Miyashitas standing on the platform with their guard and Canon Giles. By this time, Mr. Miyashita was virtually catatonic. I don't think he even knew where he was or why. He was not the only silent one. None of us spoke as we stood waiting for the call to board.

Although the morning was pleasantly warm, the Miyashitas were both dressed in their winter coats and boots. They had no room in their single suitcase each to pack these bulky but necessary items, so they wore them. Part of Mrs. Miyashita's suitcase was occupied by packets of garden seed. I saw them when she opened the case to slip in the few ounces of green tea I had managed to find for her. The seeds were tucked in among gloves and wool scarves and Mr. Miyashita's spats. She had still more packets stuffed in the pockets of her fur coat.

The conductor called the "all aboard." Mrs. Miyashita took my hand in hers and held it to her cheek for a moment. She smiled her gentle smile and spoke to me in Japanese. I did not understand her words, but I understood their meaning. I could not reply. My voice would not work. She smiled at me again, then went to stand beside her husband.

I turned to Mr. Miyashita and held out my hand to him. He looked at me and I saw a flicker of recognition in his eyes.

"Miss Jeynes," he said. He shook my hand and bowed the same polite little bow that he had on the day we first met at Greer & Western. "Is this not a splendid morning?"

I WASN'T LOOKING forward to the job of packing up the office for good. Mr. Miyashita had given me no instructions, but I knew it had to be done. Mum volunteered to help. I told her we didn't need to rush because the rent was paid until the end of June. Besides, before we could start packing, I'd have to do an inventory of all the contents, and find somewhere secure to store everything. As it turned out, I didn't need to bother with any of it. Someone—I've always assumed it was the Custodian of Enemy Alien Property—did the job for me. When I got to the office Monday morning, everything had been removed. And I mean everything—the art, the filing cabinets, the darkroom equipment, the furniture, the stock ticker, the coat rack, the coffee pot, even the tiny jack pine. There was not so much as a paper clip left behind. The safe with Mr. Miyashita's cash in it was gone too. The Custodian had made quite a haul.

I walked to the Miyashitas' house, but once again the Custodian had been there before me. The locks had all been changed, so the key that Mrs. Miyashita had given me did not work. I peered in the windows. The house was as empty as the office. So was the garage.

I never did know for certain where all the Miyashitas' belongings went except for the house itself. It stood empty until January 1943 when the government gave permission for the Custodian of Enemy Alien Property to dispose of all Japanese Canadian property. The next week, the house was bought for a song by a Calgary businessman who'd been too old to join the fighting but not too old to stay home and expand his business and his bank account. He did very well out of the war. After he died, his children sold the house to a real-estate developer who knocked it down to make way for the apartment building that stands there now.

Many years later, in the late 1980s, I think, Terps and I went to an art auction that featured Western Canadian works. There, on the block, was Mr. Miyashita's big Gissing of the Turner Valley oil well. Two of his Marmaduke Matthews watercolours came up too. I wondered where they had been all those years. I didn't have the heart to bid.

I know Canon Giles was right, that I did the best thing for Mr. Miyashita by not going to the police. At least I know it in my rational mind. But in my heart, I still feel that I betrayed him. Illogical as it may be, I have carried the guilt of that betrayal with me all my life. I still feel sick with shame when I think of it.

MEGGIE TOLD ME over today's martini that they're throwing a surprise party for me at this week's memoir class. Apparently our fellow memoiristas think that my leaving this place upright and on my own two feet is worth a celebration. Here at Liver Spot Lodge, it's customary to leave feet first. Jerome and Sally will be there. And Darren from physiotherapy. Meggie says Darren regards me as one of his triumphs. It's going to be quite the occasion—Janice's special home-baked cookies, real china

275

cups for the tea and coffee, glass glasses for the fruit juice. Courtesy of Jim and Meggie, there'll even be a little bubbly for those of us who still like to bend an elbow. Meggie says that we should have a martini before we go, just to get in the spirit. I pointed out that if we start pouring down the gin at one o'clock in the afternoon, we'll both be asleep before the party starts.

"At least we'd have an excuse," Meggie said. I assumed she was referring to certain members of our class who tend to nod off, especially during the read-aloud sessions.

"Well, I certainly can't finish my notes and drink martinis too," I said, sounding so self-righteous, not to say downright prissy, that Meggie burst out laughing.

"Now c'mon, Kay, be honest," she said. "Whether you finish or not, it won't be because of the gin. You know very well that neither of us has ever managed to drink an entire cocktail at this place. Matter of fact, if I poured yours in a thimble and tossed in an olive, you still couldn't get through it. So don't go blaming our martinis for not finishing your notes."

I hate to admit it, but Meggie is right. I have only one day and two nights left before I go home, and no one to blame but myself if I don't finish. That's why I'm still sitting here writing although it's almost eleven. From now on, there will be absolutely no more excuses and no more rambling allowed. This time it's The End or Bust.

WE DID NOT hear from the Miyashitas for almost two months. Mrs. Miyashita could neither read nor write English, and by then Mr. Miyashita was lost too deeply in his own misery to write for her. He had not spoken since they left Calgary. The letter, when it did come, was written by Mrs. Ito, a neighbour of the Miyashitas at the New Denver camp. Rose Ito was a second-generation Canadian born in Vancouver. She could speak her parents' language but had never learned to write it. She and her two young children had been assigned to the New Denver camp. Her husband was sent to a road camp somewhere in the Kootenay region. Mrs. Ito was a good woman and a kind one. She took the Miyashitas under her wing and did her best for them. At first, she only wrote what Mrs. Miyashita dictated to her, but before long she started to add a page or two of her own news to the letters.

The detention camp was not surrounded by fences or barbed wire. In theory, I suppose both Mrs. Ito and the Miyashitas may even have been free to leave. But where could they go with no money? Japanese were not allowed to work or attend school outside the camps so, in the unlikely event that two elderly people did find work, they would not be able to take the job. Mrs. Ito was a trained seamstress and probably could have found work. But even if she had been allowed to work outside the camp, how could she leave her children? I also find it appalling to note that, with what little money they did have, internees were expected to pay for their own food. Living conditions in some camps were so bad that the Red Cross actually sent in relief parcels. Can you believe that? Relief parcels in Canada?

After the war, I went to visit Mrs. Ito. We spent a day together, and she told me things that she could not have said in her letters from the camp because they would never have got by the censor. She described the system of barter that had developed early on at New Denver. She'd had the presence of mind to bring the head of her sewing machine with her, so the ability to mend other people's clothes became her currency. For Mrs. Miyashita, it was her garden produce. With the help of Mrs. Ito and other neighbours, she planted a big vegetable garden that first summer. Even though it had been put in a week or two late by local gardening standards and probably violated at least a dozen of the regulations for internees, the garden flourished. It kept much of the camp in fresh vegetables for the summer. Early in the autumn, doubtless in violation of still more regulations, Mrs. Miyashita organized the digging of a big root cellar. Its contents got many of the same people through their first winter.

Mum and Dad and I tried to help. We shipped care packages to the Miyashitas and later to Mrs. Ito as well. Food rationing was in effect by then, and Mum, the keeper of our ration books, always put aside some of our allotment to send to New Denver. Mrs. Ito was very careful to thank us for the contents of each parcel item by item so we could tell what had made it through and what hadn't. Not much of the tea or coffee we sent was still in the box by the time Mrs. Miyashita opened it. Early on, we had foolishly tried sending money. Since internees couldn't cash money orders or cheques, we sent cash. The Miyashitas never saw a penny of it, so we quit trying.

By then I was working as a typist at Royalite, but right after Thanksgiving I left for Ottawa to work as a clerk for the Department of Agriculture. I continued to save up my tea and coffee rations, and anything else I thought might be useful, and send them home to Mum so she could include them in the parcels for New Denver. I remember that I once made a great find, a pile of used clothing for Mrs. Ito's children. We sent her thread and cloth as well, and writing paper for her letters. After the Miyashitas died, we continued to send parcels to Mrs. Ito.

Looking back, I'm surprised Mr. Miyashita survived that first winter. Shelter in the camp was limited to uninsulated shacks that the government had thrown up as housing for the internees. The shacks were drafty, literally freezing cold. Those who had brought winter coats and boots generally slept in them. But despite the miserable living conditions, Mr. Miyashita did not get so much as a slight sniffle until the spring. Right after Mrs. Miyashita had finished organizing and planting her second New Denver garden, he came down with a terrible cold. One of the other elderly detainees was a doctor who had trained in Tokyo before moving to Canada. The doctor tried his best with the limited resources available to him, but when the cold developed into pleurisy, there was very little he could do. Mr. Miyashita died on May 28, 1943. Mrs. Ito told me that after Mr. Miyashita's death, Mrs. Miyashita simply gave up. She died four months later.

By the time we met, Mrs. Ito had moved to the Okanagan Valley with her husband and children. It was their ambition to own an orchard, and eventually they were able to buy a small one near Kelowna. They made a great success of it too. I took the bus to Penticton in order to give her the money I had kept safe at home since my Hong Kong trip. After our experience with sending money during the war, I certainly wasn't going to trust a sum like that to the mail. I'd long since cashed the travellers' cheques and exchanged the foreign currencies. Together, they added up to more than a thousand dollars. I was certain that the Miyashitas would have wanted Mrs. Ito to have their money.

IT'S A BANNER morning here at Foothills Sunset. There were times I thought this day would never come, but here I am, bags packed and waiting for Sally to load me in her car and take me home. I have lots of time before she gets here, so maybe I can finish my notes by telling how I met Ken. That was in Ottawa in 1945 and the war was still on, but now that I think back, it feels as if he belongs after the war, to the part of my life that began when we were married and Sean was born. I guess that's another problem for memoir writers—how do you know where to stop? However, I do know you shouldn't make decisions when you're tired, and I have to admit that I'm a little weary from yesterday, what with saying goodbye to everyone and finishing up my packing and almost arriving late to my own surprise party.

As usual, it was Meggie's makeup job that cut the time so fine. Five minutes to go, and she was still messing around in front of her mirror. The whole business seemed to be taking much longer than usual, maybe because she'd put in some extra effort with the mascara and eyebrow pencil in honour of the occasion. I was beginning to get a little antsy by the time she moved on to the eyeliner. We were both sipping our pre-party martinis, so perhaps they contributed to the delay. In spite of the gin, her hand was remarkably steady, and everything seemed to be landing in approximately the right place. At last, with a swipe of her trademark Scarlet Passion and seconds to spare, Meggie declared her face a done deal. It was a new face too, at least one I'd never seen before. The eyeshadow was much darker than usual and the eyeliner's sharp, upward curve swooped almost to the hair at her temples.

"Well?" She struck a pose. "Do I look surprised?"

She looked like a startled raccoon, but I refrained from saying so.

"Very," I said.

"Excellent." She paused for a moment. "So is the guest of honour ready to look surprised?"

"Well, I'll give it a try, but I'm no actress, so anything that could pass for real surprise is probably beyond me."

"I figured as much," she said. "That's why I did my makeup like this. See—I look surprised enough for both of us."

"But, Meggie, that doesn't make any sense. You're the one who planned the party, I'm the one who's supposed to be surprised."

"Picky, picky, picky. Don't be so literal, Kay. You're starting to sound like poor old Dave. It's the thought that counts. Consider my new paint job your going-away present."

"Well, thank you," I said. "It really is the perfect gift. It'll take a lot of pressure off me when we make our entrance."

"Hey! What are friends for?" She grinned and opened her eyes even wider. "Now aim your walker and lead the way. Be damned if I'm plopping a pair of specs over this masterpiece."

Ah, Meggie, I'm going to miss you.

MY THANKS TO:

Hero Miyashita, my dear friend and neighbour of thirty-five years, who kindly allowed me to use his name for a character in this book.

My husband, Don Buckle, for his editorial advice and patience.

Betty Wilson, Frances McLean, Ruth Horlick, and Margaret Brooke, for their memories of coming of age during the period in which this book is set.

Ian Wilson, who talked to me about learning to fly in the British Commonwealth Air Training Plan and about serving as both a pilot instructor and a pilot during the Second World War.

The late Patrick McCarthy, pilot and writer, who contributed his memories of joining the Canadian Air Force directly out of high school and of serving as a pilot stationed in England for much of the war.

The late Rob Scott, for his personal memories of the Pan American Clipper at anchor in San Francisco Bay.

Dave Moberg, manager of guest services at the Banff Springs Hotel, for a tour of the hotel and for his comprehensive knowledge of its history.

John Aaron, now retired from the United States Geological Survey in Reston, Virginia, for a first-hand account of his visit to Midway Island.

Grant Reddick, Dennis Thompson, and Cynthia Downe, for their memories of the Calgary they grew up in.

Martha Gould and Ingrid Olson, for their gifts of time and professional expertise on every book I have written.

Don Kerr, poet, and Walter Gantner, scholar, for their time and advice.

Ruth Linka and her team at Brindle & Glass, and Heather Sangster at Strong Finish, for the enthusiasm and support they brought to this project.

Those friends who read *Flying Time* in manuscript form and made many excellent suggestions for its improvement.

Meghan Macdonald, my agent and friend, for her steadfast kindness and for her faith in this book.

SUZANNE NORTH was born and raised in Calgary, and now lives in Saskatoon. She is the author of the Phoebe Fairfax mystery series and has written for magazines and CBC Television, as well as for documentary films. She has also worked variously as a bibliographic searcher at a university library, a waitress, a high school teacher, a television announcer, a pianist at a ballet school, and an unbalanced bookkeeper. *Flying Time* is her first literary novel.